HARRIET BEAMER
STRIKES GOLD

Center Point
Large Print

Also by Joyce Magnin and available from
Center Point Large Print:

Harriet Beamer Takes the Bus

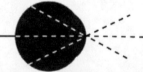

**This Large Print Book carries the
Seal of Approval of N.A.V.H.**

HARRIET BEAMER Strikes Gold

Joyce Magnin

CENTER POINT LARGE PRINT
THORNDIKE, MAINE

This Center Point Large Print edition is published in the year 2013 by arrangement with Zondervan.

The text of this Large Print edition is unabridged.
In other aspects, this book may vary
from the original edition.
Printed in the United States of America
on permanent paper.
Set in 16-point Times New Roman type.

ISBN: 978-1-61173-857-5

Library of Congress Cataloging-in-Publication Data

Magnin, Joyce.
  Harriet Beamer strikes gold / Joyce Magnin. — Center Point Large
    Print edition.
    pages ; cm.
  ISBN 978-1-61173-857-5 (library binding : alk. paper)
  1. Large type books. I. Title.
PS3601.L447H36 2013b
813′.6—dc23
                                                                2013014901

For the lunch ladies at
Lynnewood Elementary School

HARRIET BEAMER
STRIKES GOLD

Chapter One

Harriet Beamer rarely sulked. It wasn't on her top-ten list of favorite things to do. Smiling, looking on the bright side, was always preferable no matter what the circumstance. But today she felt a little sad and sulky as she peered into the yard at the birds—crows mostly—and the trees and green lawn with spotty crowns of dirt here and there. She took a deep breath and let it out her nose. It was a pretty view, especially with the mountains in the background. But still, there was definitely something different in the air from what she was used to, and she wondered.

Maybe moving to Grass Valley, California, to live with her son and daughter-in-law was a mistake. She missed home—back east, Pennsylvania. She missed her friend Martha and hoagies and scrapple and, worst of all, Henry and she were still . . . nervous around each other. She had hoped that once she moved in—lock, stock, and massive salt and pepper shaker collection—she and Henry would figure out how to finally discuss the elephant in the room. That had not happened.

Harriet slipped into her red Converse sneakers and tied them tight. She liked the way they went with her white Capri pants, the ones with the little blue anchors on the cuffs. Red, white, and blue. She felt quite patriotic and nautical.

"But they started this," she told her reflection in her bedroom window as she pulled a brush through her short, gray hair. There was a time when she considered dyeing it—perhaps back to its original brunette, but she always thought of an excuse not to. "They insisted I come live with them. They said I was too old to take care of myself."

She was pretty much working herself into a perfect snit when the phone rang. Her cell phone. The fancy one she had purchased for her big trip from Pennsylvania to California. Harriet grabbed the cell from the night table and saw it was Martha calling. Her heart raced a tiny bit. Martha always knew when Harriet was feeling sad.

"Martha," Harriet said. "I am so glad you called."

"I was worried about you." Martha's voice held a twinge of melancholy.

Harriet sighed as she sat in the blue, wingback chair near the bedroom window. "I miss you," she said.

"And I miss you. Are you okay?"

"Not really," Harriet admitted. "I mean, I'm not sick or anything. It's just that I feel a little . . .

listless today. Maybe even sad or at least blasé. I'm not sure moving here was such a great idea."

"Of course it was a good idea," Martha said. "Just give it more time."

Harriet always tossed the stale bread to the birds, and now she watched a crow the size of a Labrador Retriever puppy swoop down to steal a piece from a tiny sparrow. "You big bully," she said.

"What's that?" Martha asked. "Who's a bully?"

"Oh, it was just a big crow swiping a piece of bread right from a sparrow."

"If it's come down to you watching thieving crows, then maybe you are ready for some new excitement."

Harriet pondered this through a moment until a light bulb turned on in her brain. "Let's do something about it then. You should come out for a visit. A nice, long visit. It will be like old times."

Harriet listened to several seconds of silence before she said, "Well, what do you think?"

"I don't know," Martha said. "I . . . I guess I could come . . . now. Considering that . . ."

"Considering what?" Harriet asked.

"Nothing," Martha said. "It's nothing."

Harriet did not believe it was nothing. But she also knew Martha tended to be a private person but would spill her guts when the time was right. She'd let the comment go for now.

"Are you sure it would be okay with Henry

11

and Prudence? Won't they feel imposed upon?" Martha asked.

"They'll be fine. After all, it was their idea for me to come to live with them. And they must have known I'd want to entertain a houseguest every now and again."

"I suppose, but I don't want them to feel put out."

"They won't. There's plenty of room." Harriet glanced around the small bedroom. It was not the smallest room in the house. The third bedroom, the one Prudence had converted into an office, was by far the smallest room. Harriet's room was next in line of smallness. Still, it had been a very long time since Harriet had occupied a bedroom that felt so tiny. Finding a way to fit Martha in for a week would take some rearranging. It would be like fitting two feet into the same shoe.

"We'll make it work, somehow," Harriet said. "I mean, the house is small, but I believe there is always room for friends." Harriet's Basset Hound, Humphrey, ambled by and flopped at Harriet's feet. She reached down and scratched behind his ear. "I'll talk to them tonight over dinner."

"As long as you're sure."

"I am," Harriet said. "Now, enough of this worrying. Let's pick a couple of options for dates so I can clear it with Prudence and Henry. She is so very organized, you know. Makes me crazy.

Everything in its place, a place for everything. Not that I'm a slob or anything, but sometimes I—"

"What about your salt and pepper shaker collection? Don't tell me she's got a place for them too."

"Ha, you won't believe it, Martha. You just won't believe it." Harriet shook her head. "My collection is still mostly in the garage. In boxes. Doesn't that just fry your cookies? I've been able to set a few around, but Prudence didn't like my monkey shakers or my gnome shakers on the windowsills. She said they creeped her out."

Harriet, who knew Martha very well, could almost see the ensuing expression on her friend's face through the phone lines. Shock. Utter and total shock. Everyone who knew Harriet knew just how important her salt and pepper shaker collection was to her, how large and monumental it was, and about the love and devotion that went into caring for it over nearly twenty years.

But "I'm sorry" was all Martha said. Not exactly the outrage Harriet had expected to hear steaming through the phone. It was almost as though Martha didn't find it all that upsetting. And this lackluster reaction convinced Harriet even more that there was definitely something heavy on Martha's mind.

"Are you all right, dear?" Harriet asked. "You seem a little distracted."

Martha sputtered a few syllables until she finally said, "I'm sorry. No . . . I'm fine."

"As long as you're sure. You'd tell me if you had a problem?"

"Certainly, Harriet. I'd tell you."

"Well, we both know that's not true." Harriet opened the window. "Scat, you crows. Honestly, why do the big guys always pick on the little guys?"

"Now, what about your collection?" Martha asked. "She won't let you display them?"

"Yes, I just told you most are still in the garage. In boxes." Harriet took a deep breath. "Martha, I know you said everything is fine, but frankly, dear, you *do* seem distracted."

Martha let go what sounded like a nervous giggle. "Harriet, I told you, I'm fine. Really. It's just that . . . that sometimes I wish you had never left."

"There's a lot of that going around today."

"What do you mean? Is everything okay? Is there something else going on with you and the kids?"

"No," Harriet said. "I think I'm just sore about my collection."

"Maybe you can find a compromise," Martha said. "Put them in a display cabinet. It *is* your house now too."

"That's just it. It doesn't feel like my house. I feel like a guest. The guest who never leaves, like I'm the stinky fish left in the refrigerator too long."

"Now you're just being maudlin."

"A little. Maybe. But lately I've been thinking that I have been put out to pasture and it might be time to sell my collection. You know, before the . . . the Grim Reaper comes knocking on my door."

"Now stop it," Martha said. "You have not been put out to pasture. Isn't that what that whole cross-country trip was about? Didn't you learn anything?"

Harriet felt a tiny bit ashamed of herself. "Yes. You're right. But is it too much to ask that my collection, something so important to me, be part of my life here?"

"Of course not. You need to be honest with Prudence. Tell her how you are feeling."

Harriet swallowed. "I can't stand the thought of them in those boxes in the garage. They need to be free, Martha. Free and on display."

Martha chuckled. "I agree. But please, Harriet, don't sell. Don't do something you will regret. Maybe you could just start getting more of them out one set at a time. You know, just kind of sneak them in, introduce them slowly into the décor."

Harriet laughed. "I can just see the reaction from Prudence if she saw a turtle looking at her from the kitchen counter."

"So what? She'll get used to it."

Harriet shook her head. "No, the woman does not like change. And she's got eyes like a hawk. Notices everything. She can spot a piece of lint from twenty paces, and then she's right there with her DirtDevil. The other day she got all flustered because I dropped my tea bag into the sink. It's not plutonium, for crying out loud. It's Red Rose."

"She got mad?"

"No, not mad. Let's just say she let me know the proper place for used tea bags. I had every intention of tossing my tea bag in the trash."

Talking about tea made Harriet desire a cup, so she carried the phone out into the kitchen. It wasn't a long walk. The house was a ranch style built around 1974. Harriet liked the layout well enough. She especially enjoyed that there were no stairs to climb. The kitchen was the biggest room in the house. Henry had said the previous owners built on to the original floor plan. The kitchen now boasted a fine granite island and lots of wood cabinets—all white, stark white, with pretty yellow door knobs and one set of cabinets that had doors that were all glass to show off Prudence's collection of Fiesta dinnerware with bright colors and inviting shapes.

While Harriet and Martha continued to talk about Harriet's new life but not about Prudence in case Henry walked in from his den, Harriet filled the kettle with water and set it on the stove to boil. She retrieved two teacups and saucers from the cabinet before remembering that Martha was on the phone, not in the kitchen. She returned one teacup and saucer with a sigh, dropped a tea bag into the other teacup, and then sat down at the round kitchen table.

Finally Harriet said, "But hey, why are we discussing all this on the phone? We can talk when you get here. Just come as soon as you can. And stay at least a week, more if you can."

"Well, okay. Let me check on some things first and get an idea about airfares, and then I'll get back in touch with some dates."

"Spectacular," Harriet said.

"It will be," Martha said. "I'm so excited to be seeing you."

"Me too. I love you, Martha."

"I love you too."

Harriet tapped the phone off and set it on the kitchen table. Misty-eyed, she felt memories of home flooding back. Could it have been three whole months since she arrived in Grass Valley? It was already early September, and time was certainly whizzing by at breakneck speed, although Harriet felt she had been standing still.

"I feel like I'm in the eye of the hurricane, Humphrey," she said. "Everything is whirling around me, and I'm moving like a sloth." She leaned down and rubbed the dog behind his long, ridiculous ears. "I really need her to come. Or I just might go stir-crazy."

"Are you okay, Mom?"

Harriet looked up. Henry was leaning against the kitchen counter. He was wearing his usual Dockers and a green Polo shirt with the insignia of a golf club his agent took him to once. He held a coffee mug in one hand and a Little Debbie snack cake in the other. Henry had a weakness for Little Debbies.

"Oh, Henry, I didn't hear you come in."

"I needed to come up for air, and I need more coffee. I've been writing since six this morning. I heard what you told Humphrey. Why would you go stir-crazy?"

Harriet waved his words away. "Don't pay any attention to that. Just the ramblings of an old woman."

"Mother. Cut it out. You are not an old woman. You have more energy than me sometimes. But I will say that I'm a little concerned about you." He took a bite from the small chocolate cake.

"Concerned? About me? Why?" Harriet sipped from the little, delicate teacup with purple violets rimming the brim.

Humphrey let go a woof.

"I just think you need to be doing more," Henry said. "If there's one thing I've learned it's that you might be seventy-two—almost seventy-three—but you are not ready for the pasture."

Harriet smiled. "Well now, that's nice to hear but—"

"Maybe if you got out and did something. Made some friends. Got involved with something."

"Well, speaking of friends, I was going to wait until dinner when Prudence is home, but I might as well tell you now that I've invited Martha for a visit. Won't that be nice?"

Henry coughed. "Martha? But, Mother, you should have spoken to Pru and—"

Harriet rested the teacup on its saucer. "Now, Henry. You told me I should feel at home here."

"Of course you should. I was only saying that having Martha here is fine as long as the dates are good for Prudence. That's all I was saying."

"I'm sorry, dear. I have been a little edgy lately, haven't I?"

"It's okay, Mom. But that's why you need to get out. Most days, you spend all day in the house. You bought that Vespa scooter so you could get around town easily."

"I know that, dear, and I have used it . . . many times."

"And you need to make new friends. I wanted you to buy a car. But you insisted on buying yourself a scooter. You said it made you feel hip. But you can't very well take friends around with you on that thing, can you?"

"I do like the scooter. It's cute, and the helmet

makes me feel young. But the truth is, I'm too old to make new friends. And, frankly, there is no one at that church we go to that I would feel comfortable with. I think that's why they keep asking me to take nursery duty. I'm everyone's grandmother."

"It is a younger crowd, I know," Henry said. "But there must be some way to meet people your age."

Harriet fiddled with a salt shaker. It was shaped like an obelisk, a crystal obelisk with a silver cap. "I suppose I could see if there is a salt-and-pepper-shaker club near here."

"That's the ticket. I've wondered why you haven't done that by now." He poured more coffee from the carafe, which was now down to the dregs, into his mug and stirred in a splash of Half and Half. Then he grabbed a second Little Debbie from the opened box on the counter.

Harriet continued to fidget with the salt shaker—it wasn't even one from her collection. She felt her hackles go up again. She suppressed the urge to allow her frustration to boil over. And without looking at Henry, she said, "Maybe it has something to do with the fact that I haven't even spent any time with my collection since I got here. I want to set up my display, but Prudence says there is no room and . . . and . . . oh what's the use? I should just sell the entire collection and be done."

Henry swallowed coffee and leaned against the counter. "Now you're being a martyr."

"Maybe so, but the fact remains that there is no room for my collection, and you know how important it is to me. Each and every shaker has a special meaning."

"I understand. But you have to see Prudence's point of view. It's a small house, and she has it decorated how she likes, but . . . I'll speak to her and see if we can come up with something. We really do want you to be happy."

Sandra Day, Prudence's uppity cat, hissed at Humphrey and sent him dashing into the living room. She then sauntered past Harriet, rubbing against her shins. Harriet tolerated the cat like she tolerated a pickle on her plate at a restaurant. She did not like pickles of any kind.

"I put up with her cat," Harriet said. "And poor Humphrey. Sandra Day just terrorizes him. And frankly, I don't think Prudence really gives that cat the attention she deserves. She's still one of God's creatures even if she is a cat. She can't help that, you know."

Henry sat down at the table. "Prudence and Sandra Day have an understanding. Now listen, don't you miss getting together with your salt-and-pepper-shaker friends, even if you are not exactly enjoying your collection right now?"

Harriet shrugged. "I guess. It's just hard to be without the things I'm so familiar with. It's been tough enough getting used to living with you and Prudence, and, frankly, dear . . . Now, you know I love Prudence like she was my own daughter, but"—Harriet leaned closer to Henry—"she can be a little difficult."

Henry smiled. "I know. Especially lately. It's been hard for me also. She's been so moody. Yesterday she yelled at me for leaving one sock—*one sock*—on top of the hamper and not in it."

"Yes, and if I didn't know better I'd say she was—"

"Oh Mom, don't even say it. Don't even think it. We've been trying again for months now, and nothing is happening."

Harriet sighed and patted Henry's hand. "A grandchild would definitely give me something to do."

"Please, Mother, I think I would know if my wife was pregnant."

Harriet laughed. "Of course you would, dear."

"What's that supposed to mean?"

"Nothing, dear. Geeze. Talk about being on edge. Now, if you'll excuse me, I want to take Humphrey for a walk."

"Okay. And I should get back to work. And really, Mom, we want you to feel at home, and I promise we'll do whatever it takes to help."

"Okay. So I guess we'll discuss Martha's visit over dinner?"

"Sure, Mom." Henry snagged a third Little

Debbie. But he put it back in the box when Harriet wagged her finger at him.

"You eat too many of those," Harriet said. "They're not good for your cholesterol."

"Oh, my cholesterol is fine." Henry glanced around the kitchen. "What's not fine is the rest of this house. It's so small. And with another adult living here . . ."

Harriet felt her eyebrows rise. "We can make it work. I'll need to set up another bed in my room."

"I know, Mom. If only . . . well, if only the whole house had rooms proportionate to the kitchen."

"Henry, you're making much too much out of this."

"We do have that old double mattress in the garage still, unless Prudence had it hauled away to make room for your shakers."

Harriet laughed. "I hope you are not suggesting that Martha and I share a bed."

"Why not?"

"Henry. No. Just no. And besides, Martha snores like a stevedore. It's going to be rough enough."

"All right. I'll do something."

"And please, Henry, a real bed. Not one of those blow-up mattresses you throw on the floor. This is a home, not one of those city crack houses."

"What's wrong with an air mattress?"

"Everything, dear. Everything. Especially at our age."

Chapter Two

Harriet clipped Humphrey's leash onto his collar. "I don't like you in this thing," she said, "but they insist." Back east, Harriet mostly let Humphrey loose in the yard. And when they did go for a walk, Humphrey sidled close to her side, only straying long enough to visit a telephone pole or a hydrant.

Humphrey looked up at Harriet under his wiry eyebrows. He hated the leash also.

"But it's a nice day for a walk, don't you think? And Henry is right. I *do* spend too much time indoors. Just don't tell him I said that."

Harriet pulled open the front door and breathed in the fresh mountain air. She really did like Grass Valley, especially the town's history and what she called an artsy fartsy feel—but not in a bad or pretentious way. It was a place where you might expect to see Jack London or Mark Twain stroll out of a cornfield. Or maybe hear Aaron Copland's *Fanfare for the Common Man* whenever you opened a door to the outside. A place of original art and ice cream cones. She understood why her author son liked it here.

Before Henry and Prudence moved here, Harriet read that Grass Valley, a relatively small town with a population around thirteen thousand, sits in the foothills of the Sierra Nevada Mountains and has its roots in the California Gold Rush of the mid-1840s. And Prudence told Harriet that it supposedly got its name when a group of men searching for lost cattle came upon a "grassy valley." Harriet thought that was quaint and all, but she especially enjoyed downtown Grass Valley, which still maintained its rustic, Western look. And as she pulled slightly on Humphrey's leash, she thought she might ride the Vespa into town later and do a little shopping.

"Let's go, boy."

But before she could take a first step down the porch steps, Henry called for her.

"Mom," he said when he caught up with her on the porch. "I have a suggestion."

Harriet felt her eyes roll even though she didn't tell them to.

"No, no, it's a good suggestion," Henry said. "Why not stop at Mrs. Caldwell's house today? Like I told you before, she makes great pie, and I think she could be a good friend."

"Oh, there you go mentioning that woman again. You'd think she was like your Auntie or something. You go over there so much."

"I like her. She's easy to talk to. And she already

loves Humphrey from our visits with her when I used to take him for his walks. You've been here three months and all you've done is wave to her from a distance."

"Oh not again, Henry. I told you, I can't just walk up to someone's front door and say, 'Hi, I'm Harriet. Want to be my friend?' For crying out loud, I'm seventy-two years old, not seven. People would think I'm senile or off my meds or something."

"Mother, you've been seen riding a bright yellow Vespa up and down the block a few times. The neighbors already think you're off your meds." Then he laughed. "I'm kidding, Mom. No one thinks that."

"Yes, but it's still weird to just walk up to someone's door. What if she's sick or still in her bathrobe or hasn't washed her hair in a couple of weeks or is on a chocolate binge? No respectable person wants to be interrupted in that state."

"Then let me call first."

Harriet stepped off the porch with Humphrey at her side. "No. Not today. Perhaps another day. After Martha's visit."

"It's the fourth house up, the white one with the yellow trim—in case you change your mind. And by the way, Mrs. Caldwell always has clean hair."

"Okay, okay, I know which house. You've told me a dozen times," Harriet said without turning

26

around. Now, why would he be noticing Florence Caldwell's clean hair?

She and Humphrey walked onto the sidewalk. "I don't know why I'm so . . . so afraid to make new friends. I'm sure this Mrs. Caldwell is very pleasant, but I'm not ready or something. And with Martha coming, I really don't see the need." She stopped while Humphrey sniffed a telephone pole. "I want to go home. That's the God's honest truth. I want to go home to Pennsylvania."

Humphrey let go a loud woof.

"Don't you dare tell the kids, though. It would break their little hearts. Well, at least Henry's."

Harriet paused to let a car back out of a driveway. She watched it head down the street before she walked on. "Did I ever tell you how I crossed the Royal Gorge in a tram car, Humphrey? I rode 1,178 feet above the Arkansas River in a box the size of a small elevator with twenty other people, including one woman who was screaming her lungs out the entire way—and no, it wasn't me. Now, if that doesn't take guts I don't know what does. It was scary but so invigorating."

The dog stopped, sat on his haunches, and looked up at her as if to say, "Only a hundred times, Harriet."

"I want to feel invigorated again, like I did on the road, on the busses. I'm turning into an old fuddy-duddy living in this development."

Harriet walked a few more paces when she

spotted the pretty house with the yellow trim. The bright sunshiny color looked inviting against the white house and the endless blue of summer sky. "It is a beautiful day. Just some wispy clouds."

Just as Harriet and Humphrey reached the yellow-trimmed house, the door opened and a woman walked out.

"Now isn't this a handy coincidence, Humphrey. There she is—Mrs. Caldwell. I bet you dollars to donuts that Henry called her and said to be on the lookout for me, the doddering old woman and her hound. I just bet he did."

Harriet needed to think fast. If she just turned on her heel and set off toward home, she was certain Mrs. Caldwell would be insulted, and she didn't want that. On the other hand, if she kept moving forward she most assuredly would be sipping coffee and eating pie very shortly. But she was curious about why Henry had taken such a liking to this woman, and maybe she was a little jealous. Perhaps she'd investigate, just to satiate her advanced curiosity.

"She looks friendly enough. A little younger than me, but at least she's not some thirty-year-old kid like everyone else around here."

Humphrey and Harriet moved closer to the house. Mrs. Caldwell waved with a vigorous hand raised in the air like she was flagging a rescue plane. "Yoo-hoo," she called. "Yoo-hoo!

Harriet." And then she motioned for Harriet to come over.

"Oh dear, Humphrey. I guess we have no choice. Darn you, Henry Beamer."

Humphrey pulled on the leash. Pie. She has pie.

"I bet you want pie," Harriet said to the dog. "Henry told me he took you here and about how you two ate pie with her. It's a miracle you didn't get a bad case of the collywobbles."

"It's about time you came for a visit," called Mrs. Caldwell. "I was starting to think you didn't like me. Come on in."

Mrs. Caldwell met Harriet at the fence. She pushed the picket gate open with her left hand while she extended her right, criss-crossed. "We should have a proper meeting. I'm Florence Caldwell. I cannot believe it's taken us this long to shake hands. Although"—and she let a small chuckle escape—"I have enjoyed seeing you tooling down the street on your scooter. You are a riot, Harriet Beamer."

"Henry has told me how much he's enjoyed visiting you."

"He's such a nice boy," Florence said. "And so talented. A regular Ernest Hemingway living in our midst."

"Thank you," Harriet said. "I don't know where he gets his talent from. I have trouble writing a grocery list."

The next thing Harriet knew she and Humphrey

were inside the house, sitting at Florence's kitchen table. Harriet immediately understood why Henry liked to go there. Florence's kitchen reminded her of the one she left in Bryn Mawr, Pennsylvania. It was the West Coast twin of the kitchen Henry grew up in, with the pots hanging on the wall and the refrigerator humming in the corner. Even the Formica-topped table with its four, red vinyl-seated chairs was familiar. And the smell—well, the two places were interchangeable with the aroma of fresh coffee and cinnamon, with a hint of leftover tomato sauce that was probably pooling in the garbage disposal. This was home to Henry, a home away from home.

The tiny hint of jealousy had turned into a large green-eyed monster. "This is a lovely room," she said as she used all her powers to tame the monster.

"I just made a pot of coffee," Florence said. "French roast with a hint of hazelnut."

"That would be delightful," Harriet said. As soon as the word left her mouth she wanted to reel it back in. Now she was just sounding pretentious and silly. Who says "delightful"? She went back to surveying the kitchen, which opened up into a family room with a large window overlooking Florence's backyard. Harriet saw a small, wrought-iron plant stand on the right side of the window that reminded her of a staircase, and each step had a row of African Violets in terra-cotta pots. Harriet had grown African Violets back home.

"And I made an apple pie yesterday," Florence added.

"Henry loves your pies. And well, they really are quite scrumptious." There she went again. Quite scrumptious. Henry would never say, "Quite scrumptious." But she did feel the need to confess that she enjoyed Florence's pies.

Humphrey, who was resting under the table, let go a quiet woof.

"And Humphrey also," Florence said. "He always enjoys a slice—unless you'd prefer he not have any."

"Maybe just a very small slice. Eating too many apples sometimes gives him the collywobbles."

Florence laughed a hearty laugh. "Collywobbles? Honestly, you are a nut."

Harriet ignored the remark and watched Florence slice two large pieces of apple pie. And one smaller Humphrey-sized slice.

Harriet took a small bite and let it sit in her mouth a moment before chewing. She let all the cinnamon and allspice, apple goodness swirl around before chewing. She couldn't help it. The pie was that good. Memorable even. "Oh dear," Harriet said. "This is the best pie I have ever eaten. I mean that sincerely. You should have a shop."

Florence only smiled. "My daughter keeps

trying to talk me into opening a bakery, exclusive to pies. But in this economy? No thanks."

"Well, thank you very much. It's delicious. So do you have one child, then?"

"Yes. She's grown now, of course."

Harriet nodded. "Henry is an only child." How she hated that phrase—as though there was something wrong with having just one child. Martha had one child too.

"I know," Florence said as she took a bite of pie. "He told me."

Harriet chewed, swallowed, and then sipped her coffee. Florence probably knew everything about Henry. Maybe he even told her why he sold his father's business. Maybe it was easier to talk to Florence than to his own mother. She was surprised he hadn't visited Florence since Harriet had come to live with him and Prudence. Or had he and just not mentioned it? She didn't always know where Henry was when he went out. But Florence certainly had not been over to visit him.

"So how are you enjoying Grass Valley?" Florence asked after a pause.

Harriet looked into the backyard as though the answer to Florence's question was out there with the rose bushes. "It's lovely. Nice weather. Always smells like pine trees."

"You don't sound convinced." Florence finished her last bite of pie.

"Oh, it's not that I'm not convinced. I guess

I'm just feeling a bit homesick." Henry was right. Florence Caldwell was easy to talk to, and she kind of reminded her of Martha.

"Perhaps you should get involved," Florence said. "Make some new friends. I mean, besides me, of course. Henry said you collect salt and pepper shakers. I'm not certain, I've never heard of one, but there might be a club nearby."

Bells rang like Big Ben in Harriet's head. Her suspicions about Henry calling this woman when she had expressly told him not to were probably right. "Did my Henry put you up to this? Did he call you and tell you to invite me in for pie and to talk me into—"

Florence smiled. "Don't be upset, Harriet. He just loves you. He wants you to be happy."

"I know. I just don't know my way around here. Prudence is way too busy with her fancy dancy job, and Henry is always on a deadline or something. And he doesn't like me driving his BMW, not really. For heaven's sake, it's a car. And I'm a good driver—well, most of the time, and it's not like I can ride my Vespa everywhere. Don't get me wrong, I like my scooter—it's so cute—but sometimes you need four wheels and . . ." She stopped talking. Now she was just running off—diarrhea of the mouth, as Martha would say.

"They are busy. So is my daughter. But maybe I could take you around. Show you the sights.

We could visit a gold mine or go into town and visit the shops. There are some lovely places around. Do you like art? There is a lovely gallery in town—The Bitter Herb on Mill Street. I know the owner. She's my daughter, Mabel."

Harriet finished the last bite of her pie. "That would be nice, but . . . did you say gold mines? Are they real? I mean, I know this town has that kind of history—the Gold Rush and all—but I didn't know they still had mines."

"Of course. This part of the country is famous for gold mines. One of the most famous is the Empire Gold Mine. It's a park now, a tourist destination. But still very cool. What do you say we go now?" Florence picked a piece of crust from the pie.

"To a gold mine? Today?" For the first time in three months, Harriet's heart quickened.

"Sure, it's early. Not too hot yet. Empire is only up the road a piece. And I'll drive. Don't think I want to share your scooter. Just because it can accommodate two passengers doesn't mean you should." Florence rubbed her behind probably from just thinking about it. "And best of all, I don't have to go into work today."

"Oh, do you work?"

"Part-time. At my daughter's gallery. But I don't work on Wednesdays."

"Oh for goodness sake, that's wonderful. Then you get to see her all the time."

"You would think that would be a good thing, but when we're at the gallery, she's strictly business. She's my boss. And she has no trouble letting me know it."

Harriet wrinkled her nose. "Eww. That's uncomfortable. Why do you work for her?"

"Oh, it's not as bad as all that. And she needs me. Helps hold her overhead down." Florence leaned back in her chair. "And believe you me, I am not shy about telling her when she's overstepped a boundary."

Harriet noticed the salt shaker on Florence's counter. It was a short, fat, round ball made of melamine, probably manufactured in the 1950s. They were pretty popular back then, and she had several like it in her collection. Different, bright colors. "I guess I would love a visit to a gold mine. I've never seen one. Even in my cross-country trip I never ran across a gold mine. A few doggy-type land mines at the bus stops, but never gold."

Florence laughed. "Then it's settled. Let's go."

Harriet tugged Humphrey's leash. "I just need to take him home, and then I guess I'll be ready to go. Should I wear anything particular?"

"No, what you're wearing, capris and sneakers —I love your red high tops—is perfect for the gold mine. But bring a sweater. It can be cold inside some of the buildings."

"Oh, maybe I can find a salt and pepper shaker set. Do they sell souvenirs?"

Florence nodded her head. "Not sure if they have salt and pepper shakers. I never looked for them there. But yes, they do have a souvenir shop."

When Harriet and Humphrey left to make their way back to the house, Harriet stopped about halfway there and thought a moment as Humphrey visited another telephone pole. Florence seemed like a nice woman. Maybe even someone she could befriend. Perhaps her jealousy was uncalled for. "But, Humphrey," she said, "Martha will always be my *best* friend."

"Henry," Harriet called as she opened the front door, "I'm back from my walk."

Henry appeared in the living room. "How was it?"

"Your scheme worked, dear. I had coffee with Florence—"

Humphrey ambled past them and flopped on the floor near the couch.

"It wasn't a scheme, Mom. I just want you to have fun."

"I know." Harriet patted Henry's cheek. "I know. And hey, it worked. I'm going to a gold mine with her today."

Henry leaned down and kissed his mother's cheek, leaving a small, chocolate crumb. "I'm proud of you, Mom. I know that was hard."

"You know something, Henry? Making friends

on the road—on the bus or train—was easy. But here? It's different for some reason."

Henry looked into Harriet's eyes. "Maybe because on the road you can't just get up and leave. Catch the next bus."

"Henry, dear," she said walking toward her room, "don't go getting all Sigmund Freud with me. I'm much too old for that."

"Just saying, Mom. I'm just saying."

"Okay, now you better get back to work or whatever you call it. Writing, I suppose."

Henry folded his arms. "What's that supposed to mean?"

"What? What does what mean, dear?"

"Writing is work. Just because I don't swing a hammer like Dad doesn't mean I don't work."

Harriet clicked her tongue and snorted a breath from her nose. "Oh, Henry, don't be that way. I didn't mean anything by it."

"Right, well, just for the record, writing is hard work. Maybe even harder in some ways than what Dad did."

Harriet almost let go a burst of laughter but thought better of it. "I know, dear. Now, you go on. Florence is picking me up in just a few minutes."

"You mean you're not taking the scooter?"

"Ha, ha, very funny. Not this time, and don't make fun of my Vespa. It's pretty handy. It might come in handy someday, even for you."

"Okay, okay. Have fun."

Chapter Three

Harriet and Florence enjoyed their tour of the Empire Gold Mine, even if it was a little tiring. "I don't think I walked around that much even when I was making my trip across the country," Harriet said on the ride home. "But it was fascinating—and such pretty grounds. Lunch was good too."

"Yes, the mine owners had quite the life back then."

"And the gardens. Just gorgeous. Reminded me a little of a place back home—Longwood Gardens."

Florence turned the car onto Main Street.

"I guess I must have known there is a lot that goes into getting gold from rock, but all that science and stuff and those poor miners traveling so far into the earth . . ." Harriet shivered. "Gives me the willies."

"And what about the mules?" Florence said with a quick thump on the steering wheel. "They spend practically their whole life miles below the earth's surface. Seems pathetic."

"Yeah, I'll say. I could never put my Humphrey

down there. He'd be scared out of his mind."

"There are other types of mines," Florence said. "Above-ground mines. They're called placer gold mines."

"Placer?" Harriet was intrigued.

"Yep. That's when the gold is deposited above the ground in gravel beds and creeks. It's a lot easier to mine a placer lot than dig under the mountain."

"So the gold is just lying around? Who deposits it?"

Florence laughed and nodded. "Yes, it's just lying around, and Mother Nature deposits it. The gold has weathered loose from the rock it was embedded in and then floats downstream—in a matter of speaking. There's a lot of geology behind a placer mine. The miners dredge it out with machines that separate the gold from the rock."

"Wow, that does sound easy. And you can find chunks of gold?"

"Not always chunks. Small bits and pieces, some larger stuff, I would imagine. It takes time. But it can be done. I guess some people actually make a good bit of money doing it. Some folks even still pan for gold in the streams around here."

"Wowie zowie, imagine that. Finding gold. And you can keep it?"

"Long as you have proper right to it."

By now Harriet's imagination was running rampant as she watched the view of the Sierra Nevada Mountains whiz by. She imagined herself wearing a mining helmet with a little light on the front and cowboy chaps somewhere in those mountains, kneeling at the bed of a stream, picking gold out of a metal pan and maybe even shouting "Eureka!" But she was certain Henry and Prudence would never take her gold mining.

The women drove on, turning off Main and toward home. Harriet could not help but still be intrigued by the idea of gold mining. She looked into her souvenir bag at the trinkets she purchased at the Empire Gold Mine, a huge and difficult operation she was certain in comparison to one of these placer mines Florence talked about. Harriet had purchased two sets of salt and pepper shakers, each with the words Empire Gold Mine stamped on them, three pencils for Henry, and a paper-weight for Prudence. She had briefly entertained the idea of buying a baby bib, but, of course, so far there was no news from Henry and Prudence on the grandbaby front.

"Fat lot of good these will do," she said, holding the shakers.

"What do you mean?" Florence asked. "They'll hold salt and pepper. I'm sure they're usable."

"Oh, no, I'm sorry. They're perfectly good shakers. I was just thinking out loud. Are there still active gold mines around here?" She said that last part to avoid talking about her collection currently in exile in the garage.

"Oh sure," Florence said. "Some of them are serious endeavors, and other places are more for entertainment, and I guess there's a handful or so of people who still think they can strike it rich."

"Really? You mean anyone can hunt for gold?"

Florence turned onto their street, Butterfly Lane. "Well, sort of. There are places where you can try your hand at panning for gold for a fee, and I think you can still get a lease on a mine—if you have the money, the time, and the equipment. But no, mostly the professional mining companies take care of our gold supplies."

Harriet twisted her gold wedding band around her finger and wondered if maybe, just maybe, the gold had come from Grass Valley. "Now wouldn't that be a hoot—talk about destiny."

"Excuse me?" Florence said. She pulled the car into Harriet's driveway.

"Oh, just me thinking out loud again. I was wondering if the gold in my ring could have come from here."

Florence shrugged. "I guess anything is possible."

Harriet pushed open the car door. "Well, Florence, thank you for a wonderful day."

"Thank you for coming, and stop by anytime."

"Or you can mosey up here anytime. I'm not a

pie baker, but I'm sure I can open a box of something or other. Henry always has those Little Debbies. Can't eat them myself." Harriet smiled into Florence's eyes. They were nice, crystal-blue eyes.

"Thanks," Florence said.

Harriet walked into the house feeling like she had made her first California friend.

"Henry," she called as Humphrey trotted up to her, wagging his tail and dancing a jig. Harriet patted his head. "Did you miss me, pooch?"

Humphrey said, "Woof."

"Hi, Mom," Henry said. "Did you have a nice time?"

"I had a very nice time, and you were absolutely right. Florence is very sweet, and I learned a lot about gold. Did you know you can still mine for gold around here? And that not all the gold is buried way far under the mountains? It's just lying around in streams and riverbeds."

She looked at Humphrey and imagined him wearing a small mining helmet and two saddlebags bulging with gold. It made his belly sag even more. "Nah, you would not make a good gold mule." Humphrey looked at her with relief in his eyes and trotted away.

"I'm glad you had a good time," Henry said.

"My feet are tired, but I thoroughly enjoyed visiting the gold mine and walking around the grounds. I bought Prudence a paperweight. It looks like a giant gold nugget."

"Oh, that's thoughtful, Mom. I'm sure Pru will be delighted."

"I loved the grounds. The mansion and the fountains, and there's even a reflecting pool. I reflected. But only for a minute or two. I reflected on how rich the Bourns must have been." Then she laughed. "They ran the place for a time. Gold barons, I suppose."

"Good, Mom. But I think I should get back to . . . to work." He moved closer to Harriet. "Look, Mom, I'm sorry I jumped down your throat before. It's just that sometimes I think you disapprove of what I do for a living, disapprove of me for not following Dad's foot-steps."

Harriet shook her head. "If that were true, would I have brought you these?" She reached into her Empire Gold Mine bag and pulled out the three pencils.

She watched a smile spread across Henry's face. "Ah, that's so nice."

"This one here"—she handed it to him—"is fancy. You tilt it, and the mule moves with the gold. Isn't that clever?"

"It sure is. Thank you."

"You're welcome, son." She patted his cheek, something she did often and sometimes to Henry's annoyance, but mostly he liked it. This time he caught her hand in his and patted it. "I really need to get back; it's already three o'clock and, by the way, Prudence called and said she is going to be late. She has an errand to run."

"Okay. I can start dinner in a little while," Harriet said, "but I think I'd like to rest first for a bit."

"Thanks, Mom," Henry said. "Not for resting. I mean for handling dinner. It's a big help. I have to get this chapter done—today."

"Another Western, dear?" she asked even though she already knew.

"Yes, the continuing saga of Turtle Creek."

Harriet pulled her Empire Gold Mine shakers from the bag. "When I was in Dodge City, I finally figured out what you see in cowboys."

"Really? You never liked cowboys."

"Now, I didn't say I like them, I just said I figured out their appeal. There's a difference, dear. Now, I better set these salt and pepper shakers down somewhere. Maybe you wouldn't mind if we actually used them." She swallowed. "No, on second thought, I'll just add them to my collection in the garage." She emphasized the word *garage*.

Henry didn't say a word.

Harriet smiled. "It is my hobby, although you'd never know it—around here."

"Mom," Henry said. "I told you we are working on it. But listen, I was going to wait to tell you this, but Prudence and I have a surprise for you that might make you feel better."

"Really, Henry? A surprise? For me? I love surprises."

"Yes, a big surprise, and I think you are really going to like it."

"Tell me," Harriet said.

Henry shook his head. "Nope. Not until Prudence comes home. Because, Mom, it was her idea."

Harriet sighed. "Okay, okay. Leave me hanging." She yawned. "Maybe I'll even take a little nap before starting dinner."

"Good idea," Henry said. "I have cowboys stuck in a cave-in." Henry kissed his mother's cheek. "Have a good rest."

Chapter Four

Henry sat down at his desk and looked over the blueprints. It was hard to read the plans without thinking of his dad and not feeling bad for not following in his father's footsteps and for selling the business, Beamer's Beams and Buildings.

"But it wasn't my calling, Dad," Henry said.

"You were the builder. God made me a writer. How long do I have to feel guilty about it?"

Humphrey trotted into the den, wagging his tail.

"Humphrey," Henry said, "I thought you were taking a nap with Mom."

Humphrey let go a quiet woof and plopped down on his rump. Henry patted his head. "I can't wait to give Mom the surprise." Humphrey swished his tail. "She is going to hug the stuffing out of me. And she might feel just a wee bit sorry for thinking Pru didn't care about her and her collection. This was all Pru's idea."

Humphrey swished harder. "Look at this. Mom will have her own addition on the house. She's been talking about her collection a lot. Well, now she'll have a place for it."

Humphrey barked. "You are so right. I am a good son—even if I don't quite measure up."

He rolled up the plans, secured them with a rubber band, and set them next to his desk.

"We'll tell her tonight, over dinner." He unwrapped a snack cake. There was something about the super sweet goodness that aided his writing. Little Debbie was his muse. Humphrey still looked at him with a look that only a dog could give.

"Sorry, old man, you can't have any. Chocolate is not good for dogs."

Humphrey lay at his feet.

46

Henry read through the words he had written that morning. For the most part he was pleased but was unsure of his next move. He had already decided that the cowboys needed to stay alive.

"What do you think, Humphrey? I have three cowboys stuck in a cave. Do we blast them out?"

Humphrey whimpered and closed his eyes.

"Yeah, that's the ticket. Dynamite."

It was nearly six-thirty when Harriet roused from her sleep.

"Oh goodness," she said out loud. "Visiting a gold mine was hard work. I slept like a rock." She looked around the room. Even though she had been sleeping there for three months, sometimes, especially if she slept during the day, she had to reorient herself and remember she was not in Bryn Mawr anymore.

"Humphrey," she called. But he didn't come. "Now, where did that silly pooch get off to, I wonder?" She looked around. "Should have named him Houdini."

She yawned and slipped off the bed, visited the bathroom, and then headed toward the kitchen to prepare dinner. Her stomach growled. But first she stopped at the den, where she found Humphrey fast asleep at Henry's feet and Henry typing fast on his keyboard. Harriet coughed.

"Mom," Henry said, looking up. "How was your nap?"

"Fine," Harriet said. "How's it coming? Did you get the boys out of the cave?"

"Yep, we blasted them out with dynamite."

"Ah, that's nice, dear. You always did like explosions."

Henry scratched his head on that one a second but then quickly remembered the time he tossed the firecracker into the trash can. And about the time he made the vinegar, baking soda, and chocolate syrup volcano that exploded all over the kitchen. He had quite a mess to clean up.

While Henry went back to his keyboard, Harriet glanced around the den. It was a nice room at the back of the house with cream-colored carpet and lots of bookcases jam-packed with books and little tchotchkes Henry had collected through the years. The walls had pictures of him and Prudence, one of Humphrey, and several framed writing awards. Henry sat at a black desk strewn with notebooks and books and pens. The desk probably came from IKEA, not that there was anything wrong with it. It was just that Harriet thought Henry deserved real wood.

"I was just going in to start dinner. I thought spaghetti and meatballs sounded good."

"Fine," Henry said, not looking at her and not taking his fingers from the keyboard.

Harriet waited another few seconds, then spotted the roll of blueprints. "What's that?"

"What's what?" Henry said, still not looking.

"Standing next to your desk. It looks like a set of blueprints."

Henry grabbed the papers and placed them on top of a high bookcase. "No, no, Mom. They're just . . . storyboards for the novel. You know, mapping out the plot."

Harriet smiled. "Uh huh. I'm going to make dinner. Did Prudence say what time she'd be home?"

"A little later than usual, so probably by seven, seven-thirty."

"Okay. That's gives me plenty of time. I've had a hankering for spaghetti and meatballs." She repeated herself because she was fairly certain Henry had not heard her the first time.

"Are you sure? I can make dinner if you want."

Harriet waved the thought away. "No. I want to, really."

"Okay, Mom. Spaghetti and meatballs it is."

Humphrey opened his eyes and said, "Woof."

"I knew that would get you," Harriet said. "He loves spaghetti and meatballs."

"So do I, Mom. Especially the way you make them."

Prudence was not exactly a good cook. Harriet was surprisingly okay with that. She knew being a lawyer meant long hours and dedication, and that just because a person is born with ovaries that doesn't mean she is able to cook. Henry had become the chef in the family. Another talent

Harriet couldn't figure out. Max had boiled water and toasted bread—that was about it. Well, there was that one time he tried to bake a frozen pizza when Harriet was sick in bed with the flu. Harriet had quite a mess to clean up the next day. He put the pizza in the oven upside down. How he could have made such a blunder remained a mystery. Max refused to discuss it. And Harriet could make a few things well—like spaghetti and meatballs. But she was nowhere near the culinary skill level of Henry and his amazing gourmet meals. But she appreciated the way Henry enjoyed the few good meals she could make.

"Well, you are the great cook around here. I'd love for you to teach me some dishes sometime."

"Sure, Mom. Maybe when I finish this book," Henry said, once again without looking away from the computer monitor.

Harriet assembled all the ingredients for her meatballs. Humphrey sat nearby, knowing he was in for a treat very soon. "Now, I'm not giving you raw meat," Harriet said. "It gives you the runs."

Humphrey whimpered and lay down under the kitchen table.

"Patience," Harriet said. "Patience."

She mixed her ingredients, formed her meatballs, and started frying them in a touch of olive oil. It felt good to be cooking for a family again, although she had to learn to remember to adjust the ingredients. Back in Pennsylvania, Harriet was often content with a salad and soup, even the occasional pizza or cheese steak or Chinese from the Sampan. Oh, how she missed the Sampan. They made the best spring rolls.

Fortunately, the last time she made spaghetti sauce she had made plenty, and so there was sauce in the freezer that made the meal preparation that much easier.

"You see, Humphrey, I knew we'd use this sauce eventually."

As the meatballs sizzled, Harriet's thoughts returned to gold. She kept wondering what it would be like to actually find a gold nugget. What did raw gold feel like? She twisted her wedding band again.

"What do you think, Humphrey? Is it rough or smooth? I know it's heavy, and I also know it's not magnetic. I mean, magnets don't stick to it. But that's about it."

As she stirred the sauce, her thoughts wandered to a streambed where she could see the treasure shimmering in the crystal-clear mountain water. But she shook the reverie from her brain and returned to her meatballs, which would become round, brown nuggets of rock if she didn't pay attention.

Once the meatballs were nearly cooked through, she put one aside to cool for Humphrey. Then she dropped the rest in the simmering sauce.

"Okay, you can have it when it cools," she said. "But for now, maybe you should go out and peedle your wee."

Humphrey liked that idea and sauntered to the deck door.

"You're a good boy," Harriet said. She slid open the slider door and let Humphrey out in the backyard. The fresh air was nice and, as always, smelled of pine. She followed Humphrey out, sat on a deck chair, and listened to the birds warbling in the trees. Maybe she could get used to California, she figured. But something still tugged at her heart. And who knows, maybe Martha would fall in love with the town and move out. But maybe not. Martha had her son, Wyatt, to consider, even though he was an adult. But it was times like this, when she was relaxing on the deck, that being able to share the time with a good friend sounded the most inviting.

Florence appeared from the side of the house. She carried a pie.

"Yoo-hoo," she called. "I was knocking on the front door but no one came, so I thought you might be back here. I saw your Vespa in the driveway and figured you'd be home." She climbed up the deck steps. "I brought you a pie. Lemon meringue. I hope you like lemon. I made it after we got home from the mine. I thought Henry might appreciate it."

"Hi," Harriet said. "Sure, Henry likes lemon

meringue, but you didn't have to bake."

"I know. I wanted to. My way of saying thanks for a nice day." She sat next to Harriet. Humphrey tootled up the steps and lay down near Florence. She rubbed his belly. "There's a good doggie."

"I should be thanking *you*," Harriet said.

"Ah, no matter. We can thank each other. What are friends for?"

"But you didn't have to bake us a pie."

"Ah, it's nothing. What's a little meringue between friends? Just make sure you return the pie tin. I have four, a matched set. They're special. They were my mother's. Sometimes I think that's why my crust turns out so good. Baked in a hundred-year-old tin."

Harriet smiled. She definitely liked Florence Caldwell, but she still nursed a twinge of jealousy about Henry. Did she bring Henry pies before Harriet was in the picture?

"I will be sure to get it back to you. And thank you. Let me just go put this in the kitchen, out of the heat."

"Sure thing. Mind if I sit a spell?"

"No. Make yourself comfy."

Henry was in the kitchen stealing a meatball.

"Hey," Harriet said. "Wait for dinner."

"Oh, is that a Florence Caldwell pie?"

"Yes. She just brought it. She's on the deck."

"Great. I've missed her pies. We haven't seen Florence much lately. I think she's been giving you some space until you got settled in, Mom. I'm so glad you two met today." Henry wiped sauce from his lips and headed to the deck. Harriet set the pie on the counter and went to the door to look outside. She saw him give Florence a kiss.

"Thanks for dessert," she heard him say.

"Thanks for the dessert," Harriet mimicked.

She gave her sauce a quick stir or two, smacked the spoon against the side of the pot, and then set the spoon on the little pumpkin-shaped spoon rest. But Harriet felt a little ashamed. "She's a nice lady," she told herself. Jealousy was a stupid emotion.

Harriet, Florence, and Henry sat on the deck awhile. Florence told Henry about the trip to the mine, which, of course, Harriet had already recounted. But he hung onto her words as though he had been hearing the story for the first time.

Harriet tried to get a few words in edgewise, but the two of them were so busy yakking she turned her attention elsewhere. In fact, her thoughts turned to the surprise Henry said they had for her.

Humphrey, who had run off after a rabbit, ambled back onto the deck. The dog nuzzled Harriet's hand like he could still smell raw meat.

"I washed my hands, you silly animal," Harriet said. She leaned back and took in more of the fresh air as she listened to the conversation.

"So you just set off dynamite and saved the cowboys," Florence said. "If only everything in life were that easy."

Maybe that was it. Maybe Harriet needed to take a deeper interest in Henry's work. She made a mental note to pay more attention. But Henry stood just a few seconds after her revelation and announced he needed to get back to Cash and Polly, his main characters—even though it wouldn't be long until Pru got home.

"Oh, you go right ahead," Florence said. "Write some good words. I need to be heading back to the ranch myself."

Harriet walked Florence to the front of the house.

"Thank you again for the pie. I'd love to invite you for dinner tonight, but Henry said they have a surprise for me and I have to talk to them about my best friend, Martha, coming for a visit."

"Oh, that's fine. I understand. We'll do it another day."

Harriet smiled. "Thank you, Florence." She willed herself to forget about her jealousy.

Florence touched Harriet's shoulder. "I hope the surprise is one you've been wanting."

"It's not," Harriet said. "Not yet anyway. But right now I better get back to the meal. I want to make a nice big, nutritious salad."

Chapter Five

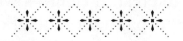

It was just a little before seven-thirty when Henry looked up from his work and saw Prudence standing at his den door. She had a funny grin on her face and was holding her briefcase in one hand and a small, yellow, plastic bag in the other.

"Hi, honey," Henry said. "How was your day? Why are you standing there like that? You look like you just got made partner or something."

Prudence walked over and kissed Henry's cheek. "I had a terrific day. And not only that, but I have a feeling it's going to get a whole lot better."

"You mean when we tell Mom our plans? I know she is going to fall off her rocker. She saw the blueprints today in my den; they were rolled up. I told her they were plans for my book. I think she bought it."

"Well, that will be fun, but . . . Henry, I stopped at the drugstore on my way home."

"Uh hum," Henry said, looking back to his monitor.

Prudence tapped the desk. "Aren't you going to ask me why?"

"Okay, why?" He looked up from his work and pulled Prudence onto his lap. "Why did you go to the drugstore? Run out of shampoo?"

Prudence jiggled the bag. "I bought one of these today."

"What? A tube of cortisone?"

"Henry." Prudence pulled herself to her feet. "Look."

Prudence reached into the bag and removed a small pink and blue box. "Not exactly." She waved it in front of his face.

"Prudence, is that a—"

"Yep. Come on. Let's take it for a spin."

Harriet called Humphrey into the house. "Come on, I just heard Prudence drive up. Time to put the pasta in the pot."

She removed the lid from the boiling water, dropped an entire pound of thin spaghetti into the pot, and gave it a quick stir. "Okay, Humphrey, dinner in nine minutes."

Harriet set the kitchen table using the everyday stuff at first but then remembered the surprise Henry mentioned. "Maybe we should eat in the dining room and use the good dishes and maybe even have a glass of wine with our pasta." Then she thought a moment and said to Humphrey, "Yep, wine. Then if Prudence doesn't . . . imbibe, we'll know, and Henry's asking me this morning not to talk about babies and mentioning some surprise for me was a smoke screen." She laughed a little like a mad scientist.

Humphrey let go a low woof and curled into a ball in a corner.

So she set the table with pretty cloth napkins, which she quickly folded to resemble swans—a trick she learned from a waiter on her trip across the country. She lit two white candles and opened a bottle of red wine she found tucked away in the dining room breakfront, so it could breathe.

She stepped back and looked at her handiwork. She might not be the world's best cook, but Harriet Beamer could set a nice table.

"Oh, Humphrey, it's lovely." Harriet stood for a moment and sighed. She really had missed caring for a family. She felt kind of bad for thinking negative thoughts about being here this morning.

The timer dinged and startled her. Harriet dumped the spaghetti into a metal colander. Steam rose from the pasta as the water drained into the sink. She prepared plates for the three of them, using Prudence's Fiesta dinnerware plates. She gave Prudence the olive green one, Henry the bright orange plate, and herself the turquoise one. Humphrey, who happened to like leftover spaghetti, would have to wait—although she did still have a meatball cooling on the counter for him. And Humphrey knew it too. He sat in front of the sink waiting like a child.

"It's coming," Harriet said as she patted his head. "It's coming."

Harriet was just about to slice a loaf of crusty Italian bread when she remembered how persnickety Prudence was and washed her hands free of any possible doggie contamination.

"Nothing personal, boy."

She set the sliced bread, the salad, Florence's pie, and the filled plates on the table, and the oregano, garlicky aroma filled the dining room. It was still light outside, but the sun was on the downstroke, and the house was pretty much in shadows from the trees. The candles flickered sweetly. She turned on Henry's iPod, and smooth jazz filtered through the room. Yes, this was definitely a celebration dinner—no matter what the big surprise was.

Next, she went into the living room expecting to see the kids. But they weren't there. So she called down the hall. "Henry! Prudence! Dinner!"

She waited but did not hear them coming. She called a second time and still nothing. "Oh dear, the meal will get cold. Cold spaghetti is fine for breakfast but not for dinner."

She walked closer to the master bedroom and was just about to call but stopped when she heard giggling and what she was certain was smooching.

"Good grief, can't they wait until after dinner?"

She was just about to knock on their bedroom door when it opened and out walked Henry and Prudence still giggling and holding hands.

"There you are. I've been calling," Harriet said. "Soup's on, and it's getting cold."

"Sorry, Mom," they said together. "We had to . . . we had something to discuss," Prudence said.

"Well, I hope it's about the secret. I'm busting."

"Oh, you'll find out," Henry said.

Harriet led the way to the dining room as Sandra Day sashayed past as though she had been privy to the conversation.

"What's this?" Prudence said. "A fancy dinner in the middle of the week?"

"Yep," Harriet said as she picked up the bottle of wine. "Henry said you two have a good surprise, and I am hoping it is a good surprise worthy of a celebration. Wine, dear?" she asked Prudence.

Prudence rested her palm on top of her wine glass. "Oh, no thank you. Not tonight."

Harriet looked at Humphrey with raised brows. "That's A-okay with me," she said.

Henry stood. "That reminds me, Mom, I need to go get your surprise." He glanced at Prudence. Harriet noticed the look on Prudence's face. Confusion. The same thing Harriet was feeling.

"Where are you going, honey?" Prudence asked.

"To get the . . . you know, the special surprise—for Mom. The one we've been working on."

"Oh yeah, I forgot. It's in your den."

The den. Now Harriet was about as confused as she ever was in her life. The only surprise she could think of was the one she had been waiting a very long time to hear, but how on earth could Henry go to get it? This was making no sense at all. Her excitement deflated like a balloon. She was most definitely wrong.

But off Henry went as Harriet and Prudence sat staring each other down like two wrestlers until Prudence, who had not stopped smiling, looked at her plate of spaghetti. She rolled a meatball around with her fork. "It looks delicious, Mother. And smells divine."

"Divine?" Harriet said. "Who talks like that? Come on. What gives? What are you two up to?"

But Prudence only smiled. "You'll see, Mom. Patience."

Henry returned, carrying the roll of blueprints or, as Harriet was told, the storyboards she spied in Henry's den. Her heart sank. It wasn't the surprise she had been hoping for at all. And why would she care about Henry's book plot? That was his business.

"Oh," Harriet said, "maybe we should just eat

first. The spaghetti is getting cold. The surprise can wait."

To which Humphrey said, "Woof."

"Good idea," Prudence said. "I'm starving. I had a very big day." Then she smiled.

Henry said grace, adding a very cryptic ending to his usual dinner prayer. "And thank you so much for the big news."

Harriet said, "Amen," and then, "I think a glass of wine would be nice."

"Um, sounds good," Henry said.

"Oh, none for me," Prudence said for a second time. "I'm . . . watching my weight." Then she giggled again, and that was when Harriet could not contain her thoughts another minute.

"Hold on just a cotton-pickin' minute. What is going on? Those are not storyboards, and you"— she looked at Prudence—"are positively glowing. And, frankly, dear, I have never heard you giggle so much in all the years I've known you."

"I've never known her to giggle so much either," Henry said.

Prudence smiled and dropped her fork on her plate. "Isn't that what they say about . . . about pregnant women?"

Harriet felt her eyes grow almost as big as oranges at that moment. Her heart beat fast as a wave of pride and excitement washed over her. For an instant she thought the room went black like before a faint. But it didn't. If anything the room brightened. "Oh dear, you mean it? You . . . you're . . . a baby? I knew it. I knew it all the time. Those storyboards were just a big fat decoy."

"Yes," Henry said. "We're preg—well, Pru is pregnant. But we, she and I, are having a baby."

Harriet cried. She sat right there and cried into her spaghetti. "I'm so happy. I have to call Martha." Then she looked at Henry and jumped up and hugged him. Then she hugged Prudence, who started to cry, and then Humphrey whimpered and Henry swiped tears from his eyes.

"Well," Harriet said. "I can't eat. I'm too excited to eat."

"You might not be able to eat for a week," Henry said. "There's more. Another surprise."

"More?" Harriet said. "How can there be more? Pregnant is pregnant. Unless you're having twins and, frankly, I don't know if those fancy dancy tests they have nowadays can tell you that this early on."

"No, no," Henry said. "It's not twins—well, at least we don't know if we're having twins. We have another surprise."

"Okay, okay, tell me. But remember, I've already had one heart attack."

"Henry," Prudence said. "I think we should eat first. After all, Mom went to all the trouble to prepare it."

Harriet sighed again. She patted Prudence's hand. "You know, dear, you are absolutely right.

We should eat—especially you. A pregnant woman needs to keep up her strength."

"Oh, I really am going to watch my weight gain," Prudence said.

Harriet laughed. "That's nice, dear. You go right ahead and watch." Then she looked at Henry, who was munching a meatball. "We all will."

"Okay, okay," Henry said. "Let's eat. Second surprise later. Over lemon meringue pie. Now, why don't you tell Prudence about your trip to the gold mine?"

Harriet's heart sped. "Oh my goodness, I had the most wonderful time visiting the Empire Gold Mine. I went with that Florence Caldwell down the street. You know, Henry's friend. She's the one who gave us this lemon meringue pie. Anyhoo, she took me, and it was spectacular."

Prudence finished chewing and said, "That's great. It's a really neat place."

"Yes, yes it is," Harriet said. "And I learned so much about gold and gold mining. Did you know not all gold is under the ground? Some of it is just hanging out in rivers and gravel beds just waiting to be picked like tiny little flowers."

"I did know that," Prudence said. "Placer mines are all over the place. Ha, maybe that's why they call them that."

Harriet shook her head. "I bet it's because that's where Mother Nature just happens to place the gold nuggets."

Prudence twisted more strands of spaghetti around her fork. "I don't think there are many real nuggets around. Not like you think. It's mostly dust and little specks."

"A nugget's a nugget no matter how small," Harriet said.

Prudence laughed. "All right, Dr. Seuss, but it takes a lot of tiny nuggets to make one worth its weight."

"I still think it's fascinating. Florence said I could even find a place that will let me pan for gold. In a stream."

"Oh sure, there are lots of places like that around. But you won't get rich."

Harriet slipped a piece of meatball to Humphrey, even though he had already eaten the one she cooled for him. "Oh, I know that. I'd need a lease on a larger plot of land."

Prudence nodded her head. "I think it's time for that incredible-looking pie." Apparently, Prudence wasn't going to watch her weight so closely that she wouldn't eat a slice of a Florence Caldwell pie.

"I'll say," Henry said with just a little too much gusto for Harriet's liking. She knew she had to stop feeling jealous of Florence Caldwell, but still, Henry never really fussed over *her* cooking — or anything else Harriet did for that matter. Oh geeze, why was she letting herself think this way? She willed the negative thoughts away.

"Just a small slice for me," Harriet said. "Too much lemon upsets my stomach."

"Okay," Prudence said. The conversation quickly turned to talk of baby furniture and baby names and even morning sickness until Harriet all of a sudden had a terrible thought. A thought she wasn't sure she should even say out loud. The possibilities were just too awful. So she grew quiet and finished her meal—including a second glass of wine.

But the silence didn't last long. She didn't want to upset Prudence or Henry, but she just had to ask. Harriet could not hold it in another minute. So the second Henry swallowed the last of his lemon meringue pie, she said, "What about me?"

"You?" Henry said. "I don't understand. You're going to be a grandmother. Of course, you'll need to decide what you want little Henry or Henrietta to call you."

"Henrietta!" Prudence said. "I am not naming my child Henrietta."

"Why, dear?" Harriet asked. "It's a lovely name. It was my mother's."

Prudence shook her head. "I'm sorry, Mother. It's just—"

Henry laughed. "She's lying, Pru. Her mother's name was Louise."

Harriet laughed. "What I mean is, what about me? You made me move here, and you must admit this house is small. Three bedrooms, and I can't imagine Prudence will give up her office or you your den, Henry. So that means my room will become the nursery and—"

Henry stood. "Relax, Mom. That's the other surprise."

"What? You're sending me back to Pennsylvania?"

"No," Henry said. "Let me tell you. We were planning this even before we found out Prudence is pregnant." He looked at Prudence, and Harriet was fairly certain she saw his eyes twinkle with tears. Then he grabbed the roll of papers. "Come on, let's go in the living room. There's more room to spread out."

Humphrey also followed Harriet into the living room and flopped at Prudence's feet once she sat down in the big, overstuffed chair. "See that," Harriet said. "He knows he's going to be an uncle."

Henry took a breath and spread the pages out on their big ottoman.

Harriet looked at them. "Why, Henry, I was right. They are blueprints. Were they your dad's? What are they for? The Bryn Mawr house?"

"No, Mom, we had them drawn up. Look." He pointed at the page.

Harriet tilted her head this way and that as she scanned the drawings. Her heart swelled as she realized what she was looking at. "Oh, Henry. Oh, Prudence. I'm . . . I'm. . . . I don't know what

I am. I can't believe you want to do this for me."

"Of course we do," Prudence said. "You mean a lot to us. And now you will mean a lot to little Penelope or Horatio."

"Horatio," Henry said. "You're kidding, right?"

Prudence chuckled, and Henry went back to the blueprints.

"This right here is the brand new mother-in-law suite we are having built. You'll have your own space, your own little apartment. Your own sitting room, bedroom, and bathroom."

Harriet was speechless a moment, and then she said, "Oh my goodness gracious, I'm going to cry again. Just sit here and cry. It's just too much good news. Whoever thought you could have too much good news? First finding out about the baby"—she sniffed—"and now this."

"We know it's been hard, Mother," Prudence said, "especially where your salt and pepper shakers were concerned. We thought this would give you enough space to display them and to feel like you still had your own place."

Harriet lost it at that point. This was just too much. First a grandchild and now her own suite.

Harriet realized it was too late to call Martha back east, and the rest of the evening was quiet. Joy-filled but quiet. Henry and Prudence snuggled on the couch through a documentary on Iceland, which was a lot more interesting than Harriet thought it would be. Soon, Prudence yawned and they decided to go off to bed.

Harriet had wanted to discuss Martha's visit, but there was already so much news and excitement that she decided it could wait until morning. Henry, however, brought it up just before he and Pru excused themselves.

"So, Pru," he said stroking her hair, "Mom has invited her friend Martha out for a visit."

Prudence sat up straighter. "Really? When? Will she be staying long? I'm so busy at work now, and with the baby news—"

"I told her it would be fine," Henry said. "They haven't picked dates yet. They wanted to wait to see how it fit with your plans."

Prudence stood and paced like she was in a courtroom. "We're not really set up for guests. And the builders will be here." Prudence lifted Sandra Day from the back of the chair and stroked her fur.

Harriet felt tears well in her eyes. She knew Prudence would want to wait a while before having houseguests and for good reason, but she so wanted Martha to visit.

"Martha can sleep in my room," Harriet said, trying to keep the tears from spilling. "You'll hardly notice her. And as for the builders, what's the big deal? They'll just go about their business."

Henry grabbed Prudence's hand. "Come on, honey, sit down."

Prudence flopped back on the couch with a sigh.

"I think it will be good for Mom to have her friend here. It will help keep her occupied while the building is going on and . . . and all."

"I have been feeling a little bored," Harriet said. "I don't even have my collection to fuss over and—"

"That's why we're building the addition," Prudence said. But then she appeared to have second thoughts about what she'd just said.

Prudence stood again. "Okay, Mother. Look, I'm sorry. I guess I might be a little anxious about everything happening all at once. It will be fine for Martha to come. Just pick a date."

"Any date?" Harriet asked.

"Any date," Prudence said.

"I'll call Martha in the morning," she said. Harriet patted Humphrey's side. He had been lying at her feet the entire evening.

"Good," Henry said. "But for now I think we should all head off to bed. It's been an exciting day."

Harriet stayed up a little while longer, watching the news and the beginning of *The African Queen*. She could watch Humphrey Bogart movies forever. But she must have been more tired than she thought because she woke just as Humphrey and Katharine were about to go over the falls. "Oh dear. They'll make it, they always do." She clicked it off because she was starting to feel tired.

Humphrey yawned wide. "Come on," Harriet said. "Maybe you should go out one more time. Our bladders aren't what they used to be, especially after all the excitement we had tonight. And I don't want you to wake me up at 3:00 a.m." Humphrey sighed and skittered out the deck door as soon as Harriet opened it.

Harriet stood on the deck and imagined what it would be like to build the addition and then move in. At first it seemed so exciting and wonderful, but the more she thought about it the more she realized it would probably be the last home she'd ever have.

"Oh dear," she said and wiped the nasty thought from her mind. "Harriet Beamer, you stop thinking like that. You still have plenty of adventures ahead of you. And you are going to be a grandmother. Now, that's an adventure." She turned her thoughts back to happier possibilities.

She imagined the addition, *her* addition, with vinyl siding—white but real wood shutters painted light blue to match the rest of the house trim. She would hang delicate white curtains and find the most perfect cabinets and shelves for her collection. Of course, she would need a rocking chair so she could rock the baby.

Humphrey ambled back up the deck steps. "It

would be just like the baby was visiting Grandma," Harriet said to him.

Humphrey yawned wide and looked up at her. His eyes seemed even more bloodshot than usual, but in the low light it was hard to tell for sure. "Isn't it funny, Humphrey," she said. "We are getting two additions."

The pooch shook his head and let go a low noise—not exactly a growl. Bassets did not tend to growl; they were just too laid-back and easygoing for that sort of thing. But the sentiment was there.

"Okay, enough fun for one night. Let's go to bed. We can dream of great adventures and babies."

Chapter Six

The next morning Henry was wide awake at six. He had a difficult time sleeping. No matter how hard he tried, he could not keep his eyes off Pru, wondering, worrying for her. The excitement of the new baby was both wonderful and terrifying. He dressed in the usual tan Dockers and a dark blue golf shirt. Someday Henry would learn to play golf, but for now he didn't mind just looking like a golfer. He watched Prudence sleep for a minute or two more. She was always so pretty—and now she was even prettier than ever, if that was possible. He pushed her hair off her face and kissed her cheek.

She stirred a little and he smiled. And as Henry watched, he couldn't help but feel a twinge, no, maybe a pang of concern. Prudence had lost two babies. He supposed it was only natural that he would feel just a wee bit nervous. "Please, Lord," he whispered, "don't take this baby too."

Henry finished dressing and made his way to the kitchen for his morning routine—coffee on the deck when the weather was nice and then off to the den to start writing. He found Harriet already in the kitchen. And the coffee already made. She was picking at the leftover lemon meringue pie.

"Mom," Henry said. "You're up early this morning. Are you all right?"

"Oh sure, son," she said as she grabbed the coffee carafe. "I'm just so excited about . . . oh, about everything. When will the builders get here? I guess we'll have to dig a foundation first and then—"

"Whoa, slow down." Henry took the mug of coffee Harriet offered and sat down at the table. "How much joe have you had?"

"Just three cups. I've been here for a while. I

keep thinking about how wonderful it's all going to be—a baby and a mother-in-law suite, which I think we should call the Grammy Suite. Don't you just love it? That's what I've decided I'd like the baby to call me. Grammy, with a "y," and, oh, of course Martha's visit. Life is practically perfect."

Henry laughed. "Okay, okay. I know you're excited, but it's not happening today. With Prudence being nine weeks along, the baby is not due until the spring, and the builders are not starting the job until a week from Monday. Today is Thursday, so that's eleven days from now. It's supposed to take two months start to finish, inside and out."

Harriet slumped into a chair. "Oh, that's okay, honey. I'm just so excited. And at least I'll be in by Christmas—before Christmas. I can have my own tree."

"That's right, Mom. It will be nice for you to unpack your collection." He grabbed a fork and dug into the pie with Harriet. "But I still think you should find a way to stay busy at least until Martha gets here. Then you two can do things together."

"I will," Harriet said. "I promise I will find something to occupy my doddering old brain. But first I'm going to call Martha today and give her *all* the good news. I just wish I was sure how Prudence really felt about having her come."

"She's all for it, Mom. Pru and I talked last night, and she's fine with it."

Harriet shook her head.

"Honestly, Mom. She is."

"Really. Just like that?"

Henry nodded. "Yep. She's just got so much on her mind now and . . . hormones and all."

Harriet nodded. "Hormones. Can't live with them and can't have babies without them. Pain in the neck, hormones are. Geeze, wait until she's fifty, then you'll see some serious hormones."

"Mom, please. It's early in the morning."

"Oh, sorry, dear. I know you have a squeamish tummy. Well, I imagine Prudence is going to want to slow down all her office activities. I can't say I'm not glad. That's got to be stressful."

Harriet sipped her coffee. "And I, for one, would like it if she quit the town council. She doesn't need that stress—especially now and with her history."

Henry picked at the pie. "I know, Mom. I've had some concerns. And speaking of concern, no more coffee for you."

"I'm just saying, dear. You need to consider these things. Stress is not good for her."

Henry pushed the now empty pie tin away. "I know. I just want to let her make that decision. Okay?"

Harriet raised her hands. "I'm not saying a word."

"Uh huh. For now, you just concentrate on you. Find a salt-and-pepper-shaker club or something, join a women's Bible study, get ready for Martha's visit, and before you know it they'll be gluing the drywall—"

"Taping, dear, you tape drywall."

Henry smiled and said, "Now see, this is why I'm not a builder. You know more about it than me from living with Dad all those years."

"Yes, yes, well, that's obvious."

"But," Henry said, "that doesn't give you the license to meddle and bother the workers and tell them what to do. We've hired a very reputable company."

"I'm sure you did. What company?"

"Prudence hired them. I think their business is called something like Day and Knight Home Design. That's knight as in King Arthur."

"Oh, that's nice. My new home is being built by a knight. I hope he's good."

Harriet smiled, and Henry watched her eyebrows lift like two gothic arches. "No, no, it's two women. They're very experienced and come highly recommended. In fact, Pru tells me they did the addition on the Hannigans' house up the street, that big house with the gorgeous addition on the side with the tall windows and brick chimney."

"Oh, that place? I've seen it while walking Humphrey. And I have to admit I've admired it. Are you sure you can afford something so—"

Henry coughed. "Well, that's where you *can* be helpful. We were giving that some thought last night too, and, well, we should have asked you first, but it was before we knew about the baby and, well, gee, Mom—"

"Spit it out, Henry. What can I do for you?"

"Mom, we need your money."

Harriet laughed so hard she spit coffee. She couldn't say she was surprised, but still, she also didn't think they would go ahead and plan such a building project without some kind of money.

"Really? But didn't you plan?"

"Of course. We've been approved for a loan. But now, with Prudence being pregnant and all, and who knows what will happen with her job . . . She might want to quit for a while."

Harriet smiled. "Nah, I doubt she'll quit, but she will need to . . . make some choices."

Henry refilled his mug. His favorite mug, the one he got on his honeymoon in Hawaii. "Well, can you see your way clear? Consider it a baby gift."

"That's quite a baby gift." Harriet ran some numbers through her brain, not that she was ever very stingy with money. She enjoyed being generous.

"Okay, look, the way I see it, it's all God's money, and I'm just here to re-distribute it, you know? And this is a good cause."

77

"You mean it, Mother? You'll help us out?"

Henry looked up. It was Prudence, dressed and ready for work. "You mean it?" she said again. "We just thought we'd ask, what with the baby coming"—she touched her belly—"or do you want time to think about it?"

Harriet took a deep breath as Humphrey ambled next to her. "No, no. What's there to think about? It's only money, and you know what they say: I can't take it with me. I'll go down to the bank today. Just tell me what to transfer to your account and it will be done. I'd rather you guys write the checks."

"Oh, Mother," Prudence said, "thank you."

It looked to Henry like a moment when Prudence might want to hug Harriet, but Prudence stepped away. "I'll just grab breakfast at the office," she said.

Henry stood. "Are you feeling okay this morning? No morning sickness?"

"No. And I didn't have any morning sickness before, so . . ."

He kissed Prudence. "Have a nice day. I love you."

"I love you too," she said.

Then Henry spoke to Prudence's belly. "I love you too." Only he said it in a baby voice.

Harriet waited until she heard Prudence pull the SUV out of the driveway to ask Henry about something that had been on her mind but she never thought the time was right to ask.

"Tell me about Prudence's mother. She never talks about her."

"Oh gee, Mom, do we need to do this now? You know her mother ran off when Pru was a teenager, right?"

"Yes, but, well, has she ever spoken to her? I mean, since?"

"She tried a few times, but her mother never returns her calls or letters."

"That's sad. Do you think now, with the baby, she might try again? If there is ever a time when a woman needs her mother it's when she's pregnant."

Henry shrugged and sipped his coffee. "I wouldn't know, but if she wants to try to get in touch I guess it will be all right. But I don't want to pressure her about it. And you shouldn't either."

"Oh, I won't, dear. It makes me heartsick, though."

"Yeah, me too."

Henry sat back down at the table. "So what are your plans today, Mom? Besides the bank."

Harriet, who had just poured another cup of coffee despite Henry's warnings about too much caffeine, told him. "Oh, no plans, dear—except, well, I might hang around in town. Do a little shopping. Maybe poke around for some curtains for my new Grammy Suite."

"Shouldn't you wait until after it's built before you buy anything? Get the right size?"

Harriet clicked her tongue. "*I* know how to read a blueprint, dear. I can get the window dimensions. And besides, I just want to do some looking."

Henry shook his head. She would never stop rubbing it in.

"Okay, but don't forget to call Martha. And don't take any wooden nickels. Whatever that means."

Harriet patted his cheek. "That's what your daddy always said."

Chapter Seven

Harriet watched Henry make his way into the den to write. She was proud of her son, but every so often that niggling frustration about the way he sold his father's business and chose a totally strange occupation reared its ugly head. She knew it was ugly. She wanted to make peace with his decision. But in her heart of hearts she thought that if Henry had stayed with the family business it would have somehow kept Max alive, like a legacy.

Harriet suddenly remembered Martha went to her Bible study on Thursday mornings, so she resolved to call her later in the day when she got back from shopping. She loaded the dishwasher and then took Humphrey for his walk. She made a point to pass the Hannigans' house to get a better look at the new addition.

The house was a typical California split-level —nothing too spectacular except the addition. It was gorgeous, even to Harriet who tended to enjoy high standards when it came to things like house additions and Grammy Suites.

"Not bad, not bad at all," she told Humphrey. She stayed a minute and admired the details around the windows, the bright, white shutters, and the bright red door, the perfect match for the house. "I can't wait to see what these Day and Knight gals can do."

She was just about to walk on when the Hannigan door opened and out stepped who she assumed was Mrs. Hannigan.

"Hello," the woman called. "Can I help you?"

Harriet shook her head as a wiggle of embarrassment went through her. "No, no, I was just admiring your addition."

"Oh, thank you. We like it."

Harriet patted Humphrey's side. He was acting like he wanted to walk on. "Just a minute, boy," she said. "Yes, well, my son just hired the same builders you used to put an addition on our house."

"Oh, the Day and Knight girls. You won't be disappointed. I highly recommend them. Now, which house is it?"

"Just down there. Three or so houses. The one with the big maple out front."

"Oh, the lawyer's house?"

"Yes, yes, Prudence is my daughter-in-law."

That was when Mrs. Hannigan seemed to change her tune a fraction or so. "Oh, really," she said. "The new member of the town council?"

"Yes, that's her. I'm very proud of my Prudence."

And that was when Mrs. Hannigan put her nose in the air and turned away and stormed back into the house.

"Goodness gracious, Humphrey," Harriet said. "What in the world was that all about?"

Humphrey sat back on his haunches and sniffed the air.

"You know something, don't you? You've been here longer than me."

Harriet looked at the house one final time and said, "Come, Humphrey. Just because the outside of a house is pleasant doesn't mean the people inside are pleasant also. For goodness sake."

Harriet made her way back to the house. She paused on the sidewalk and looked at her son's home. It was a fine house with a nice porch with wooden spindles. Prudence kept the window boxes nice with poppies, and she kept an unruly trailing verbena inching its way up a trellis in the front yard that gave the place character.

Still, though, it was small, and an addition would help. She already knew from the drawings that it would have a roof that pitched to match the existing house. It would be one story high, built on the west side. All in all, Henry and Prudence made a great choice. She could hardly wait for construction to begin. But for now she would concentrate on getting money transferred and preparing for Martha's visit.

Harriet unclipped Humphrey's leash and let him dash into the house unencumbered. She hung the leash on the coatrack and then went straight to the den. "Henry," she called. "What is with that Mrs. Hannigan? When she found out where I live and that Prudence is my daughter-in-law, she turned all sourpussed. We were having a wonderful conversation about her new addition until then." She took a breath and sat down in the rocking chair Henry had in the den along with another comfy chair.

Henry, who had kept on typing, stopped and said, "So, you ran into her, did you? She's just being a sore loser. Her know-it-all son, mealy-mouthed Clancy Hannigan, ran for the council and got all upset when Pru beat him out in the election."

"Oh, is that all? Well, why is she so snooty about it? I'm sure the election was fair. Or was it,

Henry? Is there something underhanded going on? Is Prudence a corrupt politician?" She wasn't serious but couldn't resist the urge to pull Henry's chain.

"Mom, don't get excited. Pru is not corrupt. Clancy Hannigan was a sore loser. That's all. The voters decided who got the seat. And believe me, they made the right choice."

Harriet swallowed and glanced around the room. "Um, well, do you think she'll be able to continue her duties with the baby coming?"

"Again, Mom, that's her choice. The council doesn't meet more than twice a month, and it's really not as stressful as you think. It's small town politics, Mom. Trash can policies and leaf collection."

"Okay. I just think we should make Prudence's life as stress free as we can. I plan to help with that."

Henry looked at his monitor. Harriet could see his eyebrows rise in the reflection.

"No, really, dear. I'll be nice. I'll stay out of trouble. I just meant I'll help out around the house as much as I can. I can certainly help out where the builders are concerned. Answer their questions. Make a decision if one needs to be made. That way Prudence can stick to lawyering and . . . and whatever it is a town council does. And growing that baby."

"But . . . but, Mom, we have everything under

control. Why don't you take up a hobby, I mean besides your salt and pepper shakers? Or spend more time with Mrs. Caldwell. Or better yet, get ready for Martha's visit."

Harriet snorted air out of her nose. "Why, Henry James Beamer, I think you are trying to silence me. Keep me out of the way."

"No, no, Mom, I just . . . I just don't want you to get stressed either. You already had one heart attack."

"Oh, well, in that case . . . but, really, dear, I won't be a nuisance, and I'll stay out of the builders' way."

She crossed her fingers behind her back. Maybe.

"Great. Now, look. I need to get another two thousand words written today. Why not go into town like you said, get that money transferred?"

"Can I take the car?"

Henry's eyes grew wide. "My car? My BMW?"

"No, dear, the antique Düsseldorf you have parked in the driveway. Of course the Beamer." She shook her head. "I still cannot believe you did something that funny. Henry Beamer bought a Beamer."

Henry laughed. "I know. I know. But believe me, I hadn't even thought of it until after the car was in the driveway for six weeks. A neighbor pointed it out."

"Well, can I?"

"Take the car?" Henry swallowed. "Why not the Vespa?"

"Oh, I suppose I could, but I am going to the bank to transfer—"

"Okay, okay, but drive slowly. No fancy driving, both hands on the wheel, don't open the sunroof, and be careful where you park. You know where the keys are."

"Thank you, son. I won't harm your precious car."

By ten o'clock, Harriet had changed into a pair of pink capris with little seashells at the cuff and a pink-and-white striped shirt. She felt a little like a candy cane with a pudgy belly, but the light green cardigan she added helped pull the outfit together. Next she laced up a pair of black Converse sneakers. She had bought them a couple of weeks ago. Chucks were now her favorite shoes. She never wore anything else.

It was one o'clock back east. But as excited as she was to tell Martha all the news, maybe calling her after instead of before going to town was still the best idea. Martha would probably have checked some flights and dates by then.

"Now, Humphrey," she said. The pooch was sitting at the front door as though he were going along. "I can't take you with me this time out."

Humphrey whined and lay down on his belly.

"I'll bring you a donut or two. Nice and warm. Fresh from the bakery."

It was a typically beautiful day. Expansive blue skies, lots of sun, and the ever present smell of pine. Henry's car sat in the driveway. A late model BMW, black with a pecan-colored leather interior.

Harriet slipped into the driver's seat. It fit like a fine leather glove. She had taken Prudence's SUV out a few times, but this was only the second time behind the wheel of Henry's car. And the first time he had been riding along. She usually rode the scooter into town to pick up her medications. She'd been on extra meds since the heart attack—including a low-dose aspirin. Harriet adjusted the seat, using the fancy electronic adjustments Henry showed her, next the mirrors, and then she buckled her seatbelt.

It was easy backing the car out of the driveway, plenty of room and driving the BMW was like skating on butter—smooth. She took a deep breath, said a quick prayer, and took off down the street toward town. She thought about where she'd go and what she'd do. The new Grammy Suite was exciting, so maybe she would look at some paint chips as well as curtains. Maybe she'd stop at the furniture store she saw the last time she was in town. But first she needed to stop at the bank. That was the priority. Her thoughts were going fifty miles an hour when she slammed on the brakes. She almost ran a red light. Harriet stopped, and the car lurched a little, but at least she wasn't in the middle of the intersection like last time. That's what had made Henry so nervous since.

The light turned green and off she went into the downtown area. The ride was pretty usual for a while, nothing too spectacular, except she did like seeing the mountains in the distance. But once you hit the shopping district, it brightened up into rows of stores and businesses with a decidedly Western theme. She pulled into the parking lot directly across the street from her bank on Church Street.

"There now, that wasn't so bad."

She grabbed her purse and got out of the car, making certain to lock it. Henry told her that locking it automatically set the car alarm. She stood there looking at the automobile as it emitted three short beeps indicating the alarm had been armed. "Car alarms. Geeze. In my day we just left the dog in the car . . . or the kid."

Harriet looked around. She especially enjoyed the more artsy fartsy places with local pottery and crafts. Maybe she would pick up something pretty for Prudence as a congratulations gift or something homey for her new suite. After all, according to the blueprints, she would have a fairly large sitting room. Of course, there was no kitchen, but that was okay, and the bedroom was a good size. Large enough for Martha—the next time she came. She crossed the street and headed into the bank. First things first. "Get it done," she said. "Then forget it. It's only money."

She approached the teller with the deposit slip Henry had given her. She couldn't help but feel a little strange and wondered if the teller, a nice young man named Joseph, would be suspicious at all. Would he wonder why she was depositing so much money into her son's account? Did she have to explain?

"It's not like there's a rule or anything," she said not meaning for her words to be heard. But when she set the deposit slip on the counter the words slipped with it.

"Excuse me?" Joseph said.

"Oh dear, I'm sorry, I was just thinking out loud." He must think she was senile. And she didn't want that.

"I was just wondering about the deposit. If you'd be curious about why I was putting so much money into my son's account."

Joseph continued tapping his keyboard. "No, that's not my business. As long as you have the money."

"Oh, I do. You see, well, Henry, that's my son, see his name is right there." She was so nervous. "He's building an addition onto his house. For me. And I'm the bank, so to speak." Then she let go a nervous giggle that made her sound even more ridiculous.

"That's sweet," Joseph said. "Sounds like you have a good boy there."

"Oh, I do."

Joseph pushed the deposit receipt toward her. "All done, sweetie. You have a nice day, now."

"Oh, oh, thank you." Harriet took the small slip of paper. She looked it over. Her balance had dwindled considerably since she sold the house back east. "Oh well," she said to Joseph. "You can't take it with you." She crammed the slip into her handbag and strolled out of the bank feeling both relieved and stupid. The air was fresh and had a little bit of an autumn snap to it.

Harriet walked down the street and rounded the corner onto Neal Street and then down to Mill.

Her first stop was to a baby boutique, where she couldn't help herself and bought three pairs of booties, a baby bonnet—with yellow trim— and a bib that read "I Love Grammy" on it over a big red heart. Next she wandered into a store that carried decorations and small pieces of furniture for the home. Inside, the store smelled delicious. She saw many things she liked but left without purchasing anything. She would wait until the suite started to take shape.

As she walked on she noticed many things about the downtown area that she liked. The old movie theater, which she had never been to, storefronts shaded by green awnings, and lots of friendly looking people.

But soon her stomach growled, and since her feet were a little tired, she turned into a small café called Rachel's—a quaint little place with booths and tables. The waitress, wearing a black apron over jeans and a pink shirt, seated her sort of near the back and away from the window. Harriet was none too thrilled about that, but it was okay.

The waitress handed her a small menu. "Can I get you something to drink?"

"A coffee would be nice," Harriet said. "With cream."

Harriet looked over the menu. There wasn't too much that interested her that morning—except the French fries. She enjoyed French fries and it was nearly lunchtime, so she decided that's what she would have. Coffee and French fries. And then she made a mental note to find a donut shop on her way home. Humphrey was partial to glazed.

Harriet's thoughts tumbled like socks in the dryer. So much had happened in the last twenty-four hours. It was like dreams were coming true, left and right—grandchild, the Grammy Suite, Martha coming, and now, finally, she would be able to display her collection. Could life get any better?

Chapter Eight

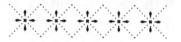

Harriet looked around the café as she sipped coffee and waited for the fries she'd ordered. She noticed a woman sitting on one of the spinner stools at the counter. She was wearing jeans and a dark blue jacket. Her hair was cropped short, and she wore black shoes. Somehow, she looked out of place. But Harriet wasn't sure why.

Then after her fries came, Harriet dipped one into the small puddle of ketchup she made on the edge of the plate, and just as she brought it to her mouth a young woman—a girl, really—sitting close by caught her eye. She looked tall, skinny, and was wearing a dark green shirt and blue shorts. The girl's hair was short and pitch black, a color Harriet was convinced never occurred in nature unless it was oozing out of the ground. And she had several tattoos on her arms and one on her neck, which gave Harriet the heebie-jeebies, not because of the subject, which was a thorny rose, but because the thought of having a neck tattoo was disgusting. Still, Harriet thought she was pretty, and who was she to judge a book by its cover? Look at what happened at the Hannigan house.

The girl was sitting all alone. Now, Harriet had several such encounters on her cross-country journey, and most of them worked out just right. She often ended up offering some older, womanly, sage advice and moving on. But now, now that she lived here, she thought better of approaching the girl. But she did kind of remind her of Lacy, the college student who helped her buy a new phone and learn to use a GPS.

She dipped three more fries and ate them. They were tasty, probably the best fries she had ever eaten—well, except for the ones on the Boardwalk at Ocean City, New Jersey. But she couldn't stop looking at the girl, who had finally noticed her. Uh oh, Harriet thought. Maybe she'd come over and say something, maybe something nasty.

Then Harriet watched as the girl slowly walked over to her, sat down across from her at the table, and introduced herself.

"My name is Lily. I saw you watching me."

Harriet felt a little flustered and embarrassed and maybe even annoyed. Why in the world would this young girl just approach her like that? She willed herself not to turn bright red and said, "I'm sorry, you just kind of reminded me of a friend back home. That's why I was staring. Except she didn't have tattoos, that I could see any-hoo, or a pierced eyebrow. What is that, dear, in your eyebrow? A vulture? And her hair was plain, old mousy brown, not black like yours . . . Excuse me, dear, but that can't be your natural color."

"I was born blonde," Lily said. "But I went black. It's a statement."

"Um, it certainly is."

The girl sipped the soda she had carried with her.

Harriet reached her hand across the table. "My name is Harriet Beamer."

"Nice to meet you," Lily said, shaking Harriet's hand. She sucked the last of her soda through the straw.

"Can I buy you another soda or pop or whatever you call them out here?"

The girl dug around in the ice at the bottom of her glass with the straw. "Sure. Thanks."

Harriet raised her hand to get the waitress's attention. Usually a good judge of character, Harriet decided to give Lily the benefit of the doubt, and the café was kind of crowded. She felt safe enough.

"How old are you, dear?" Harriet asked.

"I'm seventeen."

"I thought you might have been younger."

Lily shook her head. "Folks are always saying that. But my birthday is next June, and I'll be eighteen then."

Harriet looked into Lily's eyes, which were the color of the Mediterranean Sea—at least, the sea on brochures. There was a hint of sadness and maybe even fatigue. But why would a teenager be fatigued unless she wasn't sleeping well? And why wasn't she at school?

"So, Lily," Harriet said, "I'm curious. Why did you come over here?"

Lily looked away from Harriet. "You were staring at me. I thought I'd give you a close-up."

Harriet clicked her tongue. "Now, now, no need for sarcasm. I explained to you why I was looking."

Lily let go a nervous laugh.

"Shouldn't you be in school?" Harriet asked.

Lily looked away again, only this time she took a deep breath and blew it out her nose. "I don't go to school—not anymore. I'm just waiting here for my dad. He's down at the assay office in Nevada City. He'll be by soon to take me home. He always leaves me here when he goes to the assay office."

"Assay?"

"Yeah, you know, gold. He's getting some rocks checked out."

Harriet felt her heart begin to quicken. "You mean your father works in a gold mine?" She could hardly believe her ears. After all she had learned about gold yesterday with Florence, she was immediately smitten by Lily's remark and the sheer uncannyness of the situation.

"No, no, he's just panning for it now. He'd like to lease a mine but . . . well, since Mama died we've just been scraping by. Dad got real depressed and lost his job, and now we just do what we can."

"Goodness, no wonder you are so skinny. Does it cost a lot to lease a mine? Can you make money?"

The waitress came by.

"Changed your seat I see, Lily," she said. Then she looked at Harriet. "Is she bothering you?"

"No, of course not. We were having a nice talk."

Harriet glanced at Lily, who cracked a generous smile.

"Please bring Lily here a grilled cheese, some fries, and a Coke."

"Okay," the waitress whose nametag read Cindy said. "It's none of my business."

Harriet tried to establish eye contact with Lily again, but Lily kept looking away.

"What was that all about?" Harriet asked. "Should I be worried?"

Lily played with a straw wrapper. "No, she just doesn't like Dad and me. Says we're freeloaders, always looking for handouts. But that ain't true. My dad will work, and so will I."

Harriet reached across the table and patted Lily's hand. "It's okay. Some people can be so mean-spirited."

Lily smiled, exposing two perfect dimples. "We ain't freeloaders. It's just since . . . since Mama . . ."

Harriet patted her hand a little harder. "Now, now. Don't you be embarrassed; I completely understand. Now, what were you saying? Does it cost a lot of money to lease a, you know, to lease a mine? More importantly, can you make money?"

"Yeah, I'll say," Lily said. "You can get rich. You don't think all those folks during the gold rush got all the gold out of them mountains, do you? No siree, they didn't. My dad says there's tons of gold just ripe for the pickin', as he says. Plenty."

"That's just what the tour guide at the Empire Gold Mine said."

"Yep," said Lily. "You been there?"

"Yesterday. I went with a new friend, Florence. I guess you don't know her, but even she talked about a type of mine called a . . . a place—"

"Placer," Lily said.

"Does your dad know much about the placer mines they've got around here?"

"Oh sure, my dad knows all about every kind of mine."

The waitress retuned with Lily's sandwich, fries, and Coke. "Thank you," Lily said. And then she turned to Harriet. "Thank you."

"My pleasure, dear," Harriet said. "Enjoy."

"Thank you," Lily repeated. "Yeah, and my pop

knows this guy who has a big mine. He leases off sections of it to regular folks like us. 'Course, whoever leases the land has to afford all the equipment to get the gold out of the ground." Lily turned the ketchup upside down to put some on her plate and then munched a fry soaked with it.

Harriet's curiosity grew. "Really? And your pop is sure about this?"

"Yep, he's some rich dude, named Crickets. They call him Old Man Crickets." She laughed lightly.

Harriet nibbled one of her own fries. "Really? It's for real?"

Lily nodded as she chewed. "Dad's seen it, the mine. Up in the hills. The thing is, Old Man Crickets is getting too old and wants to just lease it to folks, a small plot at a time to get at the gold hiding up there. Pop says it'll take some machines and manpower."

"Oh. Sounds expensive."

Harriet might not have known anything about what kinds of machinery were necessary to get at the gold, but she figured it might cost a pretty penny. Otherwise everybody and their Aunt Fanny would be digging for gold.

"Well, it costs a little. But Pop knows some fellows who'll give him a good deal. He just needs a backer. You know, a silent partner. Someone to sit back, write the checks, and wait for the money to roll in. That's what Pop says anyway."

Harriet grew quiet. Her stomach did a little flip-flop, and she felt a check in her spirit but chalked it up to caffeine. Maybe people were just more hospitable and friendly than back east. This was almost too uncanny to be really happening. Her first thought was to jump right in, but maybe she should talk to Henry and Prudence first. And she should get proof that the mine even existed. But Harriet had money. She could invest.

Harriet watched Lily consume the food like she hadn't eaten in days. She really did seem much younger than seventeen—fourteen or fifteen.

"It's always been Pop's dream to strike it rich," Lily said. A dab of ketchup sat like a red pimple on her cheek.

"Well, it sounds intriguing, Lily. I might be interested in something like that, but I would need to discuss it with—"

That was when Lily's phone rang. "Excuse me. It's Dad."

"Hi, Dad," she said into the phone. "Really? That much? Sounds like we get to eat burgers tonight."

Harriet smiled and ate another fry.

Lily seemed to be listening for a long minute until she finally said, "Oh no, well, we have to find a backer soon, real soon."

Lily listened another few seconds.

"Look, Dad, I'm with a new friend. I'll call you right back." She tapped off her phone and set it on the table.

"That was Dad. He got $102 for the gold he panned this morning. But he says Old Man Crickets is about to lease the mine to some fat cat corporation unless Pop can get a backer real soon to go in on it with him. He's on his way here right now."

Harriet swallowed and glanced around the café. Her eyes darted everywhere but to Lily. She needed to think fast. She thought again about her visit to the Empire Gold Mine and what the tour guide said about gold in the mountains. Maybe she could take it slow. Maybe she could work out a deal that even Prudence and Henry would think was a good one.

"I really hope Dad can find a partner. Old Man Crickets really likes him; he was career army and was my dad's superior when he was in Afghanistan."

Harriet swallowed. She had always had a soft spot for vets.

Chapter Nine

Henry sat at his desk, trying to write the next sentence, but his thoughts kept leapfrogging from the baby to his mother, who was out in town with his car. He didn't know which thoughts were more frightening. Actually, he did know. His heart sank like a lead balloon as he remembered how hard it was when Prudence lost the first two babies. Once was hard enough, twice was almost unbearable, but the thought of a third time was impossible. "I don't ever want to go through that loss again," he told Humphrey.

Humphrey looked at him under his wiry eyebrows, through forever bloodshot eyes that were always sad even when the dog was not. Henry patted his head. "Not this time, old man. This time God is going to give us a baby—to hold."

Humphrey relaxed and settled back down on the floor.

Henry turned back to his story. Another Turtle Creek saga. His fans had fallen in love with Cash and Polly. His author wheels turned as he read over the words he had written earlier. "Maybe, Humphrey, maybe it's time for Cash to become a daddy."

And then with a burst of what Henry called amazing grace, he began typing. But he had only written a paragraph when his cell chimed.

"Drat," he said as he picked it up. "It's Mom. Oh dear, she crashed the car. I knew it. She needs to stick to the Vespa."

He tapped Answer on his phone.

"Mom? What's wrong?"

"Oh, Henry dear, why do you always think something is the matter?" Harriet glanced across the table at Lily. "I'm fine, the Beamer is fine. I . . . well, I'm at a most darling little café downtown, and I met a most charming gal. Her name is Lily and she—"

"Mom," Henry said, "can this wait? I'm in the middle of writing, and I've told you how hard it is to be disturbed."

"Oh, well, I wouldn't want to disturb you, dear. I can make my own decisions. It is my money, after all."

"That's nice, Mom. You buy whatever you want." Henry continued typing. "I'm sure it will look just fine in the Grammy Suite. Oh, did you deposit that money?"

"Yes, dear, I deposited the money this morning."

Harriet glanced at Lily and watched her eyes grow big.

"Terrific. Thank you again, Mom. We really appreciate it. Now, you just buy whatever you want."

"Okay," Harriet said. "I'll buy whatever I want."

Henry tapped off his phone and continued typing. Humphrey scrambled to his feet and nudged Henry's leg.

"Oh, not you too. Do you need to go out?"

But Humphrey only folded back down and closed his eyes.

"Good boy. I'm sure whatever Mom is buying will be okay. And yes, I'm sure she's bringing donuts home."

Harriet tapped off her phone. "Well, I doubt we can fit a gold mine in the Grammy Suite." Then she smiled at Lily, who had just eaten the last bite of her sandwich.

"Finish your fries," Harriet said.

Lily shoved three fries into her mouth and chewed before saying, "They say gold is a great investment for, and I don't mean no disrespect, but for older people. Women especially."

"They do?" Harriet said. Having finished her own, she snagged one of Lily's fries before Lily could actually finish them. "I guess it couldn't hurt to talk to your dad." Harriet took a deep breath. She couldn't believe she just said that. "How much would you need? Can I see the mine?"

"Dad will tell you all the figures. And of course we can visit the mine. Can't go all the way up the mountain to the source, but we can get close."

Harriet's heart raced. "Do you think I'll see some gold?"

Lily smiled. "I'm sure of it. I'm sure you'll see some gold—probably just specks, you know. The big stuff has to be separated from the gravel and sand."

"Oh, I know that," Harriet said. "I remember that from my visit to the Empire Gold Mine."

Lily turned her head as the café door swung open.

"Dad," she called. "That's my Dad," she told Harriet.

Harriet looked at the man walking toward them. He was tall and burly and wore a cowboy hat and boots, rugged jeans, and a light plaid shirt. His hair was blond, like Lily's probably was in reality.

"Howdy," he said, tipping his hat.

"Daddy," Lily said. "This here is Harriet Beamer. I was telling her about the gold mine lease and Old Man Crickets."

"Oh, okay," he said. He grabbed a chair from a nearby table and sat down. "Nice ta meet ya, ma'am. My name is Winslow G. Jump. But call me Win. Ha! All my friends do because knowing me is a Win for you."

Harriet watched Lily turn away like any embarrassed teenager would.

Harriet extended her hand. "Nice to meet you, Win." She thought he sounded like a politician.

The waitress came by and asked Win if he wanted anything. "Go on," Harriet said. "Order whatever you want. My treat."

Win leaned back in his chair and patted his belly, which was kind of round and jolly. He wasn't exactly starving. "No, no, nothing for me, pretty lady. But my little girl and me are gonna eat good tonight."

"You really got all that money from the assay office today, Dad?" Lily asked.

"Sure did, little filly, enough for hamburgers and dessert, a big slice of that red velvet cake you love so much."

Lily smiled wide. "I'm proud of you, Dad." She turned to Harriet. "He had to work hard for that. Panning is not so easy."

"No, no, sure ain't," Win said. "Not like it would be if we could just get into Brunner's Run. The machines do most of the work. We just have to dig and keep the water flowing."

"So, Dad," Lily said, "is the mine lease still available or did Crickets sign it off to someone else already?"

"No, no, he didn't lease it yet. But he's close. I

105

don't think he has a choice. He's ready to retire and get out of the gold game, and he'll lease Brunner's Run to someone else unless I can find me a backer and take over."

Harriet took a breath. She felt another stronger check in her spirit but thought it was the fries coming back. "Maybe I can help."

She watched Win's eyes grow wide. "Really, ma'am? Are you sure? You'd only need to make a piddly little investment at first. Just to secure the lease and then—"

Lily interrupted. "We can talk about all that later. If you really want to help, maybe we should get to the bank so Daddy can get back to Crickets before it's too late."

Harriet watched Win smile at Lily. "Easy to tell who has the brains in this family. But patience now, gal. I don't want to rush Mrs. Beamer into anything."

Harriet chuckled. "I don't know anything about the gold mining business, but from what Lily's been telling me you seem to know an awful lot about gold and gold mines."

"I sure do. I've been studying on it for quite some time. Just looking for the right opportunity, and I'm pretty confident that Brunner's Run is it."

Harriet felt her heart skip a beat and touched her fingertips to her sternum. "My son just told me to buy whatever I want, but I just wonder if I know enough to be an investor. What will I have to do?"

"Oh, that's not a problem," Win said. "We'll take care of all the details. All you got to do is sit back and watch the money roll in—after you sign the agreement, of course. And naturally, I'll get a percentage of all the gold we find."

"Of course," Harriet said. A small investment wouldn't hurt too much. She would talk it over with the kids later.

"Okay. I can't believe I'm saying this, but where do I sign?" Harriet said.

"I got the papers right here in my pocket. Not much to it really." He reached into his breast pocket and produced two pages that looked very official to Harriet. "My goodness, but look at all that small writing," she said.

"Oh, just a bunch of legal mumbo jumbo. Basically, all it is saying is that you now have the right to mine for gold on a section of land known as Brunner's Run. Up there in Downieville."

"Downieville?" Harriet said. "I thought it was here, in Grass Valley."

"Oh, all the best placer mines are in Downieville," Lily said. "Everybody knows that. And it's not far. Just a few miles up route 45 North—the Golden Chain Highway."

Golden Chain Highway. Harriet liked the sound of that.

"I guess going to the bank would be the right

thing," Harriet said. "But I would like to see the mine."

She tried to sound knowledgeable and in charge. After all, she was an investor now.

"No problem," Win said.

Lily coughed and said, "I already told her that we couldn't climb all the way up the mountain, Dad. Maybe just stop down below, at the bottom of the stream. You know, where we saw all that gold that time."

"Hot diggety dog," Win said. "You are absolutely right. We can't expect you to climb a mountain, now can we, Harriet? But we can show you the run, the small place where the gold has a tendency to pool sometimes. But don't you worry. We'll get that gold too."

"Okay," Harriet said. "I can't wait."

The waitress set the check on the table. Harriet took it and left a generous tip. The three new friends headed for the door. On her way out, Harriet passed the woman sitting on the spinner stool, the woman who, though it was only now registering for Harriet, had seemed terribly interested in what was happening at their table. The woman dropped a book she seemed to be reading and smiled at Harriet as she retrieved it.

Harriet crossed the narrow street with Lily and Win. But with each step her anxiety seemed to grow until finally it grew to a point where Harriet felt too nervous to get into Win's truck with them. She remembered what happened in Reno when that sad, suicidal man kidnapped her. Now, there was a risk she took, and it turned out okay.

"Would you mind if I followed in my car?" she asked. "It's parked just over there."

"Oh, no trouble," Win said. "I'll drive nice and slow so you don't get lost. You'll know it because it has some fine-looking steer horns on the front. See it, right over there?"

Harriet suppressed an eye roll, thinking how cliché that was, but she chalked it up to being in the Old West as she spied the truck parked only a few spaces from Henry's BMW.

"That's my car right there. The black BMW."

Harriet saw a look pass between Win and Lily. It made her stomach jump, but she suppressed that also.

"So I'll just meet you there," she said as she unlocked the door.

"You bet," Win said.

Harriet climbed into the car. Her heart pounded like a trip hammer.

"Here goes nothing," she said as she turned the ignition.

She pulled the car onto the street just behind Win. Lily waved at her from the truck window. "Follow us," she called.

Harriet followed close behind the obnoxious, blue pickup. She couldn't help but notice some rusty spots on the sides near the wheel wells. But she figured that was pretty much par for the course after what Lily already told her, even if Win didn't seem all that down and out. But she chalked it up to him wanting to be strong for Lily. It couldn't be easy raising a daughter all by himself.

After making their way through town, they took a left turn onto Route 49 and stayed on the Golden Chain Highway for about forty miles. Harriet had never travelled this road before, but it was wide and safe enough as it seemed to make its way through the mountains and the mountain towns. She followed close behind Win and Lily.

Their next turn off the highway took them into a small town Harriet thought for certain must be Downieville. It seemed even older and more Western than Grass Valley with rows of stores and businesses with balconies just like in the movies. They crossed a small bridge over a river.

That river could have gold in it, she thought.

But they didn't stop there. They kept driving up and up and then down on curvy roads, past houses. Harriet smiled when she saw a sign with a picture of a man panning for gold. She thought maybe they had just passed a place where she could pan if she wanted. But no, she was about to embark on an even better adventure and, best of all, she didn't have to do any of the work. She snuggled back into the plush car seat. Yep, that was the way to go.

Win finally pulled over onto a grassy area. Harriet pulled the BMW behind and climbed out. She looked around. The area was like a dried meadow except for a creek babbling down a hill. The creek looked like it came directly down from the mountain. The water was clear and clean and, even though it was hard to believe, the air smelled cleaner than in Grass Valley. Harriet took a deep breath and smiled.

Win sidled up to Harriet. He seemed to be admiring the car.

"It's my son's," Harriet said. "If he knew I drove it this far from town he'd be—"

Win, who towered over Harriet like John Wayne, touched her shoulder. "Maybe you should run it through the car wash before you take it home."

"Good idea."

Lily pointed toward the creek. "That's Brunner's Run."

Harriet thought the small babbling stream was quaint, but how in the world would it ever produce gold? "Where's the mine?" she asked.

"Oh, that's way up in the mountain. We can't climb there," Win said. He pointed to the top of a pine-tree-covered mountain. "Way up there."

"Then how can I see the gold?" Harriet asked.

"Oh, at the run. Come on. You can see gold specks all over."

Harriet followed behind them. They were

walking kind of fast. "Specks?" she called. "I thought I would see some nuggets."

Win stopped and reached into his pocket. "Like this?" He held a shiny gold chunk. "This here nugget came from our mine."

Harriet smiled. "Oh, it's so pretty. Can I—"

"Hold it?" Lily said. "Sure."

Win placed the nugget in Harriet's opened palm. "So this is gold." It was much smoother than she expected but lumpier.

"Sure is," Win said. "It's inside that creek there, hiding in the gravel beds. I could sell this for a pretty penny, and I was thinking I might have to until you came along. No wonder I call it my good luck charm."

Harriet chuckled. "Don't you mean your gold luck charm?"

Lily laughed. "That's a good one, Dad. I like Harriet."

They walked on until they got to the edge of the grass where the water began.

"Lookee there," Win said. "In the water. See all that sparkly stuff?"

"Gold?" Harriet said in barely a whisper. "That's all gold."

"And that's just the dust," Lily said. "The real stuff, the money gold, is up higher, still big and heavy enough to stay where we can get at it. That's why we need money. It takes machinery to get in there."

"That's right," Win said. "Crickets has one machine working, but we need another."

Harriet took a breath. "I can't wait to tell Henry about this." She pulled out her camera to snap a picture.

Win grabbed her hand. "Oh, now, hold on a second, Harriet. I know you're eager, but Old Man Crickets won't appreciate it if you go taking pictures of his mine before the paperwork is signed."

Harriet dropped her phone in her purse. "Of course. I'm sorry."

"But hold on, I was saving these for the right moment." He reached into his pants pocket. "Had these in the truck. Pictures of your mine, Harriet. The place way up yonder." He pointed.

"Oh, let me see."

Win showed her a picture of what looked like a wasteland, scrub brush, and a small, shallow creek. A backhoe was on the right and also a funny-looking contraption that looked like a long box with water running down it.

"What's that?" Harriet asked.

"That's your mine."

"No, I mean that." She pointed to the box.

"That's what you call a sluice box. It helps to separate the gold from the other rocks and ores."

"Now, how does it do that?"

"Well, gold is heavy. It sinks. Whatever ain't gold is washed away."

"Oh," Harriet said. "So that's my mine?"

"Your little section of it. Just as soon as you sign the papers and, well, you know, give me the money. We can bump up operations and be producing gold right quick."

"So what do you say, Harriet?" Lily asked. "Will you help us?" Her voice sounded like a little girl needing Christmas to come.

Harriet couldn't help it. Her heart was beating so fast she had to will it to slow down. She had never been so enamored with anything in her life.

Chapter Ten

Henry stared at the computer screen. He hated it when the screen stared back. Mocking him, egging him on like a playground bully. Didn't the computer know he had run out of words for the day? But with being so close to a deadline, he had to keep pushing.

It was hard to write. He couldn't help but think of Prudence, and every time he did, the worry crept back in. He did his best to give it to God. But still the worry persisted. Most of the time, when he got stuck in that kind of a loop, he could use it to his advantage in his writing. He could channel those feelings and use them to help his characters express themselves. But he was tired. He had spent too much valuable sleeping time watching Prudence sleep. Like she was going to explode or something or because he could hardly believe she was carrying his child. Still, tired was tired no matter the reason.

"Maybe that's it, Humphrey. Maybe I'm tired. It's hard to be a brilliant writer when you are tired. I suppose it's hard to be a brilliant dog when you're tired."

Henry patted the dog's head. The dog gave him a look, and then arched his wiry brows.

"I suppose that's true," Henry said. "I am blessed to be living my dream."

Henry checked his calendar, another procrastination trick. "The builders are coming a week from Monday," he said to Humphrey. "That might help. Maybe." Maybe having all that activity around him would be a good thing. It could be distracting. Or maybe he just had to get over it. Prudence was fine. The baby was fine. Even his mother was fine.

"Mother," he said looking at Humphrey. "Where do you suppose she is? I hope she's not up to something." He felt sort of bad for not letting her finish what she had to say earlier.

But she'd tell him later. For now it was good

to be alone. Or so he tried to convince himself.

"Now back to work, old man."

Humphrey tilted his head and settled into his sleeping position.

The instant Henry poised his fingers over the keyboard his phone jingled. "Drat!" He looked at the name. "Martha? Why would she be calling my number?"

Humphrey was not so much interested.

Henry tapped Answer. "Hello."

"Henry," Martha said, "I hope I'm not disturbing you."

"No, no," Henry said. "I can use a little break." He took a breath and leaned back in his chair.

"Okay, as long as I'm not disturbing you."

"No, not at all. What's up? How's back east?"

"Beautiful. The leaves are changing already. That sugar maple in your . . . well, your old front yard is gorgeous. Always the first to turn."

Henry could see the tree in his mind. "It always was so pretty."

"I've been trying to reach your mother. But she hasn't answered her cell. I was hoping she was home, if that's where you are."

"No, sorry, she isn't here. She went out a while ago."

"I rang her phone ten times in the last two hours. I'm beginning to get worried that she fell into a ditch or something."

Henry smiled. "I doubt she fell into a ditch, but

that is odd. She always answers her phone or calls back pretty quickly. Maybe she has the phone somewhere else and she can't hear it. Or she could have the sound off. She's done that too. Or she left it in the car."

"You're probably right. But I really wanted to speak to her."

Henry pulled a yellow pencil from the pencil mug on his desk and drummed with it. "She went into town to do some . . . shopping. I expect her home pretty soon. I'll make sure I tell her you've been calling and to check her phone."

"Okay, well, I was just wondering . . . has she . . . well . . ."

"Told us you are coming?"

"Yes."

Henry sensed nervousness in Martha's voice. "Yep, she told us. And we'd love to have you."

"Are you sure it won't be an imposition? I could stay at a hotel or a bed and breakfast."

"Nope. In fact I think it will be great for Mom. She's been kind of knocking around the house like a stray pinball." Henry assumed his mother hadn't reached Martha yet if she didn't know it was okay for her to visit. That meant she didn't know about the baby either. He wouldn't tell. He'd let Harriet share the good news.

"Well, thank you, Henry. I guess I'll go ahead and buy my ticket."

"Yep. Anytime. Tuesdays are generally the

cheapest days to fly, and we'll be happy to come get you."

"I'd be flying into Sacramento, is that right?" Martha said.

"Yes. It's about an hour or so drive. But don't worry about that. It's our pleasure."

"So is this coming Tuesday okay? I know it's short notice. And I hope a two-week stay is really all right."

Henry was surprised the visit would be so soon, but he'd explain to Pru.

"Yep. Say, how is Wyatt?" Henry asked. He decided to change the subject just in case he sounded hesitant.

"I haven't heard from him in a few years. Last I knew he was in school but not very happy."

Martha seemed to sputter a little. "Oh. He's . . . he's doing okay."

"Good," Henry said, even though he sensed something wasn't quite right. "And how about you? Mom mentioned something about a health scare."

"Oh . . . um, that. Well, it turned out to be nothing. I'm fine. Gonna live to be a hundred."

"That's good to hear. Now, you go ahead and book your flight, and I'll tell Mom you called."

"Thank you, honey," Martha said. "I can't wait to see California."

"You might not want to go back," Henry said.

"Oh, I'd need a pretty good reason to move

118

lock, stock, and barrel across the country."

"I know," Henry said. He drummed the pencil. "It will be good to see you for however long you stay."

"You too," Martha said.

Henry tapped off the phone. He looked down at Humphrey, who had started to snore. "Now where do you suppose Mom is?"

He tapped in Harriet's number. No answer. "Um," he said to Humphrey. "That's strange. I hope she's okay."

A little more than an hour later Harriet had handed Win a sizable bundle of cash and was standing outside the bank shaking his hand. Win had said that cash was preferable because he could get it to Old Man Crickets and into the hands of the workers faster and secure equipment without delay. She signed the several official-looking papers and was feeling a tad anxious. So anxious that her hand wobbled when she wrote her name and so her signature was not as pretty as it usually was.

"Now don't you fret," Win said. "I'll get these copied and get you your copies right quick."

"Okay, dear." Harriet needed to catch her breath. She was starting to feel a bit winded from the whole ordeal. She might be spry and active, but she was still seventy-two and the last few hours had been a bit of a whirlwind.

Win folded the pages and stuffed them into his shirt pocket. He smiled at Harriet through yellowing teeth, and for the first time Harriet noticed a wide gap between his two front teeth.

"All you need to do now is sit back and wait for the mine to start producing and then rake in the cash." A small puff of coffee-laced breath swirled around.

Harriet liked the sound of that, especially now with the baby on the way and considering how much money she had just forked over to pay for her new Grammy Suite.

"Thank you, Mrs. Beamer," Lily, who had been very quiet through the transaction, said. "This is going to help so much." Lily hugged her. Harriet enjoyed how it felt to hug Lily back. She enjoyed young people and thought maybe she and Lily could be friends. "Oh, dear, you can just call me Harriet. I'd like us to be friends, not just business partners."

Lily pulled back and said, "I'd like that."

"On second thought," Harriet said, "I could be like your grandma."

Lily's eyes twinkled. "Really? I ain't never had a grandma. Not like a real family." She looked away.

"Well, you do now, and I'm just tickled pink to be part of it," Harriet said. "I can't wait to see the gold come out of the mine."

"Now, now, hold on there," Win said. "Like I

120

told you, the actual placer is way up on the mountain. All you have to do is wait down here."

Harriet looked up at Win. "That's what I meant. I'm really not all that interested in climbing mountains. Not anymore." She took Lily's hand. "I'll just count on you two giving me some first-hand reports."

"Alrighty then," Win said with a tip of his cowboy hat. "I'll be in touch real soon."

Harriet swallowed. "Okay. I guess I better be heading home. I think I've been gone a lot longer than Henry expected. I'm sure he's worried sick over that car."

Win shook her hand. "Now this has been an exciting day."

"It certainly has," Harriet said. "Never in my wildest imaginations have I imagined something like this happening to me."

She looked into Lily's eyes. "And I made a new friend."

Harriet strolled with a little less of a spring in her step across the street to the parking lot. The day had turned into much more than she had planned. That was for sure. If someone would have said she'd be the proud investor in a gold mine earlier that morning, she would have said they were crazy. But nonetheless, here she was with a lease and feeling an odd mixture of pride and fear.

The BMW was a little dusty and grimy from

the ride to Downieville. "I better get you washed," she said. "Henry will have a conniption fit if he sees all that dirt."

The nearest car wash she could find was a little farther away from downtown than she liked. It was the kind you drove through, and as often as she did she still felt a little claustrophobic as the giant rollers and huge rubber wipers did the job. The car wash was also one of the ones that sold gas, which was a good thing since Harriet thought she should gas up the car also after driving it all that distance.

Once she was out on the straightaway toward home she started to weigh the pros and cons of telling Henry and Prudence about the gold mine. On the one hand it would be nice to have all that free legal advice, but on the other hand she didn't want them telling her she was foolish and wasting her money. No, she'd wait a while to tell, maybe after she had a couple of real gold nuggets to show them. Then she could say she is saving for her grandchild's college education. What parent could argue with that? Nope, she'd hold off on telling and enjoy keeping her secret to herself. Well, she'd tell Martha.

Martha! In all the excitement, Harriet hadn't arrived home when she had wanted to call Martha. She would need to call the minute she got home. Harriet put pedal to the metal and sped home, keeping a close lookout for the police.

She looked at herself in the rearview mirror as she passed a cow pasture. "Goodness, Harriet, you look a mess." She felt like a mess also, tired and excited. "You are going to be so excited for me, Martha," Harriet said out loud. "Of course, you can't tell a soul, not a living soul."

Harriet pulled the car into their driveway on Butterfly Lane just as a Fed Ex truck stopped in front of the house. Harriet waited a second until the driver, a young woman, jumped out. She went to the back of the truck and opened the lift. Oh, to be that nimble.

Harriet climbed out of the car and started toward the front door but had only gotten two or three paces when she heard her name.

"Are you Harriet Beamer?" the driver called.

"Yes. Yes, I am," Harriet said. "Do you have a package for me?"

"I do," the driver said. "But I wanted to meet you. I feel like I know you already. Henry has told me so much."

Harriet couldn't help but feel a little confused. "I don't understand. Are you and Henry friends?"

"Well, kind of. I delivered all those packages you were sending. Henry said they were salt and pepper shakers. You've become kind of a legend at the depot."

Harriet smiled. "Oh for heaven's sake. Me? A legend? All I did was send my collection and the shakers I found in my travels across the country."

"Well, even so. We got a kick out of it. At least I did. And here's another package addressed to you. From Maggie Valley, North Carolina."

"Oh for heaven's sake. It must be from Ricky and Shawna." Harriet smiled at the driver. "They're my Native American friends—Cherokee to be specific. They took me stargazing. I think stargazing is one of the most spectacular things a person can do." Harriet signed for the package. "Thank you very much. I wonder what they would be sending me."

"Probably more shakers. You are a hoot and a half, Harriet Beamer," the driver said. "Have a nice day."

"Thank you—I think."

Harriet carried the smallish, brown package into the house. She gave it a slight shake but didn't hear anything. She set it on the ottoman as Humphrey trotted over. His tail was wagging a mile a minute. It had been a long day without her. Harriet patted him. "Hello, puppy," she said. "Did you miss me?" Sometimes Harriet wondered if Humphrey worried that every absence meant she was off on another adventure and that he could very well be stuck inside the belly of another airplane on his way to who knew where.

"I told you I'd be back," she said with her most reassuring tone and several pats on his side. He responded by falling onto his back so she could get in a good belly rub also. And that was when she remembered she had forgotten to stop at a bakery. "Oh, Humphrey. I'm sorry. I forgot your . . ." She didn't dare say the word *donut,* hoping he might have forgotten. And why remind him just to get him upset? That didn't seem right. After a couple more good rubs, Humphrey scrambled to his short little legs and trotted off, but not without giving Harriet a disappointed, mournful look.

He never forgets.

That was when Henry appeared in the living room. "Mom," Henry said, "where have you been? You've been gone all day. I was starting to worry. You didn't answer your phone. I called several times." Henry stood in the doorway between the living room and his den. He had a pencil sticking from one ear, and his arms crossed against his chest like he was reprimanding a tardy child.

"You did?" Harriet said. "Oh for crying out loud, Henry, I'm sorry. I didn't hear the phone jingle." Harriet rifled through her bag—it was a large thing, more of a tote bag, with a bright yellow background and covered with flowers. She loved the bag as it had served many purposes over the last year, from carry-all to weapon. "I know I brought the fool thing with me. Where is it?" She removed a small flashlight, her favorite Moleskine notebook, two pens, a wadded up Kleenex, six pennies, a pack of orange Tic Tacs, and a tube of hand lotion concocted with oatmeal.

"Life was definitely easier when we weren't all in communication every minute of every day," she said. "All it does is lead to unnecessary worry."

Harriet found her phone wedged between a small copy of the New Testament she carried and a red wallet crammed with coupons she never used.

"Here it is," she said, holding it up obviously so Henry could witness the fact that she had taken the phone into town with her. "See, no need to worry, dear. I had my phone."

"I can see that," Henry said. "But it's only good if you turn it on. Otherwise it's a paperweight."

"I know that, son. And if I needed you, if I ran the car up a telephone pole or into a moose, I would have turned it on and called."

"I'm sorry. I'm just worried about a lot of things right now."

Harriet looked into her son's Hershey-chocolate-bar-colored eyes. "I know, honey. But you have got to calm down. Prudence and the baby are doing great. You're the one who isn't, and if you keep up this level of worry, by the time the baby is born you'll be a babbling, gray-haired, worrywart stringing beads at a mental hospital. Isn't that what the good Lord says, worry is not going to add a single . . . whatever it is . . . to your life. Worry just subtracts."

"I know. It's just—"

Harriet patted his cheek. "She'll be fine. The baby will be fine. I know."

"Thanks, Mom. But where have you been?"

"Oh, well, I told you where I was going. I went into town and got a—"

"Is that a package?" Henry said.

"Yes. It just arrived. It's from my friends in Maggie Valley."

"That's nice."

Harriet opened the package and pulled out two, gold, star-shaped objects. "Oh, that was so sweet of them," Harriet said. "They remind me of the night we went stargazing."

"Oh, that is thoughtful," Henry said.

Harriet shoved the wrappings into the box. "I think Humphrey needs to go out."

"So did you buy anything?" Henry asked.

"I did."

"Where is it? In the car? Do you need help carrying it inside?"

Harriet couldn't help but burst into laughter. She recovered quickly, thinking about a gold mine in the living room, and looked away from Henry. "No, no, let's just say it will be delivered when it's time."

"Oh, good idea. And we don't have moose in Grass Valley."

"No? Then what do you have?"

"Bears. Grizzlies and elk."

"Okay, I will definitely call you if and when I

meet a grizzly bear in downtown Grass Valley."

"Oh, and another thing," Henry said as Harriet checked her phone. "I spoke with Martha today."

"Oh dear," Harriet said. "She called my cell phone ten times. I missed every call."

"That's why she called me." Henry sat on the couch and tied his shoe laces. "She's making plans to come on Tuesday. I told her that's fine."

"Really? This Tuesday?" Harriet said. She sat on the couch and untied her sneakers. "That's wonderful, but oh dear. Tuesday? I have so much to do to get ready."

Henry stood. "She sounded great, Mom, and is so pleased to be coming. We had a nice conversation."

"Henry," Harriet said practically leaping from the couch. "Did you give her the good news? The baby news?"

Henry chuckled. "No, don't worry. I saved that for you."

Harriet sat on the edge of her bed with Humphrey at her feet.

"I suppose I can tell you," she said as she reached down and patted his side. "But you have to promise not to tell a soul."

Humphrey didn't move much except to swish his tail slightly.

"I leased a . . . a gold mine. There I said it. Out loud. I can hardly believe it." All of a sudden

Harriet was struck with a case of what she called monkey nerves. "A gold mine, Humphrey. Mommy leased a gold mine."

Humphrey looked up at her with a decidedly incredulous expression and then laid his head on her foot with a whimper.

"Oh dear. I hope I didn't make a terrible mistake."

Humphrey let go a woof.

She changed into more comfortable clothes, jeans and a light sweater. She placed her Chucks near the closet and then grabbed her cell phone to call Martha.

"Martha, you are not going to believe it," Harriet said the instant Martha said, "Hello."

"Harriet," Martha said. "I've been trying to reach you all day."

"I know. I'm sorry. I have been having quite a busy day. My phone was in the bottom of my tote. I never heard it ringing."

"Well, I wanted to tell you that I could come soon. I spoke with Henry earlier and he said Tuesday would be fine."

"I know. And I'm so happy. I can't wait to see you, but you haven't heard the big news. Prudence is pregnant." Harriet's heart skipped a beat. She was so excited to say the words out loud. "Prudence and Henry are going to have a baby."

"Oh, Harriet, I am so happy for you. For you

and . . . and everyone. When is the baby due?"

"In the spring"—she did a quick cipher on her fingers—"April, I think. A spring baby. Isn't that just so sweet? Henry was a winter baby and winter babies can be difficult."

"Congratulations," Martha said. "That is wonderful, wonderful news."

"Thank you, and of course you will be Aunt Martha."

"Now you just want to make me cry."

Harriet almost mentioned Wyatt, but thought better of it. Wyatt had yet to marry, and Martha never talked much about becoming a grand-mother. Especially lately, now that she thought about it.

"Don't cry, dear. This is a joyous time and not only that but . . . but there's something more."

"More news?"

Harriet took a deep breath, glanced out the bedroom window, and thought a moment. No. News of the gold mine was better delivered in person. And she would keep the news about the addition until Martha got there too so she could see her face. "Nothing. I will tell you when you get here, but it's a secret. You'll have to promise not to tell the kids."

"Okay. I'll promise."

Chapter Eleven

The next couple of days flew past. Harriet busied herself with getting everything ready for Martha. And Henry had located a bed and had it delivered in record speed. And now it was Monday, the day before Martha's arrival. Harriet could hardly contain her enthusiasm. She looked over the room before having breakfast, imagining what it would be like to have her best friend in the world staying with her.

"Will you look at those curtains? They're nice, but they could use refreshing."

Harriet wanted something brighter. New curtains could bring a room a complete new look.

Later that morning, she and Florence Caldwell went into town together and bought a few things, including the curtains—bright yellow with pink flowers—and three sets of brand new sheets. Nothing to be jealous about over curtains or sheets, and Florence was a pleasant shopping partner.

"Not much beats brand new, Egyptian cotton

sheets," Florence had said as they stood in line waiting to pay for their treasures.

"So smooth," Harriet said. Then she laughed. "Do you remember the sheets we slept in as newlyweds? Egyptian cotton was never heard of."

"I do remember. I think I used the cheapest sheets for ten years of marriage. It was like sleeping on sandpaper some nights.

"Your friend will be very comfortable," Florence continued. "You must be very close."

"That will be seventy-five, twenty-two," the cashier said.

Harriet swiped her card and went through the menus before answering.

"We are close," Harriet said as she slipped the card back into its spot in her wallet. "I don't know what I would have done if I didn't have Martha right after Max died. She helped me through some pretty shaky weeks."

"I hear that," Florence said. "There is nothing like a good friend."

Harriet smiled. "I know she'll love these curtains." It was nice that Florence understood about Martha.

They made a couple of other stops in the store before heading to the car. Harriet purchased a small bud vase and a pair of warm socks. "It's not cold yet," she had said. "But these are so cuddly. Keep my tootsies toasty."

Florence pulled her minivan onto the main street. "Where to?"

"Oh, I don't know. I could eat."

"Good idea."

"I ate at that little café, Rachel's. It was kind of nice."

"Oh, Rachel's is a good spot. Let's go. And Harriet, lunch is on me."

Harriet did not argue, considering all the money she had been putting out in the last few months. Her reserves were nearly depleted, which made the whole gold mine enterprise that much more important. She hadn't told Florence about the lease. She wanted Martha to be the first person to know. But she was beginning to think she should, especially since she had yet to hear from Win or Lily since their initial transaction or get copies of the signed papers. Over lunch. She would tell Florence over a veggie wrap and fries and get her advice.

Florence parked in the lot, and the two made their way to Rachel's Café. It was a little before one o'clock and the place was hopping. But it didn't take long to get a seat. Many of those waiting were getting take-out.

The same waitress, Cindy, led them to the table Harriet had sat at before, promising to bring coffee right away. And as they passed the counter, Harriet once again saw that woman from the other day, leaning over a book. She couldn't put her finger on it, but there was something odd about her. She stood out like a broken toe.

"I think I'll have grilled cheese," Florence said.

"Veggie wrap and fries for me," Harriet said with a glance toward the strange woman.

"What's up?" Florence asked, turning toward where Harriet was looking. "Do you know her?"

Harriet turned her attention back to Florence. "No. It's just that she was here the other day when I . . . I . . ." She could not say the words. Now, all of a sudden, she was filled with utter embarrassment and couldn't get the words out.

"When you what?" Florence asked.

Cindy set down two cups of coffee. "Where's your little friend today?" she said to Harriet.

Harriet's heart sped. "I . . . I don't know. She's really not my friend. We had just met that day."

Cindy shook her head. "Uh huh. Can I take your orders?"

"What was that all about?" Florence asked after Cindy left.

Harriet let go a huge sigh. She tried to stall as long as she could, dumping Half and Half into her coffee, stirring it as though she were trying to make butter, looking every which way but at Florence.

"Okay, here's the thing," Harriet said. "The other day I was in here, and I met this girl, Lily.

134

She was waiting for her father, who was at the assay office."

Florence stopped her right there. "Oh no, I think I know where this is leading. Did you get snookered into buying some fake gold nuggets? Fool's gold?"

Harriet felt her eyebrows rise and her cheeks flush. "Well, not nuggets. At least not per se, not exclusively."

Florence let a small chuckle escape her mouth. "Then what? What did you do?"

"Okay, okay. I leased a mine. Well, a section called Brunner's Run."

For a second or two, Florence didn't say a word or make a sound.

Harriet glanced around the café. The woman was still leaning over her book, although she had seemed to shift more toward Harriet and Martha.

"Okay, you say you leased a mine. Tell me about it," Florence finally said.

Harriet proceeded to explain the whole thing. Florence seemed to know quite a lot about placer mines and such, and that actually gave Harriet a certain amount of comfort. But still, she found it necessary to ask, "Do you think I was scammed?"

Florence chewed her sandwich and looked pensive a moment. "Not necessarily. There are plenty of legitimate mines and leases around, but I guess you should be careful. Get Prudence to check it out."

Harriet swallowed. "I can't. I haven't told them, and I won't tell them. Not until I have made a profit."

"You know that could be a long, long time."

Harriet pulled a piece of cucumber from her veggie wrap and set it on the side of her plate. "I don't like cucumbers. Pre-pickles, that's all they are. Slimy pre-pickles."

"You should tell Henry," Florence said.

"I can't, and, Florence, please, promise me you won't tell either."

"Okay. I promise."

Harriet looked into Florence's eyes. "I'm serious. I'll tell him when I'm ready."

"I promise."

After having little success at home, Henry had gone to his favorite coffee shop that morning to work, leaving a note for his mother so she'd know where he had gone when she got back from shopping with Florence. A place called JavaScone. It had a nice ambience, artsy with original paintings by local artists on the walls. Rustic wood tables with tiny votive candles and a seemingly endless array of sweets. *A Horse with No Name* was playing in the background when he got there, and Henry hummed along as he chose a vanilla latte and a blueberry scone.

He sat down at the only remaining table near the window and opened his laptop. It was a particularly hard chapter to write since he made the tough decision that Polly would lose the baby. Writing about it brought back some painful feelings, but Henry had learned to use those emotions to write better, richer, truer.

He remembered sitting in the hospital cafétéria while the doctor tended to Prudence after losing their second child. He wondered if he would ever be a father. If maybe it was his fault. Maybe there was something wrong with him. Henry reached way down deep inside his heart and wrote:

Cash wiped tears from his wife's eyes. Then he kissed the one, large tear that escaped and had rolled down her cheek. He kissed it to taste it, to try to really understand what it was like for her to carry a baby for nearly nine months only to have him die just days before he was ready to be born. But he couldn't know, not really. All he could really know was that there was a huge void inside of him now. A void that would never, ever be filled.

Cash felt his hand turn into a tight fist. Why, God, why wasn't this child born just one day earlier?

Henry looked away from the screen and broke off a piece of scone.

But that's the way it should be. He didn't want the new baby to fill the void left by the two that were with Jesus. He didn't want to forget them—ever.

Henry went back to his story and kept typing, pleased and not so pleased with the words he was writing. "I can always re-write," he thought.

He looked at the screen, then at the scone. He sipped his latte, and that was when he noticed a tall burly man wearing a cowboy hat walking toward him. He was with a girl, probably his daughter, Henry thought. The two sat directly across from Henry.

The cowboy hat the man wore intrigued Henry. It was a vintage, black, rancher-style Stetson made of beaver fur felt and probably had a satin lining. Henry knew this from his research and thought perhaps he was the only one in the restaurant who knew. He smiled and went back to his work, kind of wondering about the appeal of cowboy hats in the twenty-first century.

"I like her," the girl said. "She's a nice old lady. I don't want her to get hurt, not like before."

Henry looked up again. It was hard not to eavesdrop. After all, it was in the writer's handbook that eavesdropping could be a good way to learn something about dialog, not to mention find a plot.

"I like her too, darlin'," the cowboy said. "But she'll be all right. Widows like her have all kinds of money. She'll be okay."

Henry watched as the girl sipped a soda. "I hope so, Pop. I like this one."

Henry wondered if they might be up to no good. He paused from his work to listen more.

"I'm gonna have to call her today," the man said. "Arrange for more money." Then he leaned back and patted his paunch. "Costs a lot of money to keep a gold mine humming."

Gold mine? Now Henry was really intrigued. This could be just what he needed for his book. What if Cash discovered gold? It would solve all his troubles.

Henry wrote a few notes about it in his notebook: Research gold mines. Grass Valley. Mining supplies in late nineteenth century.

He sipped his latte. Yep, a gold mine could be just what the doctor ordered. He went back to work, only stopping for a JavaScone sandwich for lunch.

Florence dropped Harriet off in front of the house.

"There's Prudence's car," Harriet said. "I wonder why she's home. I hope she's okay. And Henry's BMW is gone."

A flashback of Henry's call that Pru had suffered yet another miscarriage surfaced in her mind. She looked into Florence's eyes. "I'd invite you in but I think I better check this out."

Florence waved. "Sure. Call me if you need anything."

Harriet closed the car door and hurried up the path. She pushed open the door and Humphrey trotted right to her. He let go three short woofs, a signal usually that something was wrong.

Harriet dropped her packages. "What is it, boy? Where's Prudence?"

"Over here." She heard Pru's voice but didn't see her.

"Where?"

Prudence poked her head over the back of the couch. "Here."

"Are you okay, dear?" Harriet asked. "What's wrong? Where's Henry? Should I call the doctor?"

"No. I'm fine. And Henry left a note that he went to a coffee shop to work. I was just feeling a little nauseated and thought I would work at home, but I've got to tell you, I feel awful."

Harriet sat next to her and patted her knee. "How far along are you again?"

"About nine weeks. I waited a long time to take the test. I wanted to be sure."

"Then you're right on schedule for morning sickness if you're going to have it."

"But it's afternoon," Prudence said.

"Yeah, well, it can hit anytime. It's normal. Right as rain. Nothing to worry about. I mean you're not . . . spotting or cramping, right?"

Prudence shook her head.

"Okay, you're fine. The baby is fine. Maybe some crackers."

Harriet looked into Prudence's eyes. She saw

something she didn't think she had ever noticed before. It was a little sad and a little dreamy.

"Are you okay?" Harriet asked. "I mean, besides the morning sickness?"

Prudence looked away for a fraction of a second and then turned back to Harriet. "I guess I've been thinking about my mother lately."

"I guess you have. It must be so hard. You miss her terribly, don't you?" Harriet continued to pat Prudence's knee.

Prudence squirmed a little on the comfy couch. "I don't know if I miss her terribly or if I'm angry. But some days, like today, I sure miss having a mother around—to help and . . . you know, be with me."

"You have me."

Prudence smiled. Her eyes now glistened with tears. "I know. And I really am happy you're here with us. Henry is also."

"And I'm glad to be here. I can't think of anywhere I'd rather be."

Harriet touched the side of her face. "How about if I go get those crackers and some tea?"

Prudence smiled.

"Be back in two shakes of a lamb's tail. Now, you just rest."

Harriet set the kettle on to boil and had just located the box of soda crackers when the back deck slider flew open. Humphrey bolted for the door and was outside lickety-split. Harriet jumped, but then she laughed when she saw Florence standing in the kitchen holding yet another pie.

"I thought you all could use something sweet," she said. "When you didn't call, I thought probably everything was all right over here." Harriet decided not to be jealous, that Florence evidently had just-walk-right-in-the-door privileges here. She could tell that Florence really cared about the kids.

"Another pie? You must bake a pie every day."

"Pretty much," Florence said, putting the pie on the table. "Blueberry today. How's Prudence?"

"She's fine. Morning sickness. Her first time. She never got sick with the others."

Florence nodded. "I hear that's sometimes a sign. Being so sick you want to die is a good thing when you're pregnant."

"I had heard that also," Harriet said. She arranged eight crackers around a small plate and set a blue teacup in the center.

"Crackers are good, but pie is better," Florence said.

"Maybe we should let her stomach settle first."

The kettle whistle blew, and Harriet made three cups of tea and carried it all out to the living room on a vintage Pepsi tray—the one with girls on a beach having way too much fun drinking Pepsi. The slogan read, "The drink that satisfies."

"Here we are," Harriet said in a sing-songy voice.

"Thank you," Prudence said, sitting up straighter. "Hi, Mrs. Caldwell."

"Now haven't I told you a dozen times to call me Florence. And, you know, crackers are good, but I brought pie."

Harriet watched Prudence's eyes light up. She did like Florence's pies. But Prudence looked at Florence and said, "Thanks, but maybe just the crackers for now."

Harriet patted Prudence's knee. "You just let those crackers settle, and then we'll think about blueberry pie."

Florence stayed for a few more minutes before she excused herself. "As long as all is well here, I think I'll skedaddle."

"Thank you for stopping by and for the pie," Prudence said.

"No need to show me out."

"Would you let Humphrey inside?" Harriet asked. "Oh, and pick up your special pie tin from the lemon meringue pie. It's on the counter. I forgot to give it to you this morning when you picked me up."

Harriet enjoyed her time with Prudence. It was the first time in, well, ever that the two of them had spent so much time together just talking. It seemed now they had something in common. Prudence seemed to enjoy the stories Harriet told of her pregnancy and Henry's delivery.

"Let's just say he took his time," Harriet said.

"Three false alarms and thirty-six hours of labor. I thought maybe I was giving birth to a hippo. And don't get me started on Max, for goodness sake that husband of mine . . ."

Prudence's eyes grew wide. Harriet changed the subject.

"So the builders are coming next Monday," Harriet said. "I am just so excited."

"Yes, yes," Prudence said. "Bright and early."

"How long did they say the project will take again?"

"Two months, start to finish."

Harriet did the same quick calculations she had done before. "That means I really will be in my own place by Christmas."

"Yes," Prudence said. "Then we'll get started on the nursery. I figured Christmas would be a good time to start." Sandra Day jumped onto Prudence's lap. Harriet liked to see Prudence give the cat some attention, although she knew that some cats, like Sandra Day, didn't require much, not like Humphrey.

"Sounds good to me," Harriet said. "Have you got any thoughts on décor?"

"For your Grammy Suite or the nursery?"

"Well, dear, I thought that I would decorate my suite. I was talking about the nursery."

"That's what I thought. No, not really. I just know I want the nursery light and airy and full of books and pictures and soft things."

"Ha, that's pretty much how I was thinking about the Grammy Suite."

Prudence yawned and patted her tummy. "Do you think I'm showing yet?"

"Well, maybe a little. But don't rush it." She smiled as she took off her sneakers. "Say, I bought a few things for Martha's visit. Would you like to see?"

"Sure," Prudence said. "But I am pretty certain I have a little baby bump going on here."

"Darling, the baby is the size of a peach pit right now."

Harriet had just picked up her bags when she heard her phone jingle. "That might be Martha," she called to Prudence. "Will you excuse me?"

"Sure," Prudence said. "Take your time. I think I'll rest a bit."

Henry closed his laptop. He had had enough writing for one day. He checked his phone. It was almost three o'clock. He tossed his trash into the can and stuffed his computer into his leather messenger bag. The cowboy and the girl had long gone, but Henry was still very excited about the prospect of having a gold strike in his new book.

"How hard can gold mining be?" he said to himself on the way outside. "A pick, an axe, maybe some pans and, presto! Gold nuggets."

Feeling quite pleased with his new plot twist,

Henry walked down Main Street. He passed Rachel's Café, but he wasn't hungry so he went on to the Viking Bakery. He had promised Harriet he would bring donuts home for Humphrey.

"Six glazed, please." He ordered extra because Prudence might enjoy something sweet. "Warm ones if you have them."

"Just out," the girl behind the counter said. "Only six?"

"Oh, make it a dozen."

Henry was feeling so good. There wasn't much that could burst his bubble that day. He paid for the donuts, and as he opened the bakery door he noticed their bulletin board. His eyes fell on a flyer that read, "Gold mines for lease. Don't get duped. Call the professionals."

"Now there's a sign if ever there was one." He peeled off one of the telephone tabs. "For research." Henry didn't think he would ever actually invest in anything as sketchy as a gold mine. But with the baby coming, who knew?

Chapter Twelve

"Don't stop ringing," Harriet said as she searched her bag.

But unfortunately, when she found her phone tucked in the very bottom of the large bag, the jingling had stopped.

She looked at the screen. It was Win who had called, not Martha. She felt both disappointed and excited. Maybe they struck gold.

Humphrey followed Harriet onto the deck. She wanted to return Win's call out of earshot of Prudence.

"Harriet," Win said. "How are you?"

"I'm fine. I'm sorry I didn't pick up when you just called. I couldn't get to my phone. It was stuck in the bottom of my tote again."

"Oh, that's no trouble at all, darlin'."

"I'm glad. So what's up? Good news, I hope."

"Well now, in a matter of speaking it's good news."

Harriet sat down at the deck table where the sun was warm. "Uh oh, I don't like the sound of that, Win."

"Now, it's nothing huge. It's just that the boys have been working awful hard. In fact, too hard. We don't have the machinery to keep up with how much gravel and dirt they're going through. That's where you can help."

"I can?" Harriet imagined herself climbing the mountains and using a shovel or pickax or whatever it was they used up there. "But how?"

"That's easy. The boys are asking for a second sluice box and another trommel too."

"Trommel?"

Win laughed. "Why don't you just meet us down at the bank before it closes, and I'll explain it to you."

"But I just this minute got back from town. Can it wait until tomorrow?" But then she remembered. Martha was coming.

"Okay. I'll just slip my sneakers back on. How much do you think you'll need?"

"Not much, darlin'. A paltry amount when you consider how much gold we're fixin' to get out of all that dirt we move through the trommel."

"Sounds exciting," Harriet said. She had images of great mounds of dirt being forced through a giant flour sifter. But that couldn't be right, could it? "I can meet you at the bake . . . I mean bank in a half hour or so."

"I'm already here," Win said. "Lily and I will just wait right here for you, pretty lady."

"Okay." But then she remembered Henry was

gone and had taken the BMW. "I guess I can take the SUV if Prudence doesn't need it," she told Win. "My Vespa would take too long."

"You mean one of them bitty scooters?" Win said.

Harriet thought she might have detected a certain amount of derision in his voice. But then he chuckled. "That's super cool, Harriet. I knew you were one special lady."

Harriet tapped off her phone. "Trommel? Sluice box? Gold mining sure takes a lot of equipment."

She patted Humphrey, who was looking at her like she had just lost her mind. "Now, don't you start worrying. I'm certain it will pay off."

Harriet went back inside and checked on Prudence first.

"How are you feeling?" she asked.

"Much better," Prudence said. "In fact, I would love a slice of that pie if you wouldn't mind."

"Course not. I'll go get it."

Harriet sliced into the pie. The nearly purple juice flowed like lava and the sweet, succulent aroma lifted to the air. It smelled sweet and refreshing and healthy. "Blueberries always did smell clean," she said. She dropped a chunk of crust on the floor for Humphrey, who lapped it up like there was no tomorrow. Next Harriet poured a glass of milk. "One percent," she read. "It's whole milk now."

"Thank you," Prudence said as Harriet set the

plate and milk on the ottoman they used as a coffee table. It was soft and thick, and the serving trays always came in handy, otherwise the milk would spill onto Prudence's carpet.

"Now, don't you worry about the dishes," Harriet said. "I'll clean up when I get back."

"Back? Are you going out again?"

Harriet swallowed. "Yes. I . . . I forgot something. Do you mind if I take the SUV? I won't be long." Prudence said she didn't mind her taking her car, but Harriet was thinking. Now she'd done it. She'd lied. Harriet did not like to lie. It was one thing to just choose not to tell someone something, but to out loud lie was quite another. Harriet's heart sank.

But as she made her way to the door, she justified the lie by thinking of the baby's future college career.

Henry jiggled the donut box as he entered the house. Humphrey came running.

"Here you go, boy." The dog leaped with about as much joy as a Basset could muster. Henry fed him the donut. "Nice and fresh."

"Hey."

Henry looked up. Startled. "Mom? You sound funny."

"It's me," Prudence said.

Henry looked toward the couch and saw Prudence.

"What are you doing home? Are you okay?"

"Yes. Just some morning sickness. Your mother was here taking care of me. I'm fine now."

Henry leaned over and kissed Prudence. "Um, blueberry. Pie?"

"Florence brought it over. Pretty tasty."

"I have donuts." He set them on the coffee ottoman before joining Prudence on the couch.

"I'll have one of them too."

"So where's Mom now?"

"She took the SUV back into town." Prudence readjusted herself. "Said she forgot something. She was out all morning buying things for Martha and then having lunch with Florence."

"Wait. That's tomorrow. Martha arrives tomorrow—at one o'clock. Isn't that—"

"I know," Prudence said. "I didn't put it together until now, but we have that ultrasound appointment at one. There's no way you can do both."

Henry touched Prudence's cheek. "I am not missing the ultrasound. Martha will just have to wait at the airport. She'll be fine."

Prudence caught Henry's hand in hers. "I really want you there. Doctor Kate said it's early for the first ultrasound, but given my history she said she'd feel a little better having it done. Guess I'm considered high risk."

"I like the idea too. I can't wait to see the baby."

Prudence sighed. "How was your day? Get much done?"

Henry nodded. "Great. Great day. I got a lot done, and I came up with the perfect twist. A gold mine. I think Cash is going to discover gold."

Prudence let go a small laugh. "That's brilliant. And perfect for the setting. There was a lot of gold mining going on in these parts."

"I know," Henry said. "Still is. I saw an advertisement for leasing a mine."

Prudence shook her head. "No. Don't even think about it. Too risky. And it takes years."

"I know." Henry settled back into the couch as Humphrey ambled by, asking for a second donut. "Mom will kill me but . . . okay." He fed one to the dog and then handed one to Prudence.

"As long as Mom doesn't think she's driving into Sacramento by herself."

"Just tell her no," Prudence said.

Henry let go a nervous laugh.

By the time she got to town, it was four o'clock. Harriet parked the SUV, dropping the gearshift into park with a thud and a sigh. She checked her face in the rearview mirror and brushed her fingers through her hair. Oh well, good enough. She saw Win and Lily standing outside the bank, waiting. She was feeling mixed emotions. On the one hand she was glad that she finally heard from Win, but on the other hand she was feeling nervous since telling Florence Caldwell about it. It wasn't that Florence had told her to run in the other direction, but she was not all that positive or enthusiastic either.

After taking two deep breaths, she started across the street. The closer she got the easier it was to see that Lily looked, well, a little slutty. She was wearing dark blue shorts that were so short and tight that a passerby could see way too much. Her white T-shirt was cut way too deep. But Harriet took solace in the fact that Lily wore a pair of bright yellow Chucks.

Of course, Harriet still did not like Lily's tar-black hair. She wondered if she could talk Lily into letting her pay to have it brought back to its natural glory. If that was even possible.

"Hello there," Harriet called with a quick wave.

Win turned his head in her direction. "Hey there, darlin'," he called. Win gave Lily a look and then took her hand as they walked toward Harriet.

"Hi, Lily," Harriet said.

Lily glanced first at Harriet and then locked her eyes on the street. "Hello, Mrs. Beamer."

Harriet felt her brow wrinkle. "Now, what did we say about that? I want you to call me Harriet unless it's just too hard. I know it can be—hard, that is—to refer to an elder by their first name."

A smile crept across Lily's face. "Okay, Harriet," she said.

"Now ain't that just so sweet," Win said. "I'm glad to see the two of you gettin' on so well."

Lily sidled near Harriet and walked beside her.

"Well now, tell me about this . . . trommel, was it? And another sluice box?" Harriet said.

"I'll be tickled to tell you all about it," Win said, "but maybe we should step into this here coffee shop and talk."

Harriet read the sign that hung by two chains over the door. Clancey Hannigan's.

The trio took a small table after ordering their drinks. It was one of those places that didn't have wait service. Just kids behind the counter, probably college students, who made coffee with pretty designs in the foam. Harriet's was a gorgeous leaf design that she just hated to mess up. And somehow, one of the students managed to form a pretty sun shining in Lily's. Her father had given her permission to drink coffee, thanks to Harriet's urging.

"So tell me," Harriet said after she sipped. She tried to sip at the edges and ever so carefully as to keep the design from shifting. But she knew it was short-lived.

Win on the other hand stirred his latte. And this made Lily shake her head and say, "You know, Pop, you got no class. No class at all. You don't appreciate fine art."

"Fine art? It's coffee and milk foam. Art schmart. Now, if you ever saw those paintings they do on the black velvet, you know, of the Grand Canyon and Jesus, now that's art."

Harriet nearly choked on her foam.

"It's garbage," Lily said.

"Now, now," Harriet said. "To each his own."

"But you can't be serious. Those paintings are not real art."

"I agree. My friend Martha is an artist. Now, she does what I suppose you would call real art."

Lily folded a piece of straw paper. "I do art. I like to draw."

"And she's pretty good," Win said. "But I keep telling her that art is no way to make a living."

"I'd like to see some of your drawings some-time," Harriet said. "And I'm sure my friend Martha will. She's the expert."

Lily shrugged. "Maybe. I'm not very good."

"I bet you are a good artist," Harriet said, wondering why Lily's father was not being more supportive.

"Any-hoo," Harriet said, "I'm a little pressed for time, and if we are going to the bank . . . But I sure would like to learn more about gold mining."

"Sorry, Harriet," Win said. He glared at Lily, who had chosen to sit closer to Harriet.

"Sorry, Mrs. Beamer," she said.

Harriet patted her hand. "It's all right, dear."

"Now let me tell you about trommels," Win said.

Harriet smiled wide. It was like being let in on ancient secrets.

"A trommel is kind of like a washing machine, or a great big sifter. It turns"—he made a motion with his finger—"like this, sifting through tons of dirt and gravel. The heavier stuff, hopefully the gold, falls through the trommel into the box below."

Harriet nodded her head. "I think I understand."

Win sipped his coffee, leaving a bit of foam on his lip, which he wiped with his hand. "We already got one up on the site. We call it the beast because it just does so much work. Sifts through tons of dirt and gravel."

Once again the image of the giant flour sifter popped into Harriet's mind.

"You see"—Win took a pen from his pocket and drew on a napkin—"it looks a little like this." He drew an image of a machine with a large cylinder attached to some sort of rigging and motor. "Now, inside this here large tube are a bunch of screens and things that sort through the gravel and size the ore and pebbles and tiny rocks and things."

Harriet understood the theory, but she really didn't see how the machine could tell the difference between the gold and the ordinary rock.

Win scribbled a little more on the page and

pointed to a box. "See here? That's the sluice box. We run water through it and it washes off the ore and helps sort the gold. The bigger junk rocks are extracted and the gold stays in the sluice."

"Then you just pick it out?" Harriet said.

"Yep. All there is to it."

"It really is pretty simple," Harriet said. "And I guess it beats kneeling by the river with a pan."

"Hot diggety dog," Win said. "You got that right. And I got the sore knees to show for it. Now, you just don't worry your pretty little head over all this technical stuff. You let ol' Winslow take care of that."

Harriet looked at Lily. "How are you enjoying your latte, dear?"

"It's good," she said. "Thank you."

"Are you sure you don't want a treat, a small something to tide you over till dinnertime?" Harriet thought Lily looked too skinny. "A vanilla scone?"

"No, thank you. I'm fine. The coffee kind of took my appetite away."

"As long as you're sure. I saw they have cheesecake. I'd be happy to get you a slice, maybe with raspberries."

Lily's eyes widened. Harriet figured you could tell a lot about a person by how she reacted to cheesecake. Harriet reached into her bag and pulled out a ten-dollar bill. She pushed it into

Lily's hand. "Now you get a slice while your pop and I talk business."

Lily glanced at Win. He nodded his head. "Maybe get it to go."

"Good," Harriet said, turning to Win as soon as Lily had left. "Now, how much do you think you need? And please, remember I have a grandchild on the way."

"Well now," Win said. "Ain't that a blessing, just a doggone blessing. I'm happy for you. Do you know if it's a grandson or granddaughter?"

Harriet finished her drink. "Not yet, and maybe my son and daughter-in-law will want to be surprised."

Win reached across the table and took Harriet's hand. He sniffed. "Well, I'll just never forget the morning my Sally, God rest her soul, presented me with the most precious bundle of joy. My Lily. She was the prettiest little thing I had ever seen." He took a breath. "Still gets me choked up."

"Ah," Harriet said. "That's so sweet. But, well . . . can I be honest with you?"

"Wee doggies, little lady. If you can't be honest with your business partner, who can you be honest with?"

Harriet fiddled with the salt shaker. Standard restaurant issue. Nothing memorable. "Don't get me wrong but, are you sure of this . . . this mine?"

Win leaned back in the chair. "As sure as sure can be. As sure as I am that the sun will shine tomorrow. As sure as I am that God is in his heaven."

Lily returned with the cheesecake.

"Now, what do you say we mosey over to the bank and finish our business," Win said.

It didn't take long for Harriet to hand over more cash to Win.

"Cash on the barrelhead always gets the best deal," he always said.

"That's fine," Harriet said. "Now I guess I should be on my way. My friend from Philly is arriving tomorrow."

Harriet watched Lily's eyes grow wide with interest.

"Would you like to come along with me right now, Lily?" Harriet asked. "I have a little shopping to do." She really didn't, but something inside told her she should spend some time alone with Lily. And another hour wouldn't matter much.

Lily looked at her father. He hesitated, hemmed and hawed, but then finally he agreed that Lily could go along with Harriet. But only for an hour or so.

"I'll meet you at the café, at Rachel's," Win said, looking at his watch.

"Thanks, Pop," Lily said.

"Good," Harriet said. "We won't be long."

Win took hold of Lily's hand. "Would you excuse us a second? I just want to have a couple of father-daughter words with Lily."

"Sure," Harriet said.

Win led Lily a few paces away, out of earshot.

Harriet watched as Win seemed to have something mighty important and serious to say. Lily wasn't saying a word until Harriet was pretty certain she saw Win squeeze her wrist a little too hard. Most of the time, Win and Lily appeared to get along pretty well, but she supposed that the stress and worry of being a single parent could get to him now and again. Maybe he was telling her to mind her manners and not overstay her welcome.

Harriet and Lily headed toward the shops. "Now, I don't know if I told you this, Lily, but my son is having an addition put onto his house. It's a mother-in-law suite, but I think that sounds so . . . old. So I'm calling it the Grammy Suite." She looked at Lily who didn't seem to be paying attention.

"Is everything all right, dear?" she asked Lily.

Lily smiled, but it was a forced smile, the kind that has so much truth behind it. "Oh sure. I'm all right. I was just thinking about how nice it is to shop. Pop never takes me—unless it's to the Goodwill. That's where I got these Converse sneakers. Or sometimes we snag clothes out of those clothes collection boxes in parking lots. I've raided lots of drop boxes all across the country."

Harriet felt her heart drop just a little. Something just wasn't adding up. "All across the country?"

Lily stopped walking for a fraction of a second and then sped up. "Yeah, like I said before, Pop and I have to keep moving because of jobs."

Harriet stopped in front of a small boutique. "But maybe now with the gold mine your traveling days could be behind you."

Lily let go a nervous laugh. "Yeah, right."

Harriet looked at the store window. It was filled with a lovely assortment of household treasures —statues of birds and small boxes that could hold any little treasure you'd want. There was a dolphin lamp and a perfect little Goldilocks and the Three Bears lamp that appeared to be handcrafted. "Now, that would be just right for the nursery. I don't think you heard me tell your father that I'm going to be a grandmother."

Lily didn't say anything.

"You know what?" Harriet said. "Here I am thinking about myself, and you have such a need for some new clothes. What do you say we take care of that? Let's get you some more . . . stylish clothes." She didn't dare say what she really thought.

"Really? You mean it?"

"Sure do."

That was when Harriet saw a true smile on Lily's face.

"And then if we have time, I'll come back and get that lamp. I can always take it back if my daughter-in-law doesn't like it."

"Thank you," Lily said. "But . . . I don't want to be a problem."

This time Harriet's heart broke just a little.

Henry assumed his mother would be home soon. It was nearly six o'clock, and he had already fired up the gas grill on the deck. This was something that Humphrey especially enjoyed. The grill always meant hot dogs. He watched intently as Henry worked. It was a perfect evening for steaks and salads. And there was enough potatoes au gratin left over from when Harriet made them to make a nice side dish. She always made extra.

He even thought he had time to whip together a nice peach cobbler and fresh whipped cream. But he needed to check the fridge. Yep, a full container of heavy cream. And there were six, large peaches on the counter. Prudence's boss, the senior partner at her Sacramento law firm, had given the peaches to her. It seemed his wife had an incredible garden, including a small orchard of fruit trees. She was always sharing the fruits or vegetables of her labor.

At one point, maybe even while he was still running his father's construction business, Henry imagined himself a chef at a four-star restaurant. But he never pursued it. It seemed the writing virus never left him, even when he prayed for it to go away, prayed that God would give him another mission in life. But the desire always came back stronger. But now with the baby on the way, Henry was thinking about alternative means to make ends meet. It was hard to make it as a writer, and if Prudence didn't want to work anymore, he would have to do something about their income.

He closed the refrigerator door with his foot as his arms were full of various ingredients. Maybe cooking school was in the future. Or, who knew, a bestseller.

Henry assembled the ingredients for the cobbler and got to work. And it wasn't long before he had the peaches prepared and the cobbler mixture—flour, sugar, and milk—ready to go.

Humphrey was sticking close by, ready to lap up anything that might spill on the floor.

"The secret is the cinnamon," Henry told Humphrey. "You wouldn't think peaches and cinnamon make a good taste combo, but they do."

Henry mixed sugar, cornstarch, and a little water, for the peaches, together and set it on the stove to boil. He stirred it constantly. "This is where it takes patience to be a chef," he said.

Humphrey whimpered.

"Ah, you don't care. You just want to eat."

He added the peaches, folded them into the mixture gently, and then poured the whole glorious, wonderful smelling mixture into a pie tin. Yes, he knew that was a little unorthodox, but he preferred to make peach cobbler in a pie tin. Actually it was Florence Caldwell who gave him the idea.

Then came the final step of mixing the cobbler part, the batter, which he dropped by spoonfuls onto the peaches.

"Now, we just bake for thirty minutes or so and there you have it."

He set the timer.

"So, Humphrey, did I tell you about the cowboy I saw at JavaScone? He was talking about gold mines. I wish I had talked to him. Maybe the next time I go to JavaScone he'll be there, and I can ask him a few questions."

Humphrey said, "Woof."

Harriet and Lily finished their shopping. Lily was very pleased with her new clothes and even some new underwear.

"Thank you," Lily said when they were standing in front of the café. "I haven't had new under-wear in a long time. Pop says I don't need it."

"Do you?" Harriet asked.

"Kind of. Makes me feel pretty and, you know, all . . . womanly."

Harriet patted Lily's cheek. "You are beautiful. And I'm not saying to dress all flirty and flaunty, no siree Bob, but I am telling you it's okay to look nice and feel nice."

Lily dropped her shopping bags and threw her arms around Harriet, who in turn dropped her tote and hugged Lily back.

Harriet thought Lily wanted to say something else, but Win strolled out of the café. "There you are. I was wondering when you'd show up."

Lily picked up her bags. "Hi, Pop. Harriet got me the nicest clothes."

"Did she now?" Win said. "You can show me later. Right now, it's time for meat loaf."

Harriet waited a second or two for Win to say thank you or something, but he never did. "I guess I need to get home also. I'm sure Henry has been cooking. He's quite the chef, you know. You'd think he was trained at the Cordon Bleu."

"Thank you again, Harriet," Lily said.

"Okay, now, you two run along for dinner. I just thought of something I forgot," Harriet said.

Harriet still thought she needed to show up at home with something for herself. She did not want Henry to get suspicious. She walked past several shops until turning into The Wild Onion, a store boasting fine home furnishings. She was nearly knocked over by the sweet potpourri when she entered, a mixture of balsa and rose-hips, sage and vanilla, and maybe a hint of cinnamon—according to Harriet's nose. It smelled nice enough, just a little too strong.

The store carried many specialty items like flower arrangements, vases, brass and stone statues of horses and angels, garden ornaments, shiny gazing balls, and the like. But her eye fell almost immediately on a small, wrought-iron plant stand.

She ran her hand over the cool, black metal. It was twisted and gnarled like vines and had two shelves for plants. And two gargoyles. One on each shelf. At first she thought they were just taking up room, but then she liked them. The stand gave her a twinge of homesickness. Harriet had gotten quite good at raising and propagating African Violets. Perhaps she could again.

"Oh, that's a lovely piece. Handmade right here in Grass Valley."

It was the voice of a middle-aged woman, short, a little dumpy, and Harriet thought she had the prettiest face, almost angelic. She also thought she had been pegged for a tourist. But that was okay.

"Oh, I do like this little stand. How much is it?"

"That's three hundred and twenty-six dollars. It's all hand-wrought by a local craftsman. It's the only one like it."

Harriet liked that idea but not the price. She had already spent a king's ransom since coming to Grass Valley. But she really hadn't bought anything for herself, for her new Grammy Suite. "It would be like owning a work of art," Harriet said as she touched the ear of the gargoyle on the left. "It's very . . . interesting, different. I like it."

"It is a work of art," the woman said. "It's so pretty. And even the gargoyles were handmade, casted and sculpted by the artist. A woman by the name of Zee Blush."

"Zee Blush?"

"Yes. She's rather eccentric."

Harriet glanced around the shop. She saw many things made from grapevines and burlap. Nothing else spoke to her the way the gargoyles did. "I think it will work just perfectly under one of my windows. I'd like to keep African Violets on it."

"Oh, that would be lovely," the woman said.

"Do you think violets would like gargoyles?"

"Oh, certainly. Gargoyles are lucky."

"I didn't know that. Not that I believe in luck very much, but that's neither here nor there. I'll take it."

A few minutes later Harriet left The Wild Onion with the plant stand, a bag of potpourri, and two candles that smelled like butter cookies. It was a touch awkward carrying the items back to the SUV, but she managed. After all, she had managed to lug a tote bag and a wheelie suitcase across the country, so a three-block walk with a plant stand was a piece of cake.

Chapter Thirteen

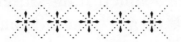

Henry was pretty much ready for dinner. All he needed now was for Harriet to come home. He had the steaks rubbed and ready to go. Six ears of corn ready for the grill and the cobbler had come out of the oven looking as good as any cobbler on the cover of *Food Network Magazine* or *Bon Appetit*. And the smell in the kitchen was an amazing blend of spices and sweet and smelled just the way late summer or early fall should smell.

"You know something," he said to himself out loud, "you really can cook."

He assembled dishes and utensils, glasses and napkins—the ones with the purple dots on them—and carried them out to the deck.

Prudence was happily sitting there looking over some legal papers, the kind of stuff that, frankly, made Henry's brain hurt.

"I thought we'd eat out here," he said. "Long as the bugs don't bother us." It was still warm enough to eat outside but not for long. Henry looked out over the yard and the mountains. Fall was definitely settling in, and soon he would bring the deck furniture inside and grilling would be difficult at best.

Prudence did not look up from her pages. "That's a good idea. It's such a nice evening."

Henry set the table as Humphrey sauntered past. Although it was hard to tell, Henry thought the dog was looking a little forlorn. "Have you heard from my mother?" he asked Prudence.

"No, I thought she'd be back by now. It is getting late."

"I hope she's okay. I worry about her sometimes. I don't want her to get into trouble."

"Oh, what kind of trouble could she get into?" Prudence said. "She'll come home, wagging her tail behind her."

Henry sat down at the table. "Do you think we'll be able to barbecue once the builders get started?"

"Sure," Prudence said. "Maybe not while they're working, but I don't see why not after they've left for the day."

"I can't wait to see it—the building, I mean. Mom's gonna love it."

"Me either," Prudence said. She looked at him. "Henry, why do I get the feeling you have something else on your mind? Are you worried about me? Or is it your mother? Your new book?"

"Oh, a little of everything, I suppose, but, well, mostly I'm worried about money. I mean, can we afford the lifestyle we've gotten used to? And what if you want to quit working? I'm just a writer."

"Henry, we'll be fine. I promise."

"I guess, but—"

"But what?"

"What would you think if I went to culinary school and became a chef? Got a real job with an actual paycheck?"

Prudence swallowed and then burst into laughter. "Really? You? Wow. If that's what you want. I mean, you are a really good cook. But to do it all day long? Could you? And what about your writing? You love to write."

Henry stood, moved behind Prudence, and put his hands on her shoulders and massaged lightly. "I don't know. I'm just thinking it might be more steady. My father always had steady work. I mean, he didn't get paid unless someone bought the houses he built. But it wasn't like writing. You know?"

Prudence reached back and took one of his hands. "Henry. You're doing great. But if you want to go to culinary school, that's fine too."

"Sometimes I wish you weren't so supportive."

"What in the world does that mean?"

Henry took a deep breath through his nose. "It just means if you were the demanding sort of wife, you'd just tell me what to do."

Humphrey leaped up, well, more like he hauled

his low belly off the ground, and headed toward the deck. He trotted right past Henry and Prudence.

"She must be home. I swear that dog knows it's her coming from a mile away."

"Okay," Prudence said, "now don't forget we have to talk about the airport run tomorrow."

"That's right, I almost forgot."

"Henry, yoo-hoo, Henry," he heard his mother calling. "I'm home, dear."

"On the deck," Henry called. "Getting ready to grill some steaks."

"Come see what I bought today."

Henry smiled at Prudence. "I better go see what she bought. I kind of blew her off the other day."

"Okay. I'll go see too. And then can we eat? I'm starving."

"You bet."

Harriet stood in the living room. "Isn't it spectacular?" she said. "Don't you just love it?" She was holding her new plant stand so they could both see.

"Um, yeah, what is it?" Henry said.

"It's a plant stand," Harriet said. "It's going right under the south window of my new Grammy Suite."

"Are those gargoyles?" Prudence asked, moving in for a closer look.

Harriet touched one of the grotesque figures. "Yes. Aren't they sweet? The whole thing, gargoyles and all, was made by a local artist. An eccentric woman named Zee Blush. It's one of a kind. An original Blush."

"That's nice, Mom. Real nice," Henry said. "You can keep it in your room until the building is done."

"Henry," Harriet said. "You hate it, don't you?"

"I didn't say that," Henry said. "It's just . . . different."

"Well, I like it," Prudence said. "It's . . . whimsical."

"Thank you, dear," Harriet said. "I'm going to put African Violets on the little shelves."

"That will be so pretty," Prudence said.

"I also got some candles and potpourri. Martha likes potpourri."

Meanwhile, Humphrey moved closer and sniffed the plant stand.

"And speaking of Martha," Henry said, "she arrives tomorrow."

"I know," Harriet said. "I am so excited."

"So are we," Prudence said. "Let's start dinner and we can discuss the details."

"Details?" Harriet said, following Henry and Prudence outside. "What details? Her plane lands, she gets off, goes to baggage claim, and I snag her from the sidewalk like the brass ring on a carousel."

Henry dropped three steaks on the grill. Prudence and Harriet sat down at the table to start on their salads of baby spinach.

"Mom," Henry said, "there's a little problem."

Harriet's heart pounded. "Problem? Did something happen? Is she still coming?"

"Yes, of course," Prudence said. "It's just a slight scheduling conflict. I have to get an ultrasound tomorrow."

Harriet looked at Prudence. "Ultrasound? Isn't it a little early for one of those?"

"The doctor thought it was a good idea considering . . . my history. I made the appointment before we were sure of Martha's arrival time. I'm afraid it creates a conflict."

"Conflict? Why should it create a conflict?" Harriet said. "You guys can drive the BMW and I'll take the SUV."

"No, Mom," Henry said.

Harriet dropped her fork. "Wait. You don't expect me to ride the Vespa all the way to Sacramento and then bring Martha and her luggage home on the back like I was Jed Clampett or something?"

"No, no, of course not," Henry said. He sat down at the table. "I just meant that I don't want you to drive by yourself all the way to the airport. It's a long drive. I'd rather go with you, but it means Martha might have to wait a couple of hours."

"Yes, Mother," Prudence said. "Henry will take you after our appointment. I'm sure Martha will understand. She can have lunch at the airport.

173

There's a lovely restaurant called La Bou, where she can get a sandwich and have a terrific view."

"No, she's having lunch with me," Harriet said. "I'm going myself. I'll be fine. I have a GPS. Remember? For heaven's sake, I made it clear across the country by myself; I can certainly find the San Francisco airport."

"Sacramento, Mom. It's Sacramento."

Harriet looked at Prudence. "He's so easy."

Prudence laughed. "I know."

"Are you sure, Mom?" Henry asked.

Harriet picked up her fork and stabbed a spinach leaf. "Of course I am. And I'll only be alone going one way."

Henry went back to the steaks and opened the grill cover. Savory smoke poured out. "As long as you're sure," he said, waving away the cloud.

"Thank you, dear. I'll be fine. You just go and have a nice ultrasound."

Henry looked at Prudence. "Yeah. It will be exciting."

Harriet felt a wash of pride and joy fill her heart. She sighed and let the feeling grow like ripples on a smooth lake. She was pleased with Henry's accomplishments, but more so, Harriet was proud of the man she and Max raised. In that brief moment that passed between Henry and Prudence, Harriet saw so much, so much love and concern and joy. She was convinced that seldom did any mother get to experience something so sweet. And yet, in those few seconds, Harriet also felt disappointment. Why couldn't Henry continue in his father's business, and why had he kept selling it a secret?

Harriet poked at a crouton, trying to keep a threatening tear from dropping onto her plate. It was the secrecy and the hushed phone calls through the whole transaction that troubled her the most. Was it her fault?

Henry served the steaks, perfectly charred with nice grill marks and just the perfect amount of juices.

"I hope it's how you like it, Mom."

"I'm sure it is, dear. You always know what's best for me."

Henry took a step back. "What is that supposed to mean?"

"Nothing. It's just that you're good at making choices for me without asking."

Henry dropped the serving plate onto the grill. "Here we go. I've been waiting for this, Mom. You just can't let it go. I did the right thing. For you and for me."

"How was selling your father's business, the one he built from . . . a jar of nails, a hammer, and one customer good for me? It was . . . it was all I had left of him."

"Maybe this isn't the best time," Prudence said. "Let's talk after dinner."

"No," Henry said. "Let's have this out now."

"There's nothing to have out," Harriet said. "It's over."

"Mom, listen. If I had kept the business I would have destroyed it. It wasn't for me."

Humphrey trotted onto the deck and laid his head on Harriet's knee. He looked up at her with wide eyes. Harriet patted his snout and rubbed behind one ear. "Even Humphrey knows what you did was underhanded and unfair to your father's memory."

"Oh, so Dad would have preferred me to sink the business in Chapter 11 and leave you nothing. Mom, you forget, you made out pretty well on the deal."

"Money," Harriet said. "It's not just about money."

Henry took a huge breath, which he let out slowly as though he were counting down seconds. "No. It's not just about money. But I mattered also."

Humphrey ambled to Henry and laid his head on his knee.

"I don't care to discuss this anymore," Harriet said. "We have a big day tomorrow."

"Well, well, well," Prudence said in her best lawyer courtroom voice. "I think the two of you have much to discuss, but I recommend eating the elephant one piece at a time."

"Good idea," Henry said. "Let's just enjoy our dinner."

After a couple of minutes of silence, Prudence asked, "So what have you got planned for Martha's visit?"

"Planned?" Harriet said. "I . . . I don't know. I hadn't planned anything. I've been so busy with getting my room ready, and the baby news, not to mention the Grammy Suite."

"I'm sure you two will find plenty to do," Prudence said.

"I'm sure we will," Harriet said.

Henry pushed some potatoes around on his plate. "Who's ready for peach cobbler?"

"Oh, you made cobbler?" Harriet said, hoping to diffuse things.

"And homemade whipped cream," Prudence said.

"I'll be back in a flash," Henry said.

Harriet gathered the dinner plates. And as she did, she couldn't help but notice that Prudence was all of a sudden looking a little pale.

"Are you okay, dear?" she asked. "Did that little . . . kerfuffle upset you?" And here she was the person telling Henry to watch Prudence's stress level.

"No, no, I'm glad you two are talking but—" Prudence leapt from the table and made a mad dash inside to the bathroom.

"Is she all right?" Henry asked when he returned with the cobbler and dessert plates. "I've never seen her run so fast."

Harriet smiled. "Morning sickness can hit anytime."

Henry flopped into his chair. "I don't like this, Mom. She wasn't this sick with the . . . before."

"As hard as it is to believe, honey, this is actually a good thing. As long as she stays busy and happy. This will pass, probably very soon, and believe me, your baby will grow strong and healthy."

"But it's taking so much out of her. She's so tired."

"Par for the course, Henry. She's just coming up to the end of her first trimester. It could last a few weeks. It lasted almost the whole time for me."

"I hope you're right, Mom. I'm thinking about asking her to stop working. I have even thought about going to culinary school so I can get a real job."

"Really?" This was the first Harriet had heard about that idea. "But Prudence will never quit now. She can work right up until the baby's due date. And you should let her if she wants to. No, Henry. She'll know when she needs to stop working. Trust your wife and her doctor."

"I know but—" Henry put his hand on his stomach. "I don't feel so good."

"Sympathy pains," she said. "Did I ever tell you your daddy took to his bed for three days because he said his stomach was upset, and that he had swollen ankles and headaches?"

Henry laughed. "No. Did he really have swollen ankles?"

"Just his ego was swollen."

Henry filled a dessert dish with the cobbler. "But how can throwing up every day be healthy?"

"It just is," Harriet said. "Did you forget the whipped cream?"

Henry's eyes darted. "Oh, sorry, I'll just go get it."

But just then Prudence returned to the table carrying the stainless mixing bowl brimming with fluffy whipped cream. "Sorry about that." She laughed.

"Henry is worried," Harriet said.

"I know." She sat down and patted his hand. "Do you know he stays awake at night staring at me? He thinks I don't know, but I do. I can feel his eyes boring into me."

"Ah, poor thing. He's just so worried."

"I know. I guess I am also," Prudence said. "That cobbler looks awesome."

"Really, dear," Harriet said. "You outdid yourself. That's quite a cobbler you made."

Harriet's thoughts turned to Max. "I guess maybe you're more like your dad than I thought."

"How's that?"

"You both like to build things. With your daddy it was buildings. With you it's seven-layer fudge cakes and Beef Wellington and cobbler. You probably would do very well in culinary school if that is what you decided to do."

Chapter Fourteen

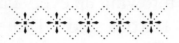

Harriet could hardly sleep that night. She was so excited for Martha's arrival. She saw pretty much every hour on the digital clock until three when she must have finally dozed, because when she opened her eyes again it was nearly six-thirty. She sat up, rousing Humphrey from his sleep. She figured Humphrey did not share in her sleeplessness. The hound could sleep through Armageddon if he wanted to.

She hurried to the kitchen to make coffee—for her and Henry. Prudence had sworn off coffee for the time being. Sandra Day, who was lapping water from her bowl, seemed in a rare good mood. She only hissed once at Humphrey, who then sat on his haunches and waited patiently until Her Majesty the Queen had eaten and sauntered off to visit the litter box.

Stupid cat. Humphrey chomped down his breakfast. *At least I pee outside like a respectable animal.*

Harriet made oatmeal because it was wholesome and comforting and there was a crispy chill in the air. And she remembered how oatmeal calmed her stomach when she was carrying Henry.

She checked the clock.

"Martha gets in at one o'clock," she told Humphrey. "Can you stand it? It took me almost a month to cross the country, like I was a pioneer, but she does it in about nine hours—given the layover."

Humphrey swished his tail.

"I guess you'll be happy to see her again too."

Humphrey swished a second time and then let go a low woof when Harriet heard a light rap on the deck slider.

"Florence," she said. "What's she doing here so early?"

"Yoo-hoo," Florence called. "Harriet!"

Harriet opened the slider. "Good morning. What brings you out so early?"

Florence walked past Harriet into the kitchen as Harriet closed the door.

"Henry asked me to stop by. He said you might need some company for the drive into Sacramento."

Harriet nearly burst out loud laughing, but fortunately Henry appeared.

"Oh, hi," he said.

"So what is this? Driving Miss Daisy?"

"Mom," Henry said. "It was just an idea."

"Not a very good one. I told you, I'm fine to go

alone." She turned to Florence. "No offense, dear, but you understand."

"Of course," Florence said. "I just want to help if I can."

"I'm fine. You can just go on home. I'll get to the airport and back with no help."

"I'm sorry, Florence," Henry said.

Florence shrugged. "No problem, sweetie. I'll just get going. But I'm here if you change your mind."

"Thank you," Harriet said.

Harriet waited for the slider to click shut. "Henry, how could you? We've had this discussion."

"I know. I'm sorry. Can we just drop it? I don't want Prudence to hear us arguing again."

"I made oatmeal and coffee," Harriet said. "But, Henry, you really must trust me. I can drive to Sacramento. Easy peasy."

"Coffee sounds good," he said as he sat down at the kitchen table. "I didn't sleep so well."

"You look tired. Something on your mind?" As if she didn't know.

Henry grunted.

"Thought so," Harriet said. She poured coffee into Henry's favorite mug. "I told you to stop worrying, but I guess that's an impossible request. I bet you stayed awake all night staring at Prudence."

Harriet placed the mug in front of him, and then poured a splash of Half and Half into it and stirred. "This will help. You have a big day. I think you should have oatmeal also."

Henry sipped his coffee. "Ah gee, thanks, Mom, but I'm not hungry. My stomach—" He stopped talking.

"Then oatmeal is the perfect thing. It will settle your tummy, and you shouldn't go to the hospital on an empty stomach. You don't want to eat hospital cafeteria food."

"Okay, okay. I'll eat some oatmeal. But just a little. With brown sugar, raisins, and Half and Half."

Harriet laughed. "Of course."

Harriet prepared his breakfast and then joined him at the table. "Where is Prudence, anyway?"

"I left her in the bathroom. I guess she's showering and dressing. She'll be along."

Harriet looked at her son. She suddenly saw him as a twelve-year-old boy sitting at the table back east. Baseball glove in one hand, corn dog in the other. And now, here he was a published author and soon to be a father. She let go a sigh and wished Max was still alive. Then she grabbed his hand and squeezed it. "I love you."

Henry swallowed. "I love you too, Mom. Can you believe it? I think it's finally going to happen this time. I've been so . . . so worried, you know, because—"

Harriet let go of his hand. "It's time. And it's time for you to believe it also. I think today is going to help you more than you'll know."

"You know, Mom, I have never prayed so much and so . . . so fervently over anything in my life."

"I know. Just like your dad, except . . ."

"Except what?" Henry chewed his oatmeal.

"I'm just gonna say it, Henry. I think your father was a lunatic while I was pregnant with you. A sheer, sweet, loving lunatic. He wouldn't let me carry the newspaper inside the house. I didn't have to vacuum for six months, and the day you were born? He carried me into the hospital."

Henry looked at Harriet. "So, what's wrong with that?"

"Nothing, dear. Eat your breakfast."

A few minutes later, Prudence joined them. She looked smart in jeans and a purple blouse.

"Good morning," she said. She turned to her profile and showed off her tummy. "Are you sure there's not something here?" She pulled her blouse tight.

"Um, come to see it," Harriet said, "I think I see a small . . . bump."

"Is that bad?" Henry said. "Is something wrong? It's too soon, isn't it?"

"No, no," Harriet said. "Relax. Maybe really thin women show sooner."

Prudence placed her hand on her stomach. "I thought so, Mother. I'm so excited. I can't believe we're going to see our baby today."

"Sit, both of you," Harriet said. "You need oatmeal in your stomach."

"Don't fight it, honey," Henry said.

"But I don't think I'm supposed to eat before the ultrasound."

"Nonsense," Harriet said. "You eat and drink. And then drink some more."

"Are you sure?" Prudence asked.

"Did the doctor tell you to stop eating?" Harriet asked. "It's just an ultrasound; it's not major surgery."

Prudence sat, and Harriet set a tumbler of milk in front of her. "I guess the oatmeal does sound good," she said.

Henry patted Prudence's hand. "What's wrong, honey?"

"I'm just nervous. I don't want there to be anything wrong."

"There won't be," he said. And for the first time he believed it.

"That's right," Harriet said. "You are going to have a beautiful, healthy baby."

Harriet placed a bowl of steaming oatmeal with raisins and brown sugar in front of Prudence. "I'm glad you're here," Prudence said.

Harriet needed to catch her breath. "Oh, so am I, dear. I am so glad I'm not back in Bryn Mawr sitting on the edge of the couch wondering how you are doing. I like being part of it all."

Henry laughed.

"What's so funny?" Harriet asked.

"No, no, I'm sorry, Mom. I just had a funny image of you sitting on the couch talking to your salt and pepper shakers, wringing your hands with worry."

"I wouldn't put it that way," Harriet said. "And I figure as long as the salt and pepper shakers don't start talking back, I'm doing fine."

By eleven-thirty Harriet was ready to leave for Sacramento. She had chosen a lovely driving outfit. Light blue slacks, red Chucks, of course, a pretty pink blouse with a lacy, white collar.

"Drive carefully, Mom," Henry said. "Call me when you get there. Remember, you can wait in the cell phone lot until she calls you. They have boards with flight information so you'll know just when her plane lands."

"Henry," called Prudence. "Let's go."

Harriet opened the tailgate and helped Humphrey into the back. "There you go," she said.

Humphrey said, "Woof."

She set the GPS in the SUV and waited until Henry had pulled the Beamer onto the street before she set off herself. She sailed a quick prayer that all would be well with the baby.

Harriet turned onto the Golden Chain Highway. Route 49. From there it seemed like a straight trip. It was the same route she had taken to Downieville, except the opposite direction. She had just settled back into the comfy seat for the longest part of the ride when her cell rang.

Remembering all the warnings Prudence and Henry delivered concerning cell phones while driving, Harriet pulled to the side and parked. Her first thought was that it could be Martha calling to say the flight was delayed or something. The phone continued to jingle as she dug around in her purse. "Fool thing," she said. "Where are you?"

She snagged it just in time. It was Win.

"Hello," she said.

"Well, good mornin' there, darlin'," Win said. "I was just calling to give you an update."

Harriet was amazed at how quickly her mind rolodexed through all the possible things he could mean. Maybe they struck it rich. Maybe the mine was dead.

"Oh boy," Harriet said. "I hope it's good news."

Win coughed. "Let's just say I got good news and I got bad news."

"Well, tell me the bad news first," Harriet said. "That way I can enjoy the good news longer. And hurry if you can, I'm on my way to the airport to pick up my friend."

"Well, as it turns out, we're gonna need to get an extra backhoe up to the site as soon as possible. We need to dig more gravel to get into the trommels."

"The beast?" Harriet said. "You mean the beast?"

"That's right, and now that we have two beasts it only makes sense that we should move more gravel. Gotta push a whole lot of bad dirt to get to the good."

"Oh dear," Harriet said. "I . . . I wish I could see this place in action. See some of this gravel and maybe even some of the gold. Have you gotten any out of the mine at all?"

Win coughed again. "Well, now, these things take time and lots of patience. But I suppose if you really want to traipse all the way up the mountain to the site, I guess we could arrange it— for another day, of course. I'd have to get a man down to help us drive up and then hike the rest of the way."

Harriet swallowed. "Oh, I guess I'm not up for all that. And what with my girlfriend coming and all."

"I don't want you to worry. I'll tell you what. I'll have some more pictures taken and you and Lily can meet up and she can go over them with you. Would that help?"

Harriet sighed. "I guess so. It would be prudent, I suppose, to see the new equipment."

"No trouble. How about if I have the men take some pictures and send them to Lily's cell phone? And what do you say we all meet at the café around four o'clock?"

"No, not today," Harriet said. "My friend is coming."

"Oh yeah, you did mention that. Tomorrow then?" Win said.

"I'm not sure. I'll let you know."

Harriet tapped off the phone without asking Win about the good news. The bad news was enough. She would address that tomorrow. For now she had to get Martha.

The remaining ride into the city was uneventful and the airport was easy enough to find. She simply followed the signs to the cell phone lot, found a spot with an ample view of the arrivals board, and waited for Martha to call. She called Henry. They were still waiting for the technician. "I'm here, darling, safe and sound. Not a scratch on me, the car, or Humphrey."

"I wasn't worried," Henry said.

Harriet laughed. "Have a good ultrasound. We'll see you at home."

Humphrey barked. "You got that right. In my day we waited inside the airport at the gate like people, human beings," she told Humphrey who had managed to get into the backseat. "We weren't worried about terrorists and bombs."

Martha's flight landed on time. Now all she had to do was wait. The plan was that Martha would call once she got her bags and Harriet would only have to drive up and get her. But when thirty minutes passed after the flight had landed,

189

Harriet worried. Martha should have made it to baggage claim by then.

She waited another five minutes before ringing Martha's cell. No answer. She called six times and still no answer. She checked her messages and recent calls. She checked for smoke signals. Nothing from Martha. She was certain she had the correct day and time. Where on earth was Martha?

Her heart pounded. She turned to Humphrey. "Oh dear, what if something happened? Where is she?

"I'll call Henry. He'll know what to do. No, I don't want them to worry. Not today. She'll call."

Henry and Prudence waited patiently in the waiting room. Prudence couldn't hold another drop of water without bursting.

"I'm completely water-logged," she said. "I have to pee."

"But you can't. Not until after the ultrasound."

"I know. I know. But come on. My appointment was ten minutes ago."

Henry spied another pregnant woman across the room—extremely pregnant. She was smiling at them like she knew something they didn't know. Henry smiled back.

"Our first," he called.

"I can tell," the woman said. "My fifth."

"Yikes," Prudence said. "Congratulations."

The woman only nodded before she was called back into the examination area.

Henry watched her work her way out of the seat. By the time he thought to help, she was out.

"Oh dear," Prudence said.

"You get used to it," the woman said. "You get used to *all* of it."

Henry opened a magazine. "Look at this," he said, trying to distract Prudence. "It's about a woman who grew a seventy-five-pound potato."

"No, it's not. It's about a woman who rode her bike seventy-five miles to return a library book."

"Yeah well, I like the potato story better. I wish they'd hurry."

"Me too. My bladder is going to explode." Then Prudence laughed. "I think I know how Humphrey feels sometimes. I have new sympathy for him."

"I'm sure he'll be glad to hear it."

"And come to think of it," Prudence said, "we need to find a bakery when we're finished. I need more donuts. Glazed donuts. And they need to be warm."

Henry swallowed. "Sure, honey. Anything you want."

That was when the technician called for Prudence. Henry held her hand and her water bottle as they made their way down the sterile corridor into the even more sterile, cold, and darkened room.

"It's creepy in here," Henry said, leaning over like the Hunchback. "Where do they keep the brains, I wonder?"

"Okay," the technician said, "Prudence, why don't you hop up on the table?"

Henry helped Prudence onto the table.

"Just lie back," the technician said. "My name is Jennifer."

She had a nice, soothing voice, Henry thought. She was average height, not too skinny, not at all fat, wearing a flowered medical smock thing or whatever they called them and green scrub pants.

"Okay, lie back and just roll up your shirt. I'm going to squirt some of this gel on. It's cold."

Prudence wiggled. "It is cold."

Henry sat down at her head with what he thought was a pretty good view of the monitor as Jennifer moved a benign-looking wand around on Prudence's belly. There was something on the screen, but Henry didn't know what. It looked like a fuzzy map of Asia to him.

"I guess it's like hunting for a submarine off the coast of Russia."

No one laughed.

"I understand your doctor said she'd be down to take a look."

"She did?" Henry said. "Is she worried about something? What's wrong? Is that normal procedure?"

Jennifer adjusted some knobs. "Not exactly. But we'll just wait until she gets here."

The door opened and in walked a tall, trim woman. She wore a doctor's coat.

"Hi," she said. "Sorry I'm late."

"What is it, Kate?" Prudence asked. "Is something wrong?"

"No, no," Kate said. "I just wanted to be here."

Jennifer continued to move the wand around Prudence's belly as she adjusted knobs on the machine. "Now listen," she said.

"What's that?" Henry asked. He heard a distinct rushing sound.

"That is your baby's heartbeat," Jennifer said. She moved the wand around. "Good and strong but . . . hold on, oh . . ."

"There?" Kate asked, pointing to the screen.

"Yes," Jennifer said. She adjusted the knobs.

"It sounds different," Prudence said.

"That's because it's two. Two heartbeats," Kate said.

"My baby has two hearts?" Henry said.

Kate laughed. "No, it's twins."

"Wait, what did you just say? Twins? Two babies?" Prudence said. "Are you kidding?"

"Two what?" Henry said, looking at the screen but understanding none of it.

"Two babies," Jennifer said.

"Whaaaat?" Henry said. "Are you sure? Where? All I see are black blobs and gray squiggles."

"This right here is squiggle A," Jennifer said.

"And that must be squiggle B," Prudence said, pointing at the screen. Except by now she was sobbing so hard she could hardly speak.

"That's right. Two babies. They're not identical, but there are definitely two," Kate said.

"Is that why I'm getting big so soon?" Prudence asked.

"Yes, I thought this might be why when you mentioned that to me, but I didn't want to say until I was sure."

Henry said nothing. He just stood there looking at the screen until he couldn't stand it another second, and he started to cry. "Two babies. We're having two babies? I don't believe it."

"They look great," Jennifer said.

"But we don't have twins in our family," Henry said. "Are you sure?"

"Absolutely," Jennifer said.

"Congratulations," Kate said. "I want to see you in the office next week."

"Thanks, doc," Henry said.

"You do nice work," Kate said. "I need to get back."

Henry put his hand on Prudence's forehead because he didn't know where else to put it. "Twins, honey. We're having twins." He looked at Jennifer, who was busy making adjustments. "That's all, right? Just two?"

"Just two."

Henry watched tears stream down Prudence's face. "Twins. I can't believe it."

"Can you tell if we're having boys or girls or one of each?" Prudence asked.

"Not with any accuracy. It's a little early. But definitely at your next one. That is, if you want to know."

Chapter Fifteen

Harriet now had a full case of monkey nerves. Where in the world could Martha be?

She checked her phone just in case she hadn't heard it ring. Still nothing. Nervousness turned to panic. Maybe it was her. Maybe she had the wrong day? Maybe she was losing her mind. Maybe she was . . . old. "Please, dear God," she said, "help me find Martha."

Harriet started the car. "I'll have to park and go into the terminal." Even though Harriet knew they would never tell her if Martha was on the flight or not, she could at least look around. Maybe Martha was lost. By why wouldn't she call?

Then she thought about Wyatt, Martha's son. She had his number. Surely he took her to the airport. She tapped his number. Nothing. No answer. Just a message saying the number was not in service.

"This is getting ridiculous."

She drove to one of the short-term lots, parked the car, and then headed into Terminal A. She wished she had left her tote bag in the car as she wandered through a sea of people, not knowing where she was going. She wanted to call out, "Martha," but didn't. She headed straight for baggage claim, hoping Martha was still waiting for her bags. No Martha. Just a group of Boy Scouts and other miscellaneous people.

Next she went to the first official looking person she saw, and there were plenty to choose from. But she thought the tall woman standing near one of the monitor stations looked kind.

"Excuse me," Harriet said. "I hope you can help me. My friend Martha was supposed to get off that plane over there, flight 1060, and I can't find her, and she doesn't answer her phone. I'm really worried."

"Did you try to call her? Maybe she missed her flight."

"I just said I tried. She doesn't answer."

"What about family?"

"I tried. No one is there."

"Let's go to the security office," the woman said. "I don't know what they can do, but maybe we can figure something out. Otherwise, you'll just have to wait to hear from her."

A few minutes later, Harriet entered the office and there, sitting like a lost child, was Martha. A large purple tote bag at her feet and one large, black suitcase were nearby.

"Martha!" Harriet cried. "Is that you?"

Martha stood. "Oh Harriet, I was beginning to think you'd never come."

"What happened? I was so worried."

Martha puckered her lips. And then she said, "I am so embarrassed. I lost my phone. I mean, I didn't lose it, not exactly. Well, I was at Midway Airport, you know we had to make a stop to change planes, and I had to go to the bathroom, and I had my phone in my pocket." Martha showed Harriet her pocket. It was kind of wide and kind of loose on the baggy pants she was wearing. "Anyway, it fell in the toilet."

Harriet laughed. The security people laughed. Martha cried. "I didn't know what to do. The phone was dead. I didn't have time to buy a new one before my flight into Sacramento and then, well, here I am."

"Why didn't you call me from another phone?"

"I didn't know your cell phone number off the top of my head. I just tap your name. Never bother with numbers anymore."

"I know," Harriet said. "Modern technology."

"We tried to call the house. This nice security man helped me get Henry's number. No answer."

"No one's home. They're getting the ultrasound right now, today."

"Really," Martha said. "That's great." Then she sprang to her feet and threw her arms around Harriet. "I'm so glad to see you. I've missed you so much."

"I've missed you," Harriet said. "And I'm glad you're safe. I'm glad you're here. I was so worried. I thought you were kidnapped or in a hospital or you changed your mind. Or the plane crashed, but I figured they would have told us if that happened."

Martha put out her arms and they hugged again. "I'm so glad you're here." Harriet said again.

"Me too," Martha cried.

"Let's go home," Harriet said.

Henry waited for Prudence in the waiting room while she got cleaned up and mercifully visited the bathroom. He couldn't keep from telling everyone his news.

"Twins," he kept saying. "Twins."

The people in the room applauded. Henry had never experienced anything that came close to what he was feeling at that moment. Marrying Prudence was a close second. His first book contract was pretty exciting. But this. This was extraordinary.

Henry could not stop grinning. And why not? He was going to be the father of twins. When he saw Prudence he announced it to his new friends. "Here she is, the best mother-to-be in the whole world."

"Henry," Prudence said, "don't embarrass me."

"Congratulations," said one woman sitting next to a big, burly guy. "Twins. That's awesome."

"Thank you," Prudence said.

Henry took her hand. He kissed her. "Are you hungry?"

That was when someone laughed and said, "Of course she is. She has two babies to feed."

"That's right," Prudence said. "Now I really need those donuts."

"All you have is that one suitcase?" Harriet asked Martha as they made their way through the terminal to the car after having some lunch at the airport restaurant Prudence had recommended.

"Yep. Two weeks isn't that long, and I thought maybe I could do laundry at your house."

"Of course you can. And maybe you'll stay longer."

"No, my return ticket is for two weeks from now."

Harriet thought at first that she had forgotten where she parked the car. "Oh dear. I was in such a rush and so upset I didn't take notice of my spot."

"Oh no," Martha said. "Losing me was one thing, but we need the car."

"I know. And Humphrey is in the backseat. I'm sure he's worried sick."

"Oh no," Martha said again. "Let's just start looking. But stick together."

"Right." Harriet reached into her tote bag to retrieve the keys and that was when it struck her. "Wait. The key. When I unlock the door with this thingamabob it beeps and the lights flash."

"Oh good. Start pressing the button."

Harriet did, but unfortunately there were other people doing the same thing and so they saw lights and heard cars beeping all over the place, until finally, "Wait," Harriet said. "I hear Humphrey yowling."

"It's coming from over there," Martha said.

They walked a few more paces until Harriet said, "There it is, right where I left it. I remember now."

Harriet opened the tailgate. Humphrey was quite pleased to see her and Martha.

"It's okay, boy," Harriet said. "We're back."

Martha patted his back and sides. "Hello there, Humphrey. How've you been?" Humphrey's tongue lolled out as he grinned from ear to ear. His ears even perked, although only a trained Basset lover could tell for sure.

"He's so glad to see us," Harriet said.

Martha pushed her bag into the back. "Don't worry, boy, just the one. Still plenty of room for you."

The ride home was enjoyable. Harriet loved being with Martha again. "I fixed up the room," Harriet said. "Brand new curtains and sheets."

"Oh, you didn't have to fuss," Martha said.

"Sure I did. You are my best friend."

Martha smiled and was just about to say something when Harriet's phone jingled. This time she had Martha to find it. Which she did.

"Win?" Martha said looking at the screen.

"Oh dear. Now what does he want? Would you put it on speaker, dear?"

"Who is Win?" Martha asked as she pushed the right button.

Harriet pointed her index finger up. "Hello," Harriet said.

"Hello there, darlin'."

Harriet glanced at Martha. She hadn't told her about the gold mine yet. And wasn't sure this was the best time.

"What is it?" she asked.

"I really need to schedule our appointment for tomorrow. Can we meet at the café say around ten-thirty in the morning?"

"I . . . I suppose so. Will you still have pictures?"

"Sure, sure," Win said. "But I need you to go to the bank first and meet me at the café after."

"Okay. I guess I can do that. How much more do you need?"

"Another fifteen."

201

"Hundred?" Harriet said.

"Yep."

"Okay," Harriet said with a deep breath. "I'll be there. And can you bring the copies of the papers I signed too?"

But Win had already hung up. She had Martha tap off the phone.

"What was that all about?" Harriet would have to tell her now.

"So what do you think?" Henry asked as they stood in line at the bakery. "Should we tell her?"

"Who?" Prudence was perusing the tasty assortment of bakery delights. "Your mother? About the twins?"

"Yeah." Henry pulled the number thirty-eight. They were serving twenty-two. "This could take a while. Maybe we can find another bakery."

"No," Prudence said. "This is the best one. Certainly we should. I mean, do you think you could keep the secret that long? I mean, we have a ways to go."

"Probably not," Henry said.

"Okay. So we'll tell her I'm expecting twins."

"She will die," Henry said.

"Oh, don't say that. I'm going to need her help for sure."

Henry looked around the small shop. "So we should definitely tell Mom that we just found out that we're having twins." His voice was a little louder than necessary. The bakery customers applauded and congratulated them.

"Way to go," one man said with a slap on Henry's back.

Henry could feel that he was beaming, even if it wasn't such a manly thing. He couldn't help it. Prudence, on the other hand, looked a little pale.

"You haven't eaten anything since oatmeal this morning?" Henry asked.

Prudence shook her head. "All I want is a donut. Glazed and warm."

That was when a small, older woman wearing a baggy coat and pointy glasses moved to the front. "I'm next," she said, "but take them first. She needs a donut more than me."

"Thank you," Henry said. "That is so kind of you."

"I had seven babies," she said. "Never enough donuts."

Henry swapped numbers with the lady. But he didn't have to. Everyone agreed to let the lady go right after Henry.

"Now see," Prudence said. "And people say it's a terrible world. I think it's a lovely place to raise children."

Henry ordered a dozen glazed donuts. Warmed.

Prudence didn't make it out of the store before eating one. She ate the second in the car.

"I hope Mom made it okay," Henry said. "She hasn't called since she made it to the cell lot.

I'm choosing to believe that means all is well."

"Sure it is," Prudence said. "We would have heard from her if something went wrong. She's probably home or close to home by now with Martha next to her and Humphrey in the back."

Martha dropped the phone into Harriet's tote bag. "Come on, you know you'll tell me eventually."

"Okay, but it's top secret."

"Is it something for the baby?"

Harriet shrugged. "In a way. I leased a gold mine."

Martha was silent for several long seconds until she laughed and said, "You are such a card. You did *not* lease a gold mine."

"Yes, I did. It's what they call a placer gold mine, right here in Grass Valley. Well, in Downieville, but it's not very far away."

Martha was silent again, but Harriet actually felt good that she finally let the cat out of the bag. She had been dying to tell someone besides Florence. And Humphrey. And it was nice that her best friend knew now too.

"Really?" Martha said. "A gold mine? How in the world do you lease a gold mine?"

"I leased a gold mine from a man named Old Man Crickets. That was his associate who called. Winslow Jump. Win."

Martha snorted air out of her nose like a bull. She snorted so hard her glasses popped off and landed on the dashboard, and Harriet swerved so hard she nearly ran the SUV onto a rough shoulder. "Crickets? Are you serious? Old Man Crickets?"

"I know, I know. But, yes, that's his name."

"How much did that cost? Harriet, I know you got a small fortune when you sold the house and from when Henry sold the business, but you are far from being a millionaire."

"My initial investment was five thousand for the leasing claim. And I've been paying for equipment so Win's men can work."

Martha didn't say a word. Instead, she stared out the window.

"Say something, Martha, please."

"Five thousand dollars is a lot of money. I could have used that kind of—"

"What?" Harriet said. "Money? You need money? Is that why you sounded strange the last few times we talked?"

"No. Never mind. It's nothing I can't handle."

Harriet felt the elation of the day deflate. "I wish you would have told me."

"It's over now. I only hope the claim is on the up and up. You know, there are lots of scams out there."

Harriet's spirits sank even lower. She knew that very well, but she was certain Win and Lily were not scam artists and, as usual, changed the subject. Harriet had gotten quite adept at adjusting the fan when the manure threatened to hit. "Hey, there's something else I wanted to tell you."

"There's more? Don't tell me. You bought the Brooklyn Bridge?"

"No, no. It's just a small thing so far, but, well, maybe it's pretty big, bigger than we know. Prudence and I have been trying to get along better, and I'm learning so much about her. She's not as fancy dancy as I thought." Then she laughed. "It is kind of hard to be fancy dancy with your head in the toilet."

"Morning sickness?"

"I'll say. Morning, afternoon, and evening. And she's not even in her second trimester yet."

"Oh, that's rough. Are you sure they'll want me there with all that going on? I mean, I'm glad you and Prudence are getting along. I don't want to interfere."

"Yep, because I think they kind of like it when I'm keeping busy. Henry's worried I'll . . ." She almost told her about the addition before she was ready. "Well, he's been trying to get me to make friends, like I'm seven years old."

Harriet turned onto Butterfly Drive. "This is their street."

"Very nice," Martha said. "In fact, I was meaning to say on the drive just how pretty it is out here."

"It's okay. I still miss back east sometimes.

206

There's just something about all those old, stately houses. These ranchers and split-levels are so modern or something."

"It looks like the kids are still out," Harriet said as she parked the car. "The BMW is missing."

"This is a nice house," Martha said. "Is that your scooter?"

Harriet laughed. "Sure is. Cute isn't she?"

The two friends sighed at the same time and said, "I've missed you so much." They hugged. Humphrey let go a loud woof.

"Come on," Harriet said. "Let's go inside. Believe it or not, I have more news."

"You're kidding. I don't know if I can take anymore, not after the gold mine. I still can't believe you actually did that."

"Wait until you meet Lily and Win. You'll feel so much better about it."

Harriet opened the door and stepped out.

"Lily?" Martha said. "Who is Lily?" She tugged open the lift gate.

"Win's daughter. She's a teenager. You know the type—seventeen, dark, brooding, probably writes poetry late at night."

"Weren't we all dark at that age?"

"Well, let's get your bag inside and I'll show you around."

Harriet unlocked the front door as Humphrey scooted around to the back of the house. "Welcome," she said, "to Chez Beamer." She went in and dropped Martha's bag on the floor.

Martha stepped farther into the house. "This is lovely. Prudence did a nice job decorating."

"It is nice," Harriet said. "And it's going to get a whole lot nicer."

"How so?"

"Come on in the kitchen and I'll tell you."

"I could sure use a cup of coffee," Martha said.

"It's been quite a day for you."

Harriet prepared the coffee as Martha looked around. "Now, this is a great kitchen. And look at the deck." She moved closer to the sliders. "Oh, Humphrey looks like he wants in." She pushed open the door and in he went, heading straight to his water bowl.

"Henry said it was added on a couple of years before they bought it. And speaking of adding on . . ."

Martha sat down at the table with a little bit of a thud and sigh. Obviously travel weary.

Humphrey finished lapping his water and stretched out his long body on the floor at Martha's feet. "How are you, boy?" She leaned over and gave him a good rub behind the floppy ears. "Oh, I've missed these ears."

Humphrey smiled.

The coffeemaker gurgled and the aroma of coffee swirled through the room. She opened a cabinet. "Little Debbies. That boy is in for a rude awakening one day. He eats them like they're going out of style. I don't suppose you want one?" She showed Martha a box of oatmeal creme cookies.

"No, thanks. Something about flying that always makes my stomach funny for a while, although lunch was good. Just the coffee."

Harriet set two coffee cups on the table. She chose cups with saucers instead of big, heavy mugs. A reunion between close friends called for cups with saucers.

"Any-hoo," Harriet said, "my other news is that the kids are having an addition—"

"I know that," Martha said.

Harriet chuckled. "No, no, let me finish. They aren't just having a baby. They're also having an addition built—a mother-in-law suite. Can you believe it?"

"Oh, Harriet," Martha said. "That is good news."

"I call it the Grammy Suite."

"Harriet, you are one terrific mom. And now you'll have a place for your collection. Sounds to me like the kids are trying to take extra good care of you."

Harriet was tempted to explain that she was paying for it, but decided it wasn't really about the money. It was about the love.

The coffeemaker gurgled at last and Harriet filled their cups. She set a small pitcher of cream on the table.

Martha added a splash and then lifted her cup. "Here's to a grandbaby, a Grammy Suite, and a gold mine. It's been a great day. Gee, that's a lot of g's."

"I'll say," Harriet said. And they laughed.

They clinked cups. "And here's to my dearest friend in the world," Harriet said. "Together again."

Martha sipped her coffee and leaned back in the chair with closed eyes. She let go a long sigh. "I hate to fly."

Harriet laughed. "I never knew that."

"It's the take-offs. Rattles my cage something fierce. My head still feels fuzzy."

The coffeemaker made a strange final rattle like it sometimes did, as though it had discovered a drop of water yet to filter. Harriet turned in its direction on instinct. "I wouldn't know. I've never flown."

"Don't," Martha said. "Unless it's the only way."

In a few minutes, Harriet refilled their cups, and this time she set the box of oatmeal creme cookies on the table. "Just in case your stomach is settled."

"So tell me the truth now," Martha said. "How is it, really, living with your kids? Is it strange at all?"

Harriet picked off a corner of a cookie. "Sometimes. I mean, we're family and I know that, but still, it's *their* family, if you know what I mean.

I'm the fifth wheel, the square peg, the stinky fish."

"Yeah, I guess it would be hard."

Harriet felt pensive a moment. "I wonder if that's why I bought into the gold mine."

"What do you mean?"

"Well, I guess the mine is . . . well, mine. And I'm hoping, no, praying that it will pay off big time so I can do more for them. It's time to leave something behind, something they'll look at and say, "Mom did this. Mom left this for us.""

"But you've done that, Harriet. Henry is so much like you. You just don't know it. He's your legacy, and now with the baby on the way, well, if there was ever something you contributed to, that's it."

"But what if I could send Henry to culinary school and he became a world renowned chef? He just started talking about school. Or I arranged the baby's college education?"

"I think you should let Henry decide his own future. You tried that once before, and look what happened."

Harriet felt the hair on her neck tingle. "He sold the business. In secret."

"Because he was afraid to tell you. Please, let them decide. And if you really do strike gold and get rich, then that's gravy."

Harriet reached out her hands to Martha. Martha held them and squeezed. "The best legacy you can leave them is to be happy, enjoy the time you have left, at least thirty years." She smiled. "That's what they'll remember."

"But . . . but . . ."

"No buts, Harriet. You have a wonderful son. You raised him well."

"And you have Wyatt," Harriet said.

Martha looked into her coffee cup as though it held the answer to an age-old question. "Wyatt," was all she said.

Chapter Sixteen

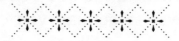

"Mom," Henry called the instant his foot hit the porch steps. "Mom!"

He pushed open the door. "Mom, we're home." Prudence followed behind.

"Coming," Harriet called. "We're coming."

Humphrey skittered out of the room before Harriet and Martha.

"Wow," Martha said. "He's excited."

"He should be," Harriet said. "He's going to become an uncle."

"Martha," called Henry. "It's so good to see you. How was your flight?"

Martha moved close enough to Henry to hug

him. "Henry, you look wonderful, and congratulations."

"Thank you. We're excited."

Martha pulled away and hugged Prudence. "Hi, Prudence. You are gorgeous. I can't believe it. A baby."

"Thank you, Martha. Welcome to California." Then she laughed.

Harriet stood near the couch and felt her eyebrows crinkle. "What's so funny?"

Prudence sat in the big chair. Humphrey trotted close and Prudence patted his side. "I see I'm not the only one getting fat around here."

Henry clicked his tongue. "You are not getting fat. And we won't ever say that."

"Okay, okay," Prudence said. "Do you want to tell them the news?"

"News?" Harriet said. "You have news?" She sat on the couch. "I guess it's good news, because you two look terribly excited."

"It is, Mom, but you should sit," Henry said. "This is pretty exciting."

Martha sat next to Harriet on the couch. "Okay, we're sitting, son," Harriet said.

"Right, right." He looked at Prudence. Humphrey sat with his head resting on her knee. Sandra Day sauntered past and leaped onto the back of Prudence's chair.

Henry nearly sucked all the air out of the room. "Okay. Are you ready?"

213

"Ready," Harriet said. She couldn't imagine what was so exciting.

"Do you want to tell, honey?" he asked Prudence.

"No, no, I think you should tell."

Henry took another deep breath and said, "Twins. We are having twins."

This time it was Harriet who nearly sucked all the air out of the room. She grabbed onto Martha. "Did you hear that? Twins. We're having twins. Well, they're having twins, but me, also, sort of, twins. I'm going to be Grammy to twins. Twins. Oh my goodness."

She leaped up and wrapped her arms around Henry. "Congratulations, Henry."

Then she gave Prudence an equally substantial hug.

"That is exciting," Martha said. "Twins. Wow. Two of everything."

"We were stunned," Prudence said. "But there they were on the ultrasound monitor. Two . . . babies. Two heartbeats. And that's why I really am beginning to show."

Henry sat on the arm of the chair next to Prudence. "Yep. Baby A and Baby B. That's what the technician, Jennifer, called them. Isn't that cute?"

Martha laughed. "He's so happy. That's nice." But then she got kind of a faraway look in her eyes that Harriet could feel in her heart. She

214

made a mental note to ask Martha about it later.

"This calls for a celebration," Harriet said. "We should all go out for dinner. To that lodge, you know the one, with all that rusticness—what's it called?"

"Half Moon Lodge?" Prudence said. "That's a fabulous idea."

After Harriet caught her breath and sat back down she said, "Well? Did you ask?"

"Ask what?" Henry said.

"Boys? Girls?"

Prudence shook her head. "No. The technician said it was too early to tell with any amount of certainty. All we know is that they are not identical twins."

"Oh, well that's just fine," Harriet said. "Now we need to get double everything."

She nudged Martha and whispered, "That gold will come in handy now."

"What was that, Mom?" Henry asked. "Did you say something?"

"I'm just glad we're building the extra rooms. It's really going to come in handy."

Harriet and Prudence locked eyes. Harriet felt so much emotion well up inside of her she thought she might burst. "Oh, Prudence," she said, "I am so happy for you."

"I know you are, Mother. I just wish . . ."

"Wish what?" Harriet asked.

"Well, you know, my own mother . . ."

"Yes," Martha said. "This must be bittersweet for you."

Prudence said. "It's okay."

"Now, you should try not to think about it too much," Harriet said. "We might never know why it worked out like this, but try to rest assured that God has got you and those dear sweet babies in the palm of his hand. He's got his reasons."

"I know, Mother," Prudence said. "Do you really think he has my mother in the palm of his hand?"

Harriet looked at Henry. "Maybe not the same hand," she said. "But I know he loves her too, and if you two are meant to be reunited someday then you will be. For now, all you need to do is take care of yourself."

"Thanks, Mom," Henry said. "In fact, why don't you rest before we head out for dinner, honey? I'll wake you in plenty of time." He kissed her head.

"Okay. I am a little tired."

"That actually sounds good," Martha said. "It's been a long, trying day. I'd like to rest before dinner also. There is the time difference to contend with."

"Oh, that's right. And was your flight especially tiring?" Prudence asked.

Harriet laughed. "Let's just say we had to play a little game of hide-and-seek. Martha dropped her phone at Midway Airport in the toilet and had no way of getting in touch with me."

"Oh no," Prudence said with a little giggle. "I did that once. Sometimes if you set the phone in a bowl of rice it will start working again."

"Really?" Martha said. "I hadn't heard that."

"Hide-and-seek?" Henry said as though he was just hearing it. "You mean Martha was lost or you got lost? I knew it. I knew you'd have trouble."

"No," Martha said. "I was the one who got lost. Your mom was terrific. And here I am, safe and sound."

Harriet smiled at Prudence. "Are you okay, dear?"

Prudence touched her stomach. "I'm glad you're here to . . . teach me. I don't know anything about taking care of a baby and now all of a sudden I have two. Two, Mom. Two babies. What if I don't wake up when they cry? I usually sleep like a rock. What if I drop one? What temperature is the right temperature for a bottle? And . . . should I use the bottle or breast-feed. Can you nurse twins?"

"Prudence," Harriet said. "Calm down, honey, before you explode. You will know. I'll teach you some things, like routines and schedules and the proper way to swaddle an infant. They like that, you know. But most of it will come to you because God gives it to you. He's the best mother of all. And the best teacher."

"Mothering is an instinct," Henry said. "I think you're going to do great."

Prudence looked at Henry. "Sometimes I . . . sometimes I worry that I might not be able to do it, like my mother. She had to run away. I won't do that, will I?"

Harriet shook her head so hard she thought it might snap off. "No, of course not. For one thing, I won't let you and, for another, you're not your mother. Your father did a pretty good job raising you all by himself."

"That's right," Henry said. "And you'll have me."

"My father did the best he could," Prudence said. "I miss him too. I know he would be so happy to meet his grandchildren."

Harriet's thoughts quickly turned to Lily and Win. For a split second she considered telling Prudence. Not on account of the gold mine but because maybe Prudence could help Lily.

But no, Prudence didn't need that right now.

"Now, look," Harriet said, "you go take a nap. You need your rest. I'll call you for dinner."

"Come on, honey. I'll tuck you in," Henry said.

Harriet and Martha waited until they heard the bedroom door shut before speaking. "What do you really think?" Martha asked.

"About what?"

"Prudence's mothering skills."

"Let's just say I wouldn't be surprised at anything. Remember, this is a woman who wears

Versace to the grocery store and has a near fit if one of the couch pillows lands on the floor."

Martha laughed. "She's in for a few surprises. And with two? I'm glad you're here."

"Me too. But you know, the poor dear never had a mother of her own to show her what to do."

"That's true," Martha said. "But the learning curve is steep, and even those of us who had role models made mistakes."

"Come on," Harriet said. "You haven't even settled in yet. Let me show you our room."

Chapter Seventeen

The next morning Harriet and Martha rose fairly early, even though Martha's body clock was not yet on California time. Harriet had not slept all that well considering Martha's snoring, but she wouldn't tell her that. And Humphrey had done a pretty good job of sawing wood himself.

"Good morning," Martha said as she sat up in bed.

"Morning," Harriet said. "How did you sleep?"

"Like a log. I can't believe I slept so well."
She hung her legs over the side of her bed. "I
thought I would have trouble the first night or
two, but I was really tired."

"I'm so glad." Harriet yawned.

"How about you?"

"Fine," Harriet said. "Although I will admit that
I might have been kept awake from time to time
thinking about everything."

"You have a lot to think about," Martha said.

Harriet took a breath. "You know, you're
absolutely right. Here I was complaining to you
about how bored and lonely I was, and now I'm
almost overwhelmed with things to do and think
about."

Martha slipped her bathrobe over her shoulders.
"So what shall we do first? I want to see everything."

Harriet took another breath. This time she let it
out slowly. "Well, first we should have breakfast
and then I need to meet Win at the café at ten-
thirty."

"Oh yes, the call from yesterday."

"Yeah. He needs more money."

Martha sat back down on her bed. "Harriet, are
you sure about this guy? Have you checked it
out?"

Harriet cinched her bathrobe around her waist.
"I didn't think I needed to. Wait until you meet
Win and Lily. You'll see what I mean. And

besides, he said he'd have pictures of the actual mine for me today."

"Okay, but . . . but . . . well, this is your call. I'll try to keep an open mind."

Henry had risen early also. He was already sipping coffee and writing by six and had managed to complete another chapter. Feeling pretty good about the book, he thought it looked like a French toast kind of day. He leaned back in his chair. "Yep. I think it's going to be a good day."

He saved his file for the third time. "I'll be back later," he said.

That was when Humphrey ambled into the den and let go a woof. "What's that, boy? You say you need to go out?"

Humphrey wagged his tail.

"All right, I'll let you out. Mom must still be sleeping."

Henry slid open the deck door, and Humphrey scooted out and made a mad dash for his favorite bush.

"All-righty then," Henry said. "French toast with raspberries."

He was whisking eggs and milk when Prudence appeared in the kitchen, looking a little like a wrung-out dishcloth. Henry stopped whisking. "You don't look so good."

Prudence sat down at the table. "I don't feel so good."

He sat across from her. "Are you sure this is normal?"

Prudence shrugged. "According to your mom and every mother at the office, it is perfectly normal."

Henry was not about to let his anxiety show. "Then we don't worry. Maybe something to settle your stomach. Some tonic water with a splash of cranberry juice?"

Prudence shook her head. "Nothing yet . . . but maybe a couple of crackers."

"Sure thing. I'm making French toast."

"None for me," Prudence said. "I think I'll shower and get ready for work."

Henry set three crackers on a plate near Prudence. "Work? Are you certain you're up for it?"

"I have to. Court today."

Henry went back to his egg mixture. "Look," he said with his back turned. "Maybe you should quit." He waited. He soaked two slices of bread in the mixture and set them in a hot, buttered pan before turning around.

"Did you hear me, honey?"

"I heard. And I've thought about it, but we'd never make it without my salary."

Henry felt his heart sink through the kitchen floor. "I'll get a job."

Prudence shook her head. "No. You'll never get your books written."

"I'll do whatever it takes. I can work at night."

"Check your pan," Prudence said. "No, I just have to get through this part of it. Everyone says it goes away. Usually."

Henry flipped the bread and dropped another slice into the eggs. "Just promise me you'll not overdo it."

"I promise."

That was when Henry noticed Martha standing at the kitchen doorway. "Good morning," he said.

Martha looked at him with wide eyes. "Morning. Smells good in here."

"Come on," Prudence said. "Coffee is on and Henry is making his famous French toast. I'm just going to go shower and head off to work."

Martha smiled at Prudence. "It really does end."

"Thanks. You have a good day with Harriet. I'll be home for dinner."

Henry handed Prudence a glass of bubbling Coke. "Just a few sips. I'm sure it will help."

Prudence sipped the Coke. "Starting to feel better already."

"I heard what you said about Prudence quitting her job," Martha said once Prudence had left the room.

Henry flipped the bread. "I wish she could. I wish she would never have to work again."

"Oh now, that might not be best for her. But I understand. It would be nice if she could quit, at least for a while."

"There's just no way. I don't make nearly enough writing books. That's why I'm thinking about culinary school, but that could just make it worse, what with tuition and books and whatever else I might need. Not to mention the time away from home."

Martha poured coffee into a mug. "Well, maybe something will happen to change all that."

"Like what?"

"Oh, I don't know, but things have a way of changing. Maybe your mom—" Martha stopped talking.

"Maybe my mom what?" Henry said.

"Nothing, Henry. I just mean people have been affording babies forever. You'll figure it out."

After breakfast and making a grocery list, Harriet and Martha went into town in Henry's BMW. They stopped at the bank first and Harriet withdrew the money Win requested. Martha's eyes grew when she saw that much cash. "I hope you know what you're doing. Maybe it would be better to just give the cash directly to the kids."

"Martha," Harriet said, "don't be so pessimistic. Now, come on. The café is just down the street."

The same server was there to greet them. "This is my friend from back east, Martha," Harriet said as Cindy led them to the usual table.

"Nice to meet you."

Martha took the seat across from Harriet.

"Are you expecting the others?" Cindy asked.

"Yes," Harriet said.

"Okeydokey. It's a little early for fries, but—"

"Oh, not today," Harriet said. "We had a lovely French toast breakfast. Just coffee."

"This is nice," Martha said, looking around.

"It is nice." Harriet glanced around. She spied that same woman sitting on the stool at the counter again. She leaned over the table. "Do you see that woman over there? Dark blue pants. Sitting at the counter reading a book."

"Yes?"

"She's always here, I mean, there, sitting over there. Every time I come in. There she is. Isn't that weird?"

Martha shrugged. "I don't know, if she's always here when you are doesn't that mean you're always here?"

Harriet had to think about that for a second. "Well, yeah, I guess, but there's something strange about her. She looks . . . out of place."

"Maybe she's a spy."

"Oh don't be silly. Why would there be spies in Grass Valley?" Harriet said. She glanced at the woman again and saw Lily making her way toward them.

"Oh good, there's Lily. Now you'll see what I mean."

Martha turned. "Is that her? With that black hair?"

"Yes." Harriet still couldn't get used to the black hair, but she was pleased as punch that Lily was wearing one of the outfits she bought her. Green shorts with a pretty blue blouse tucked in and a multi-colored striped belt.

"Lily," Harriet said. "You look adorable."

"Hi," Lily said with a wave. She stood by the table. "Thanks."

"This is my friend Martha from back east. The one I told you about. She'll be visiting for a while."

"Hi," Lily said.

"Go on, sit down," Harriet said. "Where's your dad?"

"He'll be here soon."

Harriet couldn't help but notice that Martha's brow had wrinkled like a cheap suit. "What's wrong, dear?"

"Nothing," Martha said. "I was just wondering why she isn't in school. Is it a holiday?"

"I don't go to school," Lily said.

"So you graduated?" Martha said.

Lily shook her head.

"She dropped out on account of moving around so much with her father," Harriet said. "But who knows, maybe when we strike it rich you can finish school and go to college."

Lily sucked louder on her straw. "Oh, that'll never happen. Believe me."

"Oh now, she doesn't mean that." Harriet looked at Martha. "We'll strike it rich."

"No," Lily said. "I just meant I'm not smart enough to go to college."

"Pish," Martha said. "You certainly are smart enough."

"Smart enough for what?" Win said as he took a seat.

"College," Martha said.

"Oh, that," Win said. "She don't need college. And you must be Martha, Harriet's friend."

Martha nodded. "And you must be Win."

"Dad," Lily said, "stop making decisions for me. Maybe I'd like to go."

"Now hold on, girlie girl, I'm not saying anything new."

Lily folded her arms against her chest.

"Don't worry. You can go if you want," Martha said.

Harriet was surprised at how quickly Martha thought she could speak into Lily's life. It wasn't like her. "Maybe we should get down to business."

"Good idea," Win said.

Cindy came by. "What can I get for you?" she asked Win.

"Now I know it's a little early for lunch, but could I get a cup of coffee and French fries for my sweet little filly here?" He touched Lily's hair. Harriet saw Martha wince when she jerked away. "And I'll just have a grilled cheese, no pickle, and chips," Win said.

"Grilled cheese sounds good," Lily said. "If we can afford it today."

"My treat," Martha said.

"Why thank you, ma'am," Win said.

"Be right back," Cindy said. "And would you like a Coke, sweetie?"

"Sure," Lily said.

"So, how long will you be staying?" Win asked Martha.

"Two weeks," Martha said.

"Unless I can convince her to stay longer," Harriet said.

Martha smiled. "We'll see."

After a few minutes of idle chit chat, Cindy returned with their orders.

Harriet watched Win give Cindy a quizzical look.

"Now I know," Win said. "Didn't you used to work at the bakery in Nevada City?"

"Yeah," the waitress said. "But I do better here. We never got tips at the bakery, and all I did was stand behind the counter and pass out donuts and cupcakes."

Harriet snapped her fingers. "That reminds me," Harriet said. "I have to get donuts for Humphrey."

"Humphrey?" Lily said. "Who is Humphrey?"

"My dog. He's a big, fat Basset Hound with ears that drag on the floor when he walks and an insatiable appetite for glazed donuts. Didn't I tell you about him?"

Lily laughed. And that was when Harriet realized that that was the first time she had heard Lily laugh. Laugh in a way that sounded genuine.

"Donuts?" Lily said. "That's funny. Your dog eats donuts." Then she looked at the table. "I had a dog once. But we had to give her away after Pop and me started moving around so much."

"But," Win said, "as soon as we make enough money to buy us a pretty little house on a pretty little street, we're goin' right down to the pound to pick you out a new pup."

Lily shook her head. "Right. I'll believe that when it happens."

"Now, now, dear," Harriet said. "You must have faith. Faith is the most important thing in life. Well, that and family."

"That's good," Win said. "You tell her about family and how important it is. In fact, you came out here to live with your son, isn't that right?"

"Yes. And his wife. And now they're having twins. Can you believe that? Twins."

"Congratulations," Lily said. "That's nice. You never told me much about your daughter-in-law. Lots about Henry, but not much about her."

Martha pulled her coffee mug from her lips. "That's because Harriet never really thought much of Prudence. Until now."

"Prudence?" Lily said. "That's her name?"

"It suits her," Harriet said. "No, really, she's a terrific woman. I'm so proud of her. She's a lawyer."

Win coughed. "A lawyer, you say."

"Yes. And a good one. She even serves on the . . . the . . . what do you call it?"

"City council," Martha said.

"Yes, that's it. She's very smart and knows all about the law."

Lily grabbed two fries and dipped them in the ketchup. "These are really good fries."

"I know," Harriet said. "But not as good as some I used to get at the Jersey Shore."

"Oh yeah," Lily said. "Pop and me lived near there for about three months once. Someplace called Browns Mills."

Win bit into his grilled cheese. "I was just wonderin' somethin'," he said. "Have you told Prudence and . . . and Henry, of course, about the gold mine?"

"Nope. I was gonna, but then I decided to keep it secret for a while. Until after we strike it rich. Keep it a surprise."

Win let go a long breath. "That's good. I mean, that's right nice of you, Harriet. Surprises are always fun."

"I hope so. I'm thinking I could get them a big head start on the babies' college education."

Win finished his sandwich in only four or five bites. "Anyway, that's all nice, but first we have to find the gold, and in order to do that we need to move more gravel and dirt."

"Right," Harriet said. "I guess that's where the backhoe comes in. Are they terribly expensive?"

"Oh, you got it all wrong, darlin'. We don't buy a backhoe. Nobody buys a backhoe. We just need to rent it for a while. A few weeks before the rainy season starts."

"A few weeks?" Harriet swiped one of Lily's fries. "It's gonna take that long to strike gold?"

Win smiled wide. Cindy came by and asked if they wanted anything else. "No, darlin', we're just about to leave."

"Maybe even longer than that," Lily said.

Martha felt a kick under the table she was certain was meant for Lily.

"Let's just see how far we get before the rains come."

"Can you still work the mine in the rainy season?"

"You can," Win said, "but it can get pretty sloppy up in those hills. We'll play it by ear."

Harriet finished her coffee. "You know what I remembered?" she said.

"What's that?" Win asked.

"I remembered you said you had good news too only you never told me."

"Oh yeah, yeah, well, in a way the good news has already been told and has gotten kind of watered down. I was hoping you'd ask for the good news first."

"What would you have said?" Harriet asked.

"Yeah, Pop, what would you have said?"

"I would have said that we were moving so much dirt and rock and working so hard that we needed the other backhoe. That is good news. It means we're getting close. More to dig through. Leastways, that's what my boys tell me."

Lily patted her dad's back. "And the boys are always right, ain't they, Dad?"

"They sure are, honey. We got some of the best gold hounds on the job."

Certainly not the news Harriet had hoped to hear, but she'd take it.

Harriet folded her paper napkin and set it in her coffee mug. "Okay, we have lots to do. So maybe we should complete our business." Harriet pushed the bulging envelope across the table. This time she caught a look in Lily's eye that she hadn't really seen before. Surprise? No, it was more like she was looking at something she had no business seeing. But Harriet chalked it up to youth.

Win stuffed the envelope in his pocket. "I'll be in touch."

"Hold on a second," Martha said. "Didn't Harriet say you had pictures to show her? I'd like to see them."

"Oh right," Win said. "Lily has them in that

fancy phone of hers. Go on, girl, show the pictures."

"Martha was hoping maybe we could go visit the mine. You know, at least the section I saw. The creek, or run, I guess, with all the gold dust in it."

"Afraid that won't be possible," Win said. "All that dust has been washed clean away."

"Oh, that's too bad," Harriet said.

"Sure is," Win said. "These pictures will have to suffice."

Lily tapped her phone a couple of times and then tilted the screen so all could see.

Harriet looked at a picture of a funny looking machine sitting in a dirt pile.

"That's the beast," Lily said. She swiped through the pictures fast. "This is the backhoe, the one we just got. The sluice box. And this is the main stream."

Harriet looked at the pictures. They really didn't look all that different from the ones she had already seen. Martha didn't say a word. Not a single word.

Chapter Eighteen

Henry managed to complete another chapter even though his mind kept wandering to thoughts about the babies, money, Prudence, and the coming building project.

Prudence hadn't called, so Henry was taking that as a good sign that she had gotten past her morning sickness today.

"I hate to throw up, Humphrey. It's my least favorite thing to do."

Humphrey said, "Woof."

"Except in this case, if I could be sick for her, I would be—gladly." Henry saved his file. "Come on, old man, let's go out."

Henry opened the deck doors and Humphrey trotted directly to his second favorite bush. Unfortunately, it was on the side of the house and would probably be dug up when the builders got there Monday.

"Sorry, Humphrey, you might have to find another place."

Henry stretched his arms over his head. The way the doctor showed him. It was easy to get tired and stiff sitting at his desk all day. This was something he could never understand. Why sitting was tiring. He'd maybe go on a run a little later.

Humphrey was busy sniffing around the grass and trees, even stopping to roll on his back with his tongue lolled out. Henry sat down at the deck table. The noon sun felt warm and nice on his face. He wasn't expecting Florence Caldwell, but she showed up.

"Yoo-hoo, Henry," she called. She carried a pie onto the deck.

"Mrs. Caldwell," Henry said. He straightened himself up quickly.

"Oh, sit," she said. "Be comfy. You work hard. Most people don't know how hard artists work."

Henry liked the sound of that. Yes. He was an artist. And he did work hard.

"I brought you a strawberry/rhubarb pie," Mrs. Caldwell said.

"Oh boy," Henry said. "I could go for a slice right now."

"Coming right up." She nodded toward the deck doors.

"Certainly. Mom is in town and Prudence is in Sacramento. I'm by myself today."

"Oh, you poor thing," Mrs. Caldwell said. "Well, you just sit there, and I'll get you a slice. Do you have any ice cream? A scoop of vanilla would go just perfectly."

"We might," Henry said.

Henry sat down at the table, feeling rather good. He didn't mind being pampered a little, although if Prudence was there she would have something to say.

A few minutes later, Mrs. Caldwell returned with pie. Two slices. She sat down at the table.

"Thank you," Henry said. He tasted the pie. It was, of course, delicious. "You know, if I open a restaurant, you will come bake pies for me, won't you?"

"Why, Henry, are you thinking about doing that? I didn't know you were a chef."

"Thinking about it, yes. I love to cook, and everyone says I have a knack for it. But I would have to go to culinary school."

"What about your books?"

He swallowed. "Oh, I'd still write, but with the babies coming and all, I've been worried about money. I like the idea of a steady income."

"Only natural," she said. "But Mr. Caldwell and I always found that somehow we'd get by. No matter what. You watch. You'll do fine. Wait a minute, did you say babies? As in more than one?"

"Yes. We're expecting twins. I guess you haven't heard."

"No, I hadn't. That is exciting news." She hugged Henry. "Congratulations."

"Thanks, Mrs. Caldwell."

It was nearly three o'clock by the time Harriet and Martha arrived home, groceries and donuts in hand. Harriet figured Henry would be busy in the den and she didn't want to disturb him, so Harriet and Martha carried all the groceries inside. Well, with Humphrey's help. He kept close to her ankles. He was looking for the donuts and she knew it.

"Okay, okay. I didn't forget. Let me get my sneakers off and some of this cold stuff put away."

Harriet put the fish and raspberries in the fridge while Martha helped to empty bags. Humphrey whimpered and stared at the last bag.

"He really loves those donuts," Martha said.

"He does. It's the craziest thing. He would eat the whole dozen."

"You better not let him, dear. Only Prudence is eating for two . . . er, I mean three."

After giving Humphrey his donut, Martha suggested more coffee and Harriet happily agreed. "I bet the aroma will flush Henry out of his cave."

"You must be very proud of him," Martha said.

"I am," Harriet said. She dropped a filter into the coffeemaker. "But . . . sometimes I still feel a little disappointed."

"Disappointed?"

"I just wish he had kept Max's business. I

think they would be doing much better. No matter what he says."

"Not for you to say. He has to be who he is. And I think he's doing terrific."

"I know." Harriet sat down at the table and broke a glazed donut in two. She bit one side and chewed. "Sometimes I feel bad because he did it so sneakily. Didn't tell me until the papers were signed."

"He was afraid of hurting you."

"How do you know that?"

"He told me."

Harriet stopped chewing and swallowed a large chunk of donut. "You mean you knew—all along?"

"Not all along. But yeah, I knew. I'm sorry, Harriet, but we both thought it would be better if you didn't know. Henry had to do it. He was miserable."

"No excuse. Max wasn't always thrilled to go to work, but he did it because he had to."

"Harriet. Isn't it better to have a happy son?"

"I suppose. But, I can't seem to let this go. He's an artist. Just like you. Just like Lily."

"Lily?" Martha said.

"Yeah, she told me she draws but doesn't have much time for it anymore."

"And I bet you encouraged her."

Harriet nodded. "Sure, but . . . okay, I see where this is going."

"Right," Martha said.

"But what about Wyatt? Is he doing what you hoped and planned and dreamed he would?"

"So how is Humphrey adjusting?" Martha asked as she rubbed him behind his ears. "I know he's been here longer than you, but it's still a big change."

"I think he loves it out here. He has a much bigger yard than we had back home, and I think he likes having Henry around. They've really bonded."

Martha kissed the dog on the nose.

"He's not too crazy about Sandra Day, though," Harriet said. "That silly cat tortures him."

"I'll bet. The cat does come across a bit uppity."

"Okay, Martha," Harriet said. "Enough stalling."

Martha seemed to suck all the oxygen out of the kitchen. "I have to tell you something."

Harriet's heart sank. She did not like the tone of Martha's voice. "Uh oh, what's wrong? Does it have anything to do with that doctor's visit you told me about when I was on my trip?"

"No, that was a lie. A smokescreen. I actually had something much worse to do."

Harriet leaned closer toward her friend. "Martha, you're scaring me. What is it?"

Harriet pushed some stray hairs out of her eyes. "It's . . . it's Wyatt."

"Wyatt? What's wrong with him?"

"Well, nothing, really. At least not physically. He got himself into some trouble."

"What kind of trouble? Financial? Does he need money? I've got money."

"No, no, not exactly."

"Come on, Martha, spill it."

"He's in prison. That day you called, I was on my way to court."

Harriet swallowed. Her first impulse was to laugh, thinking it was a joke, but the seriousness of Martha's tone made her think it was no joke.

"Martha? Why? What happened?"

Martha picked at her donut, and then she slipped it to Humphrey.

"Tell me what happened," Harriet said. "What on earth could he have done? He was always such a quiet, gentle kid."

"He got himself mixed up with drugs and ended up committing armed robbery."

Harriet fell back in her chair. "No. Really? But when?"

"This happened while you were on your trip. I didn't want to tell you while you were traveling. In fact, I didn't really know anything until the police came and arrested him. Right from my house. They just came inside and took my son. The next thing I knew, he was in jail. They gave him fifteen years. Fifteen years!"

Harriet did some quick calculations. She guessed that Wyatt would be in his mid-forties, maybe older, before he was eligible for parole.

"Oh, Martha, I'm so sorry. I had no idea you were going through that. Why didn't you tell me? I would have ended my trip and come back to be with you."

"That's why I didn't tell you. There was nothing you could have done. He confessed to the crime."

Martha looked like she wanted to cry. To just break down and sob for days. Harriet could feel her pain. It was like a million pounds of weight resting on Martha's shoulders. If only Harriet could take that away.

"Go on, cry, if you want," Harriet said. "It's okay."

Martha sniffed, and then she cried. Not for long. A minute or two. She blew her nose and wiped her eyes. "He's gone, Harriet. My son is gone."

Harriet's mind had gone completely wild as she imagined all sorts of possible scenarios. She also knew it would be best to get the facts. Just the facts, as Sergeant Friday always said.

So Harriet scooted her chair over and she and Martha sat close together for the next few minutes while Martha told her the story.

"And so, like an idiot, he was high on . . . on something at the time, thought he was the Incredible Hulk or something, and he burst into the drugstore and held a gun to the clerk's head."

Harriet gasped. "How awful."

"But here's the stupid part. The gun was not

even loaded. Wyatt said he couldn't bring himself to actually load the thing."

Harriet shook her head. She knew Wyatt was not the brightest crayon in the box, but she had no idea he was just plain stupid.

"I'm sorry, Martha. Do you go visit him much? How's he doing? Don't they have programs?"

Martha practically fell off her chair, she laughed so hard. "So-called programs. They don't help much. He goes to counseling and rehab meetings. He's clean now. Or getting there."

Harriet chuckled. Clean. It was such a street term. One she never thought she'd hear one of her friends use in connection to a child, unless it meant the usual thing—clean as in scrubbing behind his ears.

Harriet hugged her friend and then kissed her forehead. "I don't really know what I can say. I don't think there is anything except that I'm here for you and Wyatt. I know he wasn't in his right mind."

"Oh, he knows he did wrong. He's very remorseful, but like we all know, life choices have consequences, and just because you say you're sorry doesn't free you from those consequences."

"But fifteen years? For a first offense? The gun wasn't loaded."

"The judge was pretty mad. And it wasn't exactly a first offense."

Harriet shook her head. "Oh no, there's more?"

"Just little things. But it added up. Shoplifting. Vandalism. Stupid stuff. I was too embarrassed to tell anyone. Even you."

"Maybe Prudence can do something." Harriet felt her heart quicken. "Yes, she's a lawyer. Maybe she can help."

"No. Please, don't tell her. The sentence is set. His lawyer has appealed and done all the necessary things. It's going to stick."

Martha wiped away tears. "I couldn't tell you but his sentencing date was two days after you left. I thought you might not leave if I told you. But the bottom line is, he did the crime."

"Who did what crime?" Henry stood near the refrigerator, looking a little surprised.

"Henry," Martha said. "We thought you'd smell the coffee."

"And the donuts? I don't know why, but I've been so hungry lately. Especially for sweets."

"I do," Harriet said. She winked at Martha.

Harriet fed the other half of her glazed donut to Humphrey and laughed. "Sympathy cravings."

"What?"

"Do you think you might be a tad jealous?" Martha asked.

"What? I am not jealous. Of Prudence? No way. I'm thrilled."

"She didn't say you weren't thrilled to pieces. But look, son, it's perfectly normal for an expecting daddy to take on some . . . well, symptoms while his wife is pregnant."

Henry laughed. "That's crazy, Mom. I am not having symptoms." He seemed to stare off into space for a second.

Humphrey said, "Woof."

"Well, I was a little sick to my stomach this morning."

Martha laughed. "I think it's sweet."

Henry poured himself a cup of coffee and added a splash of Half and Half. He grabbed a donut. "So. What crime?"

"I might as well tell you," Martha said, and she proceeded to tell Henry the whole story about Wyatt. Henry pretty much listened, stunned.

"I don't believe it. He was always a good kid."

"I know," Martha said.

"Should I call him? Can I call him?"

"You can write," Martha said.

Henry touched his stomach. "Maybe I shouldn't have eaten that glazed donut on top of the pie."

"Pie?" Harriet said. "What pie?"

"Florence brought over a strawberry/rhubarb."

Harriet shook her head.

Chapter Nineteen

The next few days whizzed by. Harriet and Martha did some sightseeing, including the Empire Gold Mine, which Martha found to be "educational and impressive." Win had not called asking for more money, which made Harriet happy. But she also realized he still had never given her copies of the papers she signed.

Henry took a break from his writing schedule to get things ready for the builders. He cleared the side yard of some rocks and dug out Humphrey's second favorite bush.

"Don't worry, old man," Henry told him. "We'll replant it."

Henry had never seen Humphrey look so despondent. It was like he had lost his best friend. But then again, he had never seen a dog look so jubilant when he dug the hole out back for the rhododendron.

Prudence weathered several bouts of morning sickness, but she still looked after her garden and the house, catching up on laundry and general housework. Florence Caldwell, whom Harriet had come to think of as simply nosey after all, came by with a batch of brownies. The kind Henry loved, with walnuts.

All in all Sunday morning arrived with peace and tranquility. But, as Harriet sipped coffee with Martha in the kitchen, she admitted that she really didn't want to go to church.

"I'm tired," she told Martha.

"Now, now," Martha said. "I think we should go. It's good for the kids, and from the sound of it you haven't been attending church much."

"I know. It's the congregation," Harriet said. "I don't believe there is a person over forty, except for Mr. Marsden, and he's so old I think he might have dated Cleopatra."

"I'll be with you today," Martha said. "Let's go."

So off they went, a little late on account of Prudence moving a little slowly. They all went in the BMW. Harriet thought Henry looked so proud he might burst his buttons.

They no sooner walked into the lobby when Harriet was asked to fill in at the nursery. Harriet clasped Martha's hand. "I knew it."

Geraldine Tubman told Harriet that little Gerry had been throwing up a lot lately.

"Now, he's not sick. Doctor said he just has a sensitive tummy."

Harriet took Gerry from Mrs. Tubman. "Oh, it's okay. Have you tried oatmeal? Good for an upset tummy."

Mrs. Tubman only smiled. She kissed Gerry's cheek. "Now, Mommy will be back right after the service."

"He'll be fine," Harriet said.

"You bet," Martha said. "We're a couple of old pros."

Harriet sat Gerry in a crib and gave him a pat on the head and a toy. "Sometimes nervous mommies make babies' bellies nervous."

The hour and fifteen minutes went quickly. Harriet and Martha enjoyed the children. Martha especially enjoyed building block towers and knocking them down.

"We just heard," said Sally Roberts after the service, a young professional woman with one child, two-year-old Scotty. "It's wonderful news."

Harriet handed over Scotty once Sally signed him out like he was a library book. Harriet understood the need for security, but she appreciated that in her days as a young mother people were more trusting. There wasn't the need for security cameras in church—especially church.

"It is wonderful," Harriet said. "I couldn't be happier. Thank you."

"And Prudence is radiant," Sally added. "And twins. A double blessing."

As the kudos and blessings came in, Harriet smiled about as wide as all outdoors. It was terrific news, and she deserved to feel every bit as proud as she was feeling.

"Praise the Lord," said Terri Higley. "I know it's been a rough go for them."

And so it went until all the children had been safely delivered back into the care of their parents. She and Martha joined Prudence and Henry in Fellowship Hall where they enjoyed a cup of coffee with a hint of Irish Cream, a lemon Danish, and the continued congratulations of nearly everyone they saw.

Prudence and Henry seemed to be enjoying the attention also. And from across the room Harriet did notice that it was true, Prudence was absolutely radiant, especially when a ray of sunlight burst through one of the windows and shone directly on her, signaling her out for all to notice. Harriet basked in Prudence's radiance.

But soon enough, the sun ray was gone, the crowd had thinned, and they were on their way home.

"That was kind of fun," Prudence said. "I'm not used to being in the spotlight without a jury bearing down on me."

"It was nice," Henry said. "I'm so proud of you."

"And I'm proud of you," Prudence said. "You looked so . . . so fatherly when you collected the offering."

"Thank you, honey," Henry said.

Harriet grabbed Martha's hand. "Such a cute couple."

"But now," Henry said looking into the rear-view mirror, "we get back to reality. The builders are starting tomorrow."

"I know," Harriet said. "I am just . . . just all atwitter. I can't wait to hear the hammers fly."

Martha laughed so hard Harriet thought she might have laid an egg. "What's so funny?"

"Can't wait to hear the hammers fly?"

"All right, all right," Harriet said. "I suppose that was a little corny. I guess I just mean I can't wait to hear the sounds of building going on."

Martha patted Harriet's knee. "I know. I know."

"I can't say I'm not a little nervous about the commotion and disruption," Henry said.

"That is true," Prudence said, "since you work at home and all."

"At least the building will be happening outside. Should be a little less disruptive," Martha said.

"Well, I am really looking forward to it," Prudence said. "Aren't you, Mother?" Harriet was looking out the window at the passing trees and the lovely view of the mountains. Everywhere she looked in Grass Valley there was a view. A place to lock her eyes and look. It was a pretty place.

"I certainly am," she said.

Harriet snuggled back into the seat. She was happy. A far cry away from how she felt just over a week ago, all sulky and wishing she had never left Pennsylvania. And why not? She was going to be a grammy, have her own addition, was part lessee of a gold mine about to strike, and her best friend was sitting next to her. What else did she need?

She couldn't help but smile when the car hit a bump. God's pleasure. She often felt God's pleasure on bumpy roads. She wondered why that was.

Sunday quickly slipped into Monday morning, and Harriet was awakened by the sound of the builders. Mostly, she heard talking and the sound of truck engines. She pulled on the same pants she had worn the day before, the same shirt, and then slipped into an older pair of Chucks without socks.

She tossed a small pillow at Martha's bed. "Wake up," she called. "Today's the day."

Martha roused from her sleep. "What?"

"The builders are here. Let's go."

Martha rolled over. "You go. I want to rest awhile."

"Suit yourself," Harriet said.

Harriet brushed her teeth, mouth washed, ran a brush through her hair, which she decided needed a cut, and dashed outside.

Henry was talking to a tall, thin woman who was deeply tanned and gorgeous. Her hair was the color of sunshine, and her teeth were so white

Harriet figured they could help guide the space shuttle in for a landing.

"Oh, oh," Henry said. "Here she is now."

"Hi," Harriet said, stepping over a small bush.

"It's so nice to meet you." The tall woman shook Harriet's hand. "My name is Daisy Day." She spoke with a southern accent, which Harriet found charming.

"And this, of course, is my mother, Harriet Beamer," Henry said with his arm around Harriet's shoulders.

"You designed my new Grammy Suite?" Harriet asked.

Daisy nodded. "I sure did. Well, me and Daisy. She's off inspecting another job at the moment. But she'll be by in just a tiddly wink. I hope ya'll like it."

"But aren't you Daisy?"

"Yes, that's right. But so is Daisy. Daisy Knight. She's been my ever-lovin' best friend since kindergarten. Both named Daisy. Isn't that just a scream?"

"Yes," Harriet said. "A scream." She looked at the bright yellow pick-up in the driveway with the words, Day and Knight, Two Daisies Design, painted across the door in purple. Henry hadn't quite told her the correct name of their business.

"What a cute name." She said the words, but she also thought that builders this cute could not possibly know what they were doing.

Daisy looked at her clipboard and then back to Harriet. "Henry told us his daddy was a builder, so you must know plenty about building. I guess we'll need to work a little extra careful, now won't we?"

Harriet didn't quite know how to respond.

"But you just don't worry your pretty little heart over it."

"I'm not worried," Harriet said. Yes, she was.

"Good. Good. But if you catch us using the wrong nail, you be sure to tell us, or if you don't want us to rabbet the lintels, well, that's okay too. You just holler."

Of course she wanted them to rabbet her lintels. It was the only proper way to build a doorjamb. Or so she thought. It was hard to tell with this Daisy. She was a fast and smooth talker.

"Well, it was nice to meet you," Harriet said. "I'm certain the addition will be spectacular."

"Oh, it will," Daisy said.

"Except," Harriet said, "I was looking at the plans and—"

"Mother," Henry said. "The design is complete."

"All I was going to say was that I would like it if you could include several built-in shelves for my collection."

"I thought you'd just buy a cabinet or something," Henry said.

"I could. I could. But wouldn't it be nice to have shelves, floor to ceiling, built right in?"

Daisy screwed up her mouth. "I don't think that would be a problem. And we certainly don't need to make that decision today."

"Right," Harriet said. "And I was also wondering if you could put a nice, deep sink in the powder room. Since that's my only running water. I'd like a place to work with my pots."

"Excuse me?" Daisy said. "Pot?"

Harriet laughed. "No, no, dear, pots. I raise African Violets."

"Oh, certainly," Daisy said. "That's not a problem."

"Why thank you, dear. Now I'll just leave you to your work. I don't want to interfere."

"Nice to meet you," Daisy said.

Harriet smiled wide. "And you too."

Harriet left Henry with Daisy and went to the kitchen where she found Humphrey near his water bowl, looking like he had lost his best friend. "What's the matter with you?" Harriet asked. "You aren't jealous of Martha, are you?"

Humphrey let go a soft woof. A woof that usually meant he was hungry and hungry for donuts. But Harriet thought he had had quite enough recently.

"It's kibble for you this morning," she said. "Here you go." She filled his dish with the small brown pellets. He gulped them down like a nervous Nellie.

"Uh oh," Harriet said. "Are you anxious about

something? You always gulp your food when you're upset."

And that was when Sandra Day sauntered into view.

"The cat," she said. "That darn cat."

Harriet patted Humphrey's head. "Well, don't you worry too much. In just a few weeks we'll have our own place. No cats allowed."

"No cats?" It was Martha.

"Good morning," Harriet said. "Yes. No cats in the Grammy Suite."

"Capital idea," Martha said with a yawn.

"Coffee?" Harriet said.

"Please. And what is that noise?"

Harriet stopped to listen. "Oh, that sweet melody is the sound of a backhoe firing up. They'll be digging the foundation today. They already have the area marked off and cleaned up." She poured water into the coffeemaker to make some more. Henry had already emptied the carafe.

"That's nice," Martha said as she sat down at the table.

Harriet smiled. The sound of the backhoe brought back a quick slideshow of memories for Harriet. She would often go to one of the building sites where Max worked. She did learn a lot, and she believed she had every right in the world to keep a close look on the addition construction. After all, she thought again, it was more than likely the last home she'll ever have. It was still a sobering and sad thought.

"Well, Humphrey, when we strike it rich, we'll just have to go on another adventure. Maybe to Europe or Australia."

Martha coughed.

"Don't be so . . . pessimistic," Harriet said. "The mine is going to strike. Any day now."

"I really hope it does," Martha said. "But I think you should be prepared. How much money are you planning on losing?"

Harriet did not appreciate Martha's comment. She had never given a thought to a gold mine budget. "I don't know, but I can't quit now."

"Quit what?" asked Henry, closing the deck slider.

Harriet shot Martha a glance as if to say, "Tell him and die."

"Collecting salt and pepper shakers," Harriet said.

"Well, why would you do that? In a few weeks you can display them all."

"I know," Harriet said. She thought about saying something else, but that would just be extending the lie even more. So as usual she changed the subject.

"How about bacon and eggs?" she asked.

"Sounds good." He sat down at the table to wait for the coffee. "How did you sleep, Martha?"

"Fine," she said.

"Listen," Henry said. "I've been thinking about Wyatt. I'm going to write to him. But I don't want to say anything I shouldn't."

"Oh, don't worry about that. The prison censors will take care of that."

"Censors? Wow. I've never been censored in all my years of writing."

"You'd be surprised what they consider dangerous or provocative or sensitive."

"Well, I'm still going to write to him."

"Thank you," Martha said. "I know he'll appreciate hearing from you."

After breakfast, Harriet cleaned up the kitchen while Martha showered and dressed and Henry got ready to slink into his cave for a day of cattle rustling.

"Do good writing," Harriet said.

Henry kissed Harriet's cheek. "Thanks, Mom. You have a good day too. Do you and Martha have plans?"

"Not sure. I think first I want to take Humphrey for a nice long walk and then maybe do a little housework. I know Prudence hasn't been feeling well, and I don't want her to have to work too hard when she gets home."

"Oh, that's thoughtful of you, but she got a lot done this weekend. She said she'd be a little late again tonight."

"I wish she wouldn't work so hard. It scares me."

"She's fine, Mom."

The coffee was ready. Henry poured some, grabbed a snack cake, and headed off to his den.

"He's a good boy," Martha said.

"Yes, he is. The best. But . . . look, Martha, you can still be proud of Wyatt. There must be some good left inside him."

Martha poured her coffee and took a sip. "Oh, there is. He is still just so sweet and quiet. A terrific artist. Sometimes I think that was the trouble. He just never fit in until he got mixed up with the wrong crowd."

"Then be proud of his art. Will they let him draw in prison?"

Martha thought a moment. "I think so. I'll have to check."

"That's the ticket, and then you can send him a sketch book and pastels or charcoal and water colors, pencils—whatever he needs."

"If they let me."

Harriet quickly finished her own coffee and set her mug in the sink. "I'm going to walk the dog. Would you like to come?"

"No, not this morning. I kind of like sitting here. It's such a nice room."

"Suit yourself."

Henry sat at his desk. The building sounds were not as loud as he thought they might be, and he was grateful for that. He stared at his computer screen, not really in the mood. The muse had not shown up that morning. It had been such an eventful week.

He heard a knock on the door. "Hello." Perhaps his muse knocked first now.

"Martha," Henry said. "Is everything okay?"

"Yeah, sure," Martha said, moving in closer to Henry. "I wanted to talk to you. While your mom is out with the dog."

"Me? Sure. Come on, sit."

Martha sat in Henry's comfortable reading and napping chair.

"I really shouldn't be telling you this," Martha said. "I promised your mom, but I don't want to see her get hurt, and I thought maybe we could head off any trouble, maybe even go to the authorities if we have to."

"Authorities?" Henry said. "What are you talking about?"

Martha sighed. "There's no other way to say this than to just say it. Your mother has leased a gold mine."

Henry burst into laughter. "What?"

"A gold mine, Henry. Your mother met some guy and his daughter at the café, and they talked her into buying into a gold mine."

"That's crazy. Even for my mother. I don't believe it."

Martha leaned forward. "It's true. I met the guy and saw"—she made air quotes—"pictures of the mine. He claims she can't see it in person because it's too high up the mountains. All he does is take money from her."

"Wait a second," Henry said. "You're serious. How much money?"

"Well, the other day I saw her hand over fifteen hundred dollars to rent a backhoe."

Henry leaned so far back in his desk chair he nearly toppled over. "This is crazy."

"I know. I thought you and Prudence could check it out."

"Sure, sure, but why is she keeping it a secret?"

"She wants to surprise you. She thinks she can provide money, help with the babies. But I think she's a little worried, even though she won't admit it, that it might not pan out, so to speak, and doesn't want to embarrass herself."

"That sounds like my mother all right. Okay, I should call Prudence. She knows people."

"Yes, you should. But please do not tell Harriet. She'll kill me."

Henry nodded his head. "Okay, okay. Give me as much info as you have, and I'll get Pru on the case."

"It could be legit," Martha said. "But . . . I have a sinking feeling, and this guy Winslow Jump makes me nervous. His daughter, if she is his daughter, is quite sweet and I hate that she is getting in so deep. Of course, she's still a minor but not for long."

Henry could hardly believe his ears. "Okay, okay," he said again. He grabbed a pen and a legal pad. "Now, tell me what you know."

"Now, remember, you can't let Harriet know. Tear up that paper when you're done." Martha told Henry everything she knew about Winslow and Lily Jump, Old Man Crickets, and Brunner's Run.

"Old Man Crickets?" Henry said.

"That's what she told me. He's the man who owns the land and apparently leases parts of it to miners, gold diggers."

"Fifteen hundred dollars?" Henry said, tapping his pen on the legal pad.

"And five grand for the lease," Martha said. "I don't know how much more she has given him."

"F-f-five thousand?" Henry said.

Martha nodded. "That's what she said."

"She should have just given us the cash if she wanted to help."

"She was thinking bigger thoughts, Henry."

"But to be this frivolous. The cross-country trip was bad enough, but this takes the cake."

"Try to understand and not be too upset."

"Is she going to see this guy again soon?"

"Probably."

"Please don't let her be alone with him—and absolutely nowhere secluded, like a mountain. Just in case he's a nut job."

"Good thinking."

• • •

After a jaunt around the block, Harriet and Humphrey decided to check out the builders. There were four men fast at work with shovels. A backhoe was lifting and dumping dirt into a huge pile. She thought about talking to them but then, no, she'd let them work. Just watch a few minutes. But one of the men spied her.

"Hello," he called. "Want to take a look?"

"Sure," Harriet said. "I didn't want to bother you." She and Humphrey stepped over a couple of smaller dirt piles. "How's it going?"

"Good." The young man, large and robust and wearing a blue T-shirt and a baseball cap, smiled. "My name is Manuel. I'm the boss around here."

"Ah, don't listen to him," called one of the other guys. "We just let him think that."

Manuel wiped his hand on his shirt and extended it to Harriet. "Notice which one of us is in the hole."

Harriet laughed. "That's right. My dead husband, Max, he was a builder. He never went into the holes after a while."

"Ah, Daisy told me you were married to a builder."

"I hope that doesn't intimidate you, young man."

"No. No. It's a good thing. Keep us on our toes."

With that, one of the other men dropped his shovel, stood on his tippy toes, and twirled with his hands above his head.

"You stop that, Gus," Manuel said. "Show some respect."

"He was just playing," Harriet said. She looked around. The area had been staked out with string. She saw a pile of cinder blocks and bags of concrete.

"So you'll probably be pouring the foundation very soon," Harriet said.

"Yep. Need a firm foundation. Then we can put in the flooring and the walls and the plumbing and the electric. All that good stuff. But the foundation? Most important."

Harriet thought that was pretty much a true philosophy in any realm.

"Thanks for your hard work," she said. "I can't wait until it starts to take shape."

"Come back here in a week, and it will be looking like a house."

Harriet shook her head as she walked away. These men could build a house, or at least a medium-sized addition faster than Henry could write a book. Harriet pulled on Humphrey's lead lightly. "I need to stop thinking that. He's doing what God has called him to do."

Humphrey sniffed around the site.

"Now that hole could hold one giant bone, huh, boy," Harriet said.

Humphrey woofed.

Chapter Twenty

Harriet found Martha in the living room looking through a *Good Housekeeping* magazine. She set the magazine on the coffee ottoman. "So what should we do today?"

"Well, you would still like to see the gold mine, at least that section with the stream."

"We don't have to," Martha said.

"Sure we do. Who knows, maybe you'll want to invest."

"Nah, not me. I don't have that kind of money."

"I still want you to see it."

"But just the streambed. I'm not climbing a mountain."

"No, we can't do that, but let me call and see what I can arrange. I'll call Lily and she can call her father. Hopefully, there will be some gold today. I don't see why not. It washes down from the mountain all the time. It can't all be washed away like Win said."

"You mean it comes and goes?"

After saying that, Harriet did think it sounded kind of strange. "Well, kind of. It must. When I went the first time with Win and Lily, it was chock full of gold flecks and specks. But Win said it can wash away farther downstream and then finally out to sea."

"Really?" Martha said. "So there could be gold in the ocean?"

Harriet shrugged. "I suppose so. But it would be almost impossible to mine, I would think."

Martha stood. "Okay. Now I am curious. Let's go see your gold mine."

"Terrific," Harriet said. "I think it would be best if we went into town first, to the café. I'll call Lily from there. But I better go tell Henry we're going out. We'll need to take his car, especially if we're driving to Downieville."

Martha put the magazine in the wicker basket near the couch. "I'll go grab a sweater."

"Sure thing. I'll be back in two shakes of a lamb's tail."

Harriet walked softly into the den. "Son," she said in a low voice. "Henry."

Henry spun around in his chair.

"Hi, Mom. What's up?"

"I just wanted to tell you that Martha and I are going to go into town—if I can take the BMW."

"Oh, sure, I guess so. What's in town?"

"Stores and things, dear. Just something to do."

"Okay, but stay out of trouble."

"Now what kind of trouble could I get into?" She spotted the opened website on Henry's computer, and her eyes fell on the words Culinary Institute of America.

"What are you looking up?" she asked.

"Oh, oh," Henry looked at the screen. "I was just . . . doing some research. Cooking schools. Just in case."

"Uh huh," Harriet said. She moved closer and kissed his cheek. "I'm glad you are a writer. You're very good, you know. But if you are serious about becoming a chef, then check it out. If there's one thing I've learned recently it's that you don't have to stay in one place your whole life."

"But that's what Dad did. He gave you security."

"True. But that was your father's choice. That's the important thing. Prudence believes in you, and so do I. Whatever you choose will be okay."

"What brought this on?" Henry asked. "Quite a change of heart."

"I've just been thinking, talking to Martha, you know, figuring things out."

"Thanks, Mom. So you're not mad at me for selling anymore?"

"No. Not anymore. Now, we won't be too long. I thought we'd drive into town, do some shopping, then maybe have lunch. You know, that kind of stuff. Maybe drive into Reno and hit the casinos."

"Mom, we talked about that. No more gambling."

"Just joking," Harriet said. Even though it did sound like fun. "We won't go to Reno. No more bets. Look where the last one got me."

"It got you right where you are supposed to be."

Harriet sighed. "If only we could figure it out for Martha."

"I know," Henry said. "I can't believe Wyatt is in prison. It must be torture for her."

"I think she should move here," Harriet said.

"Oh, she'd never leave Wyatt."

"But she'd do so well. Maybe start doing her art again."

"I agree," Henry said. "Grass Valley is kind of a mecca for artists."

"That's true," Harriet said. "That gives me an idea. Maybe we'll check out the local galleries. We'll start at Florence's daughter's place."

"Good idea."

"Thanks, son. I did raise the smartest boy."

"Have fun, Mom."

"You too, and maybe check on the guys when you get a chance."

"The builders? They know what they're doing."

"Yes, but it helps to keep an eye out. Don't want them cutting corners."

"I doubt that will happen."

"All right, son, we'll see you later, and I'll gas up the car."

"Thanks."

Harriet and Martha clicked on their seatbelts.

"I was thinking," Harriet said as she adjusted the rearview mirror. "I'd like to take you someplace before we go to the café."

"Before we visit the stream?"

"Yes, Florence has a daughter who owns an art gallery right in town. It's called The Bitter Herb. I'd like to take you there."

"Oh, really. I heard that Grass Valley has a lot of artists."

"Yep, artists, writers, musicians. All the artsy fartsy people come here." Harriet looked at Martha. "Sorry, I didn't mean to say you're fartsy."

"No, no," Martha said. "I can be very fartsy. But I hope you're not trying to convince me to move here by showing me galleries and—"

Harriet turned onto the street. "Martha, I'm shocked you would even suggest that I was trying to do anything underhanded," she said with a twinge of sarcasm.

"You've been known to pull some shady things."

Harriet smiled, "Okay, but not this time. Well, okay, this time. Why not move here, Martha?"

"You know why I can't move. I have Wyatt to

consider. I'd have to sell my house. So much work."

"Your house is lovely. It will sell quickly. And Wyatt, as much as I hate to say this, made his choice. You can't live your life just to visit him once a week—or however often you go."

Martha was quiet until Harriet pulled the car onto the main drag.

"All right. I'll visit the gallery. But no funny business. Don't go setting up a one-woman show for me or anything."

"I won't do anything. We'll just look. I've never been inside the gallery either. I bet it's all very Western. Well, not all of it. Lots of landscapes. Cow skulls and snakes. Deserts."

Downtown seemed extra crowded that morning. Lots of folks were out moving around the streets. Harriet thought she was fortunate to find a parking space in her usual lot. "Geeze, it's usually not like this around here. There must be something going on. Grass Valley has lots of events."

"Oh, really," Martha said. "Maybe we'll see something."

"Maybe," Harriet said. "But gallery first, café, and then the mine."

Harriet and Martha made their way to The Bitter Herb gallery on Mill Street and stopped outside the small shop. There was an orange awning hanging over the front window, which held some paintings—of a cowboy on a bucking bronco, a landscape of brush land, and a stream that Harriet thought was actually quite peaceful.

"Oh, this is a nice gallery," Martha said. "I like the name also. The Bitter Herb."

Harriet pointed to one of the paintings in the window. "See, landscape."

"It's lovely," Martha said. "I haven't painted anything so realistic in a long time."

"Maybe you just haven't been inspired. I mean, what does Bryn Mawr have? Huge houses?"

"Oh, stop. There are plenty of beautiful places around home. Not to mention the gardens. Remember when we would walk through Chanticleer?"

Harriet sighed. "Oh, yes, now, that is one spectacular place. You better stop, though. You might make me homesick."

"And then you can move back east. And we'll visit Chanticleer and Longwood as often as you'd like."

Harriet laughed. "With twin grandbabies on the way? Sorry, Charlie."

"I know, I know. Come on, let's go inside," Martha said.

Harriet pushed open the door and a little bell jingled overhead. "Don't you love it? I hope Florence is working today. I didn't think to call her before we left."

The gallery ambience felt light and airy with white walls covered with paintings. There were stands with small statues scattered about in what Harriet figured was no particular order.

Florence was sitting behind a desk, an ornate thing with curved legs and gold inlay. A small lamp that looked better suited for a bedside table sat in the right corner, and piles of papers and catalogs nearly covered the desk.

"Hello, Florence," Harriet said.

"Harriet," Florence said as she looked up from her paperwork. "I am so glad you decided to come visit the place."

"Thanks. You remember my friend, Martha."

"Yes." Florence held out her hand. "Did Harriet tell me you do stained glass?"

"You have a lovely gallery. And yes, guilty as charged. But I also enjoy pottery."

"Oh, that's terrific. I'm glad you like the gallery. It's really my daughter's business. She is in the back doing . . . something. Framing, maybe."

"Now that's an art unto itself," Martha said. "I have always admired people who understand framing."

Florence sat back down behind the desk. "It's time-consuming. She can take hours on one painting. What with choosing the right mat, the correct frame, cutting the mat, and getting the glass. It's quite a process."

"Yes. I'll stick to stained glass and pottery."

"Well, look around," Florence said. "No pressure."

Florence's daughter came out from behind a curtain. "Hello," she said.

Harriet had never met Mabel. But she immediately liked the way she looked, tall and willowy. She hid her hair under a babushka, but Harriet supposed that was very Bohemian and artsy fartsy. She was slipping gloves off her hands.

"Did I hear someone say stained glass?" Mabel asked. She wore a flannel shirt, red and green, and jeans that were cuffed at the bottom. Harriet noticed she was barefoot and thought that must be terribly dangerous while working with nails and glass. But she didn't say anything.

"Yes. I did," Martha said. "I dabble a little. Nothing too amazing."

"Oh, I would love to see your work sometime. I would love to have some stained glass in the gallery. You'd be surprised how many people look for stained glass for their homes. It's just so hard to find, unless you want old stuff and that can be risky."

"Oh, well, I would like to share it with you sometime, but that would be a little hard considering my stuff is back east."

"Well, maybe you can send me some pics. Or do you have a website?"

"A website? Me? No, I just enter my stuff in

271

local shows, flea markets, that kind of thing. I've never had a showing."

"Um, that's too bad," Mabel said. "But, please, send me some pics. Maybe we can work something out."

"Okay," Martha said.

"Wow," Florence said. "Talk about hitting it off. These two haven't even been properly introduced."

"Oh, I'm sorry, Mom," Mabel said.

"Any-hoo," Florence said, "this is Harriet. You remember I told you about her. And this is her friend Martha from back east."

Mabel laughed and shook Martha's hand. "Yes, I gathered that." Then she shook Harriet's hand. "And it is a pleasure to meet you. Mom has told me so much about you and your son—is it Henry?"

"That's right," Harriet said. "He's an artist also."

"He is?" Mabel said. "I thought he was a writer."

"He is," Harriet said. "He paints with words."

Mabel smiled. "That's a nice way to put it."

The four women chatted a little longer until Martha grabbed Harriet's hand. "I would like to see more of the town. It's so lovely. Just like you said, like walking onto a Western set."

"Everything but wooden sidewalks," Mabel said.

"You have a lovely gallery, Mabel," Martha said.

"Thanks," Mabel said. "And, please, send me those pics."

"I will."

"Oh, did I ever tell you about Dodge City?" Harriet said as she and Martha left The Bitter Herb. "They had wooden sidewalks. Made the most interesting sounds when you walked on them."

"Okay," Martha said. "I went to the gallery. Now I want to see your gold mine."

Chapter Twenty-One

Henry put a frantic call through to Prudence. Her secretary answered.

"It's Henry, Marge. Is Pru available? It's kind of important."

"Sorry, Henry. She's in a meeting. With the bigwigs. No disturbing allowed. Can it wait?"

"I suppose. When do think it will be over?"

"They just went in like ten minutes ago. I'd give it an hour."

"Okay, just have her call me."

Henry tapped off the phone. He thought about calling the police and telling them his mother had been sold a lease on a gold mine, but that was certainly not illegal. At least not yet. And he didn't really have anything to go on except the few things Martha told him. No, he'd wait for Prudence to return his call.

He sat in his comfy chair for a while, worrying, even though he really didn't have the facts yet. "Maybe it's for real," he said. "Maybe Harriet Beamer will strike gold and we'll all be rich."

Humphrey ambled into the den just as Henry thought to get back to cattle rustling. "Did you know about this?" he asked the dog. "Mom's . . . gold mine?"

Humphrey lay at his feet and whined.

"I know she is just trying to help us, but really, a gold mine? What was she thinking?"

The phone rang. "Pru," he said.

"What's up? Everything all right?"

"I'm not sure. Wait till you hear this. Martha came to see me this morning, and she told me that Mom has leased a gold mine."

Silence.

"Pru?"

More silence.

"Honey? Are you there?"

"Yes, what did you say?"

"I said my mother has leased a gold mine from some guy she met at the café in town."

Prudence laughed so hard Henry thought she might pass out.

"No, really. She did," he said. "And you need to check it out. See if it's legit."

"Hold on," Prudence said. "You're serious."

"Yes. I'm serious, Pru. She's handing over lots of money to this guy."

"But how is that even possible? How does someone meet a guy at a café and lease a gold mine? These are legal matters."

"That's what makes us so worried. It was all just a little too easy sounding."

"Okay, okay, give me names, all the info you have, and I'll see what I can do."

"There's this guy named Winslow Jump who knows a guy they call Old Man Crickets who owns a gold mine called Brunner's Run—" Henry laughed. "This sounds so silly."

"Did you say Old Man Crickets?"

"I did."

"And she bought into this?"

"Leave it to Harriet Beamer."

"Did Martha say where this alleged mine is located?"

"Downieville, a place called Brunner's Run. That's all we know."

"Okay, I know there are scams out there. But there are also legitimate mines so maybe, just maybe, your mother got mixed up in the real thing."

"I hope so, Pru," Henry said. "I'd hate for her to lose all her money to this guy."

"Yeah, okay, well, let me see what I can dig up. I know a guy at the FBI who owes me a favor."

"Okay, should I do anything?" Henry drummed his desk with a pencil.

"Try to keep her from giving this guy any more money until we get it figured out."

"I'll try, but I don't know how."

"Stall her. Don't let her go into town. Pretend you're sick. Martha will help."

"But, Pru, they're already in town."

"Oh gee. Well, let me go so I can do some investigating."

Henry tapped off the phone. "Humphrey, maybe I should mosey into town and see what I can do."

He looked at the screen. "Sorry, Cash. It looks like you'll need to rest awhile."

"Can't you just imagine your work in the gallery?" Harriet said.

"Mabel does have a nice gallery," Martha said as they walked down the street toward the café. "I could see having one or two of my pieces there."

Harriet and Martha walked on toward Rachel's.

"You sure could have a display there. Sometimes I don't think you believe in your own talent."

"Maybe. But mostly I never really thought about going public. My art has always been so private."

"I can sort of understand that," Harriet said. "But maybe it's time to share your talent. Think of the people you could bless."

"Bless?" Martha said. "With my pottery and stained glass?"

"Don't knock it. Didn't they use stained glass windows to teach Bible stories?"

"Yes, but me? Bless people?"

Harriet and Martha stopped out front of the café. "Yes. You," Harriet said, before they went in.

A waitress took them to the table in the back. Martha sat facing the kitchen. It seemed Harriet always liked to face the door.

"Listen," Martha said. "I've been giving it a lot of thought."

"Giving what a lot of thought?"

"Your gold mine."

"Oh, that's nice, dear."

"I think you should tell the kids. Let Prudence check it out. If it's all on the up and up, then great. If not, you've gotten out before you lose everything."

Harriet appreciated the way Martha looked out for her. But it was getting a little annoying even though she didn't say so. Didn't Martha think Harriet learned anything on her trip across the country? She could take care of herself. Then she had a thought.

"Who knows," Harriet said, "maybe you'll lease a little lot of your own."

"Maybe I will."

Harriet tapped Lily's number. "I'll call Lily. She gave me her cell phone number the day we went shopping."

"Hi, Lily," Harriet said. "It's me, Harriet."

"Oh, hi, Harriet. What's up?"

"Well, I was just wondering what you were doing. I promised my friend Martha that she could see Brunner's Run today. Might see some gold."

"Oh, oh, I don't know if I can," Lily said. "I had some plans."

"It wouldn't take too long. Please?"

There was a long pause before Lily said, "Okay. Dad and I had plans to visit some relatives in Nevada City today. I guess we can stop by town first. I'll ask him."

"Good. Martha and I are at the café. You know, the usual place."

"Okay, give me a little time. Maybe an hour."

"Fine. We'll just stay here. We're at the usual table." Harriet tapped off the phone.

"There, she'll be here in about an hour."

"What about her father?"

"She's going to tell him. And see if he can come too."

The server stopped at their table. "Can I take your orders?"

"Sure," Harriet said. "I would love a cup of coffee and maybe a slice of apple pie."

"Sounds perfect," Martha said.

"Okeydokey," the server whose nametag read Tammy said. "I'll be right back."

"She's different," Harriet said. "I usually get Cindy."

Martha fiddled with the salt shaker. "I miss your collection. You haven't even talked about it. Have you lost interest?"

"No, not really. It's just that while it is still in the garage I find it hard to . . . care much, and the gold mine is taking up so much of my time and brain space."

"I understand," Martha said. "Since Wyatt went to . . . went away, I haven't done any art."

"Maybe talking to Mabel about getting a display will help get you motivated again."

"Maybe," Martha said. "But I just don't know anymore. It all seems like so much bother."

Harriet picked up the pepper shaker, the nothing special, just your basic restaurant style glass shaker with the silver cap. "Are we getting old?"

"Nah," Martha said.

Tammy brought their coffee.

"Thank you," Harriet said, and as she did she glanced past the server and spied that same woman sitting on the same stool and, if she wasn't mistaken, reading the same book.

"Look over there," she said. "There's that woman again. I think she's up to something. Doesn't she look like someone who is up to something?"

"Your imagination is getting the best of you."

"No, really. Maybe she is a spy."

Martha opened a small Half and Half container. "I worry about Lily."

"I know you do."

"What if this whole thing is a scam and she's involved? What a terrible start to the rest of her life. Maybe for her sake you could speak to the kids. Let Prudence check it out."

Harriet swallowed coffee. "I can handle this. Just give me a little more time. I've already decided that if it doesn't produce a gold nugget or two very soon I'm going to . . . to renege or cancel or break my lease, whatever they call it."

"If you can."

"What? I'm sure I can cancel the lease. I mean they can't force me to keep giving him money, can they?"

Martha sipped coffee. "I don't know. That's why Prudence should have looked at what you signed."

The server brought their pie. "Enjoy."

"Thank you," Harriet said as her stomach went a little wobbly.

Martha poked at her pie. "Are you sure we can't just drive up there ourselves? I mean, how big is this town? You'll remember the spot once we get there."

"Maybe," Harriet said with a mouthful of apple. "Let's give Lily a few more minutes." Harriet smiled. "Martha, I can't wait to see the look on your face when you see all that gold floating around in the water. Of course, it's just gold dust, but it means there's bigger stuff higher up the mountain."

The two managed to pass the hour chatting. Mostly about old times. Mostly about husbands and kids and even grandkids, something Martha was now convinced would never happen for her.

"You know," Harriet said. "I don't think we did too bad. Considering."

Martha grew quiet. "At least your son didn't end up in prison."

"You aren't still blaming yourself, are you?"

"Well, yeah, sometimes. I must have done something wrong to raise a criminal, for heaven's sake."

"He made his choices. I'm sure you taught him right from wrong." Harriet stirred her coffee even though she had stopped drinking it. "I suspect Wyatt got too curious about the drugs and it got away from him. You know what I mean. He couldn't help it."

"I guess, but it's not like he was a wild-eyed

maniac off his noodle when he did it. The lawyer said he planned the whole thing, start to finish. Only the finish wasn't what he planned. He got caught. Surveillance camera. You have no idea what it feels like to see your son on a surveillance tape. All grainy and stupid with his hood pulled over his head and holding a gun. It's . . . like another world."

Harriet's heart filled with empathy. No, she really had nothing to compare to that experience, but she did know what it felt like to feel betrayed. But no, this was almost too awful to imagine. There was nothing to compare.

"I am so sorry for you," Harriet said. "I don't think I could even imagine what it felt like."

"It is weird," Martha said. "There are things you sort of prepare for—failures in school, the wrong friends, even drugs in a way. But armed robbery? Why would a mother even think that was possible for her child?"

Harriet still stirred. "You can't prepare for that. That's why it's so awful."

Martha looked away and then back at Harriet who hadn't taken her eyes off her. "Sometimes I wish I could just run away from it all, find a nice quiet place to create my art and live out whatever years God has left for me. In peace. Start over."

"Like we've been telling you, Grass Valley is a great place."

"I can't leave Wyatt. He'd have no one to visit him if I moved clear across the country."

"Can he get transferred to a California prison?"

Martha shrugged. "I don't know. Never thought about it. I could always check, but it's not like he's at a university."

Harriet looked at the time on her phone. "She should be here."

"She'll get here. Don't worry." Martha fooled with her napkin, folding the corners down and then smoothing it back out.

Harriet thought it was a very nervous thing to do.

"There she is," Harriet said, pointing toward the window.

Lily saw them and waved. Harriet and Martha waved back.

"Hi, Lily," Harriet said. "You made it. Where's your dad?"

"He said I could come alone. He had some business in Nevada City."

"Okay," Harriet said. "Just us girls."

Lily smiled and sat near Martha.

"Would you like something to eat before we go?" Martha asked.

"Sure," Lily said. "The usual, I guess."

Harriet got Tammy's attention and ordered a basket of fries.

"You and your fries," Martha said.

"They're the best," Harriet said.

"Sure are," Lily said.

Harriet thought Lily seemed more relaxed without her father nearby.

"I would drive to Brunner's Run myself," Harriet said. "But I'm not exactly certain I'll find it."

"Oh, it's pretty easy," Lily said. "But I don't mind taking you. Not like I got anything better to do."

"What do you like to do?" Martha asked.

"Oh, I don't know. I used to like to draw and stuff but not so much anymore."

"Remember, I told you Martha is an artist?" Harriet said.

"Oh, yeah." Lily practically beamed at Martha. "That's so cool."

"I like to work with stained glass and pottery. I've even painted but not so much anymore."

"Wow, yeah, I'd like to paint." Lily looked at Harriet. "But living with Pop and moving so much, well, it's just hard."

Tammy set the large red basket with the wax paper and a mountain of fries in the center of the table. "I brought a little extra," she said. "You can all share."

"That's nice of you," Harriet said.

"Yeah, thanks," Lily said.

Martha snagged two and squeezed ketchup onto them.

Lily laughed. "I've never seen anyone do that.

Most folks just squirt it all over or make a puddle."

Martha smiled. "Aw, but this is the way to do it, just a thin line of ketchup. That way you get ketchup with every bite."

Lily picked up a fry and did the same. She ate it and said, "You know, I think you're onto something."

"Why thank you, sweetie," Martha said.

Henry couldn't help it. He was pacing the den, waiting for Prudence to call. In fact, he was about fed up with waiting and was seriously thinking about going into town and bringing his mother home and having a serious discussion with her.

"Humphrey," he said, "she could be in danger. What if this Winslow Jump guy is a kook?"

Humphrey paced with him.

"Maybe I should just drive into town and—" He stopped pacing. "She has the car. That means I'd have to take the scooter." He sat down at his desk. "Stupid scooter."

There came a knock on the deck sliders. "Who can that be? The police, maybe? Or Florence with pie."

Humphrey said, "Woof."

"Okay, okay, it's not the best time for pie. Don't judge me." Henry headed for the door. It was Daisy Day standing on the opposite side of the screen.

"Hey, Henry," she called with a wave. "Just checking on things. I wanted to say hi and see if ya'll had any concerns or questions."

Henry pulled open the screen. Humphrey skittered out the door between them.

"Oh, hey, Daisy. Nope. No questions. It seems to be moving right along. Everything's fine. Fine as can be."

"Are you all right?" Daisy asked. "You seem a little flustered. Too much caffeine, maybe."

"No, no. I'm fine. Waiting for an important call."

"Well, okay. As long as you're sure, but you might want to taper off the java."

Henry let go a nervous laugh. "As a matter of fact, I was going to tell you that I think Manuel and his men do some mighty fine work."

"They sure do," Daisy said. "The best in town."

Daisy and Henry stood looking at each other for a long few seconds until Henry perked up and said, "Hey, speaking of mighty fine work, guess what?"

"What?" Daisy said with a glint in her eye.

Henry walked onto the deck and joined Daisy. "Now, this doesn't have anything to do with the addition." He smiled. "Well, now, I suppose it is an addition. Prudence and I just found out we are having twins."

Daisy clasped her hands across her heart.

"Well, bless your heart, isn't that just the most wonderful news. Congratulations."

"Thank you. We were pretty surprised. It's still sinking in."

"Then I guess the addition is right on time. You might want to consider bumping out the other side of the house and adding another room someday. Babies have a way of growing."

"Oh, maybe, but not for a while, fortunately."

Henry's cell jingled. He pulled it from his pocket. "Prudence," he said looking at Daisy. "I'm sorry, but I have to talk to her."

"Go on," Daisy said. "And tell her I said congrats."

Henry waved and closed the slider. "Pru?"

"I have some bad news."

Chapter Twenty-Two

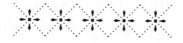

Harriet paid the bill while she and Martha waited for Lily to return from the restroom.

"You said it was about an hour's drive," Martha said. She looked through a spinner rack of postcards. "This is a nice one." She showed Harriet an image of downtown Grass Valley with a view of the mountains.

"Yes, about an hour, give or take," Harriet said, looking at the card. "It's not a bad ride, and Downieville is such a cute town. Very small."

"Downieville?" said the cashier. "That's where I was born."

"Is that right?" Harriet said. "Well, it's an adorable town."

"I hear there's lots of gold up there," Martha said with her eyes on Harriet.

"Oh, heck yeah," the cashier said. "It's all over the place—if you know how to get it and where exactly to look. And you got the money and time."

Harriet coughed. "Do you know anyone who struck it rich?"

The cashier laughed. "No, not really. But I got a brother-in-law, the lazy so and so, who keeps thinking he will." She set a receipt on the counter for Harriet to sign.

"Maybe he will," Harriet said.

"When pigs fly," the cashier said. "When pigs fly."

Lily finally made her way back from the bathroom.

"Sorry it took so long," she said. "But I wanted to call my pop. Make sure of the directions."

"No problem," Harriet said. "I hope you didn't disturb him."

"No, he's . . . not that busy."

Lily sidled next to Martha as they walked to the car.

"I never drove in such a fancy car," Lily said. "Just my pop's truck. And it's so bouncy. He says it needs shocks, whatever they are."

Martha opened the door, and Lily slid into the backseat. "Buckle up."

"So I just get out on that Golden Chance Highway?" Harriet said.

"Pop said it was the Golden Chain," Lily said.

"Okeydokey," Harriet said. She made all her necessary adjustments, set her hands at two and ten, and said, "Brunner's Run, here we come."

"Downieville or bust," Martha said.

Harriet looked in the rearview mirror in time to catch Lily rolling her eyes.

"Oh, Harriet?" Lily said. "Can you take me to Nevada City after we're done at the stream? Pop said he'd meet me at the diner there."

"Sure thing," Harriet said.

Harriet was just starting to think how pleasant the ride was when Martha started to speak with Lily about the gold mine.

"So has your father ever actually found gold?" she asked Lily.

"Sure. Some. Small stuff, dust mostly. He pans."

"But he really believes there is gold in this . . . this . . . what do you call it?"

"A placer mine," Harriet said.

Martha turned and saw Lily shrug. "That's right. A placer mine. He thinks this could be our ticket."

"I hope he's right," Martha said.

Soon Harriet crossed over the little one-lane bridge into Downieville.

"Welcome to Downieville," she said. "Isn't it just the cutest place you've ever seen?"

"It is small," Martha said. "Looks like a scene from a Western movie. And oh dear, what's that? An elk?"

Harriet looked. "Yeah, sure is," she said looking out toward a large meadow. "That's an elk. And a big one."

Lily laughed. "You guys crack me up. It's just an overgrown deer."

"But he's spectacular," Harriet said.

"Whatever," Lily said. "Now, remember to look for the little turn off."

Harriet started up the hill, the hill with the narrow, winding lane. She practically had to hug the car against the mountain. "Hang on," she said. "It gets a little bumpy."

"And scary," Martha said. "Couldn't they make the road a little wider?"

Harriet drove on, taking the curves slowly. Keeping both hands on the wheel.

"Over there," Lily said. "Pull in over there."

"Oh, I remember this," Harriet said. She parked

the car off the road on a clearing. "The stream is just over there."

"Where?" Martha asked. "I don't see anything."

"It's kind of hidden behind those trees," Harriet said. "I told you it wasn't big."

"Can we get out? Take a look?"

"Sure," Harriet said. "Let's go."

Harriet stood on the bank of the small creek with Martha. "See it?" she said.

"See what?" Martha asked.

"The gold," Lily said. "See those specks and glittering dust? That's the gold."

"Really? That's it? I can hardly see it. It doesn't look like gold," Martha said. "And if it is gold, why don't we just get it out of here?"

"Small potatoes," Harriet said. She pointed up the mountain. "The bigger stuff is way up there."

"See, look there," Lily said pointing. "There's a tiny piece." She bent down and moved the rock. She placed a teeny-tiny gold speck on Martha's palm. "It's like Harriet said, the bigger stuff is up yonder."

Harriet watched Martha shield her eyes to get a better view of the mountain. "And we can't go there?"

"No," Lily said. "It's not a good idea. Too dangerous. And you would have to hike part of the way."

Martha took a breath. "Has your father said when they expect to produce actual gold?"

"Oh, any day now, I'm sure," Lily said. "The guys will let Pop know when they've got something to talk about. Pop says it takes a lot of time to produce enough gold to count."

Harriet watched Martha shake her head as though she still didn't believe there really was a gold mine.

"You can keep that," Lily said to Martha.

"Oh, okay, thanks."

They walked back to the car.

"So is this your dad's hobby?" Martha said. "I was wondering what he did for a real job."

"Martha," Harriet said with a twinge of frustration. "Why are you giving her the third degree?"

Martha opened the door and got in. "I'm not. I'm just curious."

"It's okay," Lily said.

Harriet glanced at Lily in the rearview mirror after they both got in the car. She was looking out the window. "Oh, he does a lot of things," she said. "Especially since Mom died. He goes from job to job."

Martha turned around. "I didn't mean to pry, sweetie. I was just wondering, that's all. It just seemed to me that making money looking for gold is . . . is a little slow."

"We do all right," Lily said.

"Did he ever work a real job?" Martha asked.

Lily shrugged. Harriet pushed the key button and the car beeped.

"I don't know," Lily said. "Maybe. Maybe before Mama died."

Martha reached back and took Lily's hand. "I'm sorry, honey. I don't want to dredge up memories. I was just wondering how you get along."

"Like I said, we do all right."

"Okay," Martha said. "Now, you buckle up and we'll get you to that diner."

Harriet found her way back to the mountain highway.

"I really want this to work out for you, Harriet," Martha said once Harriet was on the straightaway again. "I hope you strike it rich."

"I don't know about striking it rich, really rich, but we'll strike something. I have a good feeling about it."

Martha turned back to Lily, who was still looking out the window. "Don't you want it to work out for Harriet?" Martha asked.

Lily swiped something from her eye and nodded. "And my pop."

"Now, I don't have much information," Prudence said, "but I did discover that this Crickets fellow —yeah, he's a real person—has just been released from prison, about six months ago."

Henry practically fell into a kitchen chair. "Oh no. Is Mom in danger?"

"I don't think so. He's been keeping a pretty

low profile. And not only this, but it seems like this Jump guy is wanted in a few states on all kinds of charges too. He's a scam artist. But it's the Crickets fellow who is apparently calling the shots, probably collecting most of your mother's money. Jump is just his toady."

"I knew it," Henry said. "Martha was right. I'm so glad she told me. Should we call the bunko squad?"

"Bunko?" Prudence laughed. "No. I called the FBI. And, Henry, they're already on the case. They've been watching Winslow Jump for days now."

Humphrey sat on his haunches looking at Henry. Worried. Henry patted his head. "It's okay. Mom will be fine."

"What?" Prudence said.

"I was talking to the dog," Henry said. "But what do you think I should do?"

"Nothing for now. She'll come home, and we'll confront her and tell what we know. I mean it, Henry. Do not do anything. Don't go all cowboy."

"She's going to be so upset."

"For a few minutes, and then I'm sure she'll feel relieved. Maybe a little embarrassed. But at least we nipped it before it went too far."

Henry wasn't so sure his mother would be relieved after just a few minutes. "Okay. I guess . . . I mean . . . I know we have no choice. When will you be home?"

"I'll be home as early as possible. And, Henry, please, I mean it. Don't draw attention to this. Let the authorities handle it."

Henry tapped off the phone. "Humphrey," he said, "we should have let her arrange her salt and pepper shakers. I should never have told her to go out and make friends. Leave it to Harriet Beamer to find a crook, an actual criminal to make friends with."

Humphrey whined. Henry patted his head again. "I'm going down there. I can't stand the thought of her—and Martha—with some crook."

The dog barked and scrambled toward the sliders. "You want to go?"

Humphrey said, "Woof."

But then Henry remembered again that he'd have to take the scooter. Henry patted Humphrey's side. "Sorry, old man, but that means you can't go."

With no other choice, Henry strapped the bright yellow helmet onto his head and straddled the scooter. He turned the key, and the Vespa chugged to life like an overgrown sewing machine. "Here we go," he said as he took off toward town. He found the small horn button and gave it a little toot. "Just in case I need it."

Henry got the scooter all the way to forty miles an hour. The seat was hard and uncomfortable. His long legs felt cramped as he tooled along toward downtown.

"I bet she's at the café. I hope she's at the café. Where else could she be?"

That was when he heard a loud horn behind him. He swerved to the right and allowed a large ice cream truck to pass him. "That's it. My mother is getting a car."

When he arrived, Henry pulled the scooter in front of the café. "I think it was called Rachel's," he said. "Well, I'll just have to check every coffee shop in downtown if I have to." He rode the scooter to the parking lot across the street. "She better be there."

Henry opened the door, catching a glimpse of himself in the glass. He had forgotten to remove the helmet. "Nuts." He unstrapped it and went directly to the cashier.

"I'm looking for my mother. She's about yea tall with gray hair and wearing . . . shoot, what was she wearing? She was with another woman. Gray hair . . ."

"Oh, they were here," the cashier said. "They were with that girl."

"Girl?" Henry looked around the café, hoping to see his mother. His eyes landed on the woman in the dark blue jacket at the counter. She was looking right at him. He ignored her.

"What girl? I don't know anything about a girl."

"Well, she was with them. They left a while ago," the cashier said.

"When?" Henry nearly leaned over the counter and grabbed the girl by the lapels. "When did they leave? Did they say where they were going? No. Why would they tell you?"

"Well, the older woman did mention Downieville."

"Downieville?" Henry said. "What the heck is in Downieville?"

The cashier shrugged. "I only know because I told her I was born there. She said it was a nice town."

Henry slapped the counter. "Downieville. I can't ride a scooter to Downieville. But who is the girl?"

"How should I know?" the cashier said.

He looked around with nervous, darting, lizard eyes. "Okay. Thank you," he said. "I'll just have to wait for her. Did she say if she was coming back?"

The cashier's eyebrows rose. "No, sir, she didn't give me her agenda."

"Okay, okay, sorry."

His phone rang. Prudence.

"Hello," Henry said.

"Henry, you sound funny. Where are you? Did you go into town, Henry?"

"She's not here," Henry said. "The cashier said something about Downieville, but I'm not even sure." He looked out the window hoping to see his mother and Martha. "And I can't ride the scooter clear to Downieville. I bet that's why she wanted the car. She knew she was going on some . . . wild goose chase."

"That's why you need to go home," Prudence said. "Just go home and wait. I called to tell you that I'm leaving the office now."

"Good, good," Henry said. "I'll see you at home."

Henry tapped off the phone and dropped it in his pocket. He was just about to open the door when he was stopped.

"Excuse me." It was the woman in the blue jacket.

"Yes?" Henry said.

"Agent Willers, FBI." She opened a small black wallet with an ID photo and badge. "I'd like to ask you a few questions."

Chapter Twenty-Three

✳ ✳ ✳ ✳ ✳

"Really?" Henry said.

"I need to ask you some questions."

"Sh-Sure."

"Maybe we should step outside," Agent Willers said.

Henry held the door for the agent, garnering inquiring looks from pretty much everyone in the café. "This is so cool," he said. "The FBI."

"We've been watching your mother for several days now. We know she got tangled up with that Winslow Jump person, and we also know that you know he's a con artist."

Henry smiled from ear to ear, holding the scooter helmet under his arm. "We're just finding out the facts. But, yeah, how do you—"

"We don't think your mother is in any danger. We've had her under surveillance."

"If you've seen her with this guy, this con artist, why haven't you arrested him?"

"We were hoping your mother would lead us to Crickets."

Henry burst out laughing. "I'm sorry. It sounded funny. But why? How could my mother lead you to Crickets? And why should she?"

"He's the ringleader, so to speak," Agent Willers said. "Jump is his roper."

"Ah, Mr. Big. The Brains. The Inside Man. This is so cool."

"Excuse me, Mr. Beamer." Agent Willers looked into Henry's eyes. "We need your help."

"Me? What can I do?"

Agent Willers waited until a passerby moved on. "Get your mother to meet Lily at the café again."

"Lily?"

"Jump's daughter."

"Oh, the girl the cashier mentioned." Henry couldn't help it. As worried as he was for his mother, he was having a blast.

"That's right. Try to get Lily to talk about Crickets. We want him, Mr. Beamer. Fraudulent gold mines are just the tip of the iceberg."

"Really. There's more? Is it drugs? Counterfeiting?"

"You are way too happy about this."

"It's just so interesting."

"Right. You're a writer."

Henry laughed. "Man, you guys know everything."

"Look, Mr. Beamer. Just see if you can get your mother to meet Lily here. We'll take it from there."

Henry plopped the helmet on his head. "Okay.

Okay. Should we synchronize watches or any-thing?"

Agent Willers shook her head. "This is serious FBI business, Mr. Beamer."

"I know. Sorry. But you're sure my mother isn't in any danger?"

"We don't believe so. These guys are not known for violence."

"They just like taking advantage of rich old women."

"That pretty much sums it up." Agent Willers put her hand on Henry's shoulder and gave him her card with the number to reach her. "Don't worry. I'll have my eye on her the whole time. The first sign of trouble and I can have three agents in the café in seconds."

All Henry could say was, "Wow."

"That's the place, over there," Lily said. "The place with the yellow awning and the tables outside."

"The Why Not Diner?" Harriet said.

"Yeah, pretty stupid," Lily said. "But Pop likes it. And they're pretty nice in there. We've been eating here a lot."

"When was the last time you had a home-cooked meal?" Martha asked.

"Don't remember."

"Maybe one of these days Harriet will have you to her house for a real meal."

"Oh," Lily said, "I . . . I don't think my pop

would go for it. He . . . he'd rather eat here."

"Okay," Harriet said. "You tell him we at least got to see some specks."

Lily pushed open the car door. "Bye."

"Bye, sweetie," Martha said.

Harriet watched the way Lily smiled at Martha. "You two have certainly bonded quickly," Harriet said when Lily had closed the door.

"I like her. It breaks my heart to think she might be tangled up in some scam. Or that her father forces her to do his dirty work."

Harriet pulled away from the curb after Lily was safely inside the diner. "I wish you would stop it," she said. "I don't have any reason to believe it's not for real. You saw the gold."

"How do you know for certain it's gold? Have you had it tested? Have you ever heard of fool's gold?" Martha's voice had gotten a little high.

"Now you're angry," Harriet said. "Your voice squeaks when you're angry."

"I'm not angry," Martha said. "I just wish you would tell Prudence and Henry. If it's not a scam, then terrific. If it is, then you won't lose any more money."

Harriet harrumphed. "You sound like a broken record. I said I have it under control."

Henry parked the Vespa in the garage and set the helmet on the seat. "The FBI," he said. "This is so cool."

He went to the kitchen where Humphrey met him in apparent hopeful anticipation of donuts.

"Sorry, old chum," Henry said. "Not this time." He patted the dog's head, sat down at the kitchen table, and said, "We have a caper to pull off."

Humphrey whimpered.

"Don't worry, we just have to get Mom to the café with Lily and get her talking about Mr. Big."

It was at that moment Henry felt a tingle of anxiety. It seemed the excitement of the whole matter had receded into concern. "Agent Willers said we were in no danger, but . . . but what if they have guns and stuff? She said they weren't violent, but still, they could always start."

Henry looked at the clock. It was nearly four o'clock. The builders would be leaving for the day, which was good, and Prudence should be walking through the door at any minute. He had no idea when Harriet and Martha would mosey in, and this made him nervous as his somewhat enlarged imagination had a tendency to cook up the worst-case scenario in most situations. Perhaps it would be best to act like nothing was wrong until later, when Prudence was home and everyone had had dinner, and then they could discuss the whole gold mine scam.

"That's the ticket," he told Humphrey. "I'll cook."

Cooking had a way of relaxing his mind. He

would sometimes cook when he felt stuck with a book. Using a different part of his brain somehow made the words flow more easily. Maybe cooking would have a similar effect on helping him to devise a plan, a way to tell Harriet the jig is up and that she had to lure Lily to the café so the FBI could essentially move in and arrest everybody who needed arresting. "Sometimes, Humphrey, you have to be deliberate about not imagining the worst."

Humphrey didn't have an opinion. He sat near his bowl watching and maybe waiting for Henry to drop a tasty morsel. Sandra Day was nowhere in sight. She was probably hard at work sleeping. That is, after all, what cats did best and Humphrey knew this.

Henry thought a moment. What to make for dinner.

"Mom has been hinting about wanting strawberry shortcake."

So Henry assembled the necessary shortcake ingredients. "It just might make the bad news go down a little easier. And besides, there is just something so comforting about strawberry shortcake, does a soul a lot of good."

Henry patted his stomach. "Our waistlines? Now, that's a different story. Except, of course, for Prudence. She can eat all she wants."

Humphrey whimpered. "I know, I know, within reason. But she is going to love this cake. And she can have three slices—one for her, and one each for Chip and Dale."

Henry couldn't be certain, but he was fairly sure he saw Humphrey raise his eyebrows and roll his eyes.

"What? You don't like Chip and Dale?"

Henry cut the butter into his dry ingredients using a special tool he bought just for making shortbread. "The proper tools make the job easier."

He could hear the workers outside banging and hammering, and sometimes a bit of laughter would drift through the open kitchen window, and he was ever so happy it was not him with a nail gun in his holster.

He spread the shortcake mixture into two round cake pans, nicely greased and floured, making sure to create a small lip around the sides. "Now, to let these bake." He set the timer and then heard a car pull into the driveway. "That sounds like Pru's car."

He rinsed his hands and dried them on a towel. "Come on, boy."

"Pru," Henry called walking into the living room. "I am so glad you're home."

Prudence didn't look so good. She dropped her briefcase, looked into Henry's eyes, and darted right past him, making a beeline for the bathroom.

Henry followed close behind and stood in the hallway.

"Are you okay in there?" he asked.

"Yeah, I think so." She seemed to be catching her breath. "Morning sickness has become afternoon sickness. I just lost my Kung Pao. Remind me never to eat Kung Pao again."

Henry winced at the thought. "Sure. Why don't you lie down?"

"I don't want to lie down, Henry. You are always telling me to lie down. I'm sick of lying down. Maybe I don't want to lie down."

Henry backed away. "I'm sorry. I'm just trying to help."

Prudence came out of the bathroom. She patted his cheek. "No, I'm sorry. I'm just a little testy."

"It's okay, honey. Do you have any more news? Because I do. You won't believe what happened to me today."

Henry took Pru's hand and led her into the kitchen. "I need to watch my shortcake," he said. "Doesn't take long to bake."

Prudence sat down at the table. "Do we have any ginger ale?"

"Sure." Henry twisted open a bottle and sat it in front of her.

"I don't need the whole liter," Prudence said.

"Oh, sorry." Henry sat a glass near her on the table. "I have to tell you what happened."

Prudence poured ginger ale into the glass.

"Okay, but I hope you didn't do anything to give it away."

"No, no. So, I went into town to find Mom, to that café. I couldn't stand the thought of her talking to this creep anymore. But she wasn't there."

"Where was she?" Prudence sipped.

"According to the cashier, Downieville, but I had the stupid scooter so I couldn't go after her."

"That's good."

"So anyway, I was leaving the café when, get this, I was approached by the FBI." Henry said this like a nine-year-old boy who had just caught his first trout.

"What? I really wish you hadn't gone into town. I told you to let the authorities handle it."

"I know, I know," Henry said. The dinger dinged. He slipped on his oven mitts and opened the oven door. "But I was so worried about Mom and Martha." He tested his cakes by lightly pushing the centers. "Perfect."

"You could have put them in danger. I told you the FBI was on it."

"That's what I'm trying to tell you, Pru." He slipped off the mitts and dropped them on the counter. "Agent Willers approached me. She gave me an assignment."

Prudence smiled. "Henry Beamer, you are like a kid. This is serious business. That Crickets guy is trouble. They say he has underworld connections."

"Really?" Henry's heart sped. "This is getting better and better. Mr. Big is in the Mafia."

And they both knew they'd be talking to Harriet as soon as she and Martha got home.

"Hey, look," Harriet said as she parked the BMW in the driveway. "The scooter's been moved. I bet Henry had to use it for something." She laughed. "Henry hates to drive the scooter. I can just see him tooling down the street all wobbly with his long legs and big feet."

"It looks like the builders have left," Martha said.

"Yeah, I didn't realize how late it was getting, and Prudence is home already. Now, that's weird."

Harriet pushed open the front door and saw Henry and Prudence sitting on the couch like two bookends. She dropped her tote bag on the floor with a thud.

"Uh oh," Martha whispered. "They look upset."

"What's up?" Harriet said. "Did Humphrey eat your Little Debbies?"

"Mom," Henry said. "We have to talk to you."

Harriet sat in the recliner. Martha pulled the rocker next to Harriet and sat. Her eyes met Henry's for just a moment, but she knew he wouldn't give her away if this was about the gold mine.

"The jig is up, Mom," Henry said. "I know all about the gold mine. What in the world were you thinking?"

"Who told you?" Harriet asked.

"That's not important," Henry said.

"I was only thinking of you . . . and Prudence, and . . . the babies."

"But a gold mine?" Prudence said. "You leased a gold mine from a man you met in a café. In what world does that make sense?"

Florence. Harriet figured it just had to be Florence. Martha wouldn't have told.

"But he seemed so nice," Harriet said. "And . . . and he showed me the gold. In the stream. Lots of it."

"I saw it too," Martha said. "Well, a little, anyway."

"It's called salting the mine," Prudence said. She sounded a bit angry, like Harriet and Martha should have known this.

"Pru," Henry said, "no need to take that tone."

"What tone?"

"Your lawyer tone. We're not in court."

"Sorry," Prudence said. "This Winslow Jump guy was probably busy tossing gold flakes and fool's gold into the stream while his daughter kept you busy at the café."

Martha snapped her fingers. "That makes sense. I bet you that's why Win supposedly had a business meeting earlier. He was salting the stream while Lily ate French fries. Geeze. That poor young girl, doing her father's bidding like that."

"He's a crook," Henry said. "Crickets is too—a big, fat crook wanted all over the country for fraud and other charges. He's wanted by the FBI."

Harriet folded her hands on her lap. Humphrey ambled by and laid his head on her feet. He whimpered. Harriet's heart sank so low and so hard she figured it could have fallen through the floor and reached China. "I . . . I don't believe it. He seemed so nice."

"The hallmark of a good con artist," Prudence said.

Harriet let go a heavy sigh. "I should have known when I never even got copies of the papers I signed. I'm so stupid."

"No, you're not," Prudence said. "Thousands of people get scammed every year. And from what I hear this guy Crickets is a consummate pro."

Harriet looked at Martha. "You were right."

"I really wish I wasn't," Martha said. "I really wish you had struck gold."

"Okay," Prudence, who was still obviously stuck in lawyer mode, said. "I spoke with the FBI and they've been following Winslow Jump for weeks. Winslow and—I forgot to tell you this part, Henry—his daughter."

"Really?" Harriet said. "But why Lily? She's a minor, and I . . . I think she really believes her father is for real."

"Maybe so," Prudence said. "But she's still working with him."

"No," Harriet said. "Not Lily. She doesn't know. I'm sure of it." Well, she wasn't really sure, now that she remembered some of the ways Lily had seemed . . . concerned or embarrassed.

"That's for the FBI to sort out," Prudence said.

"I . . . I guess," Harriet said, feeling foolish and nervous.

Harriet felt Prudence's gaze. It wasn't condemning or blaming. It was concern.

"Why don't we get the whole, every-detail story straight from you, Mother? Where is this mine?" Prudence asked. "Exactly."

"Downieville," Martha answered for Harriet.

"Right," Harriet said. "It's called Brunner's Run."

"And how did you acquire this placer mine?" Prudence asked.

Harriet settled back in her chair and proceeded to tell them the whole story from start to finish —starting with the French fries at the café in town and Lily.

"And that's all there is to it. Win said I just have to sit back and watch the money roll in."

Harriet started to cry just a little.

"Don't cry, Mom," Henry said. "It's weird. You never cry."

"I've never leased a fraudulent gold mine from a crook before," Harriet sniffed.

"We have a plan," Henry said. "Well, the FBI does. Agent Willers. She's the woman, the agent I met at the café."

"Wait a second," Harriet said. "Is she kind of tall, skinny, wears blue, short black hair?"

"That's her," Henry said.

"I knew she was up to something," Harriet said. "She's been at the café every time I was there. I *thought* she was watching me."

"She was," Henry said. "But she needs your help now."

Harriet felt her heart beat. She touched her hand to her chest. "Oh dear, I don't know. I . . . I already had one heart attack. I don't know if I can take the excitement."

"Sure you can, Mother," Prudence said. "I have no doubt you can handle this and any other thing that might cross your path."

"You mean that? Be . . . because just last Christmas I thought you thought I was a doddering old woman ready for the glue factory."

Prudence rubbed her slightly bulgy belly. "I'm sorry if I made you feel that way. I . . . I might have been thinking it, but—"

"Pru," Henry said. "Don't."

Prudence turned her attention to Henry. "No, it's all right." She turned back to Harriet. "But after you made that trip across the country and since you've been here and the way you've become . . . well, become my mother in so many ways, I've gotten to know that you can do anything you set your mind to."

"I can do all things through Christ," Harriet said.

Henry clapped his hands once. "Well now, back to the crime at hand."

The women all chuckled at once. "He's like a kid again, playing cops and robbers," Harriet said.

"And why not?" Henry said. "I don't see any reason to be dismal about the whole thing."

"There is an element of danger," Martha said.

Harriet looked at her with wide eyes. "What danger? The FBI will be there whatever it is they want me to do, right? What could possibly happen?"

"Oh dear," Martha said. "I suppose you're right, but I'm still just a touch worried, and you must promise that you will be careful and not take any silly chances."

Harriet held up the three-finger Girl Scout sign. "I promise."

"Okay, then," Prudence said. "We're sending Mother in."

"Will I get my money back?" Harriet asked.

Prudence shook her head. "Doubtful."

"Drat. I gave that man, that . . . that rat fink almost ten . . . oh dear, I can't even say it."

Henry put his hand over his heart. "Don't say it, Mom. Please don't say it." It was bad enough that Martha had told him about $6,500 of it.

Harriet cleared her throat. She patted

Humphrey, who had not left her side. "You okay with this, boy? Mommy is working with the FBI."

Humphrey looked at her. She noticed that his fur had turned a touch gray around his eyes. "Okay, what do I need to do?" She patted Humphrey's head. Harriet had never felt so deflated in her life. Of all the crazy things she had done, including the cross-country trip by bus and the occasional helicopter, this took the cake. "I should have stuck with salt and pepper shakers. At least with them you know what you're getting."

"When this is all over," Prudence said, "and your Grammy Suite is finished, you can get back to your collection, join a club. Or if you can't find a local club, you can start one."

"That's a good idea," Harriet said, even though her aching heart was not exactly fond of the idea just then. "Now, just tell me. What do I need to do to nab this . . . this—" She had a very choice word in mind, but no, she wouldn't resort to such vulgarity.

"Agent Willers wants you to set up a meeting with Lily and get her talking about this Crickets guy," Henry said. "They're hoping she'll lead them to him."

"He's the brains behind the operation," Prudence said.

Martha let go a little noise, almost like a chirp. "Henry's right. This is getting exciting."

"Lily? I was hoping she could avoid the spotlight."

"I suspect the FBI thinks it would be safer for you to speak with her, get her to tell you what they want to hear instead of her father," Prudence said.

"And she trusts you," Martha said.

"Can Martha come with me? It might seem strange to Lily if Martha isn't with me. And I think Lily really likes Martha. They are both artists, you know." Harriet sniffed like she was holding back tears. "That poor, sweet girl. I hope she doesn't go to jail or juvie?"

"Juvie?" Henry said. "What the heck?"

"Juvenile delinquency jail," Harriet said. "That's what we called it back when I was running the streets."

Henry choked. "You? Running the streets?"

"Sure. In Philly. I knocked over a few trash cans in my day, and even . . . well, let's just say there was a certain police officer who was not very happy with me."

"Okay, okay," Prudence said. "That's a story for another day. We need to get you ready to talk to Lily. She's the key to solving this whole mess."

"Oh dear," Harriet said. "I feel like a . . . a . . ."

"Superhero?" Martha said.

"Not exactly a superhero. But a crime fighter, certainly. So should I just call Lily in the morning and arrange something?"

"Yep," Prudence said. "That's all you need to do. Set up a meeting and get her talking. Casually bring up Mr. Crickets—"

Henry laughed.

"Casually bring up Mr. Crickets," Prudence repeated with a sigh, "and see if you can get her to tell you where he lives or stays or works. Something for the FBI to go on."

"That should be easy, Mom," Henry said. "Just pretend you're giving me the third degree about my whereabouts when I broke curfew on a Saturday night."

Harriet waved her hand. "Oh that, well, you were easy. I could get you to spill your guts so easily."

"I know," Henry said. "There was no trouble getting this canary to sing."

"I hope I'm not so nervous that I blow it," Harriet said.

"You won't, Mom. Now, how about if I go get dinner ready. I made strawberry shortcake—just for you."

"Strawberry shortcake," Martha said. "Yum."

Harriet heaved a huge sigh, a sigh that seemed to fill the entire room. She knew her loved ones were all trying to make the situation appear easy, take a casual, almost comical view of things. But she wasn't stupid . . . well, except for falling for the scam in the first place. She knew she had disappointed them, that there was danger in what she was about to do, and that she had wasted a tremendous amount of money. "I think I'd like to take Humphrey for a walk, if you wouldn't mind," she said. She wanted a few minutes alone. And she had someone to see.

"I'll come with you," Martha said.

"No, it's okay. I'd rather go alone."

"Okay," Martha said. "But . . . be careful."

"I'm fine," Harriet said. "Humphrey will protect me from all the nasty con artists out there. Won't you, boy?"

"You might want to take a sweater," Prudence said. "It's getting chilly."

"I will," Harriet said. "Thank you. And I'll call Lily first thing in the morning. I'll think of some reason for her to meet us."

Harriet took a blue cardigan sweater from the coatrack and put it on—inside out.

"What *will* happen to Lily?" Martha asked. "She's only seventeen. Her mother is dead as far as we know, but who knows what's the truth anymore?"

"That poor, sweet child," Harriet said, noticing her mistake. "I should have known something was wrong, terribly wrong when I saw the color of her hair."

"Hopefully," Prudence said, "she'll turn eighteen before it hits the fan. And if she isn't found culpable in some way, she'll be exonerated. But if not, she'll become a ward of the state unless her mother is alive and can be found or another suitable relative can be located."

Harriet thought this was all starting to sound much more complicated than she thought it would ever become. "Lily told me she won't be eighteen until next June. I'll be back in just a little while." All she had wanted was a few itsy bitsy gold nuggets. And now she had an entire federal case on her hands.

Chapter Twenty-Four

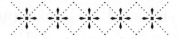

Harriet walked in the direction of Florence's house. "I've got a bone to pick with her." Humphrey stayed so close to her she could feel him against her leg. "It's all right," she said. "But . . . I wish Max was here. He'd know what to do." She sighed. "If Max was here, this would never have happened." She looked up to the heavens. "Oh, Max, you big jerk. Why did you have to die so soon?"

Humphrey stopped once to sniff around a lilac bush. But he didn't linger as usual. He found his spot right next to Harriet again. He didn't want to leave her side.

She walked on, asking God to give her some

peace about the whole thing, that peace that is supposed to pass all understanding. But she wasn't feeling it. Maybe when it was over. The air was nice, a little chilly but the kind of evening that made it easy to think. Harriet could smell roses on the breeze. She saw lights on at Florence's house.

"Maybe we should stop and . . . say hi, huh, Humphrey. What do you think?"

Humphrey said, "Woof."

"You're right. Maybe she's had some experience with this sort of thing. She seems to know an awful lot about gold mining and Grass Valley. But I can't believe she told Henry about *my* gold mine."

Harriet pushed open the gate at Florence's house. She rung the bell and waited but only for a few seconds before Florence opened the door. She was wearing a periwinkle blue bathrobe and yellow slippers that looked like they had seen better days.

"I'm sorry," Harriet said. "Were you going to bed?"

"Oh no, no, come in. I was just comfortable. Reading."

"Only if you're sure I'm not interrupting anything," Harriet said. She followed Florence to the living room.

"Is everything all right?" Florence said. "It's not Prudence, is it?"

"Prudence is fine. Everything, including morning sickness, right on schedule."

"That's good. Can I get you anything—tea, pie?"

"Oh no, thank you, Henry is making dinner and strawberry shortcake. I'll need to get back soon. I told them I was just taking Henry for a walk."

Florence smiled. "Henry's a sweet boy."

"Yeah, he really is," Harriet said. "Just like his dad."

"Are you missing him?" Florence invited Harriet to sit.

"Yes. Today and every day, but . . . but well, yes, more so today."

Florence patted Harriet's arm. "I think you have something heavy on your mind. Do you want to tell me? I can listen, and I promise I won't tell a soul. Not a living soul."

Florence tightened her robe belt and sat down on the couch. Harriet settled in a big, over-stuffed chair that threatened to swallow her, so she leaned forward just a bit.

"Really?" Harriet said with a twist of sarcasm that swirled around the room. "Really? You told on me."

"About the gold mine? I most certainly did not. I might be a lot of things but I have never betrayed a confidence. Well, not recently. But I never told anyone," Florence said.

She sounded sincere. "Well, then I don't know who, but someone told Henry and Pru about the mine." Martha was the only other person. No. She would never do that. Harriet shook her head.

"So is there a problem?" Florence asked.

"There sure is."

"Okay, well look, you go to the authorities, and they'll tell you what to do before it gets out of hand."

"Already done. The FBI is in on it. Oh, Florence, I feel so silly."

"The FBI? Really? So you got scammed."

"Fooled like it was April Fools' Day. I'm a chump."

"Oh for goodness sake, Harriet. You are not a chump. You got fooled by a con artist. These guys are experts."

"But it was his daughter, Lily, who started the whole thing."

Florence slapped her knee. "Oh, he is a pro. Trains his kid to spot a mark. Not exactly a great role model."

"And I was the mark."

"You sure were. She saw you sitting all alone at the café, and she wandered over and struck up a conversation."

"Yeah, pretty much." Harriet's heart raced like a sports car. "Does that mean she's . . . what did Prudence say? Culpable?"

Florence pursed her lips. She patted Humphrey's head. "Not sure. If she's a minor, they'll go easy on her. I hope."

"She is. She is a minor. Seventeen."

"That's the best news."

Harriet rubbed Humphrey's ears. "Even Humphrey is upset. He won't leave my side."

"So what will you do now?" Florence asked.

"The FBI wants me to help them."

"The FBI? This must be a big operation you got yourself messed up in."

"That's the consensus." Harriet looked at Florence's kind face. "I'm so embarrassed. And to think that I did this not only with the kids but right in front of my best friend. I feel awful." She patted Humphrey's head. "Just awful. I always try to look on the sunny side of life but this . . . this is too much."

Florence thought a moment. "Maybe you can look at it this way. When they nab the guys, they'll go to jail for a while and you will be stopping them from hurting another innocent person. Not to mention leading Lily into a life of crime."

"What will happen to her, do you think?"

"I think she will have to be put in state care until she turns eighteen, assuming there's no other relative."

"No," Harriet said. "Her mother died."

"I'm so sorry."

Harriet sat for another moment, quiet. "This is terrible. That poor child."

Dinner that evening was, as usual, amazing, even if the mood was sad. Henry tried to keep a lively conversation going. He talked about his new book. The babies. But it was obvious that everyone was worried.

"Okay," Harriet said. "I got us into this. I'll get us out. And I don't want to see any more long faces. I'll do what the FBI tells me."

"That's very wise," Prudence said. "Just follow the FBI instructions and everything will work out fine."

Harriet didn't say a word. She just kind of glanced Martha's way.

"Please, Mother. Let the police and the FBI handle this."

"Sure, sure," Harriet said.

Henry brought the strawberry shortcake to the table. It was incredible. Layers of whipped cream and strawberries and shortcake.

"Perfect," Martha said. "You really should become a chef. This is as good or even better than anything I've ever had anywhere."

Harriet felt so proud of Henry. "He is spectacular," she said. "Only I just don't know where he gets it. Lord knows I was never much of a cook. Strictly meat and potatoes."

"Well," Henry said, "Dad was not what you would call an adventurous eater."

"That's true, son. When he came home from work, all he wanted was a burger or steak, a potato of some sort, and a green veggie. That was it—a brown pile, a white pile, and a green pile."

"Well, that and ice cream. Remember, Mom?"

Henry patted Prudence's hand. She was busy eating cake. "My father never had less than three gallons of ice cream in the freezer all year long."

Perhaps it was the whipped cream and strawberries, but the mood had lifted. Harriet felt a little better, surrounded by her family and her friend and, of course, Humphrey, who got to sample quite a bit of whipped cream.

"So how are you feeling, Prudence?" Martha asked. "I don't think we have really had an opportunity to talk about it. Twins. I can't imagine what that would be like."

"It is wonderful," Prudence said. "God has blessed us. Sometimes I still can't believe it." She took another bite of cake. "And I'm feeling okay. I get tired and, of course, the physical symptoms are annoying, but the blessing absolutely outweighs the other."

"Two," Henry said. "Two of everything."

"Yeah, that's right," Martha said. "Two cribs, two strollers, two two-o'clock feedings . . . Goodness gracious, I'm glad you have Harriet here. She'll be a big help."

Martha insisted that she and Harriet do the

dishes while Henry and Prudence put their feet up in the living room.

"And we'll bring you a nice cup of tea in just a bit," Martha said.

"And maybe another slice of that shortcake?" Henry asked.

"Sure, sure," Harriet said. "Now you two get along. Let Martha and me do this."

The second they were out of earshot Harriet said, "You fink."

"Look," Martha said. "I had to tell. I couldn't stand for you to get hurt. And as it turned out . . ."

"Yes, but I asked you not to tell him." Harriet filled the teakettle to put it on the stove. "I'm so hurt."

"I'm sorry," Martha said. "But, I don't know, I guess with all this stuff with Wyatt I have a shorter fuse for this stuff. Wrong is wrong."

"I guess, but I'm still angry," she said as she dropped spoons into the dishwasher basket.

"Please forgive me," Martha said. She wiped her fingers on a towel.

"Okay, but . . . now, listen . . . we have to do something. We have to do something before the FBI."

Martha rinsed a plate and placed it in the dishwasher. "What? You're crazy, Harriet, but I guess I should have known you'd do some-thing."

"We have to do something for Lily. We can't

let them arrest her and make her a ward of the state or something."

"But what can we do?"

Harriet put two leftover pork chops into a Tupperware container and snapped it closed. "I . . . I don't know for sure but—"

"You can't be suggesting we warn them so they can get away. Or are you?"

Harriet wiped the kitchen table. "No, no, I guess that wouldn't be right, but there must be something we can do to keep Lily from getting into trouble and being sent to live God knows where with God knows who. It could be awful. They could send her to . . . to some abuser or crack house."

Martha closed the Maytag dishwasher door after putting in the soap and pushed the on button. In an instant the machine roared to life. "You know what? I'm surprised at you."

"At me?" Harriet asked. "Why? What did I do?"

"I'm surprised because you are usually so positive about everything. Every cloud has a silver lining—except now, all you can think is the worst. What if Lily is placed somewhere fabulous? A place that's really good for her? With people who care."

Harriet thought a moment. "I suppose that could happen but—"

"But nothing," Martha said. "We need to be positive and do what the FBI wants you to do and trust God. He's involved in this also, you know."

"I know," Harriet said suddenly, feeling a tiny bit ashamed of what she had been thinking.

"Okay, I admit it. I was going to warn her, and I know that's wrong. But maybe we can get Lily and Win to confess, to come forward and turn Old Man Crickets in. Maybe if they did that then it will go easier for them."

Martha shrugged. "I don't think it will. And besides, how could we get Win to confess without letting the entire cat out of the bag? What if he gets crazy and . . . I don't know, pulls a gun or something?"

"He won't do that."

"You can't be sure. Look at Wyatt. Who would have ever thought he would go waving a gun around, threatening people?"

"This is different," Harriet said.

Martha placed tea bags in cups and sliced more cake. "What do you propose to do?"

"I don't know. I don't know. But there must be something I can do to make this better for everyone."

The teakettle whistled.

"Look, Harriet," Martha said. "I supported your trip across the country. But I won't support you going off all half-cocked to try to make this better. Please don't do anything. Let the authorities handle it. We'll think of something for Lily."

Chapter Twenty-Five

That night Harriet lay in bed—not sleeping. The adrenaline from the excitement of the whole FBI thing surged through her veins. She kept thinking there must be some way to keep Lily from the clutches of the system. What if she could get Lily someplace safe? Maybe Lily could come live with her. Yes, that's it. She'd be Lily's foster mother. She turned onto her back. No, that wouldn't be fair to Henry and Prudence and the twins.

She tossed and turned, her head first on one side of the pillow, then the other. Still she couldn't sleep.

"Martha," she called. "Are you awake?"

Humphrey roused from his place under the window.

"Not you," she whispered. "Go back to sleep."

Harriet sunk her head back into her pillow and stared at the ceiling. There was just enough light outside to cast a strange shadow or two, especially with all the construction machinery outside. It might have been a backhoe by day, but at night it looked like a giant Harriet-eating monster.

She pulled the blanket over her head. No, that was no good.

"Martha," she called again, this time a little louder.

Humphrey scrambled to his feet. Harriet tossed a pillow onto Martha's bed.

Martha made a noise.

"Martha?"

"Harriet? What is it? Are you okay?"

"I can't sleep."

"Count sheep."

"Not working. I've been thinking about Lily."

It was at this point that Humphrey, now completely awake, went to Harriet. He sat on his rump and stared at her.

"It's not time to wake up, Humphrey. It's still nighty-night time."

"Ah, tell the dog," Martha said. "He's listening."

"No. I need to tell you that . . . that . . . What if I get guardianship of Lily, or whatever they call it?"

Martha sat up straight like a cadaver in a scary movie. "What?"

"I could take Lily."

"Harriet, that's crazy. She's probably got more problems than we know, and besides, you have grandtwins on the way. They need you. Prudence and Henry need you."

329

Harriet turned on her side and patted Humphrey's head. "That's what I thought. I just wanted to see if you thought the same thing."

"I do. Now get some sleep. You have to call Lily in the morning and get her down to the café. It's going to be a big day."

Morning finally, mercifully, came, and Harriet was first to shower. She slipped on a bathrobe instead of dressing because she wanted to get into the kitchen and prepare breakfast for everyone. Maybe it was her way of apologizing for causing trouble. Or maybe she was just trying to convince herself that everything was A-Okay, normal as usual.

She prepared scrambled eggs and a full pound of bacon. Everybody loved bacon. And she made plenty of toast. Harriet set the dining room table with cloth napkins and pretty dishes. Leaving Humphrey inside, she went out and picked a rose from one of Prudence's bushes.

"That's a nice one," she said as she sniffed the pretty pink flower. Getting back to the house was a little like walking through a minefield on account of all the construction stuff. She wanted to take a quick look at the progress.

The foundation had been poured. The rebar set, the sill plate was going in. "They might start the walls today." Everything looked good, near as she could tell.

"But we'll see what the inspector says when he comes for the first inspection."

She put the single rose into a small glass bud vase and set it in the center of the table. She folded sky blue napkins into neat little triangles and filled the water glasses from a glass pitcher she found on a high shelf in the kitchen. After everything was ready to go, she stood at the head of the table and surveyed her handiwork. "Just like at one of the bed and breakfasts I stayed at on my trip." She was actually quite proud of herself.

The clock read seven o'clock. Time for everyone to start filing into the kitchen. "Won't they be surprised?" she said to Humphrey. Henry was first to arrive.

"Morning, Mom," he said as he grabbed a coffee mug and then the coffee carafe. Only it was empty. He held it up. "Hey, what gives?"

"Everything is in the dining room today. Even the coffee. I put it in the fancy pot."

Henry's eyebrows wrinkled. "Really? Is it Sunday? Or Christmas? I must have really over-slept."

Harriet gave him a playful push. "No, no, I wanted to do something special after upsetting everyone yesterday."

"You haven't upset everyone."

"Yes, I have. Now, go on. To the dining room. It's like a bed and breakfast."

"Okay, okay," Henry said. "But you really didn't have to go to all this trouble."

"I wanted to do it," Harriet said.

Henry sat down at the head of the table, the seat farthest from the kitchen. "This is nice, Mom. Thanks for doing it."

"My pleasure." She poured coffee into his cup. "I made eggs and bacon and toast, and I found some nice orange marmalade in the refrigerator. I think Prudence will like it."

By seven-fifteen everyone, including Martha, was seated around the table. Prudence seemed a whole lot more chipper than usual.

Harriet patted Prudence's hand. "You look very happy and . . . and blissful this morning."

"I do? I guess I feel . . . blissful. And the table looks just lovely."

"Thank you," Harriet said. "Now you eat up. I can make more of anything you want."

Prudence rested her hand on her stomach. "I'm starved, and for once I feel normal. Not sick at all."

"Well, that is terrific," Harriet said. "You just stay put and I'll get you some juice. Apple or orange?"

"Apple," Prudence said.

"Good choice," Harriet said. She poured a small glass.

Martha stirred Half and Half into her coffee. "She really outdid herself this morning." Harriet could hear her in the kitchen and Martha's words made her feel proud. She poured apple juice, which was, Harriet thought, the color of gold, into a small glass and carried it back to Prudence.

"Here you are, dear," Harriet said.

"Thank you," Prudence said.

"Now come on, Mom, sit down and enjoy your breakfast. The eggs are perfect."

Harriet took her seat. She loved her family. Her friend. How often she had tried to figure out and find what it meant to feel God's pleasure. At that moment she knew exactly where it was—in her heart, with her kids and Martha. She really was quite a fortunate woman.

Harriet felt so warm and fuzzy inside it nearly tickled. And to think just a few days ago she was wishing she was back in Pennsylvania. She would be missing all of this.

"May I have the bacon?" Prudence asked.

"Certainly," Harriet said as she lifted the plate. "All you want."

"Ah, this is nice," Henry said. "You did a great job, Mom. Thank you."

"It is very nice," Martha said. "Thank you. Everything is perfect."

Prudence finished her eggs and bacon. She skipped toast, but she did put orange marmalade on her eggs. This amused Harriet.

"What?" Prudence said. "People put marmalade on eggs." She looked at Henry. "Don't they?"

"So, Mom," Henry said, "have you figured out how you're going to get that girl to the café?"

Suddenly brought back to reality, Harriet heaved one of her great sighs. "Yes, I'll just call and tell her I want to take her shopping again. I figure that will keep Win from wanting to come."

"Good thinking," Prudence said.

"Once she gets there, I'm not certain how I'll bring up Crickets' name."

"You'll think of something," Martha said. "And I'll be there."

"But remember that Agent Willers will be there too, watching. She'll make her move when the time is right."

Images of guns firing and people in blue jackets ran through her mind. She didn't want anyone to get hurt or for there to be a ruckus of any kind.

"I hope she just escorts Lily out. You know, all friendly like."

Henry shook his head. "We don't know exactly what will happen, but remember, if it gets crazy, stay low, get under the table."

"Henry," Martha said. "There will be no need to get under the table."

Harriet pushed eggs around on her plate. "So how will she know, the agent lady, how will she know when to make her move?"

"Surveillance," Prudence said.

"What? Like what? Do you think they put a bug in the ketchup bottle?"

"They probably have people listening, yes," Prudence said.

"Really?" Henry said. "This is so cool. I wish I could be there."

Harriet dropped her fork in her plate. "Won't you? Be there, I mean?"

"Well, yeah, sure," Henry said. "But I can't be sitting at the table with you. That will make her really suspicious, don't you think?"

"Yes," Harriet said. "That's what I meant. But you will at least be in the vicinity, right?"

"Me too," Prudence said. "We'll be outside, waiting."

Harriet bit off a corner of toast. "You know, I've been thinking. Do you think this surveillance stuff is why the waitress, Cindy, kept giving us the same table? I bet she's been in on it too. She might even be an agent." Harriet's heart raced. She patted her chest. "This is all getting to be too exciting."

"Anything is possible," Henry said.

"Just stay calm," Prudence said. "The FBI won't let anything bad happen."

"How can you be sure?" Henry said. "Now I think I'm getting nervous about sending Mom in there."

"I have to do this," Harriet said. "This is my caper. My gold mine. My mistake. I'll be fine. Besides, if someone has to die in a shootout, I'd rather it be me. You've got kids to raise."

"Mom," Henry said. He practically choked on his food. "Don't even think—"

"Everybody calm down," Prudence said. "There will be no guns. No one is getting shot."

"Of course not," Martha said. "Just be calm."

They finished their breakfast without a lot of chatter, and Harriet was grateful for that. All this talk about guns and people getting hurt gave her the willies. She knew she had to do the right thing. Her civic duty, in a sense. She only wished she could fast forward the day and it would be over.

"I'll call Lily in a little while," Harriet said. "It's still too early."

"Good. I'll be in the den," Henry said, dropping his napkin on his plate. "I might as well try to work. Let me know when you call her and you're ready to go."

"And I'm working from home today," Prudence said.

"Thanks," Harriet said. "It's nice to know all my loved ones will be here before the big event." That came out sarcastic even though she didn't mean it. After all, this was her first FBI sting operation.

Prudence patted Harriet's hand. "We'll be with you every step."

Harriet and Martha once again nominated themselves to handle the dishes and the kitchen. "It will help pass the time," Harriet said.

Martha cleared the table while Harriet scraped the food from plates into the garbage. She missed her Insinkerator. It was just so much more pleasant to grind the scraps. And she liked the name. A superhero name.

Harriet set dishes in the dishwasher. "I meant what I said," she said when Martha entered the kitchen.

"What?" Martha asked. "What did you say?"

"That I'm glad everyone is here for me. And . . . and I really don't want you to go back east."

Martha set cups and saucers on the table. "Oh, I wish you could get used to the idea that I can't stay. How could I? And like I've said a dozen times before, I have to consider Wyatt."

"I know," Harriet said. "And I think it's amazing of you that you love him so much but . . . and I don't mean to sound harsh, dear, but he is a grown man who made terrible choices."

"Yes, he is. But that doesn't give me a ticket to run away," Martha said. "I'm still his mother."

"There's nothing in the rule book that says we have to give up on living just because our adult children mess up. Is there?"

Martha took a huge breath. Harriet watched her lower lip quiver.

"I'm sorry," Harriet said. "I'm being terrible and I don't mean to. It's just . . . just that I need you too. And Wyatt . . . well, maybe you could fly back every so often and visit, and you still haven't checked to see if he can get transferred out here."

Martha flopped into a kitchen chair. "I've thought so much about this. About doing my art again. About feeling alive again. But I keep thinking it was me, I was a bad mother and that's why Wyatt—"

Harriet sat near her. "So staying back east alone is a kind of penance for your assumed parental crimes?" She pushed a piece of stray hair out of her eyes. "Martha, Wyatt's deplorable behavior was not caused by you. You were no worse a mother than me. Look what I did? I got my son completely turned in knots because he didn't want to build houses like his father. It's Henry's life. I have to get used that. Henry's decision to sell his father's business was his decision. That's why the business went to him. It was for his future, not mine, not really."

"I guess," Martha said.

"Think about Lily. In this case, her father is more or less forcing her to do things for him, to scam people. Right now she can't help it. But one day she'll have to decide if she's going into the family business. Her choice."

Martha thought about that a moment. "I suppose you're right. She will have to decide. She needs to go to school, become a good citizen, even if her father's in jail."

"That's right," Harriet said. "We can only take our kids so far, then it's up to them."

Harriet looked at the clock. "I'm going to call Lily soon."

"I will miss you so much," Martha said.

"Then move here, and I'll share my grandkids with you. You deserve to be happy."

"Don't tempt me." Martha put milk in the fridge. She rinsed the coffee cups and set them in the dishwasher. "Sometimes I wish there really was a way to start over. You know. A do-over. I'd be a better mother." Harriet saw a tear drip down Martha's cheek. "You know, the night Wyatt confessed—that was the worst night of my life."

"Even worse than when Jack died?"

Martha nodded. "Losing Jack was permanent. He was gone. But losing Wyatt like this . . . was . . . is different. He's gone, but not really. I feel like I'm carrying a big, heavy, Wyatt-shaped backpack all the time. Only, in my mind he's only twelve."

Harriet stood up and hugged her friend. "I'm so sorry. I wish I had been there for you. I'm so sorry."

"It's okay. There was nothing you could have done."

"I could have held your hand."

Martha swiped tears from her cheeks. "Maybe you should call Lily. Maybe you *can* keep her from getting into even more trouble."

"Come with me. I'll call from my cell."

Humphrey let go a soft whimper.

"You can come too," Harriet said. "We're all in on this thing."

Henry sat at his desk, ruminating. Percolating. Letting the characters walk all over him. Trying to shut out the unfolding events of the day. Sometimes it was necessary to let the character take the upper hand. And Henry ascribed to this philosophy as readily as any author, although there were times when he thought it was all just an excuse to procrastinate.

"Maybe I need a change of scenery."

He folded his laptop and grabbed his legal pads. Henry opened the desk drawer and removed a Little Debbie snack cake from his secret stash. He opened one, ate half of it, and dropped the rest into his shirt pocket.

"I wonder what Pru is doing?"

He called her cell.

"Henry," she said, "what in the world are you doing? I'm just down the hall, remember? Working at home today."

"I know. I . . . I just miss you and didn't want to interrupt."

Prudence laughed. "Yeah, I'm a little nervous too. I'm glad we're following your mother into town, even if we are waiting in the car. I told her we'd be with her every step of the way."

"Yeah, we can't let her be alone." Henry wandered into the kitchen and then out onto the

340

deck. He could hear the builders. "I'm so glad we're getting the Grammy Suite built."

"It will be nice," Prudence said, sounding a little distracted.

"I should hang up now," Henry said. "You're working."

"Oh, just busy work, keeping busy until it's time."

Henry sat down at the deck table. "I can't work. I'm way too nervous. Are you sure my mother isn't in any danger?"

"As sure as I can be. The FBI will take all the necessary precautions. All your mother has to do is get Lily to mention where Crickets might be and then she's done."

"I hope it goes off that easy."

Henry got up and wandered down the deck steps and toward the builders. "Okay, Pru. I guess it will be soon."

He tapped off the phone and dropped it into his pant pocket.

"Hey, Manuel," he called. "How's it going?"

"Good, very good." The building foreman looked up. "How you doing? Nice day." He looked up into the sky.

Henry stepped over some spare rebar. "It looks good."

"Thank you, man. Thank you. Today my men and me will start assembling the walls."

"Sure. Okay." He stepped over some boards

and a roll of some kind of paper. He wasn't sure exactly what it was. It all looked alike to him. "I'm going into town in a little while. So I won't be around. How's everything going?"

"Terrific," Manuel said. "Right on schedule."

"Good. Good." Henry's heart was not really in the building progress. Like Harriet and Martha and Pru, he was only passing time until the big event.

"Hey, the boss lady tells me you are getting twins." Manuel held up two fingers.

Henry smiled. "Yeah."

"Ah, man, that's cool. I have six children." He held up six fingers.

"Really?" Henry was astounded, kind of. "Six?"

"Si, six. My wife, she just tell me we're expecting again."

"Congratulations," Henry said. "That's wild."

One of the other workers tossed a wadded up piece of paper at Manuel. "There's ways to stop that from happening."

Manuel turned around. "I know that, man, but what can I say . . . I love to have babies."

Henry smiled. That was the nicest thing he had heard all day. He made a mental note that someone in one of his novels would say those exact words.

"Okay, it's all set," Harriet said as she tapped off her phone. "It's ten o'clock now and she'll be at the café in an hour and a half. And I called that Agent Willers with the number she gave Henry and told her."

"Did Lily say anything about her father?" Martha asked.

"No, she said he was out on business again. But, Martha, I feel just terrible." Harriet sat on the edge of Martha's bed. "I hate lying to her."

"Well, so what? You told her you wanted to take her shopping again. It is a great excuse for getting her to show without her father. And besides, they've been lying to you."

"I know. But is it ever okay to lie?"

"I think when a young woman's whole life is at stake, yes. It's okay to say something that might not be true."

Harriet pondered as she dressed for the day. "What does a person wear to an FBI sting operation?"

Martha laughed. "I don't know. I've never been to one before."

"Well, I don't own a flak jacket. Remind me to get one next time."

"Yeah, right," Martha said. "Me too. I should have a bulletproof vest too since I'm kind of your sidekick."

"Kind of? You *are* my sidekick. Robin to my Batman."

Martha looked out the bedroom window. "Holy Gold Nuggets," she said. "The bat signal."

"We better get to Gotham," Harriet said. She pulled on a pair of jeans and a black light sweater. She tied her red Chucks on and slipped into a black cardigan.

"You look so . . . so crime fighterly," Martha, who was wearing black pants and an orange sweater, said.

"And you look like a pumpkin, but that's okay." Harriet wrestled the car keys out of her tote bag. She had never put them back in their special key spot the day before.

"Okay," Harriet said. "Let's go now even though it's a little early. Maybe I can buy her something, a gift, and then I won't feel so awful."

"Oh, that's a sweet idea. Do you have something in mind?" Martha slipped into a pair of boots.

"Maybe. But I might change my mind. I'll see."

"Not a salt and pepper shaker set, I hope."

"No, of course not. Now, I'll tell the kids we're going. I'm glad they'll follow in their own car. I hope they don't mind going a little early."

"Right, less conspicuous that way."

"I guess. I just don't want to drive with them. Henry is such a worrywart. Come on, let's tell them."

Harriet knocked on Prudence's office door.

"Come in," Prudence called.

Harriet pushed open the door. "Okay, so Lily is

meeting me at eleven-thirty. But we want to go a little early to do some shopping."

"Okay, good. Henry and I are ready. We'll wait in the car in the parking lot until we see the FBI make their move."

"Okeydokey," Harriet said, nodding her head.

"Okeydokey what?" Henry said.

Harriet turned around and saw him standing at the doorway.

"Oh, Henry," she said. "I was just telling Prudence that we're leaving now to meet Lily in about an hour."

Henry walked into the small office. He put his arms around Harriet. "I'm proud of you, Mom. I know this is hard."

"Thank you, son. I know it's the right thing. I just don't want to see Lily get hurt."

"They'll take good care of her," Prudence said. "She's still a minor."

"That's right," Martha said. "We're going a little early to do some shopping first, so we're glad you're ready."

"We'll see you there," Prudence said.

Henry kissed his mother's cheek. "Good luck, Mom."

Harriet did not have much to say on the way into town. Her anxiety level was pretty high, and it was all she could do to get steady and to keep her imagination from running wild and possibly turn back and not go through with the whole thing.

"And what if I did?" she said out loud.

"What if you did what?" Martha asked.

"What if I just went home and forgot about the whole thing. I could just tell Win that I ran out of money."

"Well," Martha said after what seemed like a long few seconds. "I suppose you could do that. You could just run away from the ordeal and hide but then . . . what about Lily? And I don't know about you, but I think I'd be watching my back for the rest of my life. I mean how do you know what Win will do? What if he gets mad? Does he know where you live?"

"Well, I am sure he could find out," Harriet said. "But wouldn't they just arrest him if he came after me?"

"Probably . . . I guess. I don't know," Martha said. "But what about Lily?" she said again.

Harriet drove the remaining few miles in silence. Thinking. Considering all the angles. She parked the BMW in her usual parking lot across from the bank, and then watched as Pru and Henry parked the SUV where they could see the café. "For Lily," she said when she pushed the gearshift into park with a thud. "I'm doing this to save that child from a life of crime and running and bad hair dye jobs."

"For Lily," Martha said. "Harriet Beamer, I do believe this is your greatest adventure."

"Let's go," Harriet said.

"Do you know what you're going to get her?" Martha asked as they walked across the street.

"Not sure." Harriet's eyes were darting all around. She had a bad case of monkey nerves, thinking everyone she saw was an undercover FBI agent. "Look at him. I bet he's an agent," she said, pointing to a man standing near a trash can.

"Harriet, relax. Not everyone knows about this. Not everyone is a cop or an agent."

"I can't be sure about anything anymore," Harriet said.

They walked slowly down Main Street until Harriet saw a small toy and gift shop called Trinkets. "Let's go in there. I don't think I've ever been in that store."

"She's a little old for toys," Martha said.

"Maybe. But she's still a little girl in some ways. I have an idea."

It was a nice store, full of glass shelves displaying glass statues and wooden shelves with soaps and tea towels. And in the back was a smaller room with high quality toys from Switzerland and small stuffed animals.

Harriet's eye fell immediately on a small white lamb with fuzzy, curly fur and a black nose and black eyes. She picked it up. It was so soft and smelled like potpourri and comfort. "Maybe this little lamb."

"It is cute," Martha said. "I think that girl may never have had anything to cuddle."

"I know," Harriet said. "Doesn't it just break your heart?"

"It does," Martha said. "I think it's a great idea."

Harriet paid for the little lamb. "I'll just keep it in my tote until the time is right."

As they were getting ready to leave the house, Henry couldn't help himself. He knew before even opening his mouth that he was going to get into trouble for saying what he was about to say to Prudence. But what kind of husband, what kind of father would he be if he didn't say it?

"Pru?" he said.

She was taking a quick look out the window. "I think the addition is going to be so nice. I wish we could move in. Just kidding."

"Honey?" Henry said. "Sweetheart?"

"What is it, Henry? Are you okay?"

"Sure, sure, I'm fine, but . . . but I've been thinking. I . . . I . . . now, don't blow a gasket . . . but I was wondering if maybe it might be better if you sat this one out."

"What?" Prudence said. "Are you nuts? No way am I staying home while you and your mother and Martha see all the action."

"But . . . but, darling . . . the babies?"

"They'll have a blast."

"That's what worries me. Maybe you could stay

in the car then, the whole time. Or wear something to protect yourself."

Prudence's eyebrows arched. "Like what? Bulletproof maternity pants? Um, sorry, mine are at the cleaners."

"Well, don't we have anything that's bulletproof around here?"

"Now you're talking crazy. Let's just go. I think the waiting is melting your brain."

"But you have cop friends. Maybe you could borrow a flak jacket."

Prudence took Henry's hand. "Come on, let's go. Before all the good shooting is over."

Henry swallowed. "Don't even kid like that."

Harriet and Martha stopped in front of Rachel's. Harriet took two deep breaths. She looked around. She saw cars she didn't recognize and people who looked like agents all around. "What about him?" she whispered to Martha.

"Who?"

"The guy standing over there. He looks like a cop, doesn't he?"

"Come on," Martha said. "Let's just go inside."

"Okay, okay," Harriet said as they made their way into the café. "I think I should do most of the talking."

"Right, just kick me under the table if you want me to talk or do something."

Cindy seated them at their usual place. "Nice

to see you ladies again," she said. "Just two today?"

"We're expecting Lily," Harriet said.

"Good," Cindy said. She snagged an extra menu, which Harriet thought for sure was a signal, and took them to the usual table.

Harriet couldn't help but make eye contact with Agent Willers, who was at her place at the counter.

"Okay," Cindy said. "What can I get you? The usual?"

"Cokes and French fries," Harriet said. "And some for Lily when she gets here."

"Okeydokey." The waitress smiled. "I already had the order written down."

"Well, aren't you just so smart?" Harriet said. "Thank you." Then she turned her attention to Martha. "I always wanted to be a regular somewhere, you know?"

Martha chuckled and adjusted her napkin. "Harriet, my sweet friend, you will never be a regular anywhere. You are destined to go through life as an irregular."

"Now, if that weren't so true I'd take offense."

Martha smiled. "And I wouldn't be surprised if after this whole thing is over that Rachel's names a sandwich after you."

"Oh, now, there is a legacy." She smiled.

"Have you thought about what you're going to say to Lily? Do you want to rehearse?"

"I'm going to just ask her, I thought—just plain out ask her if she's ever met Old Man Crickets."

"That's good."

"And then I'll ask her where he lives, and that's when the FBI will swarm us like locusts and ruin that girl's life forever." Harriet looked at the table. "I don't know if I can do this."

Martha fiddled with the ketchup. She unscrewed the lid. "I don't see any bugs in here."

Cindy brought their Cokes. "Fries will be up in a minute."

"That's fine, dear," Harriet said. "We're not in a hurry."

Harriet sipped her drink. "Isn't that sweet, she always puts a cherry in it."

Martha looked into her drink. "Hey look, she gave me one too."

"Another signal, I bet," Harriet said.

"A signal for what? Nothing has happened."

Harriet took a breath and glanced around the small café. "Boy, am I nervous. I need to relax." She closed her eyes a second. "I can do all things through Christ."

"Yeah, can't let Lily see how nervous you are. She might catch wind before she tells you the whereabouts of Crickets and then cop a heel."

"Cop a heel? Did you just say that?"

"Hey, I watched *The Untouchables*."

Harriet shook her head. "Oh boy, here come our French fries."

"You and French fries. It's a wonder your arteries—"

"Shh, there she is." Harriet waved.

Martha adjusted her seat a little to make more room at the small table.

"Hey, Harriet," Lily said. "What's up? I can't believe you want to take me shopping again." She sat down at the table.

Harriet took a deep breath. This was going to be so hard. Lily looked very cute in another one of the outfits Harriet had bought for her. That day she wore the jeans with the ripped knees and a longish but frilly orange blouse. Her hair was still tar black, but Harriet was beginning to not mind it so much.

"Hi," Lily said to Martha. A shock of the black hair fell over her eyes. She pushed it behind her ear.

"Hi, honey," Martha said. "I'm glad you could meet us."

"Are you hungry, dear?" Harriet asked. By now her foot was tapping so hard from nerves she thought she might strike gold right there in the café.

"Sure."

"Good, because I already told Cindy to bring you an order of fries. You can have anything else you want."

"I thought we were going shopping. I told Pop we were going shopping."

"We are," Harriet said. "I just thought we'd get something to eat first."

Lily fidgeted. "Okay, I guess. But are you sure you want to buy me more clothes?"

Harriet reached across the table and took Lily's hand. "I care about you, Lily. I really do."

"Me too," Martha said. "We both do."

"Thanks," Lily said.

"So how is every little thing?" Harriet asked. "Getting along okay? It can be tough being a teenager."

Lily's eyebrows crinkled. "I'm cool. Everything is good. Terrific."

"I'm terrific too," Harriet said. "In fact, I'm super terrific."

Harriet felt Martha kick her under the table.

Cindy brought Lily's fries and Coke.

"Thanks," Lily said. She grabbed the ketchup and made a large puddle in the basket.

"Soooo," Harriet said, "you know who I was thinking about earlier?"

"Who?" Lily said, munching.

"Old Man Crickets."

Lily swallowed. Hard. "Crickets? How come him?"

Harriet attempted to look in the direction of Agent Willers.

"Well, it sounded like he was eager to lease the mine, and I was just wondering how he was doing. And if I'd ever get a chance to actually meet him."

Lily didn't look up from her plate. "He's good, I guess. Yeah, he's all right. But he doesn't come out much. Pop says he's a hermit type."

"Do you ever see him?" Martha asked.

This time Harriet kicked Martha.

"Not much, once or twice. Pop visits him mostly."

Harriet swallowed a fry. "Oh, so he lives around here?"

Lily munched. And then she sipped. "How come you're so interested in Crickets?"

"I told you," Harriet said. "I was just wanting to know if he's okay."

"Yeah," Lily said looking at her plate. "He's okay. Crickets is always okay." She squirmed a little. "I need to use the bathroom. Excuse me?"

"Oh, sure," Harriet said. "And when you get back, we'll finish our snack and head out to the stores."

"Okay," Lily said.

"She knows something," Martha said. "I can feel it in my knees."

"Your knees?"

"And my elbows. My arthritis acts up when I get vibes. You know that."

"Oh, like the time your knees and elbows told you that that nice Mr. Eckles from down the street was a jewel thief." Harriet munched a fry. "Just relax. I know what I'm doing."

"I hope so, Harriet. I wish this was over."

"Shh, here she comes," Harriet said.

Lily slid into her seat and grabbed a fry.

"So you said Crickets lives around here?" Harriet said.

"Over in Rough and Ready."

"Rough and Ready?" Martha said. "That's the name of the town?"

"Yeah. It's a cool little place. Crickets lives in a weird little house over there. I think it was on Quail Alley. He never comes out. People bring him all his food and stuff."

"Really. That must be nice," Harriet said.

"He is soooo fat," Lily said. "Pop says he weighs two tons."

Then, without warning, Agent Willers approached the table. Harriet's heart pounded in her temples.

"Excuse me," the woman said. She reached into her pocket and produced her small black wallet with a badge and ID. "Agent Willers, FBI."

Harriet put her arm around Lily's shoulder. "Don't hurt her."

"Ma'am, excuse me," the agent said to Harriet but still looking at Lily. "Are you Lillian Bagtree?"

Lily looked down at the table. She pushed a fry around on Harriet's plate.

"Are you?" Harriet asked. "Is that your name? I thought your name was Jump. That's your dad's name, Winslow G. Jump. So your name must be Lily Jump."

Lily looked up and shook her head.

"Sorry, but no," Agent Willers said. "Her real name is Bagtree."

Harriet looked into Lily's eyes. "Were you lying to me the whole time?"

"Not . . . exactly. I . . . didn't want to do it. Pop made me."

"Do you have any identification, Miss Bagtree?" Agent Willers asked.

Harriet reached into her bag and grabbed her wallet.

"Not you," Martha said. "Lily."

Lily shook her head. "No. I don't."

The agent nodded to two police officers who had appeared and were standing near the door, and Harriet noticed they were drawing lots of unwanted attention. Harriet wanted to tell everyone to mind their own beeswax, but that would have only caused a bigger ruckus.

The police officers approached them.

"Now, if you'll come with us, Miss Bagtree," Agent Willers said.

Lily looked at Harriet with the most frightened eyes Harriet had ever seen.

"No," Harriet said. "She's a minor. You can't take her anywhere."

"Sorry, but we can. She'll be released to the court's custody soon enough."

Harriet looked at Lily. "Listen. I'm going to get you out. You must do what they say, okay? Don't worry?"

"What about her father?" Martha asked the agent.

"They picked him up about ten minutes ago."

Lily stood. "I'm scared, Harriet."

"I know, dear. But try not to be," Harriet said. "I'm going to get this straightened out."

"I'm sorry, Miss Bagtree, but I have to handcuff you."

Harriet's stomach sickened. "Do you really?"

"Yes," the female police officer said. "It's for her own safety."

Harriet and the entire population of the small café watched the officers lead Lily out.

"I just don't believe it," Harriet said. "Did this really just happen?"

"They won't harm her," Agent Willers said. "And you will need to go to the FBI field office in Sacramento and make a statement and answer some questions."

"Now?" Martha said.

"Soon," Agent Willers said. "You'll be notified."

Harriet, who suddenly realized she was standing, sat down. Her stomach wobbled. "So I'm free to go?"

"Yes," Agent Willers said. "But don't leave town."

"No, no, of course not," Harriet said.

Agent Willers smiled . . . sort of. "The FBI thanks you for your help."

Harriet looked up at her. "Sure. Anytime." She spied Henry walking into the café. "Henry," she called.

Henry rushed to the table and hugged his mother. "It's all over, Mom. You did great."

"Then how come I feel so awful?"

"Because you're worried about Lily," Martha said. "I am too."

"Mom," Henry said, "she's not an innocent child. She knew all along what her father was doing. She was helping him."

"I know. But she didn't want to."

Harriet looked around the café. All eyes were still pinned to her.

"Can we get out of here?"

"Yes, let's go home," Henry said.

"Where's Prudence?" Harriet asked.

"Talking to one of the FBI agents."

Harriet, Martha, and Henry made their way through the restaurant. Harriet tried not to make eye contact with anyone. Anyone except Cindy.

"Good work," Cindy said. She reached into her uniform pocket and produced an FBI badge.

"I knew it," Harriet said.

Cindy laughed.

"I told you, Martha," Harriet said. "I told you she was a secret agent."

"Come on," Henry said. "You can leave the BMW. I'll drive us home."

Outside, Harriet saw Lily sitting in the back of a patrol car while Agent Willers was talking to an officer. "Oh, this is awful. That poor child." Harriet caught Lily's eye. "That poor child."

"Oh, look, here comes Prudence," Henry said.

"Good. I want to speak with her," Harriet said.

"About what?" Henry asked.

"That child needs a lawyer."

Prudence heard her and picked up her pace. "They will assign her one if she needs one. I doubt she will."

"Someone has to represent her," Martha said. "She's innocent."

"That's for the police to decide. But even if she is innocent, and she most likely will be found innocent, she'll become a ward of the state. They won't just let her free to roam the streets."

"Come on, Mom," Henry said. "Let's go home. Like I said, let's leave the BMW. I'll get it later."

Harriet caught one more look at Lily before the officers drove her away.

"Where will they take her?" Harriet asked.

"To the county police station, the one right here in downtown Grass Valley. They are on their way to the FBI field office in Sacramento with her father, and from what I could ascertain from the FBI just now, they're on their way to get Crickets."

"Wow," Harriet said. "I guess this is all my doing."

"If not you, then someone else, I'm sure," Prudence said.

"We're finished here," Henry said. "Let's go home."

"You and Prudence take her car," Harriet said. "I'll drive the BMW."

"Are you sure, Mom? It's been an exciting day."

"I'm sure. And you really don't want to leave your precious car alone in town, now do you?"

"I guess not," Henry said.

"Okay, Mother," Prudence said. "And besides, I would like to get an order of those fries I've been hearing about."

Henry kissed Harriet's cheek. "Straight home, Mom. No shenanigans."

"No shenanigans," Harriet said.

"Don't worry," Martha said. "I'll make sure she goes home and nowhere else."

Henry and Prudence went back inside the restaurant to get Prudence an order of fries.

Cindy was gone. Another server behind the counter took his order. "Just be a minute, sir." Then she looked at him almost cross-eyed. "Lots of excitement around here this morning."

Henry grunted.

"Well, now, look, at least your mother got out of that before she lost everything. I could tell you some stories that would turn your hair gray, young fella."

"I'm sure you could." Henry didn't want to be rude. He just wanted his fries and to get in the SUV and go home. Crime-stopping was exhausting. But he asked, "How do you know what was happening?"

"Everybody in the place knew. Well, most of us did anyhow. That Cindy—and by the way, that ain't her real name—took over for me. I spent most of the day in the back. Collecting tips for reading my magazines while she did all the work. Not too shabby."

"How nice for you," Prudence said.

"Yes siree Bob, nice for me. I'll just go get them fries."

"Mom was pretty upset about Lily," Henry said, drumming his debit card on the counter. "I hope she doesn't try anything."

"I know. I know," Prudence said. "There isn't anything she can do. Not really. It's out of her hands even though I don't know for sure what will happen to the girl. Most likely nothing. Not in a white-collar crime. But, with her father in jail and no relatives, she might have to be put into foster care until she turns eighteen."

"Oh man, that would be awful."

"Well, not too bad. Harriet said she turns eighteen in June. That's in about ten months."

"Long enough."

The server returned with Prudence's fries.

"Thank you," Henry said as he handed her his debit card.

"Come on," Prudence said. "Let's go home. Your mother and Martha are already on their way, and I think we all should be together this afternoon."

Chapter Twenty-Six

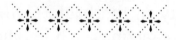

Harriet stopped at the first stop sign she came to on Main Street. Then she pulled over and parked.

"What are you doing?" Martha asked.

"I want to go to the county police station."

"Well, thank goodness. I thought you were actually gonna go home."

"What? You mean you're with me?" Harriet could hardly believe her ears.

"I can't help it," Martha said. "I like Lily. I want to make sure she's okay. She's probably scared half out of her mind. We have to at least go and make sure she's okay."

"I'm so glad you said that, because I was gonna go to the jail with or without you."

Harriet saw a nice-looking young woman pushing a stroller across the street. "Excuse me,"

Harriet called, leaning out the window. "Can you direct me to the county police station?"

"Just down there." She pointed. "Down Auburn. You can't miss it."

"Thank you," Harriet said. "Oh, and your baby is adorable."

Harriet drove ahead a ways until she could make a legal U-turn and head back to Auburn.

"There it is," Martha said. "On the right. That brown building. Looks like a log cabin."

Harriet parked the car at the police station right next to a patrol car. The same one, she thought, that brought Lily.

Martha pushed open the passenger door and stepped out. "I sure hope this is where they took her. But Prudence said it would be."

The police station was pretty small and rustic. Harriet almost expected an old timey Western jail, but it was pretty modern with computers and water fountains and mercifully a restroom, which they both used first. Harriet washed her hands and looked at herself in the mirror. "I look a fright. All this stress is not good for my skin. I think I see a new wrinkle."

Martha smiled into the mirror. "These lights are like interrogation lights. I look terrible."

"No you don't. You look sweet. As always."

They went to the lobby and waited. And waited. But no one was exactly rushing to their aid.

"I'll just find someone to ask."

Harriet approached the counter and dinged the small silver bell. A few seconds later an officer appeared from behind closed doors.

"Can I help you ladies?"

"Yes, yes," Harriet said. "Excuse me, officer, I was wondering. Was a young woman about seventeen years old brought in just a little while ago, maybe with an agent of the FBI?" She said that last part almost in a whisper like it was a big secret.

The officer shook his head. "I'm sorry. I can't tell you that. Privacy issues."

"But, but, I'm the victim. She's the—"

The officer shook his head again. "Even more reason. I'm sorry." And then he left.

Harriet's heart sank. "Dang stupid privacy laws. Don't they know we're the only friends that child has? You'd think they'd want to see us."

"Now, now," Martha said. "Let's just think a moment."

Harriet spied a bench and sat.

"Maybe if we sit here they'll take pity on me and let me visit. That's it. Doesn't she get visitors? Maybe her one call?"

Harriet dashed to the counter and dinged the bell. The same officer reappeared.

"Doesn't she get visitors? Even the worst criminals—and I'm not even saying Lily is a criminal—but please, even the worst get visitors."

The officer shook his head. "Sorry."

"Harriet, let's go home," Martha said. "Maybe Prudence will know what to do. Maybe she can pull some strings and we can visit tomorrow."

"Maybe. But what if she can't? What if Lily is sent away to some wretched foster home tonight? I'll . . . we will never see her again."

Martha grabbed Harriet's hand. "At least she's safe now. We'll figure out what to do for her at home—legally."

"Okay, okay. But I just wish I could see her."

"I know. Me too. I've grown kind of fond of Lily myself."

Harriet started to walk toward the front door when she saw Agent Willers come out of a side room, reading some paperwork. "There's the FBI lady," Harriet said.

"Agent," Martha said. "The FBI agent."

"Whatever. Let me go talk to her. Just to find out."

Harriet broke away from Martha. "Yoo-hoo, Agent Willers. Yoo–hoo." Harriet waved.

The agent stopped, startled. "Mrs. Beamer. Is everything okay? I said we'll call when we need to talk to you."

"No, it's . . . it's Lily. I'm worried about her."

"She's fine. I think she might even be relieved this is all over. She's very upset with her father. And a little frightened. But she's okay."

"So she's still here?"

Agent Willers nodded. "For now. She'll be sent

to a temporary Children and Youth Services house in a few hours."

"Where?" Martha said.

"Can't tell you," Agent Willers said. "Best thing for you is to go home and wait until you are contacted. You are material witnesses and so is Lily. But from what I hear, her testimony won't be needed. The old man is spilling his guts like Niagara Falls."

"Confession is good for the soul," Harriet said. "I read somewhere that most criminals actually want to get caught."

Agent Willers only smiled. "I'm sorry, but I really need to get going. Have a nice day. We'll be in touch." She walked past Harriet and Martha toward the front door, but Martha stopped her.

"She can come with me," Martha said. "I'll take her."

"What?" Agent Willers said. "Lily?"

"Yes. Release her into my custody. Now, I know you can do that."

"It's not that easy," Agent Willers said. "You have to go through Children and Youth Services. But for tonight, they have temporary houses they use. She'll be okay."

"Oh, I just hate that idea," Martha said. "Couldn't she just come with me?"

"Sorry," was all the agent said.

Harriet took Martha's hand. "Come on. Let's

go home before Henry gets the police looking for us."

Henry parked the SUV in the driveway. He stood there. Looking. Just looking. His BMW was not in the driveway. He heard the construction still going on out back. They had no clue about the intrigue inside the house. And Henry was glad for that.

"She's not home," Prudence said. "She should have gotten here before us."

He shook his head. "I knew it. I knew she was going to try some funny business."

He grabbed the empty French fries bag and went into the house.

Humphrey, who could smell food from blocks away, was already dancing in the entryway.

"Sorry," Henry said. "Empty. Pru ate them on the way home. No donuts." Humphrey didn't say a word. He just trotted into the living room and lay down, full on his belly, and rested his head on his paws. Henry had never seen a more dejected-looking pooch.

"Okay, donuts tomorrow," Henry called. "Right now I have to find Mom."

He tapped her name on his phone. He waited. It went to voicemail.

"I knew it, Pru. I bet she went to the county police station. I knew I should have insisted I follow her home."

"Maybe you should call the station," Prudence said.

"Good idea."

Henry followed Prudence into the kitchen. They sat down at the table.

"What's the number?" Henry asked.

"I don't know," Prudence said.

"I wouldn't call 911, right?"

"No. Call information."

"Oh, what am I so worried about? The police will tell her what to do. They'll send her on her way. If that's where she went."

"Sure she did. Where else? I would not doubt it for one minute if she wasn't trying to get Lily released into her custody."

"You think so?" Henry said. "But . . . but that's crazy. We can't have a teenager here. We barely have room for ourselves."

"Don't worry. I don't think they will release her. Not yet anyway."

Henry shook his head. He took Prudence's hands in his. "How are you holding up? Maybe you should go rest."

"I'm fine. I'm not tired. Really. I never felt better."

Henry sighed. "I need a Little Debbie."

Harriet pushed open the front door. "Yoo-hoo," she called. "Anyone home?" Of course she knew full well that both Henry and Prudence and, of course, Humphrey were all home and waiting for them. But every so often the forgetful senior citizen trick worked wonders in an otherwise difficult situation.

"I don't think they'll buy the dementia card this time around."

Martha giggled. "You just better face the music. And don't be upset if Henry is pretty angry with you for not coming straight home."

Harriet slipped off her sneakers and then hung her black cardigan on the coatrack. "I'm not worried. Too much."

"Shh, come on, they're not here. Probably in the kitchen."

Harriet and Martha strolled nonchalantly into the kitchen and waited until they were noticed.

"Mom," Henry said. "Where have you been? I gave you strict orders to come straight home. Now, where did you go?"

"Oh, Henry," she smiled. "It always makes me smile when you talk like that."

"Mother," Henry said, "did you go to the county police station?"

"When, dear? Did I go to the county police station when?"

"Don't play games."

Harriet sat down at the table and put her head in her hands. "I'm bushed. Working with the FBI is tiring."

"Well?" Henry said. He was unwrapping a Little Debbie snack cake.

Martha sat down at the kitchen table. "Yes," she said. "We went to the police station. Harriet just wanted to check on Lily. She's grown kind of fond of her. And, well . . . so have I. She really is a sweet kid. A little misguided, maybe, but that's understandable."

"I hope they treat her right," Harriet said. "The FBI lady said she's upset with her father, but I bet she misses him—considering everything."

"It's standard procedure," Prudence said. "They'd want to keep them apart. As I said, they told me they took him to the FBI field office in Sacramento. As long as you were there, did you give a statement, Mother?"

"Not yet. Agent Willers said I should wait and the FBI will call me." Harriet took a breath. "Imagine that, the FBI calling me."

The sounds of hammering drifted into the room.

"Look," Henry said, "why don't we all go into the living room? It's more comfortable and it's getting noisy in here."

"But it's a good sound," Harriet said. "It means they're framing the walls and rafters. It's the sound of normal."

Once in the living room, Prudence settled into the overstuffed chair. "How was she? Did they say anything? Did they let you see her?"

Harriet sighed. "No, they wouldn't let us see her. Not even to say a quick hello and check on her, you know? I didn't like that. But like we said, we did run into that nice FBI lady."

"Agent," Prudence said.

"FBI agent," Martha said. "She told us Lily will be going first to a children's house of some sort." She let go a deep sigh.

"Are you okay, Martha?" Prudence asked. "I bet you weren't expecting this on your vacation."

"No, I wasn't, but I'm okay. Just thinking. That's all."

"Martha offered to take her," Harriet said.

The room fell silent until Prudence said, "Really, Martha. You would consider taking her?"

Martha nodded. "I . . . I would. I know it sounds impulsive, but I've been thinking and asking God about it and . . . well, yeah, if it could be worked out, I would take her."

"Martha," Henry said with a little squeak. "You can't be serious. "She's . . . she was working with her father. Scamming old ladies."

"She was doing what she had to do," Martha said.

"I guess, but still, she knew right from wrong. She could have gone to the police."

"Really?" Harriet said. "A kid? Go to the police and turn in her father? The only family she has? Poor thing lost her mama a few years ago and everything went kablooey after that. She has no one else."

"But still. People should know right from wrong."

371

Harriet looked at Martha. She could only imagine what she must have been thinking—about Wyatt.

"I will still take her," Martha said.

"Why would you want to do that?" Prudence asked. "She's probably a handful."

"Nah, I don't think so. I think she desperately wants a stable home life. It would be good for both of us."

"I could check into it for you," Prudence said. "But don't get your hopes up. I'm pretty sure you living in Pennsylvania will make it impossible."

Martha tilted her head. "Oh, I didn't think of that."

"Why, Martha?" Henry asked. "Why would you want to take a troubled kid, I mean, at this time in your life?"

Martha's knees shook, and Harriet could see tears form in her eyes. "I guess it might have something to do with Wyatt. It's kind of like a second chance. Maybe I can keep Lily out of trouble."

"But what if you can't?" Henry said. "What if she's too far gone?"

"Like Wyatt?"

"Maybe," Henry said. "I'm sorry, but . . . you could be getting yourself into a lot more heartache."

Martha took a breath. "Oh, sweetie, there's no greater heartache than what I'm carrying these days. At least not for me. I just know in my heart

372

that I've got to at least try. Try to help that girl."

Humphrey scooted into the room. He flopped near Martha. "See? Even Humphrey thinks it's a good idea."

"Okay," Prudence said. "I'll make some calls. I can't promise this will work. I seriously doubt they'll let her cross state lines."

"Thank you," Martha said. "That's all I ask. Try. It would mean the world to me and to her."

Harriet felt tears well up in her eyes. "Oh dear, this is just . . . well, it's been such a day. Such a day."

"It certainly has been a day," Prudence said. "I think we all deserve a peaceful evening."

And fortunately, it did turn out to be a mostly peaceful evening. For the rest of the afternoon Henry and Pru worked while Harriet and Martha rested. Harriet hoped Prudence was trying to figure out a way for Martha to take Lily—if that was what Martha really wanted. Then Martha was still resting when Harriet and Henry were sitting on the deck before starting dinner, after the workers had gone home.

They heard Florence's "Yoo-hoo" around five-thirty.

"Yoo-hoo," Florence repeated. "I brought corn. Fresh corn." She carried a paper bag onto the deck. "Just bought it today. And I thought after the day you had it might be welcome."

"What?" Harriet said. "How did you know?"

"I saw a news report," Florence said. She handed Henry the bag. "Ten ears. Already shucked. Just throw them in some boiling water for a few minutes. Not too long." She seemed to have forgotten Henry was a cook himself.

"Thank you," Henry said. "But . . . but the news?"

"Now, I wasn't certain at first," Florence said. "But then I figured it just had to be your gold mine they were talking about. They arrested that Crickets fella. Showed them taking him out of that ramshackle old house up in Rough and Ready. And get this. He was in his underwear." She let go a hearty laugh. "Boxers. Baby blue boxers, and he only had a skinny T-shirt and raggedy old moccasins on too. He looked terrible. Matter of fact, he kind of looked like a big old cricket."

"So they got him," Harriet said. She leaned back in the chair feeling pretty good about the whole caper. "And I did this. I ratted him out. Well, Lily did, but still."

"Guess you're kind of a hero," Henry said.

"Yep," Florence said. "Probably sitting in an interrogation room right now, rubbing his legs together."

Harriet laughed. "The rat fink."

"Oh, I can think of stronger words than that," Florence said.

"Me too," Henry said.

"Did they mention me?" Harriet asked.

"Nah. Just something about an anonymous tip. They'll air it again on the six o'clock news, I bet."

"I can't believe it. The news," Harriet said to Florence when Henry carried the bag into the kitchen.

"Your fifteen minutes of fame," Florence said. She sat down at the table. "Say, the addition is shaping up. I bet you can't wait to get settled."

"It will be nice."

"Now, you don't seem too happy. You did a good thing. Them rustlers need to go to jail."

"It's just . . . I feel bad about the money."

"It's only money," Florence said. "Don't give it any brain space. You got twins coming and an addition to decorate."

Harriet invited Florence for dinner that evening. Henry was going to grill burgers and boil the corn Florence had brought over. But first they watched the news.

She had thought it would be kind of exciting. But no, it was actually sad. Martha nearly cried because it made her think of Lily. Henry thought Crickets looked like a gangster. "Look at the guy," he said. "I'm so glad you never had to deal with him directly."

"Yeah," Prudence said. "Men like him shoot first and ask questions later."

The air was just a little too cool to sit on the deck, but dining in the dining room was just fine.

Soon Florence called it an evening. "Thank you for the great meal," she said. "And congratulations, Harriet. Job well done." Then she turned to Martha. "And, oh, Martha, Mabel is really interested in seeing your work."

"Maybe," Martha said. "Just maybe we can work something out."

Harriet closed the shades in the bedroom. "I'm glad it's over. But . . . but finding gold would have been pretty fun, don't you think?" She then took a pair of jammies from the dresser. "I think I'll shower in the morning." She yawned wide. "I'm plum tuckered."

She turned, expecting to see Martha changing for bed. But Martha was sitting on the edge of the bed with elbows on her knees and her head in her hands.

"What's wrong?" Harriet asked.

"Oh, I don't know. Maybe I'm being rash. Maybe I should just let her go, but I can't. I can't stop thinking about Lily."

Harriet sat next to her. "You're not being rash. It's a fine idea. I think you'd be great for Lily."

"Yeah, but, what if she's more trouble than I think she is?"

"She might be, but . . . I just don't get that feeling about her. I think she really wants to be a good kid."

"That's how I feel. But . . . but . . ."

"The truth of the matter is," Harriet said, "you don't even know if you can take her. I doubt she can go across the country anyway."

"But I feel something, something inside, that is telling me I have to try. Even if I have to move to Grass Valley, I'll do it."

"You mean it? But, Martha . . ." Harriet had to sit down. She could hardly believe what she was hearing. She flopped onto the bed. The wingback chair had to be removed to make room for Martha's bed. "I can't believe what I'm hearing." She smiled wide. "I know you didn't want to leave Wyatt. But I am so happy you changed your mind."

Harriet watched a twinkle appear in Martha's eyes. "I've been thinking about it. Wyatt made his choices. He knew right from wrong, and look at what happened to him. I hardly ever see him, to be honest. And maybe now, now I have a chance to kind of start over. Maybe it wouldn't be so hard after all. Maybe I can really help Lily."

"She's almost eighteen," Harriet said. "She could just bolt out the door. You'll be taking a big risk."

"Hopefully she won't. But really, Harriet, I feel like I have to try. I know in my heart that this is right. It just feels right, you know what I mean?"

Harriet thought back to when she first arrived in Grass Valley. It had been a long road, but she knew it was right in spite of all the trials and worries. She knew she was right where God wanted her.

Humphrey ambled up to Martha. He laid his head on her knee and looked up at her. Martha patted his head. "You know, don't you, boy?"

"Okay," Harriet said. "If it's really what you want, then let's make it happen."

"It is. You know, Harriet, for months, maybe even years, I've been feeling like everything was unraveling. It started after Jack died. I didn't bounce back the way you did when you lost Max."

"I thought you did."

"Everybody did. But the truth is, it was just a show. I pretended I was doing well. I got involved with my art, and I hid there. I could shut the world out when I was working with the glass or pottery. When I threw a pot on the wheel I could smash it if it didn't go right, didn't look right, and start over. But I couldn't do that with the real stuff—like Wyatt. And then I didn't even want to do my art."

"And now maybe you have a chance to get better with Lily."

"In a way."

Just then Harriet heard Henry calling. "Mom! Mom! Come quick!"

"What in the world?" Harriet said. She and Martha dashed to the living room.

"What's wrong?" Harriet looked into her son's eyes. All she saw was fear.

"It's Prudence!"

Chapter Twenty-Seven

"It's happening again, Mom."

"Where is she?" Martha asked.

"The bedroom. We have to get her to the hospital."

Martha dashed off to the bedroom. "I'll go see."

"Okay, okay," Harriet said. "I'll go start the car. You go get her. Can she walk?"

"Not sure. Mom, why is this happening?"

"Henry, stop. Focus. Go get Prudence. Carry her if you have to."

Martha returned as Henry ran to get Prudence.

"Come on," Harriet said. "Let's get the car started."

Humphrey said, "Woof."

"She's cramping," Martha said.

"Blood?" Harriet asked with a swallow.

"Not that I saw," Martha said.

Henry carried Prudence to the car. Martha and Harriet followed.

"Now, don't worry. It could be nothing," he said. "Just relax. Don't worry."

"I'll drive," Harriet said.

"No, Mom," Henry said. "Wait here. Please. I'll drive."

"But, son, I should go with you."

"Mom, please stay."

Martha took Harriet's hand. "Let them go. We'll wait here. It could be nothing."

Prudence wiped at tears flowing down her cheeks. "But it doesn't feel like nothing. It feels like . . . like before."

Harriet leaned into the car. She kissed Prudence's cheek. "I love you, dear. I'll pray."

Harriet watched Henry back down the driveway. "I don't believe this is happening."

Prudence squirmed. "My back hurts."

"I know. I mean, I don't know. I mean, I do, but look, it's okay. I'm going to go fast. Just hang on tight. I'm running red lights if I have to."

"Okay," Prudence said. She grabbed the handle above the door. "Hurry, Henry."

Henry pulled into the ER parking lot. "Come on," he said. "Slowly." He took Prudence's hand and helped her gently but quickly into the ER. It was crowded, but Henry didn't care. He told Prudence to sit while he went to the check-in. No one was there. He waited. "Come on," he said. "Someone come."

"You have to write your name on that check-in sheet," someone said.

"Thanks." Henry wrote his name, crossed it off, and wrote Prudence Beamer and then waited some more. "Come on. This is an emergency."

Finally, a nurse arrived.

"Please," Henry said. "It's my wife. I think she's having a miscarriage. It's twins."

"Okay, sir, just calm down. We'll get to her as soon as we can."

"No. Now. You don't understand. We can't lose these babies."

"Okay, sir. Calm down. Where is she?"

Henry pointed.

"Does she need a wheelchair?"

"Yes," Henry said.

The nurse instructed a young woman in green scrubs to take Prudence the wheelchair. Prudence gingerly sat herself in it, then cried out. Henry followed as the nurse pushed Prudence toward an examination room.

"How far along is she?" the nurse asked.

"She's . . . she's . . ."

"Nine . . . ten weeks," Prudence said.

"Okay. We'll take care of her."

"Henry," Prudence said as the nurse wheeled her through the double doors. "I . . . I feel better."

"What? No, don't say that. I mean yes, say that, but . . ."

"It's not unusual," the nurse said. "But we'll check her out anyway."

"Thank you," Henry said. "Are you sure? What about the pain? How's your back?"

"My back is a little achy, but the pain is gone."

"They were like contractions," Henry said. "That's what she said. Cramps."

"All right. We'll see what's going on."

"Should we call Dr. Kate?" Henry asked.

"We have an OB on duty. He'll be in to see her."

The nurse helped Prudence onto the table. "Oh no," Prudence said. "It's . . . it's starting again. Oh Lord, it hurts."

"Settle down, honey," Henry said.

"Henry, it hurts." She leaned back on the table and cried. "It's starting again. I'm scared, Henry."

Henry held her hand. "Please," he told the nurse. "Get the doctor."

Harriet paced the living room. Humphrey paced with her. She held a fishbowl and kitty cat salt and pepper shaker set in her hands, one of the few sets she had had on display in her bedroom. She liked the way they stuck together with the tiny magnet.

"Aren't these cute?" she said. "I found them in Missouri."

"They are adorable," Martha said. "I wish you'd sit down. Let me make you a cup of tea."

"No, I can't," Harriet said. "I'm so worried. What if she loses the twins? She can't. God wouldn't let that happen, would he? Not four babies. He couldn't take four babies from them."

"Don't even say that," Martha said. She stood up. "It is a little nerve-wracking. But it is probably nothing. It usually *is* nothing."

"But this is Prudence." Harriet set the shakers on a side table. "My heart is racing. I wish he'd call."

"He will when he has something to say."

"I know, but maybe I should call—"

"No. Let's do something else. Show me the plans for the Grammy Suite. You haven't shown me yet."

"I haven't? Oh, well, then let's go to Henry's den. He keeps them in there. The builders have their own copies.

"You're a good friend, Martha," Harriet said as she unrolled the plans.

"I try. Now, you'll have to explain to me what I'm looking at."

"Okay. Well, this big area is the main sitting room. It's not real large but big enough for a couch and TV."

"So it's going to be like a little apartment," Martha said.

"And this here is a bathroom. So far it's just big enough for a shower but I think I'll ask them to change that. Make it bigger, to fit a tub."

"Won't that throw things off?"

Harriet shrugged. "A little, but they have the room. See, right here. Just bump out this wall a bit, and I was thinking I might want to have a bay window here instead of just a regular old sash type."

"Oh dear, Harriet, I wouldn't make too many changes."

"Ah, they're used to it. Builders don't mind changes."

Martha gave the plans one last look and said, "You know what we need while we're waiting? Cheesecake."

"Cheesecake?" Harriet said. "I don't think we have any."

"Ice cream then."

They sat down at the kitchen table with two spoons and a container of Rocky Road between them.

"How long has it been?" Harriet asked, looking at the clock.

"Not even an hour."

"Oh dear, it feels like forever."

"She's going to be fine," Martha said. "Those pains can be from anything. Ligaments stretching. Anything."

"I know, I know," Harriet said. She picked a nut

out of her ice cream. "But with her history . . . Why would God do this?"

Martha shook her head. "God isn't doing anything. But please. Remember, he's got this. He's in control and even if the worst happens, it will be all right. Somehow it will be all right."

Martha tapped her spoon against the ice cream container. "It sounds hollow. But I know God will help her through."

"But don't you ever ask yourself why? Why does this stuff happen? I'm seventy-two years old, and I can't figure it out."

"You never will. You can't go there. You can't ask those questions. Believe me, I tried. I looked for the reason when I watched them lead my son off to jail in handcuffs and wondered why and how this could possibly be worth it. Why did I raise a son to live a life of drugs and crime?"

Harriet swallowed the cold ice cream. "And what did you learn?"

"I learned that I can survive. Sometimes that has to be enough."

"Did it make you feel God's pleasure?"

"What? Watching them cart Wyatt away? Visiting him behind prison walls? No. But when I was finally able to release him into God's arms, then yeah, I felt it."

Harriet felt tears and swiped at them. "I am so stupid."

"What?"

"Here I am chasing a gold mine, looking for nuggets in the dirt, when all along the real gold mine was right here." She tapped her chest. "And right here." She looked around the kitchen. "The only treasure I need is my family."

"There you go," Martha said. "You're already rich."

"And so are you."

"Oh, I suppose. I have my art. I know Wyatt is relatively safe. He's made his peace with what he did and is getting the help he needs, sort of. But rich? Not yet."

Harriet closed the lid on the empty ice cream container. "Maybe you can get Lily somehow. Show her how much God loves her. Show her how to feel God's pleasure."

"Yeah, I was thinking that, before she, well, before she ends up where Wyatt is."

Harriet took her friend's hand. "I love you."

"Yeah, I love you too."

Humphrey said, "Woof."

Two hours later, it was decided that Prudence was not having a miscarriage.

"Just some growing pains, hormonal changes," the doctor said. "Nothing to worry about. But you might want to start taking it easy. Get off your feet more. You are carrying twins."

Henry cried. "That's all? Hormones? You're sure. One hundred percent?"

"Yes," the doctor said. "I would follow up with your OB tomorrow, but rest assured that you're not losing your babies."

Prudence laid her head back on the table. "Thank you, God."

Henry wiped his eyes on his sleeve. "Thank you, doctor. Thank you so much."

"You're welcome," the doctor said. "Now I'll just go get your discharge papers, and you two can be on your way."

"Thank you," Prudence said. "But . . . but, doctor, what if this happens again? What should I do?"

"Call your doctor. Or just come back. We'll always be here."

"That's right," Henry said. "Better safe."

"Yep," the doctor said. "But the babies look fine, strong heartbeats, right where they're supposed to be, and you are doing great, Prudence."

The doctor left the small examination room.

Henry, who was feeling a little lightheaded, sat on the visitor's chair as tears welled in his eyes. "I'm so happy, honey. I was really scared. I . . . I couldn't have handled it if . . . you know."

"Henry, we would have gotten through it. You are so strong. God is stronger."

"I don't deserve you, you know."

"Oh, I know that." She smiled. "But listen, maybe you should go call your mother. She's probably eaten right through that gallon of ice cream by now and paced a furrow in the carpet."

Henry snapped his fingers. "Oh, right. I'll go call."

"It's been two hours," Harriet said. "Why hasn't he called?"

"You know hospitals," Martha said. "Getting a splinter removed takes four hours."

"I know but . . . this is agony."

Martha took her friend's hand. "Come on, let's wait in the living room. More comfortable."

Harriet sat on the couch with Martha right next to her. "I can't stand it. Maybe I should go to the hospital."

"No. That's not a great idea. Henry will call."

"When?" She picked up the phone. "Ring," she commanded.

The phone rang. Harriet looked at Martha. "Weird."

"Henry," Harriet said. "What's the news?"

"She's fine, Mom. The babies are healthy. Just hormones. Growing pains. All normal."

"Oh, thank you, Lord," Harriet said.

She turned to Martha and gave her a thumbs-up. "Everyone is fine. All four of them."

Martha smiled. "I knew she was okay. Thank goodness."

"Except you sound a little wilted, Henry. Are you okay?"

"Oh yeah, just tired. It's been a crazy day."

"I'll say. Now, look, you two come on home, but don't hurry."

"Okay, Mom. And, Mom, I was so scared." Harriet could hear his tears. "I couldn't have stood it—losing the babies. Not again."

"I know, honey. Come home now. All is well."

"But she's fine, Mom. One hundred percent. The babies are right on schedule."

"I'm so pleased, Henry. Now, you give Prudence a big hug and kiss from us, okay? And then get on home. And by the way, we polished off the Rocky Road."

"Prudence said you would. That's okay. We can always get more ice cream."

Humphrey ambled by. Harriet leaned down and gave him a good scratch. "Did you hear that, boy? Everyone is fine and healthy."

Humphrey said, "Woof." He looked at Harriet under his wiry eyebrows.

"I love you too."

Chapter Twenty-Eight

✳ ✳ ✳ ✳ ✳

The next morning Harriet was up bright and early. She had spent a restless night as the events of the day before played in her mind like socks in a dryer, one tumbling over the other. She didn't want to disturb Martha, who was still snoring away, so she and Humphrey walked softly out of the room.

"Come on," Harriet whispered. "Let's make coffee."

But Henry had beaten her to it.

"Mom," he said, startled. "It's not even six o'clock. What are you doing up?"

"Same as you, I guess," she said as she sat down at the kitchen table.

"Yeah, it was pretty exciting yesterday, wasn't it?"

"Well, I don't know if exciting is the right word, but you're the writer."

Henry smiled. "I'll get you coffee."

"Thank you, dear. I hope Prudence is taking the day off."

"She is." Henry poured coffee into Harriet's

favorite mug, the one with the butterflies. "And we talked last night. She's going to quit the council. Even if it means that wimpy Hannigan takes her spot."

Harriet poured Half and Half into the mug. "Good idea. I am so glad to hear that."

"Me too." Henry sat and sipped his coffee. He had been scribbling on a legal pad.

"Were you working?"

"Oh, kind of. Sometimes I think there is a real novel I want to write. Not a Western. Something more . . . literary, as they say. I was just making notes."

"Oh, that's nice, dear."

The two sipped coffee quietly for a couple of minutes. Humphrey sat between them.

"Henry, I'm sorry," Harriet said.

"Sorry? For what?"

"You know, the whole gold mine fiasco. I'm just an old, stupid head."

Henry scribbled on his paper. "Nah, you're not a stupid head. People get caught up in things."

"It sounded so good. And there really is gold in the mountains."

"That's why people like Crickets can take advantage of—"

"Silly old ladies like me."

Henry smiled. "I was going to say people. People they think have money."

"Will you do me a favor?"

"What's that?"

"Never ask me exactly how much money I gave him."

"That much?" He sipped.

"No. Yes. Maybe. But please. Don't ask."

"Now what will you do? Find a salt-and-pepper-shaker club, I hope. There has to be one around here, at least in Sacramento."

"Yeah, I'll probably do something safer with my money, like invest in shakers."

"Glad to hear it."

They talked for a little while longer until Martha found her way into the kitchen.

"You look like you could use coffee," Harriet said.

Martha grunted. Harriet poured.

"I think I'll leave you two alone," Henry said. "I should get to work. Prudence is taking the day off so she'll probably sleep for a while."

"Oh, good," Martha said.

Henry snagged a box of Little Debbies and headed toward the den.

"Good writing," Martha called.

Henry waved.

By seven-thirty the builders were back with their machines and tools. Harriet was hoping a Daisy would drop by so she could discuss the changes. But she never got a chance to. Agent Willers called and asked her to drive into the FBI field office that morning.

"We just need you to make a statement," Agent Willers said. "And that should be it. Unless Winslow changes his mind."

"So he confessed to the whole thing?"

"Did she say anything about Lily?" Martha asked. But Harriet shooed her away.

"4500 Orange Grove, Sacramento," Harriet said as she wrote the address on a paper towel. "Across from the Tower Market. Okay. Eleven o'clock. Roger Wilco."

Agent Willers laughed. "Over and out."

Harriet tapped off the phone. "We have to go to the FBI. How exciting."

"We?" Martha said.

"I'm not going by myself."

"Did she say anything about Lily?"

Harriet shook her head. "Sorry."

"Maybe I can do something about getting Lily while we're there."

"Oh, I don't know about that," Harriet said. "That's probably handled here, in Grass Valley."

Harriet hugged Martha. "We'll figure something out. I promise. You will get Lily. Now we should get dressed and leave by nine-thirty. I don't want to be late for the FBI."

Martha giggled. "The FBI. Who would have ever believed you'd be mixed up in a federal investigation? What a hoot."

"I know," Harriet said as she walked to the bedroom. "The FBI. Hey, I wonder if they'll fingerprint me."

"You're the victim. I don't think they fingerprint victims." Martha followed her into the bedroom.

"Do you think there will be a lineup? They always looked so fun. Sitting behind the two-way glass. Picking out the perp."

"Perp?"

"Perpetrator."

"I know that. I just can't believe you said it."

Harriet and Martha changed into street clothes. Harriet chose a pretty, light blue dress with a white collar. She wore her high top Chucks.

"You're really wearing those sneakers to the FBI?" Martha, who was wearing sensible brown pants but a wild and colorful, flouncy blouse, asked.

"Sure. See." Harriet stood and modeled. "Red, white, and blue. Very patriotic."

"You are a card, Harriet Beamer."

"I better go tell Henry that I need to go to Sacramento."

"What if he wants to go with you?"

"Nah, it's just a statement. I doubt I'll be there more than an hour. There's no reason. And besides, he won't want to leave Prudence."

"He's a good husband."

Harriet took a breath. "Yeah. He really is a good husband. So much like my Max."

Harriet and Martha found Henry outside looking at the construction.

"Hey, Mom," Henry called. "Just checking. Manuel said the inspector came by yesterday and everything looks good."

Harriet kept her distance. She didn't want to get her outfit dirty. "That's nice, dear. But I've been meaning to tell you. I want to make the bathroom bigger."

Manuel dropped his hammer. "You can't." He turned to Henry. "She can't do that. It's all set."

"Mom, you can't. It's fine the way it is."

"But I want a bathtub."

"No. Sorry," Manuel said, shaking his head. "It's too late for that. You should have said something sooner."

"Please, Mom," Henry said. "It's fine the way it is."

Harriet nodded her head. "Okay, I understand."

"Let it go," Martha said. "Maybe you can still get the bay window."

"Then I want a bay window in the front. The south side."

"Now, that we can do," Manuel said. "That we can do. But you must talk to the Daisies first."

"I know. Look, Mom, I'll talk to Daisy about the bay window. But it will cost more," Henry said.

"What better place to put my money than into my home?"

"Ah, Mom," Henry said, "now, that sounds like the perfect scheme."

Harriet tried to get closer but there was just too much dirt. "Listen, Henry," she called. "I have to go to the FBI."

"FBI?" Manuel said.

Harriet glanced at Manuel. And then at the other workers. They stopped their hammers.

"Yes, the FBI," Harriet said. "I have . . . business."

"Ah, man, look," Manuel said. "Maybe the bigger bathroom would be okay. I could just push this wall here back to there and, si, yes, it could be done."

"You can?" Harriet said. "That's just peachy."

"Really?" Henry said to Manuel. "She is not going to the INS. Really. Her business has nothing to do with you guys."

Manuel slapped his forehead. "No, really, man. Wow, you had me scared."

"But I can still get my tub?"

"Sure, si," Manuel said as he turned his back. "You can get your tub. Bañera estúpida. ¿Lo que viene un jacuzzi?"

Henry pulled Harriet aside. "That was terrible, Mom. You had those guys scared to death."

"I know. Tell him I'm sorry. But you have to admit that the look on his face was priceless.

Now I really do need to get to the FBI building."

"Hold on, Mom," Henry said. "What gives?"

"Agent Willers called. She said I need to make a statement. And answer some questions."

"Maybe you should take Prudence. In case you need representation."

Harriet waved the thought away. "Nah. It's just a statement. And I'd rather she rested. Martha will be with me."

"You are like an old pro at this now."

"Hey, watch that old talk."

"Sorry, Mom." Henry laughed.

Harriet and Martha walked on toward the car.

"We better get going," Martha said.

"Call if you need to," Henry called, now standing on the front steps. "You know what? Call me when you get there. So I know you're okay. And, Mom, don't do anything."

"He's such a worrywart," Harriet said.

"Can you blame him?"

Henry found Prudence in the kitchen with Humphrey.

"Morning," he said. "How are you feeling?"

"I feel terrific," Prudence said. "I'm sorry about last night, but it felt just like . . . like before."

Henry kissed her. "Never apologize for being cautious. And please, honey, if this happens again, don't just assume it's hormones. I'd rather rush you to the hospital a hundred times than have you worry."

"I love you, Henry Beamer," Prudence said.

Henry put his arms around Prudence. "We are going to have the best babies in the world." Then he grabbed a box of cereal from the top of the refrigerator. "Honey Bunches. Want some?"

"Sure," Prudence said. "But where are your mother and Martha? I sort of thought Harriet would be in here making breakfast."

Henry joined Prudence at the table with two bowls and the milk. "The FBI."

Prudence poured cereal into her bowl. "The FBI. You mean, in Sacramento?"

"Yes. Agent Willers called and asked her to come in to make a statement. Martha went with her."

"Oh, okay, yeah, that's pretty standard procedure. She'll be fine."

"I wanted her to take you along in case she needed representation or help or something."

"Yeah, that might not have been a bad idea. It's pretty intimidating, but your mom is strong and she has Martha with her, even though they won't let Martha into the interrogation room with her."

"Interrogation room?"

"It's just a name. They just want your mother to tell her story. Then it should be over since Win and Crickets confessed to the whole thing."

"Good." Henry filled her cereal bowl and

poured milk into it. "She's a pip. And I guess she can handle herself. You should have seen the performance with the builders earlier."

"What did she do?"

"She manipulated Manuel into redoing the structure a little to accommodate a full-size bathtub in the bathroom and a bay window on the south wall."

Prudence smiled as she chewed oats. "How?"

"She mentioned the FBI and, of course, the guys thought she meant INS. They would have built her turrets and a moat if she had asked at that point."

"Oh, that's awful. And how do we know they aren't legal?"

"I think Manuel is, but if you could have seen the other guys . . . They were pretty scared."

Henry gave Prudence her cereal and then refilled his coffee mug. "I feel sort of bad for Martha. I think Martha is pretty serious about trying to take Lily."

"I know she is, but she would have to move out here. I really don't think they'll let her take her across state lines. Then, even if she does move, there could be residency issues."

"Oh, it doesn't sound too good."

Prudence stirred her cereal. "I'm afraid not."

"That's too bad. I get the feeling Martha sees it as a way of making up for what happened to Wyatt."

"Yeah, probably. But the laws are pretty exact with this stuff."

"I think I'll write to him today. Wyatt. Let him know I care. Gee, Pru, you could have stuck bamboo shoots under my fingernails and lit them on fire and I would never have said Wyatt would be in that kind of trouble."

"So he was a good friend."

"Yeah. For a while. He did get kind of distant after college. He dropped out. And I got so busy with the business and everything. I should have stayed in touch."

"Oh, well, you know what they say about hindsight. All you can do is let him know you're here for him and keep doing what you were called to do."

"Thanks. So what are you doing today?"

"Well, after I resign from the council, I'm just going to do some work here and take it easy. I guess I'll see what is happening with Lily, if they'll even tell me."

"Sounds good. You know what? I'm going to make a raspberry torte for Mom today."

Prudence patted her belly. "Chip and Dale love raspberries."

Chapter Twenty-Nine

Harriet was hoping Agent Willers would be there to greet them, but she wasn't. Instead, a very tall man who reminded her of Lurch from *The Addams Family* brought her into a sterile, boring room with nothing but a table and hard chairs. This after she and Martha were scanned, identified, and given huge badges that read "Visitor" to wear on their chests. The badge didn't even say "Hello." Harriet thought this was unfortunate.

The only good thing about the whole experience was that Harriet learned she was allowed by law to have a support person with her—as long as that person didn't say a word during the interview. Martha certainly agreed to keep silent and was just as glad as Harriet that she could tag along.

"Are they here?" Harriet asked.

"Who?" asked Agent Gilmore, or Lurch as Harriet called him—but not to his face.

"Winslow and Crickets." She sat on one side of the table. The agent sat on the other. Martha took a seat in the corner. Harriet thought she looked like she had been pickled. She sat so straight.

"No, ma'am."

Harriet felt her knees go wobbly even though she was sitting. She hadn't expected to be so nervous.

"Sorry, ma'am." Agent Gilmore showed her a piece of paper that had many lines on it. "First, tell me what happened, and then you'll need to write it all out."

"Really? Write the whole story?"

"The whole story."

Harriet sighed. "Okay."

"Now," Agent Gilmore said, "why don't you start at the beginning?"

"Okay, well, I met Lily at the café and . . ."

There was a knock on the door.

"Excuse me," Agent Gilmore said. He pulled open the door.

"Agent Willers," Harriet said. "Am I glad to see you."

"Hi," Agent Willers said. "I wanted to be here with you."

"Oh, thank you," Harriet said. "I'm glad you're here. How's Lily?"

"She's okay," Willers said. "She had a good night at a good place. They'll find a permanent place for her soon."

Martha chimed up much to the dissatisfaction of Agent Gilmore, who really seemed pretty bored about the whole thing. But maybe that was just the way the agent always behaved. "Can she please come live with me? I'll take good care of her."

"Not sure about that," Agent Willers said.

"Can you tell me what I need to do to at least try to get her?"

"Are you sure?" Agent Willers asked.

"I am," Martha said. "More sure than anything for quite some time."

"Okay, I'll check into it," Willers said.

"Can we get back to the investigation?" Gilmore asked.

"Okay, okay," Harriet said. "Like I was saying, I met Lily at the café, and she told me about her dad, Old Man Crickets, and the gold mine."

Gilmore was writing everything down.

"Keep going," Willers said. "He can write fast."

Henry was having a good writing day. He had gotten through two chapters and was re-reading for clarity and to add a word here and there. But when he heard Prudence in the kitchen, he took a break.

"Come on, Humphrey. Let's get lunch."

"Hey," Prudence said. "Did I disturb you?"

"No, no. I need to eat lunch."

"Me too," Prudence said. "How about burgers again?"

"On the grill?" Henry said.

"Why not?"

"Maybe I'll see if Manuel and his men want to join us."

"Oh, now, that's a sweet idea," Prudence said. "Maybe make up for your mother's practical joking."

Henry dashed out to start the grill. "Hey, Manuel," he called.

"Yeah, boss," Manuel said.

"I'm putting burgers on the grill. Would you and the guys like to have lunch?"

"Seriously, man?" Manuel said. "Sure. Thanks."

"Great. It'll be a few minutes."

"No trouble, man. Thanks. Hear that, boys?" Manuel called to the other workers. "Lunch is on the boss today."

Henry and Prudence formed the meat into patties and assembled buns and condiments. Prudence made lemonade, took some potato salad from the fridge, and dumped chips in a bowl. "I'm afraid I have some bad news," she said.

"What?" Henry asked.

"Nothing about the babies. It's about Lily."

"Oh, don't tell me," Henry said. "I was hoping."

Prudence followed him outside, carrying the bowls with potato salad and chips. "Well, it's not that it can't work out. But I think Martha would definitely have to move to Grass Valley to get guardianship of Lily. And that might take a lot of paperwork and take a lot of time, and then Lily would be eighteen, and then it's moot."

"Oh wow, she's going to be so disappointed." Henry dropped the burgers onto the grill. They sizzled and popped. A flame shot up from the grease, but it was quickly gone. The smell of the meat grilling was almost immediate. Henry loved that aroma. So did Humphrey.

"Do you think she'd move out here?" Henry asked.

"She might. With Wyatt in jail in Pennsylvania, though, she might not want to be so far from him."

"Yeah, that's something to consider," Henry said.

"Oh, this is just so awful." Prudence sat down at the table. Humphrey came by, obviously on the prowl for a handout. "When it's cooked," Prudence said to the dog. Then she said to Henry, "I think she might have her heart set on it."

The whole experience took nearly two hours, and by the time she was finished, Harriet felt like she had run a marathon with Humphrey on her back. She even found herself in tears at certain times, thinking about how gullible she had been. She was never so glad for anything to be over.

"Thank you," Agent Willers said. "This is never easy. But thankfully you got out before it was too late."

"Yeah," Harriet said. "Live and learn."

Agent Willers walked Martha and Harriet to the door, where they turned in their badges. "Can I keep it?" Harriet asked. "A souvenir."

"Sure, go ahead," Agent Willers said. "Drive safe now and, Harriet, don't lease any more gold mines without a thorough investigation first."

"Oh, you don't have to worry about that. I have learned my lesson."

"Glad to hear it. And by the way, thanks for helping us. You did your country a service. These guys will never hurt anyone else like they hurt you."

"Or Win's daughter," Martha said.

"Yes, I won't forget about her," Agent Willers said.

The ride home was peaceful and quiet. Neither Martha nor Harriet had much to say until they arrived back in Grass Valley.

"This has been some vacation," Martha said.

"One of a kind, I bet."

"I'll say, but I would like to see more of the town," Martha said.

"But you might need to extend your visit a little to do that."

Martha let go a chuckle. "A little? I was thinking of staying forever, remember?"

"Yeah, I remember. But what if you can't get Lily?"

"I like it here. And I really want to try to help

Lily, and I was thinking, if she can't come live with me, then maybe we can be friends. Maybe they'll at least tell me where she lives and we can see each other."

"That's the ticket," Harriet said.

"Yeah. I think I'll come back to stay."

Harriet pulled the car into the driveway. She saw that the walls of her Grammy Suite had gone up and was struck by a terrible thought. She didn't want it to be terrible. But it was, so she just had to ask.

"So, Martha, when you move out, where will you live?"

"Oh, I just assumed we'd share the Grammy Suite."

Harriet swallowed. She didn't want to be rude or unloving but . . .

"I'm just kidding. I couldn't live with you. Not for all the gold in the mountains. I'll get my own place."

"Oh, thank goodness," Harriet said. "You know I love you, but I need my space."

"And so does your collection. I'd just be in the way."

"I'll say," Harriet said.

"You don't have to be that happy."

"Hey, I smell burgers again," Harriet said. "Henry must be grilling."

Harriet and Martha went to the back of the house and, sure enough, there was a party going on with Henry and Prudence and the workers. Even Daisy Day was there with her partner, Daisy Knight.

"Hey, join the fun," Henry said. "We're celebrating."

"Celebrating what?" Harriet asked.

"Everything," Prudence said.

Harriet snagged a burger from a plate and bit into it. "This is delicious," she said. "Testifying is hard work."

"Is that your phone ringing, Mom?" Henry asked.

"Oh, yes." Harriet rifled through her bag.

"Hello," she said over the noise and music.

"Harriet? It's me. Lily?"

"Who? Lily? Oh my, how are you, dear? I am so worried. It's Lily, everybody. It's Lily."

"Oh boy," Martha said. "It's Lily."

Harriet repeated, "How are you, dear?"

"I'm okay," Lily said. "I'm staying with a nice family. For now. I miss Pop but . . . well, you know."

"Lily," Harriet said, "I am so sorry this happened."

"Yeah, me too. But I guess it will be okay. I'm kind of glad it's over."

Harriet walked away from the noise into the kitchen. "You don't have to run anymore."

"I know. But, I . . . I just wanted to tell you something," Lily said.

"What's that, dear?"

"I'm sorry. I'm sorry about everything. I'm sorry I marked you. I'm sorry I got you into trouble."

"I'm not in trouble," Harriet said. "Oh, I'm really angry about all the money, but it wasn't all for nothing. I found gold."

"You did?"

"Yep. Right here at home. It's an absolute gold mine with hot and cold running blessings. There's not a gold nugget on earth that could compare."

Lily was quiet.

"Lily," Harriet said. "Are you still there?"

"Yeah. I just wish . . ."

Martha walked into the room. "Can I talk with her?"

Harriet nodded. "Listen, Lily dear, Martha wants to say something."

Martha took the phone. "Hello, Lily? I . . . I just want you to know that . . . well, if it's all right with you, I'd like to petition or whatever they call it for you to come live with me. I'm moving to Grass Valley."

"Put it on speaker," Harriet said.

Martha set the phone on the counter and pushed the little speaker button.

"You mean it?" Lily said.

"I mean it," Martha said. "I've known it for a while. I knew I wanted to be with you from the moment I saw that silly eyebrow ring glittering in the sunlight."

"Okay," Lily said. "But when? When can it happen?"

"I don't know, and I can't even promise you. The court might say something else, but you're almost an adult. When you turn eighteen, we can be together for sure, if that's what you want."

"You mean it?" Lily said. "But . . . why?"

"Oh, someday I might tell you. But for now, it's just that . . . well, you need a home, and I need a granddaughter."

Lily seemed to be crying. "I wish it was today," she said through sniffs. "I wish I could live with you today."

Harriet held Martha's hand. "Me too," Martha said. "But I have to get back to Pennsylvania and sell my house and pack and . . . and, well, do some stuff."

"Thank you," Lily said.

"We'll stay in touch," Martha said.

"Okay," Lily said. "And, Martha?"

"Yes, honey?"

"I never got to know my real mother all that well. I know I made it sound like I knew her, that it hadn't been so long since she died. But she died a long time ago. I like to think that she was a lot like you."

Martha swiped her tears. "I love you, Lily."

Martha tapped off the phone.

Harriet wrapped her arms around her friend. "Now see, maybe, just maybe, all that glitters *is* gold. In one way or another."

"Yep. Let's get back to the party."

Harriet and Martha walked arm in arm to the deck.

"Yep," Harriet said. "I've got a real gold mine here."

The next six months whizzed by faster than greased lightning. Harriet settled into her Grammy Suite before Christmas and was as happy as a clam with all her salt and pepper shakers displayed around her. Lily, who had loved the lamb Harriet bought her, made a point to drop over almost on a weekly basis. She was studying for her GED. Harriet helped as much as she could. And Martha was in the process of moving lock, stock, and barrel across the country. Wyatt understood.

But the big news of course was the birth of the twins. A little early, but healthy.

Prudence had gone into labor on March 16, three weeks before her due date.

"Henry was a mess," Harriet said on the phone to Martha the next day. "An absolute mess. They wheeled him out of the delivery room."

"Oh no," Martha said. "How is Prudence?"

"She's recovering. They ended up doing a Cesarean. So she's sore, but she's so happy.

And the babies are so cute. Small but adorable."

"Names?" Martha asked. "Did they choose names yet?"

"Maxwell Henry, you know, for . . . for my Max." Harriet sniffed back tears. "And Emily Maxine."

"That's wonderful," Martha said.

"Oh, Martha, I can't wait for you to get here. We have so much to do, and . . ."

Harriet smiled as she continued to chat with Martha. She did have so much to do, but already she had a feeling, a feeling that maybe, just maybe there was another adventure out there.

Discussion Questions

1. Do you think Harriet handled the whole gold mine thing in the best way? Should she have consulted Henry and Prudence first?

2. What would you do if you were in Harriet's Chucks and just moved in with your son and daughter-in-law? Go looking for adventure?

3. God is often a God of second chances. It seems Martha is getting a second chance here with Lily. Have you ever had a second chance?

4. In book one Harriet learned what it means to feel God's pleasure, at least for her. But it seems it might not have taken so well in book two. What does it mean to you to feel God's pleasure?

5. Prudence never got to know her mother and many of us feel estranged from our own. How does God fill that loss?

6. Henry struggles with being a writer and wanting to have a regular job to support his family. If you were married to Henry, what would you tell him?

7. Martha says that after Wyatt's trial and incarceration she learned a valuable lesson, that she could survive. Is that good enough, to survive? Or do life and God require more from us?

8. In some ways Harriet laid down her life for Henry and Prudence, like putting up with living without her beloved salt and pepper shakers, leaving her best friend, and moving clear across the country. In what ways are you called to lay down your life?

9. Harriet is drawn to Lily almost immediately; it was almost like she was looking for someone to mother. Do you agree? Why would she do that?

10. Harriet and Henry were finally able to talk about the elephant in the room—his father's business. Do you have an elephant in your living room?

Acknowledgments

Thank you to Jimmy Rue for teaching me about gold mines.

Special Thank you to Pennsylvania State Police Commissioner Frank Noonan.

Thank you also to Pam Halter, Nancy Rue and the Crue for unflagging support.

Center Point Large Print
600 Brooks Road / PO Box 1
Thorndike ME 04986-0001 USA

(207) 568-3717

US & Canada:
1 800 929-9108
www.centerpointlargeprint.com